DEDIC

To my son, Jason and his family, for their support.

# ACKNOWLEDGEMENTS

Just Write Tuesday Morning Group for help and support while writing Dublin's Fair City.

Jean chapman's Peatling group.

Romantic Novelists' Association

My husband Dennis for your love and support.

Stephen Pomfret: Your continued support and friendship is much appreciated.

Special thanks to my publisher, Tirgearr Publishing; my editor, Christine Mcpherson; cover artist, Cora Graphics, and all the team at Tirgearr.

# Chapter One

Aileen Maguire stood up to stretch her back and looked out the bedroom window overlooking the busy Dublin street. Business went on as usual. England had won the World Cup, and men walked out of the newsagents with rolled-up copies of the morning's newspaper stuffed into their jacket pockets. But, in the bedroom above the haberdashery on the corner of upper Dorset Street, eighteen-year-old Aileen's mother lay dying.

With a sigh, she turned her attention back to the bedroom where her father was slumped in a chair by the side of the bed, his head in his hands. She picked up a cup of beef tea and held it out to him. 'Come on now, Da. You've got to stay strong.'

He glanced up, exhaustion on his pale face. 'Your mother's been rambling again,' he said. 'For the life of me, I don't know what she's on about.'

'Look, Da, you go and get your head down. I'll sit with Ma.'

Jonny Maguire stretched his tall, lean frame and stood up. His hair, the colour of gunmetal, hung limply below his ears and across his forehead. Aileen had given up nagging him to have it cut. Since Ma had taken ill three weeks ago, he had dug in his heels. He cupped his hands around the mug as if he was cold. 'You'll call me if...'

'I will, Da. Now, go on! I'll nip down and check the shop later.'

Her ma's eyes were closed but she appeared agitated, as if she was having a bad dream. Aileen pulled a chair closer to the bed and held her hand.

'Jonny. Is that you, Jonny?' Jessie Maguire's voice was but a whisper.

1

'It's me, Ma. Da's having a kip.'

Jessie turned her head towards her daughter. 'Aileen! My perfect little girl!'

'Not little any more, Ma, and not perfect either.'

As her mother gripped Aileen's hand, the doorbell jingled in the shop below. Her mother tightened her grip and struggled to sit up 'Is...someone looking after the shop?'

'Everything is fine, Ma. No need for you to fret.' Her mother appeared to have forgotten she had recently employed a woman part-time.

'You'll look after things. Your da won't...cope well without me. And watch out for Lizzy. I don't have long, so...listen to me.' Her mother's voice rasped as she struggled to breathe. Aileen stood up, dipped a cloth in a bowl of cool water, wrung it out, and gently bathed her ma's brow.

'Don't try and talk,' Aileen said, concealing her distress. 'Da will be fine, Ma, and so will you. So, please, no more of that talk.'

Her mother's face looked grey against the white cotton pillowcase. Aileen gently lifted her ma's head and helped her to suck through a straw the nourishing drink recommended by the doctor.

'I need to confess. Ask...the priest...to call in.'

Aileen placed the glass back on the side table. 'But it's only a week since he was here, Ma. What do you need forgiveness for?' Aileen kissed the side of her mother's face.

'Aileen, be a good girl...do this...for me?' Her mother struggled with the words.

'Of course I will, Ma, if it'll make you happy.' She straightened up and blew her nose. 'It's half-day closing, so I'll nip down to the church at lunchtime.'

She fluffed up her mother's pillows and tucked her in as Jessie's eyelids closed. Knowing the shop was in safe hands, Aileen lay down next to her ma, staring at the dated wallpaper and the torn piece in the corner. She had always loved this room. It was bright and airy and held many happy memories. As a child, she would climb into bed next to her parents for comfort.

Their living quarters, apart from the kitchen, hadn't been decorated since her parents moved in after their marriage in 1944, when they were both in their early twenties. Her father had been thinking of doing the place up before her ma took sick. Now it was the least of their worries.

Sighing, Aileen eased herself off the bed and made her way to the kitchen. There was a basket of washing to be tackled. She hated washday, but someone had to do it. She found it hard to believe just three of them could produce such a pile of washing each week.

She missed Ma around the place, and Da had been no help these last few weeks. With the washing, cooking, and the shop to worry about, Aileen had no idea what to concentrate on first.

For the rest of the morning, she tidied the room and prepared her mother to receive the priest. It was one of those lovely warm days when everyone wanted to be outside enjoying the sun, and by lunchtime, Aileen was glad of the walk to the church.

Later, while the priest was upstairs with Ma and Da, Aileen went down to the shop and found the part-time woman had left a list on the polished counter. As she checked through it, Aileen felt embarrassed to find they had run out of so many things. She had already reminded Da; ordering was his domain as he was the only one who could drive to the wholesaler's. The list consisted of fasteners, buttons, and reels of cotton, white lace, ladies' gloves, and nylons; there wasn't a pair in the shop. And when Aileen found the corset drawer empty, apart from the one on the dummy, she almost cried. Had Da deliberately let the stock run down? She didn't know what to think.

A knock on the shop door made her turn round. Frowning, she went to open t. 'God, Dermot, you gave me a start.'

'Sorry, just came to ask how your ma was, like.' He was holding a small brown paper parcel by his side, next to his stained blue and white striped apron.

'Come in, before anyone sees you and thinks we're open.' He smelled of meat, and she hoped he wouldn't stay long. 'She's not the best, Dermot. She's asking for the priest.' Tears gathered in her eyes, and she turned her face away.

'I'm sorry to hear that, now. Try not to upset yourself.' He handed her the parcel.

'You must stop doing this. We're eating into your profits.'

'Get away with you. It's only a few pork chops. I'll come up and cook them for you, if you like.'

'Aye, I'm sure you would.' She slipped behind the shiny mahogany counter and placed the meat in the store at the back of the shop to take upstairs later.

'I'd better get off,' he said. 'If you need anything, you know.'

Nodding, she closed the door behind him. She glanced towards the stairs and wondered how much longer the priest would be up there with her ma.

She was on the stepladder dusting the shelves when eventually he passed through. It was the older priest, his face flushed. He placed his case on the counter, took out a handkerchief, and wiped his brow.

'Did my da not make you a cup of tea, Father?' She stepped down and folded the ladder.

'No, the man barely spoke to me. But, anyhow, I must be off. I've got a few more calls to make.'

'How did you find my mother?' She placed the ladder up against the almost empty shelves.

'It's hard to say.' Shaking his head, he continued towards the door.

'Why is she so troubled, Father? My ma's a good woman.'

'You know I can't discuss your mother's confession, any more than I would yours or anyone else's, child. But if I were you, I'd prepare yourself, just in case.'

# Chapter Two

It was over a week since the funeral, and the shop was still closed. Aileen had never thought her ma would die; she was only forty-one. The pain she felt inside was like nothing she had ever experienced before, but she tried to keep her feelings hidden for her da's sake, knowing he would be feeling as much pain as she was.

Any attempt to talk to him alone was interrupted by her Aunt Lizzy, and Aileen had just about had enough of being bossed about. Everyone else had gone home, but Aunt Lizzy appeared to have taken up residence.

Aileen knew little of her ma's younger sister, and there was certainly no resemblance to her mother whatsoever. Lizzy's thin frame, her mouth tight with scorn, and her sharp features matched her tongue. Aileen could smell the chemical solution in the other woman's permed brown hair. She remembered when her ma used the Toni home perms, how she always washed her hair several times to get rid of the smell.

Aunt Lizzy's navy dress fell below her shins and was twenty years out of fashion, and her brown, block-heeled shoes did not follow any trend Aileen could remember. She had disliked her aunt on sight.

All Aileen wanted was to be alone with her da, so she could comfort him, feel his arm around her, help each other to get over their terrible loss. She thought reopening the shop would be a step forward. It was their bread and butter, and the sooner her father realised that, the better. Now her aunt was another mouth to feed.

'You'll need a bit of help around here, Aileen, with poor Jessie in the grave,' Lizzy said, twisting the silver ring on the little finger of her left hand. Aileen could not deny that with her father refusing to get involved with anything to do with the shop, everything was on her shoulders.

'You've done enough. We'll manage fine, won't we, Da?' He didn't reply.

'Course you won't,' Lizzy laughed. 'You're both grieving.' She glanced into the mirror and patted her curls into place. Then she unhooked a string shopping bag from the back of the door. 'I'm away to the butcher's to get the messages. Make Jonny another cup of tea. I won't be long.'

Aileen glared after her, gritting her teeth. 'Give me strength.' Then she looked across the table to her da. He appeared oblivious, his head in his hands.

'What does she think she's doing, Da? Why is she still here?' He glanced up but said nothing. Aileen swept back her long, blonde hair. 'We don't need her, Da.' She looked directly at him. 'If you'd help in the shop and order the supplies, we could manage. Have you still got the list I gave you the other day? If you don't order soon, we won't have a business.'

He sighed. 'The shop is a full-time job and you know how much your mother did around the place. It's kind of Lizzy to offer to help.'

Now she'd got him talking, Aileen said, 'But, look around you. She's taking over.' She scraped back her chair and stood up. 'And who told her she could move Ma's ornaments?'

'She means well.'

'You know how Ma felt about her. She wouldn't give her house room, so why are you? Do you want *me* to ask her to leave?'

'That's enough, Aileen. This is my house, and you're becoming tiresome.'

Aileen threw up her hands then placed them back down on the table and looked at her father. 'Don't you think I can manage, is that it? I can, Da. It's what Ma wanted.' She paused, but he didn't reply. 'If you could just help me, we'd be grand.'

Her da had gone into one of his silent moods, so she knew

there was no point is pursuing the argument. He was not in his right mind, otherwise he would have thanked the woman and asked her to leave days ago. 'Men are blind when it comes to the wiles of women,' she'd overheard her mother say when a neighbour's husband had run off with a barmaid. Not that Aunt Lizzy or her da were like that, but her aunt had nothing to lose by outstaying her welcome. She had no family of her own, and no husband to hurry back to. Lizzy had lived alone in a maisonette on the edge of town for as long as Aileen could remember.

Realising her da had fallen asleep, Aileen went down the passage towards her mother's bedroom. It was the first time she had been able to go inside since her aunt had changed the bedding after her ma's passing. Her father had slept in the small bedroom while her mother was ill, but now he wanted to move back. Aileen had been hesitant. It would leave a spare room, upgrading her aunt from the sofa, and Aileen didn't want to give the woman any excuse to stay longer.

Once inside, she looked down at the empty bed, stripped bare. She swallowed a sob in the back of her throat. Even her mother's pillow had been taken away, leaving her nothing to cling to. Anger, hurt, and frustration welled up inside her, and she struggled to hold it all together. Her world had turned upside down, and there wasn't a thing she could do about it.

She opened the wardrobe. Ma's brown skirt and white blouse she wore in the shop, along with three light summer dresses, dangled from hangers. Scooping them into her arms, Aileen smothered her face into them, inhaling the very last essence of her ma.

She walked over to the dressing table. Her ma's comb and hairbrush was still there, along with a bottle of Tweed perfume. At least her aunt had the discretion to leave her ma's personal things alone.

Aileen ran her hand along the flat, wooden jewellery box her da had made years ago. She lifted the lid and fingered a silver cross and chain, some pearls and matching earrings, which her mother wore on special occasions. Inside, the box had another

7

compartment where Ma kept what she termed her special things. Aileen felt like an intruder, but her need to be amongst her mother's belongings was strong. Then she saw it—a small, buff envelope lying on top of folded documents. The envelope had her name scrawled across the front.

She opened it and looked inside. A single sheet of white notepaper simply said,

*Aileen love,*
*Find your brother, and beg him to forgive me.*
*Please don't hate me.*
*I remain,*
*Your loving Ma.*

## Chapter Three

Aileen told no-one about her mother's letter. She needed to think it through carefully before making it an issue.

Dermot called most evenings wanting to take her out, and each time she declined.

'You should do as the lad says, Aileen,' Lizzy snapped. 'Change of scenery will do you good.'

Aileen's resentment towards the woman grew with each passing day, and she was close to telling her to mind her own business. But fearful of upsetting her da, she held her tongue.

Da had made no effort to go to the wholesaler's, and she was tired of trying to get through to him. She could go for the stock herself. How hard could it be? She had gone with him many times. But the keys to the van weren't hanging in their usual place.

What with the stock dwindling, and her mother's letter foremost on her mind, Aileen's head ached. She hated unanswered questions. If it was true, and she had a brother somewhere, what did it mean? Did her mother have him before her marriage to her father, or afterwards? Was it an affair? Or, even worse, had someone taken advantage of her? Was that why her ma had not mentioned it in all these years? Why would she want to bring it up now?

Her father was the only one who might be able to throw some light on it. But what if he didn't know? What would it do to him? No, she couldn't do it. For now, it would have to remain her secret.

* * *

When Aileen walked into the kitchen, Lizzy was dishing up stew on one of the hottest days of the year. Aileen stood in the doorway rooted to the spot, looking to where her mother's blue sofa and easy chairs had been moved to the far end of the large kitchen.

'Sit down,' Lizzy said, 'before it goes cold.'

'I'm not hungry. And to be quite honest, I'm sick of stew.' Aileen picked up her mother's art deco vase from the centre of the table and placed it back on the mantle where it had been before. Then she turned towards her aunt. 'What do you think you're doing, touching my mother's things?'

Her aunt grimaced. 'Petulant young hussy! Jonny, are you going to let her speak to me like that?'

Her father shifted in his chair. 'She's upset, Lizzy. Give it time.'

'Did you agree to this, Da?' Aileen pointed towards the sofa.

'Of course he did. You don't think I would have done it otherwise.'

'It's just a change, Aileen. Lizzy thinks it helps to move things around a bit.'

'Oh, she does, does she?' Aileen cried. 'I don't want Ma's things moved. She has no right to touch them.' Turning, she left the room.

It wasn't yet six o'clock when Aileen arrived outside Brogans butcher's shop. Dermot had just finished serving a customer, so it was easy for her to catch his eye.

Dermot's father shook his head. 'Go on,' he said. 'Clean yourself up first, that young woman won't wait around forever.'

'Gizza minute!' Dermot winked, whipped off his apron, and went through to the house.

'How are yea coping, love?' Mr Brogan asked.

She shrugged. 'It'll take time.' She heard a tap running out the back. 'I'm sorry to call him away so early.'

'Ah, sure, we're just about shutting up now, love, and it'll get him out from under me feet.' He chuckled. Dermot's father was a cheery soul, not unlike his son—a good sort—and although she had only been seeing Dermot a few weeks, she liked his family.

'Right, I'm all yours.' Dermot was back, running a comb through his black hair, and looking smart in a grey jacket.

He placed his arm around her shoulder as they walked down the street. Most of the shops were closing and putting up shutters, but the street was cluttered with buses, lorries, trucks and bicycles, all making their way towards O'Connell Street.

'I know it's early, Dermot, but I had to get out. Aunt Lizzy is driving me crazy. I don't know how much longer I can put up with her.'

'Ah, sure don't let her get to you, Aileen. You'll get wrinkles and spoil your lovely face.'

Her mother had once told her she had a face like a china doll. Aileen didn't think that. Lately, she couldn't get any colour into her cheeks.

'What's your da doing about your aunt?'

She shook her head. 'He doesn't appear to care. Most of the time he's in a world of his own.'

'Look, I haven't eaten, and I'm not dressed to take you anywhere posh.' He smiled.

'Will the café across in O'Connell Street be okay? They'll do us egg and chips.' They paused for traffic and then hurried across the busy street.

'Anywhere is preferable to being at home right now. I don't know what I'll do if she doesn't go home soon, I...' She felt bad to put all this on Dermot, but she had no-one else to talk to.

'Here we are.' He held open the door. 'You'll feel better once you've had something to eat.' Dermot had a way of making her feel like she wasn't alone, and she was grateful for his company.

'Here, sit down.' He pulled out a wooden chair with a red plastic seat. 'Egg and chips twice,' he said, removing his jacket. 'Is that Okay for you, Aileen?'

She nodded. 'I couldn't stomach stew three days in a row.'

'I could always tell her we've run out of stewing beef next time she comes in.' He walked towards the jukebox in the corner and slotted in the coins. A burst of the Everly Brothers' *Wake Up*

*Little Susie* brought a smile to Aileen's face.

The girl brought their food, along with a plate of bread and butter and a pot of tea. Aileen poured, then milked and sugared the drinks while Dermot tucked in. He stirred his tea and leant back in his chair.

'I'm sorry about your Aunt Lizzy, Aileen. You know, we couldn't manage without the three of us. Ma never comes into the shop; she hates the sight of blood. She sticks to the house cooking and cleaning. We employ a boy to help with deliveries on Saturdays.'

He put down his knife and fork and looked up at her. 'I'm sure Mr Maguire will get back into things soon. Your mother's death hit him hard.'

'I know.' She glanced down at her plate. 'But he knows the shop is our bread and butter.'

'Perhaps that's why he wants your aunt to stay on, you know, to help. You can't do everything, Aileen.'

She prodded a chunky chip with her fork and dipped it into the centre of the egg. The bright yellow yolk ran out over the chip, and she popped it into her mouth. 'I'd work my fingers to the bone if it meant getting rid of her.'

'That bad, eh?' He fondled his ear. 'What's happening with your secretarial course? You were quite keen a few weeks back.' He began eating again, mopping his plate with bread.

'Well, that was before, you know, Ma's heart started playing her up.' She placed her knife and fork together on her plate and bit her lip.

Dermot rummaged in his pockets and paid the bill. 'Come on, let's take a walk.'

They ambled happily arm-in-arm. City lights were coming on, but the town was quiet for a Tuesday. 'O'Connell Street's not the same without Nelson's Pillar. I still can't believe it's gone.'

'It was criminal. Now the dust has settled, I wonder what they will replace it with? Whatever it is, it won't be the same,' Aileen concluded.

Dermot took her hand. 'Look, Aileen, if you're doing nothing

Friday night, we could go to a late night showing at the Adelphia, if you want?'

'Yes, I'd like that.' Anything to keep her out of the house and away from her aunt was agreeable.

That night, outside in the shop doorway, Dermot kissed her for the first time. It was so unexpected it caught her breath. He drew her close and looked into her eyes then gently pressed his lips to hers. Surprised at how it made her feel, she relaxed against him. He kissed her again, more passionately. She drew back, her face flushed.

'I've wanted to do that for a long time,' Dermot said.

Aileen smiled. It felt good to have someone care about her. Her life had become lonely since her ma's death.

When Aileen went inside, the place was in darkness, so she switched on the kitchen light. Her father had gone to his bed. Her aunt was asleep in the armchair, her hand around the neck of a beer bottle. The fire was out.

The room had been rearranged back to how it was before. Aileen switched off the light and went to her room.

She lay awake for some time, going over things in her head—her ma's last wish, and the lovely warm feeling she had experienced when Dermot kissed her.

# Chapter Four

The following morning, her father was in the bathroom shaving with the door open when Aileen walked through to the kitchen. 'You're up early, Da. Are you going somewhere?'

He moved the razor away from his face and glanced round. 'I'm going to the wholesaler's, love.'

Aileen smiled. 'Oh, great, Da, but I've got a few bits to add.'

In the kitchen, Lizzy was stirring a pan of thick porridge. Her father never ate porridge; well, not in the middle of summer. He usually settled for a boiled egg with toast, or cereal. But since her aunt arrived, she had cooked his breakfast, so Aileen said nothing.

She could feel Lizzy's eyes boring into the back of her head as she made herself some toast and a mug of coffee. Her father came in, sat dow, and began to drink his tea, which was already poured for him.

'Are you sure you'll be all right, Da? I'll come with you.'

'No, I'll be grand.'

Aileen, who had always gone with him whenever she could, felt the blow of his refusal like a stab of pain. Unaware she was still in her dressing gown, she went downstairs to the shop and found the part-time woman searching through the needle drawer. 'We're completely out of size nine and ten knitting pins,' she sighed.

Aileen jotted it down, adding nylon stockings and knitting wool. 'Anything else?'

The woman closed the drawer. 'You've seen my list. I guess it's almost everything in the shop. When are you going?'

'This morning.'

'Well, you had better get dressed then.'

14

The day was going from bad to worse. When she handed her da the list, he raised his eyebrows. 'What's wrong, Da?'

He shook his head. 'Nothing.'

'I'll get dressed. I'm coming with you.'

'Haven't I told you? I'll be fine.'

Aileen swallowed her annoyance. She longed to be alone with him to chat, but it was plain he didn't want her with him. She made herself a fresh coffee and took it to her room and got dressed. A mumbling of voices rose from the kitchen, and shortly afterwards she heard the shop door slam.

She held back the net curtain just in time to see her aunt get into the passenger side of her father's red van. Was he taking *her* to the wholesaler with him? Aileen's heart raced.

She hurried down to the kitchen. Her aunt's enormous brown case, which had dominated the corner of the kitchen for weeks, was no longer there. 'Thank God,' Aileen murmured, sinking into her da's armchair. The woman had begun to dominate their lives.

Washing up, she threw away the remains of her aunt's thick porridge then she made herself a fresh cup of coffee and enjoyed a bowl of cornflakes. She looked around at her mother's knick-knacks, familiar to her all her life; the home which her mother had made comfortable for the three of them. Without her, everything had changed. But she was grateful that her father had, at last, seen sense and asked her aunt to leave. It would make all that had happened bearable.

The heat of the sun had gone, and she was glad of the cooler weather. The shop was quiet most of the morning, and at one point the part-time woman turned to Aileen, a worried expression on her face.

'Sure, we're losing customers every day. At this rate, Mr Maguire won't be able to afford to keep me on.'

'Don't be silly. Things will pick up once we get stocked up again.'

The woman shrugged then tried to look busy moving stock around. If she was honest, working in the drapery shop wasn't what Aileen had envisaged for herself as a career. Yet, if it meant

15

choosing between her career and her da, she knew where her loyalties lay.

Her father usually had his lunch out when he went to the wholesalers and returned just after one o'clock. Aileen had the door propped ope, waiting to help him carry in the boxes. Tentatively, she glanced into the passenger seat. There was no Aunt Lizzy, and she couldn't help smiling.

'Have you taken Aunt Lizzy to the bus, Da?'

'Yes.'

'I can't say I'm sorry she's gone. We'll be all right, so we will.'

He passed her a small box of buttons and picked up the other one himself.

'Is that it?' She glanced back into the van. 'Where's the rest of the stuff, Da?'

'There's enough here to be going on with.'

'You've got to be codding me, Da?' She gave a little chuckle. 'These will be gone in a few days. What about the corsets, measuring tapes, wool, and nylon stockings? All the other stuff on the list, didn't you take it with you?'

'I didn't need to, Aileen.'

'But, why?'

'For the love o' God! Will you leave me be?' He turned to the woman who was polishing the counter. 'I'm sorry, but I have to let you go. Take what you're owed.'

Aileen glared after him as he marched upstairs. 'Da!'

She turned to face the woman. 'Look, Eunice. He's not himself.'

'Ah, don't worry about it. I was half expecting it. It's not the same here without Mrs Maguire. She'd never treat an employee like that.' The woman opened the till and took out some money and showed it to Aileen. 'You might want to make a note.' Then she grabbed her coat and left.

Bewildered, Aileen sat down. Were things that bad? Her stomach tight from worry, she began to put the cards of buttons into the empty boxes on the shelf. She opened the other one with zips, fasteners, and safety pins, and put them away. She stayed in the shop for an hour, and not one person stepped through the door. Furious, she walked across, pulled down the shutter and locked the door.

Upstairs, her father glanced at his watch.

'What's the point, Da? All our customers have gone elsewhere. And can you blame them? What's going on? I thought you were getting back into things.'

'Yes, well, I'm doing my best.' He cleared his throat. 'Sit down, Aileen. I want to talk to you.'

She perched on a kitchen chair, trying to hide her frustration. He wanted to talk. He took off his tie and loosened his collar then removed his jacket and hung it over a chair.

'Is there something you want to tell me, Da?' Aileen had an uneasy feeling in her stomach as she leant her elbows on the kitchen table.

'It's about your Aunt Lizzy.'

'What about her? She's gone now.'

'Well, that's not quite true, because I've asked her to come and live here.'

'You've done what?' Aileen was on her feet. 'You can't be serious, Da!'

'Will yea sit down and listen!'

She sat down and placed her head in her hands.

Her father leaned forward in his chair. 'We had a long talk last night while you were out. We want you to go back to your secretarial course. It's what your mother wanted. Lizzy can help me in the shop.'

Aileen looked up. 'What shop? We haven't got one anymore. And what do you mean, *we talked it over*? She knows nothing about me, or what I want.' Furious with her da for letting the woman manipulate him again, she said, 'She'll take you for every penny, Da.' She shook her head. 'And me ma only weeks gone.'

Jonny Maguire stood up. 'It's not like that. I loved your mother.'

Distraught, Aileen linked and unlinked her fingers. 'How could you, Da?'

'You wouldn't understand.' He ran his hands over his face. 'How long will it be before you and that butcher lad, Dermot, go off? You won't think about me then.' He pushed up his shirtsleeves, revealing bony elbows.

Aileen sighed. 'Dermot and I are just friends. I'm not thinking of getting married for a long time yet.' She pushed the chair in under the table and folded her arms. 'I would have looked after you.'

'Aye! That's as might be, but I'm still a young man.'

'But Ma's sister, Da. It's not right.'

'What are you talking about? We're not doing anything wrong. Lizzy is family! And I'll thank you to show her some courtesy. While you're under my roof, I make the rules. She's coming back on Monday.'

'On Monday!' Aileen gasped. 'Why are you doing this, Da? Why?'

He sighed. 'She's lonely, and so am I. She'll take the spare room for now.' He placed his hand on Aileen's shoulder. 'Give her a chance, eh?'

Speechless, Aileen shrugged him off. Her father was never one to make big decisions on his own. He had always consulted her mother about everything. It was as if her aunt had completely turned his head.

'Well, if she's coming back, Da, I can't stay.'

'Aileen!' He reached out to her, but she turned her back and walked away.

He had always been a doting father. Now he appeared distant, uncaring of her feelings. And to betray her beloved mother so soon after her death was unforgivable. The admiration Aileen had always felt towards him dwindled.

# Chapter Five

It was Friday afternoon, and Aileen had no idea if her father expected her to open the shop again today, but she didn't care. She had the whole weekend before her aunt returned, and she wasn't going to waste her time in a shop with no stock. She had her own plans and, for better or worse, she was determined to carry them out.

The church bells tolled three o'clock when she heard her father go out. In the kitchen, she found a note saying he had gone to the barber's, and he wouldn't want any tea. Having his hair cut made no difference to Aileen now; she knew who he wanted to impress. He had left her money for groceries, something he had always done when her mother was alive, so she headed out to the shops for the essentials they needed.

Later, she put the shopping away and went for a bath then got ready to meet Dermot. She was glad she had agreed to go with him to a late night film.

When he picked her up, she thought he looked good in a grey suit, white shirt, and one of those skinny ties that were all the rage. She had washed and curled her long, blonde hair, and wore a blue summer dress and white, sling-back, high heels. She carried a white cardigan across her arm.

'You look lovely,' he said. 'How was your day?'

'Not good, Dermot, but I don't want to spoil our evening talking about Lizzy.' Smiling up at him, she took his arm as they walked away from the shop.

When they arrived in the city, a queue had already formed outside the box office, the crowd kept back by a crimson rope

19

slung between two brass poles. A group of four lads who stood in front of Aileen and Dermot were increasingly impatient, and starting to annoy a number of people by pushing each other and swearing.

The attendant walked down the line. 'Hey, you lot. Curb your behaviour or leave the queue.'

Howling with laughter, one of them stuck a finger up at the attendant and they swaggered off. Excitement fluttered along the line, and everyone moved along four places. When the barrier came down, and they finally got through, Dermot purchased two tickets from a woman with red-painted fingernails, and they stepped inside.

Aileen felt her heels sink into the rich patterned carpet on the way to the sweet counter. After selecting bonbons and liquorice allsorts—her favourites—from the tall sweet jars, they went inside. The programme had just started with the *Pathé News*, and the usherette showing them to their seats shone her torch on two plush velvet seats in the middle of a row. Aileen felt disappointed they had missed out on the back row, where she was hoping Dermot might put his arm around her. She felt in need of a hug tonight.

She was delighted when, midway through the film, he placed his arm around her shoulder and pressed his head against hers. She could smell his aftershave, and the warmth of his body close against hers helped douse her worries. When the lights went up at the interval, Dermot planted a kiss on her lips before leaving her to queue for ice cream. She felt the heat rise on her face as if she had been caught kissing behind the bicycle shed.

'Any particular flavour, or is vanilla okay?'

'Whatever you bring will be grand,' she said, hoping it would cool her down.

After the film, she had wanted to tell Dermot about the row with her da, and her plans to leave the street. But as they sat in a nearby crowded bar, she was enjoying his company so much it went from her mind.

Dermot told her funny stories about his day in the butcher's shop making her laugh. Then, just as she thought she had found the right moment to tell him, she glanced towards him—his handsome, smiling face; fingers tapping the table to the beat of the Irish music; his black hair slicked back, curling at the nape of his neck. She changed her mind. It was the first time she had looked at him this closely, and she felt a pang of regret at what she was planning to do.

'What are you thinking?' he asked, reaching for her hand.

'Oh, nothing really.' She forced a smile in spite of knowing this might well be their last date.

'God, you look gorgeous tonight, Aileen. Why don't we make a night of it? There's dancing upstairs at the Adelphia until one in the morning.'

She had no reason to rush home, and she was enjoying Dermot's company. 'Sounds like a good idea to me.'

Pulling her to her feet, they went back across the street and upstairs to the dance hall. The music had their feet tapping before they reached the dance floor.

'I'll get us a drink.' Dermot shuffled his way through the crowd. Couples shimmied and rocked to the music, all smiling and happy. She wondered if they, too, were hiding fears about their future, or just enjoying themselves, as she had done before her ma died.

The band stopped playing and, just as the dance floor emptied, she saw Dermot emerge from the packed bar holding their drinks. 'Is Cherry B okay?' he asked, placing it on the table next to her. 'They've run out of Babycham.'

'Grand, thanks.' She raised the glass to her lips.

The band struck up Bill Haley's *Rock Around the Clock* and Dermot took a quick gulp of his beer. 'Shall we?'

They made their way onto the dance floor, and Aileen was amazed to find she was partnering an expert, following his every move as if they had been dancing together for months.

The music tempo slowed to a waltz, and she felt Dermot's strong arms around her. It felt good, and when the band played *Save the Last Dance for Me*, she allowed her head to loll onto his

21

shoulder as his arms tightened around her.

Apart from her father's hugs, which seemed a long time ago now, it was the first time she had been this close to a man—and it felt good. She wasn't sure if it was the music or her emotions getting the better of her, but she wanted to stay in his arms long after the band had stopped playing.

'What's the matter?' Dermot held her at arm's length.

'Oh, it's nothing, just me being sentimental.'

Outside, in spite of the late hour, the city still bustled with young people filing out of clubs and bars. 'I've had a lovely time, Dermot, thanks.'

'Does that mean you'll come dancing with me again?' He placed his arm around her. 'I'd no idea you were such a good dancer.'

She laughed. 'You're kidding, aren't you? I was just following your very nifty footwork.'

'It proves we work well together then.' He smiled. 'My brother and I used to go dancing every weekend before he went away and my father roped me into the butchery business.'

'I thought you'd had lessons.'

'Now, who's kidding? Can you see me going to dance lessons?' He laughed and,

with his arm securely around her, they walked away from the city.

'I don't know. People can surprise you sometimes. Take my da, for instance. I'd never have thought he would choose Aunt Lizzy over me.'

They turned into Dorset Street, and Dermot released his arm and took hold of her hand. 'I'm sure that's not his intention, Aileen. Sure, I saw him drop your aunt at the bus stop the other morning when I was out on a delivery.'

She shook her head, the sinking feeling returning to her stomach. 'She's coming back on Monday.'

'Surely not!'

They were outside the draper's shop. Aileen glanced up at the windows. The lights were out. She wasn't looking forward to going in. Her da had a habit of sitting in the dark, often falling asleep in his chair. She couldn't face another row with him if he was still up.

'What is it, Aileen? Have you forgotten your key?'

'It's not that.'

'What then?'

'It's nothing.' She swallowed, not wishing to spoil their lovely evening. She moved close and kissed his cheek. 'Good night, Dermot.'

As he drew her closer and kissed her lips, her emotions got the better of her. She pulled away, not wishing him to see her tears, then pushed her key into the lock and hurried inside.

Her da slumped in his armchair, his feet stretched out in front of him, his eyes closed. Trying not to wake him, she switched the light on in the passage and slipped off her cardigan, then she fetched a light blanket from his room, gently placing it on him.

'What are you doing?' He threw off the cover and stood up. 'I'm away to me bed.'

He looked smart with his hair cut, short back and sides, but she could smell the drink on his breath; something else he rarely did. This wasn't the best time to start asking him questions, but she needed answers. 'Da, can we talk?'

He ran his hand across his face. 'Talk! At this time of the night.' He moved towards his bedroom, but Aileen wasn't going to let him just walk away from her again.

'Da, do you know anything about this note Ma left?' She unzipped the pocket in her bag. 'Please, put the light on and read it?'

He just stood there, frowning.

'Here, read it!'

He squinted, and then walked back and sat at the table. She watched his face but he showed no emotion; no sign that he was surprised in any way. Then he glanced up.

'This means nothing, Aileen. Jessie was rambling.'

'No, Da! She wasn't. Not when she wrote this. What does it mean?' She folded her arms. 'I have to know. If you know, tell me, or I'll find out for myself.'

'Oh, stop mithering and get to bed.'

'Mithering is it, Da? Well then, if you won't talk to me about it, I'll find someone else who will.'

# Chapter Six

Next morning, Aileen was up early with plans of her own. Her ma's brother, Uncle Paddy, was the one person she knew she could turn to. Dressed in a short-sleeved blouse, black mini-skirt and white low-heeled shoes, she pulled on her jacket, went down to O'Connell Street, and caught the bus to Finglas, where her uncle and aunt lived. She was edgy, and couldn't wait to get there. Hopefully, they might know something to solve the unexplained mystery of her ma's note.

It started to rain as she opened the gate and walked up the path. The garden was a blaze of colour, and she stopped briefly to inhale the scent of the roses. Her aunt opened the door in her dressing gown, her hair in large rollers.

'I'm sorry to call on you so early, Aunt Bead.'

'What a lovely surprise! Come in, love. How are things?'

'Not good, Aunt Bead. Is Uncle Paddy in?'

Aileen looked down the hall. The broad figure of her uncle—his bald head as shiny as ever, a huge smile on his face—was all the welcome she needed. 'Aileen, love.' He walked towards them and gave his niece a warm hug. A sob caught in her throat.

Bead placed her hand on Aileen's back and opened a door into the sitting room. 'Let's go in here. You'll be more comfortable.' She smiled. 'Give me your jacket. I'll hang it up. Would you like a drink, love?'

'No, thanks.'

'Well, sit yourself down,' Paddy said, sitting next to her on the sofa. 'I take it this isn't a social call, love?'

Bead tightened the cord of her dressing-gown and sat down,

crossing her legs. 'What is it, Aileen? You look like you've lost a shilling and found sixpence.'

Aileen bit her lip, her emotions getting the better of her, and she covered her face and wept.

Paddy placed a strong arm around her. 'Ah, don't cry now. It's only been weeks, and I know yea miss your ma, but things can't be that bad.' He handed her his handkerchief.

'It's worse than bad, Uncle Paddy,' she sniffed. She glanced up, playing with the buttons of her cardigan. 'I have to ask you something. Well, it's about ma. It'll drive me mad until I know the truth.'

Paddy frowned and glanced at Bead. 'Well, ask away, love.'

'Did my ma have another child? A son… I mean before she married my da, or afterwards?'

Paddy straightened up and blew out his lips. 'Where has this come from, love?'

'From this!' She took the note from her bag. 'Ma wanted me to know. Why else would she have left it where she knew I'd find it?'

Paddy read the note and passed it to Bead. 'What do you make of it?'

'I can't see her writing something like that down if it didn't mean something.'

'Has Jonny seen this?' asked Paddy.

Aileen nodded. 'He won't talk about it. Says Ma was hallucinating.'

'Well, it's the first we've heard of it.' He shook his head. 'There can't be an ounce of truth in it, Aileen love. Sure, I wouldn't lie to you. We would have known. Jessie couldn't have kept it secret.' He clasped his hands in front of him and twirled one thumb over the other. 'Does Lizzy know about this?'

'No, she'd be the last person I'd speak to about my ma.'

'I wish I knew what to suggest.'

'I can't leave it like this, Uncle Paddy. I have to know.'

'Call in at Joyce House,' Bead said. 'See what they can dig up. It might help you feel better.' She got up and sat on the arm of the sofa next to Aileen. 'Assuming it was true, and the child was born in Dublin, his birth would have to be recorded. Isn't that so, Paddy?'

'Yes, all Dublin births are registered there, but I doubt you'll find anything. Have another word with your da. See if he thinks it's worth following up. After all, he knew Jessie better than anyone.'

Aileen leaned back against the cream cushion. If her da did know, he was staying tight-lipped. 'What about Aunt Lizzy? If anything, she's made things worse.'

'What about her?'

'I wish she would go home now and leave us alone.' Aileen's eyes misted again.

'What's Lizzy doing at the shop?' her aunt asked.

'Hang on a minute.' Paddy folded his arms. 'Are you saying that Lizzy has been at the shop for three weeks then?'

'I am, Uncle Paddy.'

He sat back scratching his chin. 'You'd better tell me what's going on, love.'

Aileen couldn't contain her emotions as she told them how she felt. 'I don't know what to do anymore.'

'You poor child.' Bead leaned across to comfort her.

'Well, I'm glad you've come to us, love,' Paddy said. 'We're your family.' He stood up and dug his hands deep into the pockets of his trousers. 'Do you want me to have a word with Jonny? See if I can get to the bottom of this?'

'He won't take kindly to interference, Paddy,' Bead told him. Then she turned back to Aileen. 'Oh, Aileen love! We had no idea Jonny wasn't coping. He loved your mother, you know that. There's got to be a simple explanation for the way he's acting.'

'What am I to do? You should have heard him. I don't recognise my da anymore.'

Paddy walked over to the window. Droplets of rain raced down the windowpane. His sigh was audible, and then he turned back to face them. 'You say Lizzy's coming back on Monday?'

Aileen nodded. He came back and sat next to her, lowering his head.

'What is it, Uncle Paddy?' Aileen hooked a strand of her hair behind her ear.

He glanced up. 'Did Jessie ever talk to you about your aunt?'

Aileen shook her head and sat forward. 'Why?'

'I'm not sure if you know this, but my mother—your gran—adopted Lizzy. I can't remember the circumstances. As far back as I can remember, Lizzy was always a strange one.'

Aileen's head shot up. 'So, she's not, not Ma's real sister?'

Bead sighed. 'You didn't know that then?'

'No. Please, carry on, Uncle Paddy.'

'She wasn't your ma's favourite person. Your gran made a lot of Lizzy, felt pity for her, I think, and your ma felt pushed out.'

'Well, I can understand how ma must have felt. Lizzy's doing the same to me.'

Paddy got up and paced the small room, his hands behind his back. 'You've got to stand up to her, Aileen. Lizzy will take advantage, and Jonny's vulnerable right now.'

'Yes, but why does he let her dictate to him? It's not like him at all. I don't understand.'

Bead said, 'Happen, she'll go home soon.'

'I'm not sure,' Paddy said.

The whole situation was ridiculous and left Aileen with a sinking feeling in her stomach. She glanced up at her aunt and uncle, her eyes large with fear. 'Don't you see? If she stays, I'll have to leave.'

'Sure, that's a bit drastic, love.' Paddy sat down beside her. 'Where would you live?'

'She can stay here, can't she, Paddy? We have a spare room upstairs.'

Her uncle looked up. 'I think that's a grand idea, as long as it doesn't cause any trouble with Jonny. Do you think he'll make a fuss?'

'I don't think he will care one way or the other.'

'You could be wrong about that, Aileen. And another thing, if Jonny knew anything about a baby that Jessie had kept secret from him, he wouldn't have tolerated it all these years.'

'Da may or may not know, Uncle Paddy, but I'll not rest until I find my brother and ask his forgiveness, for Ma's sake.'

## Chapter Seven

When Aileen stepped off the bus in O'Connell Street, the rain had given way to a burst of sunshine. She felt calmer. It had been good to talk to someone who understood what she was going through.

As she turned into Dorset Street, busy with traffic and shoppers, she was surprised to see Helen Duffy walking in her direction. As they drew level, Aileen noticed the girl's dejected demeanour; shoulders slumped, her eyes cast downwards. She liked Helen, but today she was in no mood for a heart-to-heart. She felt like a fly caught in a trap.

'Helen, hello.' Aileen touched her arm. 'It's Aileen Maguire. We were at secretarial college together.'

The tall, thin girl glanced up. 'I'm sorry, Aileen. I was miles away.'

'What's wrong? Can I help?'

Helen gripped Aileen's arm and steered her into a shop doorway. 'I've gone and got myself into trouble.' Tears coursed down her face.

Aileen gasped. It was the last thing she had expected her to say. 'I'm sorry to hear that, Helen. How long have you known?'

'About a month, and I'm sick with worry. I'm four months' gone, Aileen. You know what will happen when my parents find out—and they will once I begin to show.' She sniffed. 'I called at the shop, hoping you'd be there. I asked for a corset, and your father looked at me gone out. Said he didn't have any. Do you know where I can get one today?'

Aileen saw the look of desperation in the girl's eyes, and

29

wanted to help, her own worries momentarily forgotten. 'I might be able to help.' Her da would probably play merry hell, but she didn't care. 'What about the baby's father, does he know?'

'Yes, but he's not happy. Whether he'll want to marry me now, I don't know.'

Aileen sighed. She had always hated this kind of injustice. 'It's as much his fault as yours, Helen.' Then, wishing she could extract her words, she touched Helen's arm. 'I'm sorry. It's none of my business.'

Helen lowered her head. 'I'll nip across to Clery's. I might get one there.' She moved away.

'Wait, Helen. Why don't you come back with me?'

'Can you get me a corset then?'

'I'll try.'

As they walked into the shop, the bell jingled, and her father called from the top of the stairs. 'Be there in a tick.'

'It's all right, Da, I'll see to it.'

Helen fidgeted with her hands. 'I wasn't sure you still lived here.'

'I doubt I'll be here much longer. I was helping my ma in the shop until she died a few weeks back.'

'Oh, I'm sorry. How are you managing?'

'Well, you know.' Aileen shrugged. 'It's not the same without her.' She went behind the counter and untied the laces at the front of the dummy's flesh-coloured corset. 'It might be a bit big for you.' She looked at Helen; she was so thin it was hard to believe she was in the family way. 'Do you want to try it on in the back?'

'No.' The girl held it against her and glanced towards the staircase. 'I'll take it. I can fix it up.' She appeared anxious to be off. 'Can you wrap it up before your da comes down? Do you think he knows what I want it for?'

Aileen smiled. 'I doubt it.' She cut a large piece of brown paper from the roll, folded the foundation garment into a neat parcel, and tied it with string. 'Are you still living in Christchurch Place?'

The girl nodded. 'How much do I owe you?'

'It's a little shop-soiled, so shall we say five and sixpence?'

Helen extracted a ten-shilling note, and Aileen gave her the change, surprised to find four and sixpence in the till.

'I might not see you again, Helen, but good luck. I hope things work out for you.'

'Are you leaving then?'

'Yes, I'm thinking of moving away. England, maybe. I'm not sure yet.'

'Wish I could,' she turned to leave. 'Well, it's been nice seeing you again, Aileen, and thanks for this.'

When the girl left, Aileen sighed. Poor Helen! Her life ruined. She had won a scholarship, and her parents were bound to be disappointed.

Aileen glanced round at the empty shelves; the homely atmosphere had gone from the shop. At one time, especially on a Saturday, the bell over the door had jingled all day long. Now, their long-standing customers had stopped coming in, disappointed when they could no longer get what they wanted. Aileen could hardly blame them.

When she went upstairs, her father was reading his newspaper spread out on top of the kitchen table. He was smartly dressed in a navy jumper and cords. She dared to hope this was the beginning of his recovery. He glanced up.

'What was all that about?'

'Just a girl wanting a corset, probably for her mother.'

'But I'd already told her we don't have any.'

'I sold her the one on the dummy.'

He sighed. 'I hope you told her she can't exchange it.'

Surprised that he didn't bawl at her, she said, 'I don't think she'll want to.'

She removed her jacket and used the bathroom before going back to the kitchen. Her father put down his newspaper. 'Sit down, Aileen.'

Frowning, she pulled out a chair. Was he going to open up, at last? He gave her a stern look. 'I thought you'd have opened the shop this morning. It was after ten when I got down.'

31

'I would have, Da, if you'd asked.'

'Who else is going to do it? Lizzy won't be back until Monday.'

Aileen faced him across the table. 'So, on Monday I'm sacked, is that it?'

'Don't act daft. You know you want to get back to your secretarial course.'

'What makes you think that? I was happy to work in the shop, and you made no objections before.' She lowered her gaze. 'Before *she* came poking her nose in.'

'That's no way to speak of your aunt. She's just trying to help us.'

'She's not helping, Da. She's driving a wedge between us.'

He laughed. 'Now you're being childish.'

She wasn't the one being childish. 'So, what exactly is Lizzy's role?'

'She'll take over the household chores and help me in the business.' *What business?* she was tempted to ask. 'It's best if you continue your studies. You can do a few hours in the shop when needed. Are you okay with that?'

'No! No, I'm not, Da. I can't believe you'd choose a relative we hardly know, over me.'

'Do you expect me to tell your aunt she's not welcome here? I never thought you could be uncharitable, Aileen.'

'I'm not uncharitable. She has a home of her own. I'm just trying to safeguard what we've got.'

'Don't you take that tone with me, young woman. I make the decisions around here.'

Her stomach tightened. She could hardly take in what her da was saying. She felt as if she had lost both her parents and struggled to stem the flow of tears she had tried so hard to suppress.

'Is that your final word?'

'You heard me!'

His decision couldn't have been clearer. Aileen scraped back her chair; she was sick to death of talking about Lizzy. Her throat tight with emotion, she poured herself a drink of cordial and swallowed the liquid. Then she turned to look at the man she hardly recognised as her father.

'What about Ma? She would never agree to this.'

He shifted in his chair and placed his elbow on the table, his hand on one side of his face. 'Your ma's dead, Aileen.'

'A good enough reason to carry out her last wish, don't you think?' He didn't answer. Struggling to stay calm, she said, 'I've been to Uncle Paddy's this morning.'

'Huh! Gave you some advice, did he?'

'I'm trying to understand why Ma wrote that note.'

'And are you any the wiser?'

Aileen narrowed her eyes. 'Uncle Paddy said I should ask you.'

The unexpected thud of his fist on the table made her jump. 'For the love 'f God, will you give it a rest? Our business has nothing to do with anyone else.'

'I won't. Not until you tell me the truth.' Her legs trembling, she stood her ground, reminding herself she was doing this for her ma. 'If I have a brother out there and you're not going to help me, then I'll find him myself.'

# Chapter Eight

Later that evening, Aileen prepared their tea while her father was in the shop. She had no idea what he was doing down there when the shop was closed. In spite of how she felt at his treatment of her, she got on with preparing the meal. She knew this might be the last dinner she would cook for him, and it made her sad.

She peeled and boiled the potatoes, and grilled the pork chops. She chopped and washed the cabbage, cutting it up like her ma used to, then mashed and creamed the potatoes with butter just how he liked them. The gravy made, she called him to the table. Perhaps after he'd had a good meal, he might listen to her. She was sure he was keeping something back, but it was so easy to get on his wrong side these days so she would have to tread carefully.

He sat down expectantly and began to eat. 'This is how your ma...' He paused. 'Well, you won't go wrong if you can cook as good as she did.'

Aileen smiled and picked at her food.

He pushed a forkful of potato into his mouth and cut into his meat. 'Earlier, you asked about things I find difficult to talk about. The past is the past. It's of no consequence now.' He paused and chewed his meat.

'What... what do you mean?'

'You're too young to understand, Aileen.'

'I'm not too young, Da. Why won't you give me a chance?'

He continued eating in silence. When he had finished, he pushed his plate aside. Aileen brought him his apple pie and

34

custard; she could see he was enjoying it.

'Thanks. That was nice.' He scraped back his chair and stood up.

'Why are you distant with me, Da? What have I done?'

'Nothing! You've done nothing. It's me. I just want you to leave me alone.' He shook his head and sat back down, his head in his hands. 'My wife's dead. You can't possibly understand what that feels like.'

'My God, Da! You're pathetic. You're not the only one grieving. Ma said you'd be like this, and she asked me to look after you.' She stood up. The knot in her stomach tightened, and the words tumbled together on her tongue. 'But you know what, Da?' She didn't have to ask. 'You don't want me here, do you? You want Aunt Lizzy.' She swallowed. 'What is going on, Da?'

'How dare you ask me that, and your Ma not cold in her grave! Nothing's going on.'

'So what is it then, Da?'

'I enjoy her company, and to hell with anyone who wants to make more of it.' He jumped up, knocking over the milk jug. The white liquid streamed across the floral, plastic table cover and dripped onto the floor. Aileen grabbed a glass cloth and mopped it up. Her father, without any apology, waved his hand and walked away.

Aileen sat at the table choking back her grief; her energy spent, her questions still unanswered. Where should she turn? She had no idea?

With all that was going on, she had forgotten about her date with Dermot. He would be waiting for her on the corner in half an hour. He was handsome, always whistling and happy, but the way she felt she could not raise a smile.

She lay on her bed and scribbled a note to him cancelling their date. He would be disappointed, but she wasn't ready to share her ma's secret with him. She forced herself off the bed, opened her window, and looked down. One of the neighbour's lads, playing with a ball on the pavement, glanced up.

'Can you take a message to Dermot at the butcher's for me? I'll give you a shilling.' The boy nodded then waited for her to come down. She handed him the note sealed inside an envelope and placed the money into his hand. 'Tell him I'm sorry. I'll explain when I see him. Can you do that?'

The boy nodded and shot off.

\* \* \*

The following morning, everything was as she had left it the previous evening. Sighing, she cleared the table and washed the dishes. It was eight thirty and the church bell tolled the half hour. Thinking her father was still asleep, she let him be while she made a pot of strong tea and put bread in the toaster. When she'd finished eating her toast, she poured tea into his mug. She wanted to apologise for the way she had spoken to him the previous evening.

He wasn't in his bed. The room was in disarray; the dressing table drawers were hanging open, and private papers lay strewn on the bed. Her hands shook and she placed the tea down on the chest of drawers before she dropped it. *Had they been burgled?* She rushed around checking the other rooms. Nothing had been disturbed. *Where was he?*

Cautiously, she tiptoed downstairs, her heart racing. Her da never worked in the shop on Sundays, except to stock take. Relief flooded through her when she saw him perched on the stool, reading through a document, the filing cabinet open behind him.

'Da. What are you doing? I thought we'd been robbed.' She sighed. 'Are you all right?'

'Course I'm all right. Don't touch anything upstairs, I'll tidy it up later.'

'What are you looking for?'

'The deeds to the shop. You haven't seen them, have you?'

'Why?'

'I'm selling this place.'

Aileen gripped the counter. 'But, Da! You can't.' Was he losing his mind? 'When did you decide this?'

'I'm starting a new business with Lizzy.'

'Please don't do this, Da. You haven't thought it through.'

He turned round and faced her. 'Your ma and me, we talked about moving before and after she took sick. The shop, the stairs;

it was all getting too much for her with her heart. Now I'm ready. I want a fresh start. I've saved enough, so you needn't concern yourself, Aileen.'

'Now isn't the right time.' She moved closer to him and placed her hand on his arm. 'You're still grieving.'

'How do you know what I'm feeling?' He got down from the stool and placed the papers he was reading back in the file, noisily slid it shut, then swung round to face her. 'Now's as good a time as any other.'

'But where will we live? Where will you go?'

'You can stay in digs in the city and finish your studies. It's what Jessie wanted and then, should you wish to join us, we'll not be too far from here. It'll be your home, too.'

Aileen could hardly believe what she was hearing, and she shook her head as a tear escaped and ran down her cheek. 'Were you ever going to discuss it with me, Da?'

'There's nothing to discuss.' He walked towards the stairs.

Aileen stood as if her feet were glued to the spot. She should have guessed; the shop was almost bare. Her da was setting up another business with Lizzy, and he couldn't be bothered to tell her.

This was the last straw. A feeling of loneliness engulfed her, and she went into the back of the shop and wept.

* * *

An hour later, Aileen went to the bathroom to freshen up. She knew what she should do. Why hadn't she thought of it before? She put on her white cardigan, slipped her feet into flat, white pumps, and walked the short distance to the church. Sunday masses were every half hour, so the street was alive with churchgoers.

Neighbours smiled and wished her a good morning. Usually, Aileen stopped to chat, but this morning she smiled her greeting and hurried on, her mind on questions she wanted answered.

She arrived as the nine-thirty mass had just finished. Inside, she saw the older priest shake hands with a young couple and then retire to the vestry. She gave him a few seconds, then followed.

'Can I have a word with you please, Father?' The altar boy

glanced round at her before discreetly moving into the next room.

'Yes, what is it?' The priest sounded cranky, and she wished she had made an appointment; their meeting might have been more relaxed. But she was here now and determined to make the best of it.

'I'm sorry if it's inconvenient, Father, but I have to talk to you.'

He lifted his vestments over his head and placed them down on the long mahogany counter in front of him, before turning to look at her. 'You're the young Maguire girl who lost her mother a few weeks back.' He frowned. 'I've not seen you in church much! How are you getting on?'

'I'm very unhappy, Father,' she said, ignoring the church comment. 'I found my ma's note.' She observed his uneasiness, then she opened her bag and passed him the note.

The altar boy returned and hung up the vestments before saying, 'I'm off now, Father Kelly.'

'Good lad! Don't be late tomorrow now.'

The altar boy had done her a favour. With so many parish priests, she had forgotten the older man's name. With a heavy sigh, the priest sat down, and Aileen sat opposite him on the side bench.

'There's nothing I can tell you about this. Mrs Maguire had written this before I arrived to hear her confession.' He handed back the note.

'But you knew what was in it, didn't you, Father?'

'That sounds to me like an accusation, young woman,' he snapped.

'I'm sorry, Father Kelly. It wasn't meant to sound like that. I'm so confused. Don't you have any idea?'

He shook his head. 'No. It was none of my business. I placed it in the box on her dressing table like she asked me to.'

'Please help me to understand. Da won't discuss it, and it's important to me—and obviously it was to my ma.'

He cleared his throat and leant forward, joining his hands. Then he glanced up at her. 'Don't go blaming your father. He's all you've got.'

A sob broke at the back of her throat. He had no idea. If he had, he certainly wouldn't condone what her da was up to. 'Father Kelly, I know you can't divulge my ma's confession, but please tell me about the note. I could have a brother somewhere. All you need to say is yes, or no. It's driving me mad.'

The priest stood up.

'Yes, it is true, but I can't see how…'

'I knew it. Ma wouldn't have put it down on paper if it weren't.'

'But what can you do about it now?'

Aileen's face lifted into a tearful smile. 'Well, I won't know until I try, will I, Father?'

He nodded. 'I'm afraid I have to leave you now.' He walked through to the back of the vestry.

'Thank you, Father Kelly.'

Leaving the church, Aileen had no idea where to begin her search, but she was sure of one thing, she wouldn't give up looking no matter how long it took. The priest had confirmed what she already knew, without breaking any of his priestly vows. She couldn't go back to the shop. Instead, she caught a bus to Uncle Paddy's.

# Chapter Nine

'Aileen, come in, come in.' Paddy kissed her cheek. 'We're in the kitchen. Come on down.' Aileen followed down the hall. She could smell boiled bacon and cabbage, and it revived her appetite. Bead was making sandwiches and glanced round.

'I'm glad you've come back,' her aunt said. 'Sit down. I've made a quick snack

for Paddy, but there's enough for the both of you.' She glanced wistfully at her husband. 'Even though lunch will be ready in an hour. You'll stay, won't you, Aileen?'

Aileen felt her stomach rumble. Eating at home had been almost non-existent and the smell of her aunt's cooking was too tempting to refuse. 'If you're sure. I don't want to impose.'

'Get away with you.' Bead placed a small plate of neatly-cut sandwiches on the table next to her and what looked like a doorstep in front of Paddy then went into the hall.

Aileen bit into the ham, lettuce, and tomato sandwich and helped herself to another. They were the tastiest she had had in ages. Paddy pulled over a chair. It looked far too small for him as he lowered himself down. He poured the tea and passed her a cup just as Bead popped her head round the door.

'I'm off to catch the eleven o'clock. I'll be back before you know I've gone.' She smiled. 'You have a chat with Paddy, and I'll see you later, love.' She buttoned her coat. 'Oh, and Paddy, put a light under the potatoes in half an hour,' she said, before hurrying out.

Aileen lowered her head. 'I'm sorry, Uncle Paddy, I know you and Aunt Bead are my godparents, but I can't go to mass anymore.'

'Don't let that worry you, pet.' He laughed. 'I've not been inside a church for years.

Bead still gets on at me.' He finished eating and placed his elbows on the table.

'Are things any better at home?'

She placed her cup down. 'No, Uncle Paddy. Da's still pushing me away.'

Paddy frowned. 'What's got into the man?'

'He's selling the shop.' She choked back a sob. 'He's setting up again somewhere else with Lizzy.' The knot in her stomach tightened as she related all that had happened since the previous day. Paddy pulled his chair closer to the table and began to stir his tea in silence. He leaned back and folded his arms.

'Sounds like he's more or less chucking yer out. His own daughter!'

'Oh, this is all such a mess, Uncle Paddy.' She brushed aside a wisp of her hair.

'Perhaps I should go over and have a word with him, man to man, like.'

'He won't listen.' Aileen stood up and cleared the plates onto a tray.

'Well, I'll give him no choice.' He shook his head. 'Most of this will be to do with her. Lizzy.'

'You mean about Da selling the shop?' She took the tray across the kitchen and placed it on the draining board.

'Well, I don't know about that. Jonny's his own man.'

'I don't know, Uncle Paddy? Anyone would think she had some hold over Da.'

'Let's go in the other room,' Paddy said, walking to the door. 'Leave the dishes, love, we'll do them later.'

They sat together on the sofa. Paddy knitted his fingers and held them in front of his face, his forehead creased into a frown.

'What is it, Uncle Paddy?' Aileen's eyes widened.

Clearing his throat, Paddy said. 'Look, love, don't fly off the handle now, will you? It was years ago.'

'What was? Please tell me.'

'When we were all younger than we are now,' he smiled. 'Your da and Lizzy were walking out together.'

'What? You mean they were a couple?' She swallowed and pressed her hand to her face. 'Were they having an affair when my ma–?'

'No, no, Aileen. Your da loved your ma. There was never any doubt about that.' Paddy took her hand.

'I don't understand.'

'As I said, it was years ago,' Paddy continued, 'When Jessie came back from university in England, all that changed.'

'My ma lived in England?' Aileen was astounded her mother had never mentioned it.

'She was clever; passed scholarships for God-knows-what. I know she stayed in digs for a while. She'd be about eighteen at the time.' He turned towards her. 'I know what you're thinking, and you can put that right out of your head. If Jessie had had a child over there, she would have let it slip to someone, especially Bead's cousin, Mary. They were close once.' He leaned back. 'Anyhow, as I was saying, when Jonny saw Jessie, he was smitten. He dropped Lizzy, but I'd say she's carried a torch for him all these years.'

He folded his arms. 'She had a couple of chances but turned them down. I suppose you can't help feeling sorry for Lizzy.'

'Sorry! For her? I don't. I feel sorry for my ma. It seems as if Lizzy was lying in wait. She's ruined everything, and now she's taken my da away from me.' She buried her head in her hands.

The front door clicked, and Aileen looked up. They heard Bead walk towards the kitchen. 'Does Aunt Bead know?'

'Aye, she insisted I tell you, for what it's worth.'

* * *

Over dinner, the three continued to try and make sense of it all. Regardless of how she felt, Aileen enjoyed her aunt's cooking, followed by a bowl of rhubarb pie and custard. When they had finished eating, Bead piled the dirty plates onto a tray.

'I'll make us a drink.' She glanced towards her husband. 'Would you prefer something stronger?'

'No thanks, love, I'll leave me tipple 'til later.' Sighing, he sat back on the sofa.

Aileen got up, lifted the heavy-laden tray and followed her aunt to the kitchen. She placed the dinner plates into the sink.

'The immersions on, Aileen, so the water should be hot.'

As they worked companionably together, Bead said, 'You can come and live here, you know, if things get too much for you at home.'

'Thanks, Aunt Bead.'

Aileen knew that if she were to live with her aunt and uncle, it would upset her da; in spite of everything, he was still her da and had always been a good father to her. Things had changed between them, and now it was time for her to think about her own future.

'All right, love. Leave them to drain, and we'll go back into Paddy and have our coffee.' Bead placed the drinks on a tray with handles on either side and carried it in. She sat in the armchair and Aileen settled down on the sofa next to Paddy.

'I think it's best if I move away, Uncle Paddy,' she said. 'I can't stay and watch Da sell the shop. It's too painful; Ma loved it so much.'

'Now that's a bit drastic. Where will you go? I think you're being hasty, love.' He glanced at his wife.

Bead shook her head. 'I've told her we have a room upstairs going spare.'

Paddy stood up and paced the room then, turning, he said. 'How do you think your da will take it, you going away like that?'

'There's no telling with him. But I can't stay and watch Lizzy taking Ma's place.' She sipped her coffee.

'No. I can see that.' Bead nodded.

Aileen bit her lip. Just thinking about that woman with her da made her want to retch.

'Look,' Bead said. 'If you're intent on going, I'll phone Cousin Mary in Birmingham. She runs a small guesthouse, and might be able to help. She and Jessie were good friends at one time. That way, you won't be living amongst strangers.'

Paddy clicked his tongue. 'You'll be as lonely as hell over there, Aileen.'

A tear escaped down her face and plopped onto her hand. 'Don't say that, Uncle Paddy.' She sniffed. 'If I stay, it will never be the same.'

Bead sighed as Paddy pulled Aileen to her feet and wrapped her in a hug. 'No more crying. You've done enough of that these past weeks.'

'Have you money?' her aunt asked.

'I've got a bit saved.'

Paddy fished his wallet from his back pocket. 'Here, take this. He pushed two five pound notes into her hand. 'You can never have enough.'

'Thanks, Uncle Paddy. I don't know what I'd have done without you both.'

'We're always here if you need us. Let us know what you decide, but take your time. It's a big step.'

# Chapter Ten

It was late on Sunday evening by the time Aileen arrived home. Her da was dozing in his chair. He never used to do that, and she wondered if he'd been drinking. In her room, she changed into a pair of black, mid-calf Capri pants and a red top. She had made no prior arrangement to see Dermot, and she hoped he wouldn't mind her calling unannounced. She piled her blonde hair on top with hairgrips and a spray of lacquer, then she clipped on flat, shiny black earrings. When she was ready, she gave her da a cursory glance before she tiptoed down the stairs.

As she walked towards the butcher's, she hoped Dermot had forgiven her for letting him down the previous night and crossed her fingers that he'd be in. She felt the need to talk to him. These last few weeks her feelings towards him had grown, and she would miss him once she left the street. Her happy childhood memories of growing up above the haberdashery would remain with her wherever she went.

Unlike the haberdashery, the butcher's shop had a side entrance that led to the living quarters, with plenty of yard space towards the back. The light was on in the scullery.

Aileen knocked on the green door with the black letterbox. When it opened, Mrs Brogan stood before her, drying her hands on a tea towel.

'Aileen! What a nice surprise. Come in, love.'

'I'm sorry to disturb you. Can I have a word with Dermot?' She turned her head towards the living room. 'Is he in?'

'Course he is. Go on through.'

Their living room felt homely, the sofa inviting, and the radio played soft, relaxing music. She could smell home baking, and Dermot was just demolishing the remains of a fresh scone. Mr Brogan and Dermot stood up as she entered the room.

'Aileen! I wasn't expecting you. Just give me five minutes,' he said, dropping crumbs onto the carpet as he disappeared upstairs.

'Sit down, love.' Dermot's mother threw the tea towel over her shoulder and sat down. 'How are you coping without your poor ma?'

'It's not great.' She glanced down and fiddled with a loose thread on the rib of her jumper.

'Ah, sure, I know,' the woman continued. 'I miss me chats with Jessie, God rest her. Your father's a man of few words.' She laughed. 'He must miss her all the same.'

Aileen forced a smile. 'Aunt Lizzy's coming back tomorrow.'

Mr Brogan lowered his newspaper. 'Will yea stop gassin' and make the girl a drink?'

At that moment, Dermot came back, looking smarter in a fresh pair of jeans and a white, open-necked polo shirt.

'Right, we're off,' he said. 'See yer both later.'

Relieved, Aileen stood up. It still hurt to talk about her ma, and she quickly followed Dermot out. Once they were alone, he paused to look at her. 'What's up? Has something happened?'

'Can we go somewhere and talk?'

They walked to the corner. Then he took her hand and hurried her across the street towards the city. The centre was quite lively for a Sunday night, with queues outside most of the cinemas. Aileen's heart was heavy, and she could see Dermot was no longer smiling, his brow furrowed. When they were sitting opposite each other in their favourite cafe, a coffee in front of them, he spoke. 'Is this about us, Aileen?' He placed both arms on the table.

'I'm going away.' She swallowed. 'I don't want to, but I've no choice, and it has nothing to do with us.' She paused. 'It's my aunt.'

He gulped his coffee. 'You're kiddin' me. You're letting her drive you out of your home.'

'Let me explain, and then I hope you'll understand.' She took a sip of her coffee. 'I'm going to Birmingham.'

'Birmingham!' He sat back and folded his arms, his mood sombre. 'Why go away?'

Aileen hesitated. She was going to lay her family bare, and the hissing of the coffee machine and the rattle of cups distracted her. People passed close to their table. Dermot placed his hand over hers; their eyes locked, and she found the courage to burden him with her concerns.

When she finished, she glanced up to see Dermot struggling with his emotions. He placed his hand over his face and stood up. 'I'll get us another coffee.'

She watched him walk to the tall counter and wait his turn; then she took a tissue from her bag and dabbed her eyes. When he came back, he placed the coffee down next to her, spilling some onto the saucer. 'Clumsy me. Here, have mine.' He moved the cups around and sat down. He appeared to ponder, and Aileen feared she had gone too far in revealing so much.

'Are you shocked?' she asked.

'I'm furious, although I have no right to be.' He swallowed. His face softened as he reached for her hand. 'How can he do this to you, his own flesh and blood?'

'That's what Uncle Paddy said.' She took another tissue from her bag.

'Don't go, Aileen.'

A tear trickled down her face. 'Try to understand. I can't stay living under the same roof, knowing what I do.'

'What does your da say about you going?'

'I've not told him. Anyway, he doesn't talk to me. I guess he just can't face the truth.'

'I'll help you look for your brother.' He looked into her eyes. 'I'm not going to add to your misery by trying to dissuade you from leaving. I love you, Aileen Maguire. I'll come with you.'

'That's sweet of you, Dermot. But I can't let you do that. Your father needs you. Besides, I'm staying with Aunt Bead's cousin. I'll be fine.'

'You won't object if I come and visit, then?'

'I'll look forward to it.'

The cafe was filling up. Young people pressed coins into small machines by their tables to select songs. When a blast of Elvis's *Blue Suede Shoes* filled the room, Dermot pushed back his chair and stood up. 'Let's get out of here.'

It was growing dark, and O'Connell Street was awash with lights. The queues had disappeared from outside cinemas. Love-struck couples walked arm-in-arm. Buses belched out fumes as they pulled away from bus stops, leaving a smoky smell. Men in caps chatted by the taxi rank waiting for their next fare. Life went on as usual, but Aileen felt like hers was over.

They passed the spot where Nelson's Pillar once stood—now a pile of rubble, a relic of what had once been a familiar landmark and focal meeting place for most people. Aileen loved Dublin, and with so much yet to discover, she knew she would miss everything she had come to know and love about the Fair City. But there was no point in sentiment now.

They walked hand-in-hand in comfortable silence, and Aileen felt a sense of relief to have shared her family secret with Dermot. She couldn't decipher his thoughts, but every now and then she felt the pressure of his hand on hers; the thought of leaving him brought a lump to her throat.

Without realising it, they reached the top of Grafton Street and continued towards the park. It was the middle of August, and, although there had been no sun all day, it was a mild evening. Oblivious to couples enjoying the secluded interior of the park's green oasis, Dermot sought out a bench by a tree, and they sat down.

'When will you go?' he asked.

'Next week, once I've got my ferry ticket.'

He placed his arm around her shoulder. She knew he would think it was too soon, and she was right. 'Have you thought this through, Aileen? You've hardly had time to grieve your mother, and you've no idea what it will be like living away from home.'

She had heard all this from her Uncle Paddy. 'I'm not a child, Dermot. I told you I'll be staying with Bead's cousin.' If the truth be known, she would give anything not to have to go, and for things to return to how they were before her ma died.

'I'm sorry, Aileen. I didn't mean…'

A young couple walked past them laughing, arms entwined. Aileen wished she could be that happy. She turned towards Dermot. 'I'll take my ma with me, in my heart, wherever I go.'

'I know. What I'm trying to say is, I love you and care what happens to you.'

'I think I love you, too. But…'

Dermot moved closer, and her head flopped onto his broad shoulder. 'Why don't we get married?'

The question, so unexpected, forced her to sit upright.

'Now who's being impulsive?' Yes, it would solve her problems, but she was only eighteen and had seen nothing of the world.

'Of course, we'd have to live at mine until I'd enough for a down payment on a place of our own.'

She swallowed. 'You're serious?'

He nodded. As much as she loved Dermot, if she were to marry now, it would be for the wrong reasons. Living with Dermot's family wouldn't help at all, and she had to get away from the street.

'It's all right, Aileen. I don't expect you to answer me now.' He pulled her back towards him.

'I'm flattered that you asked me. I do love you, but I don't want to marry yet. And I know you'd like me to stay, but my mind's made up.'

'Well, the offer still stands. You're the only girl for me.'

His words made her cry, only, this time, he gently brushed her tears away with his thumb.

Later, when they said goodnight, Dermot's kisses told her what she needed to know about his feelings, and it made her all the more aware of what she was leaving behind. For the first time since walking out with Dermot, he aroused in her feelings that left her wanting more.

# Chapter Eleven

On Monday morning, Aileen was up early after a sleepless night. She wondered how her da would react once she told him she was leaving. She was also curious to ask him about his relationship with Lizzy before the woman returned.

She made breakfast of bacon and eggs for them both, and,while they were still at the table, she forced herself into a nonchalant mood.

'You never said you and Lizzy walked out together, Da.'

He looked taken aback. 'My God! Tongues have been wagging.'

'Is it true?'

'We were kids. I'd hardly call a few kisses a relationship.'

'What about now?' she dared.

He leaned his elbows on the table. 'What do you mean? I've not seen Lizzy in twenty years.'

'Well, she certainly has a motive now. It could account for the way she's pushing me out.'

'That's nonsense, and you know it.'

'Is it? Have you still got feelings for her, Da?'

He glared at her. 'How dare you question me in this manner? How I feel is my business, is that clear?'

'I'm sorry, Da.' She looked down at her hands folded in her lap. 'I didn't mean to
be disrespectful.' There was so much more she wanted to say. It was crystal clear what was going on, even if her da hadn't figured it out yet.

He stood up to leave.

'Before you go, Da, I-I'm sorry if this upsets you. I'm going to Birmingham to stay with Bead's cousin. I'm leaving tonight.'

He swung round. 'I suppose this was their idea.'

'No. It was mine.'

'There's no need for you to go. Once you start showing a little respect to Lizzy, we'll all get along fine.'

'But, Da–'

He silenced her with a look. 'Now, I've things to do. Lizzy will be here soon.' And he went down to open the shop.

He hadn't taken her seriously. 'Oh, Da,' she sighed, and placed the dirty dishes in the sink and washed them.

* * *

Aileen had just finished mopping the kitchen floor when her father appeared at the top of the stairs lugging two heavy cases. Lizzy followed, a cigarette dangling from her mouth. Aileen's heart sank, and for the umpteenth time, she wondered what her father saw in the woman. Seeing her aunt again washed away any doubts she had about going away.

'I thought you'd be down at the college, Aileen,' her aunt said, taking the cigarette from her mouth. The smoke curled upwards and caught the back of Aileen's throat. 'They will be enrolling again soon, won't they?'

'No. It's not what I want to do?'

'Really!' She glanced round as Aileen's father placed the heavy cases just inside the bedroom door. 'Have you explained to her about your plans, Jonny?'

'She knows what her ma wanted for her, but the choice is hers.'

As Lizzy pulled out a chair and sat down, Aileen placed a saucer down in front of her to catch the ash.

'How was your journey, Lizzy?' her da asked. 'Was the bus on time?'

She didn't answer. She stubbed the remains of her cigarette into the saucer and stood up, removed her coat, and hung it up and sat back down. 'So what are you going to do then?' Lizzy persisted.

Aileen crossed her arms. 'I don't think that's any of your business.'

'Oh,' she laughed. 'Jessie spoiled this one, Jonny.'

'There's no need to be smart, Aileen. Lizzy's only making conversation. Put some biscuits on a plate and make yourself useful.' He placed a cup of tea down in front of Lizzy, and sat down next to her. Aileen did as her da asked through gritted teeth.

Lizzy pulled her chair closer to the table. 'Well, you're not hanging around here all day. I'll be looking after things, and once your father sells up, you're going to have to look for work.'

'No need for you to worry about me, Aunt.'

Her da stood up as if to rebuke her. He looked pathetic in a beige, woollen cardigan that sagged at the front. He said nothing, nothing at all to defend her, and she knew he never would. In defiant mood, Aileen turned and walked away.

Upstairs, she glanced around her bedroom. What would happen to her possessions? She couldn't take them with her. Once her father sold up, most of her things would mean nothing to Lizzy, and she imagined the woman throwing everything belonging to her and Ma into the bin.

Aileen's teddy and the first doll her parents had given her when she was quite young were treasured possessions, and she agonised about what to take. She couldn't fit both into her case. Her doll would have to stay where it was, on the shelf above her bed. Her jewellery box with a ballerina on top which danced and played a tune—a present from her Aunt Bead—she wrapped in yesterday's newspaper and placed it at the bottom of her case.

Her books would have to stay. She never felt lonely when she could choose from the row of classics her mother had bought for her. She picked one: *The Wit and Humour of Oscar Wilde*. Somehow it always uplifted her, and she pressed it down one side of her case, then filled it with the rest of her clothes. She couldn't possibly fit anything else in. It wouldn't be so bad if she could come home now and then and find her belongings still where she had left them, but that wasn't possible now.

Uncle Paddy would collect them for her; she only had to

phone him. That settled, she went back out to the kitchen. Her da and Lizzy were sitting together on her ma's sofa, their faces hidden behind a double spread of the *Evening Herald*. Most nights when she had arrived home after a night out, it was her ma she saw sitting with her da, reading or listening to the wireless. Seeing her aunt in her mother's place really grated.

Fighting to keep her feelings in check, she made her way towards the back of the kitchen and unlocked the door to the fire escape. It led down to their back yard and the shed where her da kept old boxes and tools. Her father got up and asked her what she wanted out the back.

'Nothing.'

He placed his hand on her arm, and for a second she thought he was going to hug her and wish her good luck. But instead he asked, 'What time does the boat leave?'

She swallowed. 'Eleven tonight.'

'You'll be needing a lift?' He pushed his hands into the drooping pockets of his cardigan.

Aileen raised her eyes to look at him. 'Don't trouble yourself, Da. Dermot's taking me.' When he sighed and made no comment, she continued down the iron steps to the shed below. Whatever had happened to her da?

She took a while to select the right size of box, and when she came back up, her da and Lizzy were not in the room. She glanced towards the coat rail. Their coats were missing. Her da never went down the pub on a weeknight, and only occasionally accompanied Dermot's da there on a Saturday night.

Back in her room, she choked back tears, anger coursing through her. She closed her case and put it on the floor, then placed the box on the bed. He hadn't even wished her a safe journey. With a heavy heart, she took her books from the shelf along with her other knick-knacks, wrapped them in newspaper, and packed them into the box. She wrapped her doll last and placed it on top. When she was ready, she took the box down the street to Dermot's.

When he opened the door, he stood back surprised. 'What's

all this?' he said, relieving her of the heavy box.

'I'm sorry to put this on you, but can you take care of these until Uncle Paddy comes for them?' She bit her lip. 'I hope your ma won't mind?'

'Indeed, she won't. Are you coming in, or are you ready to go now?'

'Can you give me ten minutes?' She kissed his cheek and hurried back up the street.

When she entered the shop, the reality of her life hit her. She thought about her ma's dying wish. Her da had been no help, although she felt sure he had information that would help her to start her search for her brother. As things stood now, her main priority was to get away from her da and Lizzy.

She stood behind the counter for the last time; the silence stretched, adding to her pent-up feelings. Powerless to change how her da felt, the knot of pain in her stomach increased. It started to rain, and heavy drops ran down the windowpane, mimicking her tears. She selected two pairs of Bear Brand nylons from the shelf and left four shillings on top of the till. Then she went back upstairs to collect her case with no idea what the future had in store.

## Chapter Twelve

Little conversation passed between Aileen and Dermot on the way to the Dublin ferry.

She closed her eyes, thinking of her future and wishing her da had come to see her off. The window wipers struggled to keep pace with the heavy rain, and she could smell lavender wafting from the dangling air freshener which fought to eliminate the meat and fish smells from the inside of the van.

Sadness she hadn't felt since her mother's funeral enveloped her. She didn't want to leave, nor did she want to say goodbye to Dermot just when she discovered she had feelings for him. The rain had eased when they arrived at the dock, and Dermot pulled into the parking area.

'The ferry's in,' he said. 'You won't have to wait long before boarding.' He lifted her case from the van.

Aileen hated long goodbyes. As they walked towards the entrance, Dermot said, 'I know I said I wouldn't make things more difficult for you, but it won't be the same without you.'

Aileen touched his arm. 'I'll miss you, too, Dermot.'

The waiting room was full, and they were lucky to find two seats where they could sit together. Dermot placed the case between his knees. 'Promise me that if things don't work out, though—and I'm not saying they won't,'—he gesticulated with his hands '—you'll come home. Ma would put you up in the spare room.' He knitted his fingers and glanced down.

Aileen placed her hand over his. 'Thanks, Dermot, I'll remember.'

The gate opened, and the crowd surged forward. Aileen felt a fluttering in her tummy and glanced over her shoulder.

'You've not forgotten anything, have you?'

She shook her head. Apart from Dermot, none of her family had come to see her off. 'Please, Dermot, don't come any farther. I'll be fine.'

He looked crestfallen, and leaned over and kissed her lips. She knew he was shy about showing his affections in public. When he handed her the case, he held onto her hand until she broke away. Keeping her feelings in check, she followed the crowd, not daring to look back; her emotions were raw.

Once she had placed her luggage in the hold, she went on deck. She wore a black and white check skirt and a red sweater her mother had knitted, with a row of cable stitching down the front. A wet, easterly wind swept across the deck. She shuddered and pulled the collar of her gabardine mac up around her neck and went over to the rail. She glanced across at the twinkling lights around the harbour where a few people had gathered.

Then she saw them. Her Uncle Paddy and Aunt Bead were standing alongside Dermot, her uncle waving his large, red handkerchief towards the ship. She stood close to the rail waving back at them with tears in her eyes.

* * *

Dermot had hoped to stay with Aileen longer, at least until she had boarded. He would have followed her through the barrier, but it was clear she wanted to go alone. He could only imagine what she must be feeling. He felt annoyed that he hadn't given her a proper kiss before she disappeared from his life. If only she had taken him up on his offer of marriage. He would have looked after her, treasured her. At twenty-six, he was ready to settle down, but he understood why she didn't feel the same.

He recalled how she had told him she loved him. And if it hadn't been for her father's strange behaviour and her aunt sticking her nose in, she would still be here in the Fair City. It was just too much for her to cope with, and now she had left home to live miles away. It just wasn't right. The whole business was just as puzzling to Dermot and his ma and da as it was to Aileen.

As soon as he returned home, his mother questioned him. 'How did it go? Did she get off all right?'

Dermot nodded and slumped down into a chair as his mother poured him a mug of tea. Dermot's da appeared in the doorway and shrugged out of his damp rain jacket.

'She's gone then?' He shook his head. 'Jonny Maguire needs his head seen to, letting a lovely young girl like Aileen go off to England on her own.' He sat down at the table and poured himself tea from the pot. 'When I see 'im, I won't be long about telling him a few home truths.'

'You keep out of it, Len Brogan.' His mother gave his da a playful swipe with the tea towel. 'You can't go wading in on people's lives.' She looked over at Dermot, who sighed and shook his head. 'Ah sure, happen the girl will come back once she's had a taste of being away from home.'

'What home?' Dermot drained his mug and got to his feet. 'You don't understand, do you, Ma? Aileen didn't go away because she wanted to. It's the fault of that no-good aunt of hers.'

* * *

The sea was fairly calm for August, but it could be unpredictable, and Aileen was glad she had taken her sea legs. If anything, the tablets relaxed her and kept her from dwelling on circumstances that had led her aboard this ship. Below deck, every seat was taken. Some passengers were lying on the floor, wrapped in blankets. Aileen found a space under a stairwell, curled up, and slept.

She was awakened a few times by the creaking of the ship, and men's coarse voices singing Irish songs in the bar. Finally, the long hours passed, and they docked in Holyhead.

She was ill prepared for the stampede as passengers lined up for disembarkation. At last, she managed to get off the ship and walked along a covered area where customs officers randomly called people over. When Aileen was called, she hauled her heavy case up onto the wooden table where it was opened. She felt her face redden as the office fingered her underwear.

'What's wrapped in the newspaper?'

'It's just my teddy bear.'

The officer beckoned to another officer, and they chatted offside. Aileen glanced over her shoulder, fearing she might miss the train. The teddy was removed from its wrapping, prodded and examined.

'Is there something wrong?' she asked. *Maybe they thought she was a smuggler or worse?*

The officer placed the teddy back in her case and placed the newspaper on top. 'No, miss.' He smiled. 'You can go now.'

Aileen hurried to catch up with the rest of the passengers, wondering what on earth they were looking for. Did she look suspicious because she was nervous? Thankfully, the train was stationary, but the small station's platform was deserted. There was nowhere she could get a warm drink; even the waiting room was closed.

She climbed on board the train, leaving her luggage in the corridor, and found a seat in one of the compartments. It felt cold and the seats smelled of damp as if they had been caught in a shower. She sat by the window, removed her coat, and wrapped it around her legs. Happen it would warm up once the train got moving.

More people crowded on board, searching for somewhere to sit, so she straightened her legs to make room. Some shared flasks of tea with one another, and she wished she had bought a fizzy drink on the boat.

It was half an hour later when the train's engine finally steamed into action and crawled its way slowly out of Holyhead. It was still dark, and she could see nothing of the beautiful scenery she had heard so much about as the train travelled through Wales. She dozed for a while and when she woke it was morning, and lights were coming on in the houses they passed. People were getting up, preparing for the day ahead; all she wanted was to put her head down and sleep.

* * *

Later, she had to fight her way onto a Birmingham train. Packed in like sardines, with only standing room, Aileen sat on her case, stifled a yawn, and told herself her journey would soon be over. It was some time before a seat became vacant, and she flopped into it, turning her face towards the window. Factories and tall grey buildings flashed by as the train approached the city and hissed into New Street Station.

She stepped from the train and stood with her case at her feet, jostled from all sides as people rushed past her to catch trains. She glanced around. At least, the station had amenities, and she headed for the waiting room and toilets. Shortly afterwards, she sat on a station seat with a mug of hot tea and a ham sandwich, contemplating her next move.

She smiled at the woman who sat down next to her, but the woman turned away. It made her all the more aware she was no longer in Ireland, where everyone spoke to everyone—even when you didn't want them to.

She gripped the handle of her case and walked towards the exit with no idea what direction to take. Outside on the busy street, she felt tired and confused. It started to rain; a fine drizzle that made her hair damp. A taxi drew to a halt next to her, and the driver wound the window down.

'Where to, love?'

'How much to take me to Hagley Road?'

'I'll get you there for five bob.'

'Five shillings!' Aileen shook her head. Someone else hopped into the taxi and it drove off.

'Hey!' A voice called out from behind her. 'You can catch a bus around the corner. It'll cost you a few coppers and get you there in fifteen minutes.'

She thanked the newspaper boy and, masking her anxiety, hauled her suitcase through the crowds along New Street towards the bus stop. Cars, lorries, and buses created a traffic jam that went the length of the street and became gridlocked at the roundabout.

When she was finally on the bus heading for Bead's cousin's house, rain was beating down. It was close to noon, and she had been travelling for hours. The conductor dropped her off at the King's Head and pointed her in the direction she should go.

Soon she found herself staring wide-eyed down a long,

broad avenue, hoping desperately that the number she wanted was nearer the top. By now the rain had soaked her hair and was running down her legs.

She passed no-one on the quiet street, and she guessed that most people were at work. Tired and weary, she trudged on, looking at the house numbers on either side of the road. Her arm ached and her case seemed to have grown heavier.

At last, she paused outside a house with a black gate and a green privet hedge and wondered what sort of reception she would get from Bead's cousin. Would she still have a room for her? And how was she going to get used to the Birmingham accent? Aileen took a deep breath, opened the gate, and walked up the path. The house was a Victorian villa with a wooden canopy over the door and a small, tidy front garden.

She dropped her case down at her feet and flexed her arm then rang the bell on the brown door. In no time at all the door opened, and a woman with a smiling face and dark curly hair stood before her.

'Now don't tell me,' the woman said. 'You must be Aileen.' She proffered her hand. 'I'm Mary. Sure, look at yea. Yea look lost. Come in, will yea.'

Relieved, Aileen stepped over the threshold and put her case down, then followed Mary down the long hallway to the kitchen.

'This won't take a minute,' she said, switching on the kettle. 'I'm sure you could murder a cuppa.' She threw a towel towards Aileen. 'Get out of that wet coat and dry your hair; it's like rat's tails.'

Aileen could well imagine how she must look, but she was too tired to care. She removed her wet things and sank into a chair.

'Well,' Mary said, breaking into her thoughts. 'How was your journey?'

'Exhausting.'

Mary removed her baking bowl and rolling pin from the table, and wiped the area clean. The plastic tablecloth showed a repeated pattern of blue sailing boats. She placed cups and saucers on the table and popped bread into the toaster. 'Would you like a cooked breakfast? This one is on the house.'

Aileen couldn't think about food. Embarrassed, she struggled to keep her eyes open. 'Thanks, but if it's all the same to you, I'll just have a slice of toast.' She felt like she was on another planet.

'Ah, sure you're tired. You've come a long way.' Bread popped up from the toaster, and she placed it on a plate. 'Well, drink your tea and eat something. You'll feel more like eating tomorrow.'

Aileen nodded. Her eyes drooped and she shifted in the chair.

'I've got three bedrooms occupied, and one small room.' Mary turned her back and filled the sink with crockery. 'I'm afraid you'll have to settle for that until such time as a bigger room becomes vacant. It's been a busy few months. Will that do yea?'

Aileen nodded. There was a room for her, and that was all she needed to know for now. 'I'm very grateful to you, Mary, for taking me in.'

Mary turned towards her, drying her hands. 'I was sorry to hear about your ma. God rest her soul.' She placed her hand on Aileen's arm. 'Losing a mother ain't easy, sure, I know all about it.' She passed the tea with milk and sugar and left Aileen to butter her own toast. 'I'll take up your luggage; we can sort things out later.'

Aileen was pleased she had remembered to exchange her Irish punts on the ship. Her throat felt dry and she gulped her tea and ate a small piece of toast, then she followed Mary upstairs and found her coming out of one of the bedrooms situated towards the back of the house.

'I hope you'll be comfy. The bathroom's across the landing,' she said, holding the door ajar. 'As I said, it's small but it's a nice room. You've a wardrobe there and a small bedside table. If yea need ought else, let me know.'

Aileen smiled her reply. When Mary left her alone, she moved over to the window that overlooked a long back garden with a couple of empty clotheslines and galvanised dustbins. Then she kicked off her shoes, stretched out on the single bed with the pink candlewick bedspread, and closed her eyes. Birmingham was a fast, vibrant city, from what she had seen of it so far. It made her all the more aware of how laid-back her life had been in Ireland. Her new life would take a while to get used to, but she was determined to make it work.

# Chapter Thirteen

When Aileen woke in a strange room, it was dark. She switched on the bedside lamp and looked at her watch. Eight o'clock. Was that morning or evening? She had been tired, but surely she hadn't slept for ten hours during the day? A cup of cold tea and a biscuit sat on the table.

She got out of bed and slipped into her shoes. Unlatching her case, she took out her wash bag and went along the corridor to the bathroom. Back in her room, she put on fresh clothes and brushed her blond hair loose. Her stomach rumbled, and she ate the digestive before making her way downstairs.

Mary was in her sitting room, knitting with the door open. When she saw Aileen, she rolled her knitting around the pins and stuck them into a ball of blue wool. 'Had a good sleep, love?' she asked, coming into the hall.

'I did, thanks. And I'm sorry about earlier. I felt dead on my feet.'

'It's all right, sure. I understand. Come on down to the kitchen. I'll make yea something to eat.'

Aileen hadn't taken much notice of the kitchen earlier; it was small and narrow in comparison to the size of the house. A grey worktop flanked both sides of the cooker, with matching overhead cupboards filling one side of the kitchen, and a square table and four chairs against the other wall. She pulled out a chair and sat down.

'Do yea like eggs?'

'Right now, I could eat anything.' Aileen laughed.

'You're not the first guest I've had from over the sea. Several hours, isn't it, the ferry? Then you've had the two train journeys. Oh, I remember it well.' She broke eggs into a bowl and beat them together with milk and a knob of butter. 'Twenty years ago now that I came here, and I slept for nearly two days. So there, ten hours is respectable.' She poured the mixture into a big, black frying pan and stood over it. 'Your Aunt Bead was just the same when she was over last. She was at sixes and sevens for days.'

Aileen smiled. Mary's accent was as broad as if she'd just walked out of Ireland. 'Can I do anything?'

'Just eat up,' she said, placing a cheese omelette down in front of her.

'This looks lovely, Mary.'

'Well, you don't want anything heavy on your stomach if you want to sleep again tonight.'

Aileen ate as Mary sat opposite her and took a small notebook and pencil from her apron pocket. 'Now, as you're family, shall we say two pounds ten shillings a week, including a cooked breakfast when yea find work?' How does that suit you?'

'That sounds very reasonable, Mary, thanks.'

'I wouldn't be doing it for everyone, mind.'

Aileen reached for her bag and took the money from her purse.

'Put that away. You needn't pay me until you find work, and believe me, you'll be spoilt for choice around here.'

'Really? That's kind of you, Mary.'

The door clicked, and Aileen heard someone come into the hall. 'That'll be Miss Brady.' Mary told her. 'She's a teacher and she works at the college. Staff meeting tonight!' Mary raised her eyebrows.

'How many boarders do you have?'

'Just two others. The teacher is on the first floor and a young girl. She's a bit younger than you; her name's Bella Smith. She's a worry, that one. She comes in at all hours o' the night.' Mary sighed. 'You might get to meet her in the morning if she gets up on time.'

'That will be nice.' Aileen was pleased to know there was another young girl in the house.

'Not if you follow her example, it won't.' Mary stood up and lifted a pile of newspapers from a chair. 'The *Birmingham Post* is here somewhere.' She looked at the date and passed it to Aileen. 'Tek it inside and have a read. I'll tidy up here and then I'll join yea.' There was something about Mary that reminded Aileen of her ma.

The front room had a settee and one enormous armchair with balding armrests; a wireless muttered on top of a sideboard, and a copper-potted fern sat on the windowsill. A frameless mirror hung over the fireplace, and a two bar electric fire was fitted into the empty grate. Aileen curled up in the huge armchair and glanced through the newspaper. Mary was right; it was full of vacancies for various jobs, but Aileen had no idea where any of them were.

When Mary joined her, she picked up her knitting and began to knit with three pins instead of the usual two. Aileen gave her a quizzical look.

'What are you knitting Mary?'

'Bed socks for me sister. She's always complaining of cold feet, so she is. And blue's her favourite colour.'

'It must be nice having a sister.' Aileen thought about the brother she might never get to meet.

'Aye. Mavis has been living in England longer than me. She was here when I came over. Whereas she talks proper English now, she tells me I'll never lose the brogue.'

'Did she ever marry?'

'Ah, sure she did, but their only child was stillborn and Ed, her better half, he died soon after that. So she's had it tough. Then I lost Ken, but sure, we have each other.'

'I'm sorry.'

'That's life.' Mary paused to count stitches.

Aileen sat forward in the armchair and fidgeted with her hands. 'Mary, can I ask you something?'

'Ask away. I won't charge yea.'

'Did you know my ma very well?'

'Well, sure, course I did. Jessie and me, we were good pals. She married Jonny, and not long after you were born, I came over here.'

'You say... I mean... did she ever tell you anything private like?'

65

Mary's knitting pins stopped abruptly, and she placed them in her lap. 'Oh, umm, in what way, love?'

'You said you were friends. I just wondered if she ever, like, told you anything personal.'

Mary looked pensive, and Aileen hoped she knew something. 'I'm not sure I know what yea mean.' She crossed her arms. 'We went dancing together and we kept in touch for a while until I married Ken. Well, you know, life takes over, and we lost touch.' She sighed. 'I was sorry she died, love, and I would have come over if...'

Aileen nodded. 'I was hoping she might have told you a secret?'

'A secret! What kind of secret are yea talking about?' Mary unfolded her arms and linked her fingers. 'What's troubling yea?'

Aileen swallowed. 'It's a bit, well...' She felt a little awkward talking about her ma to someone she had only just met. So she just came out with it. 'Did my ma have any other children, apart from me?'

Mary was on her feet. 'Glory be to God! What gave yea that notion?'

'Ma left me a note asking me to find my brother, and ask him to forgive her.'

Mary scratched her head. 'What? I mean, how? Why would she say that? Have you asked your father about this?'

'Da says she was rambling. I don't believe him.'

Mary went over and placed her arm around Aileen's shoulder. 'Look, love, there's probably no truth in it.'

Aileen sighed. 'Aunt Bead and Uncle Paddy don't believe it either. But I do. Ma wouldn't lie to me, especially as she was anxious to confess to a priest.'

Mary's eyes widened. 'She did what?' Mary looked uneasy as she gathered up her knitting. 'She could have been confessing anything, love. People can say strange things when they're close to death. Try and put it from your mind.'

# Chapter Fourteen

Aileen couldn't put it from her mind. How could she? Mary had looked shocked, and if she knew nothing about her mother's baby, Aileen's hopes were dashed.

The following morning, she woke to the sound of a toilet flushing, then footsteps running downstairs. Was that the young girl, Bella? Or was it Miss Brady?

She dressed hurriedly and went down. A pretty young girl was in the hall, pulling on her coat. When she saw Aileen, her brown eyes widened.

'You must be Bella.' Aileen held out her hand. 'I'm Aileen.'

'Nice to meet yea.' The girl gave Aileen a lopsided smile. 'Sorry, I'm late. Can't stop.

Tarra,' she shouted and headed out the door.

Aileen, disappointed not to have had a few more minutes to talk to a fellow lodger, made her way towards the kitchen where the smell of bacon frying reminded her of home.

'Sit down, love.' Mary turned and faced her, her hair in pink rollers. 'That young 'un's yampee.'

'Sorry?' Aileen pulled a face.

'By heck.' Mary laughed. 'I've picked up a few Brummie sayings in me time. It mean's crazy! Young Bella, she's a strange 'un. Do you like black and white pudding?'

'Oh, yes please. Ma always cooked it with a fry.'

'What did yea make of Bella then?'

'She seems nice.' Aileen ran her fingers across the plastic tablecloth. 'I hope I get to talk to her later. What did she mean by "tarra"?'

Mary chuckled. 'Oh, everyone says that here. Means ta-ta, as they say in Dublin, or bye-bye. You'll get used to it after you've been here for a while.'

Aileen placed her elbow on the table. 'How old is Bella?'

Mary poured the tea and then sat down, nursing her own mug with its picture of a black cat with green eyes. 'She's sixteen. To tell the truth, I'd be happier if she went back home.'

Aileen cut into the crispy black pudding and chewed her bacon. 'This tastes good.'

'Get it down yea before it goes cold.'

'Why is she living here?'

'Her parents only live in Smethwick. Not far from here, like. They've kicked her out because she's cavorting with a married man.'

Aileen gasped and almost choked on her bacon. She swallowed some tea. 'But she's only sixteen! How old is he?'

Mary shrugged. 'Old enough to know better, and she's a pretty little thing. What's worse is that she sees him nearly every night until he has to go home to his wife.' She removed her hairnet. 'Yea know what beats me?' She began taking her pink rollers from her hair, placing them into the pocket of her apron. 'Why his missus hasn't cottoned on afore; it's a mystery. Bella's never here at weekends. And you can imagine what goes on.' Mary shook her head, and her curls danced on her forehead.

'Really! You're codding me?'

'You're shocked, aren't yea? You'll find people over here more broadminded. Not that I approve, mind.'

'But what if she, you know?'

'Oh, she's not worried about that. Sez she's on the pill.' Mary shrugged. 'It's

not fool proof. Many a one's been caught out on it. I've tried talking sense to 'er. She came home sozzled a week ago. There was no talking to 'er, sure; she thinks the sun shines out his backside.'

'But isn't the pill only prescribed to married women?'

'Where do yea think she gets it?'

'No. Surely not!'

'Aye! I'm surprised that no-one's reported 'im for corrupting a minor.'

Aileen had a bad feeling about this man. Cheating on his poor wife was something she couldn't condone. But she would like to be friends with Bella. The girl was bound to be as lonely as she was, being away from her family.

'Where does Bella work?' Aileen asked, clearing the breakfast dishes.

'She works at that seed mill place down on Windmill Lane. It's only a short walk from 'ere. Why don't yea go down there and ask about a job yourself?'

Aileen nodded. 'I will after I've helped you wash the dishes.'

Mary wiped down the plastic tablecloth, and Aileen washed up in a sink full of soapy water then dried her hands. 'I'll go up and get myself ready.'

'I'll come with yea as far as the 'ill,' Mary said, removing her apron. 'I've some bits to pick up.'

A short time later, Aileen came down in a black boxy jacket and a white miniskirt and black court shoes.

'You look nice,' Mary said, slipping on her grey mac. It was the sort of thing her ma would have said, and Aileen smiled.

"Ere,' she said. 'Yea can have me spare key until I can get one cut for yea.' Mary took a gold coloured Yale key from her keyring and handed it to Aileen.

It was a warm, muggy day as they made their way down the long avenue towards the shops. It was the first time Aileen had been out since she arrived, and she was looking forward to seeing something of her surroundings.

It didn't take her long to realise that what Mary called the 'ill was, in fact, Cape Hill—a busy street with lots of shops. They crossed over and paused outside a jeweller's shop.

'This is where I leave yea,' Mary said. 'Now, if you go down 'ere, this is Windmill Lane. If you get as far as Vicky Park, yea've gone too far. I think it's halfway along on the right. Good luck.'

'Thanks, Mary, I'll need it.'

'You'll be grand. Now,' she said, shifting her large handbag to her other arm, 'can yea find yer way back?'

Aileen nodded and Mary shuffled away, leaving her to make her way down the street towards the mill. At the gate, she was met by the sound of grain being crushed in a grinder. As she advanced further in, the smell was worse than the pet shop back home. She heard the sound of water and seed being screened and washed as it filtered through a seed processor.

A man in a brown shop coat stood watching the seed fall through into containers, and another man humped sacks of raw materials inside. The man in the brown coat—stocky build and sporting a quiff—walked towards her, extinguishing his cigarette. She hoped she would be able to understand him.

'What can I do for yea, luv?'

'Actually, I'm looking for work.'

He pointed her towards the office entrance. 'Ask at the hatch.'

She nodded and went in through the open doorway. There was a wooden staircase on her left and, further along on the right, a hatch where she knocked and waited. A young girl with wavy blonde hair, cut close to her head, glanced up.

'Can I help?'

'I'm looking for work. Do you have any vacancies?'

'Hold on,' she said, and quickly lifted the phone. Within minutes, an older woman in a navy twinset and a straight, grey skirt came down the stairs.

'Hello,' she said, twirling a pencil between her fingers. 'Can you type?'

'Well, yes, I started a secretarial course in Dublin, but I had to leave before I'd taken my exams because my ma took ill.'

'Is she better now?'

'I'm afraid she died a couple of months ago.'

'I'm sorry to hear that.' The woman looked embarrassed and removed her glasses then put them back on again. 'Are you looking for permanent work?'

'Yes.' Aileen nodded.

'If you can type, you might have a job.'

'Thank you.' Aileen was surprised to be interviewed in the passageway.

'Come in here.' The woman went before her into the office and placed a sheet of paper into an Imperial typewriter. 'Can you type this paragraph?' She placed a printed sheet on the desk and pulled out a chair.

Aileen lowered herself down, feeling a little nervous. It was some time since she had done any typing, and her fingers hit the wrong key more than once. The woman whipped it from the roller.

'I'm sorry, would you like me to type it again?'

'Well, you won't be typing letters or statements, so you'll do nicely.' The older woman smiled. 'When can you start?'

'Would tomorrow be okay?'

'Fine.'

Aileen blew out her lips. She thought it rather strange that she didn't have to produce her reference, but they were obviously desperate for a typist so she wasn't complaining. She now had a job.

'We'll start you off on five pounds a week and see how you get on. Then we'll look at increasing it by ten shillings. Are you happy with that?'

'Yes, thank you.'

'I'm Miss Grimshaw. I hope you'll be happy here.' She turned to the young office girl. 'Val, can you take...' She turned back to Aileen. 'Sorry, I never asked your name.'

'Aileen. Aileen Maguire.'

'Take down Aileen's details and we'll see her tomorrow at nine.' Smiling, she inclined her head and hurried back upstairs as if she hadn't a minute to spare.

'Was that the boss, then?'

'No, Miss Grimshaw runs the accounts and generally sees to the overall running of the office staff,' Val explained. 'Mr Bill is the boss, but he rarely comes out of his office. We're lucky to see him once a week.'

'What's he like?'

'He's okay. We don't have much to do with him. Occasionally

when Miss Grimshaw's away, or busy, you might be asked to type a letter, and then you'd have to ask Mr Bill to sign it.' She laughed when she saw Aileen frown. 'Don't worry. It's not hard work, but it can be busy.' Val reached for a pen. 'Now I'd better get your details.

After a few seconds, she stopped scribbling and glanced up. 'So, you don't live far from here! How old are you?'

'I'm eighteen.'

'Really? Oh, good,' Val said. 'I'm a year older, so we should have a lot in common. You'll probably get tax stopped on your first week's wages,' the girl continued. 'But you'll get it back at the end of the tax year, or if you leave. And I hope you won't be doing that.' She placed Aileen's details into a folder and popped a sheet of paper between the roller of her typewriter. 'We've been waiting for someone like you for months. The last woman who applied was at least fifty and she couldn't even type.'

'You're codding!'

'You sound Irish. Where are you from?'

'Dublin. I just arrived yesterday.'

Bella came downstairs and popped her head round the office door. 'Hello, how are you? Have you come about the job?'

'Yes, lucky me,' Aileen said. 'I only called in on the off chance.'

'I'm pleased for yea.' She wore a blue, baggy cardigan, the sleeves covering her hands like fingerless gloves. Aileen thought she was quite beautiful, with big eyes and lashes heavy with mascara. 'Tarra.' She gave a little wave and headed towards the yard.

When Aileen was leaving, she saw the man in the brown shop coat, his arms tightly wrapped around Bella; the way he was kissing the young girl made Aileen blush. They were standing against the shed, in full view of anyone who walked in or out of the yard. Aileen paused for a second before she hurried out. If he was the married man Mary had talked about, she had every reason to worry.

Although she felt she ought to, Aileen said nothing to Mary. She didn't want to land Bella in any more trouble than she was in already. Besides, she wanted to get to know the other girl and find out what she was up to. So she put what she had seen in the yard out of her mind.

Later, as she sat with Mary in the front room, writing letters home, she couldn't help wondering what it was that attracted Bella to a man that old. He must be in his thirties!

# Chapter Fifteen

The following morning, Aileen had butterflies in her tummy and she could only manage a small piece of toast.

'To tell the truth,' Mary said, her expression downcast, 'I've had nothing to eat myself, worrying about that young 'un.'

'Where is she? Has she left already then?'

'I've not seen hide nor hair of her since she left yesterday mornin'.'

'Really! Should we be worried?' Aileen pulled on her jacket and slipped her feet into a pair of low-heeled shoes.

Mary followed her into the hall. 'Blesses an save us, Aileen, I don't know.' She started up the stairs, then said, 'I wish I hadn't agreed to take her in.' She sighed. 'If yea see 'er at work, tell 'er I want a word.'

Aileen nodded and placed her letters for posting into her bag. She wondered where Bella had been all night.

Outside, the sky was overcast and she hoped it wouldn't rain. A cold wind blew at her hair and around her ankles as she walked towards Cape Hill. She popped her letters into a postbox on the corner. The traffic was heavy, and she crossed at the pelican crossing.

She knew she could rely on Dermot and her Aunt Bead to reply. But she hoped her da would reply when he read her letter, and reconsider his decision to sell the shop. She longed to know how he was coping. If it hadn't been for her aunt, she'd still be at home looking after him and the shop, like her ma had asked her to.

Her mother's last request weighed heavily on her mind, but there was little she could do about it until someone decided to tell her the truth. In the meantime, she had a new job that she was looking forward to.

It was a bitter cold day. The wind swept through the yard and along the corridor, and Aileen closed the office door quickly behind her. Val was hunched inside her jacket, staring into space.

'I'm a bit early.'

'Sorry,' Val said. 'I was miles away. If you're warm enough, you can hang your jacket on the coatstand.' She rubbed her hands together. 'I'm keeping mine on. It's bloody freezing in here.' She began sorting through the paperwork. 'About time we had some proper heating.'

Aileen smiled in spite of the cold. A one bar, infrared heater hung on the wall, too high up to be of any use. Their desks were linked together so they were facing each other, and with only one typewriter between them, she wondered what she was supposed to do. Val placed a pile of dockets and sheets in front of her. 'You can be looking through these until your typewriter arrives.'

Miss Grimshaw hurried in. 'Oh, there you are, Aileen. Are you settling in okay?'

'Yes, thank you, Miss Grimshaw.'

Smiling, she bustled out again, and Aileen began scanning the work in front of her. Some of the handwriting made no sense to her whatsoever and might as well have been written in Chinese.

The office door opened, and a short man of about fifty, in a grey suit, burst in with a typewriter in his arms. He placed the black Remington down on Aileen's desk. 'I hope you'll be happy here, Miss Maguire.'

'I'm sure I will, thank you.'

He glanced over at Val, head down typing, and her jacket now around her shoulders. He rubbed his hands. 'I'm sorry it's not very warm in here. I'll have someone put up a partition by the door to keep out the draught.'

'The sooner, the better, Mr Bill,' Val said.

Aileen was surprised at the casual way in which Val had addressed the boss, but he just nodded and went down the corridor towards his office.

'He's a nice old sod,' Val said. 'Better than some I've worked for.' She was a fast typist; three times faster than Aileen. 'If you get stuck with anything, let me know.'

'How many people work here?'

'Miss Grimshaw and three others in accounts, including Bella—two are part-timers. Alan and Bob in the yard; you, me, and the boss.' She half smiled. 'Oh, and we have a company sales rep, Mr Pickering. He covers most of the West Midlands.' Val shrugged and tugged at the sleeves of her jumper. 'We don't see much of him. Just as well. He's a bit strange.'

'What do you mean?'

'Doo no. There's something about him that gives me the creeps. Good at his job, though, according to Miss Grimshaw. I think that's everyone.' She continued to type.

The work was simple; it was the handwriting that Aileen had problems with. 'Whose writing is this?' She held up one of the sheets.

'That'll be Alan's. Some will be Bob's, but mostly Alan, as he takes down the orders. I'll do that one, and when Alan comes in, I'll ask him to write clearer until you get used to it.'

Aileen passed it across, then picked up the next one and began to type. Val leant across the desk. 'Can I ask you something, Aileen?'

Aileen glanced up. 'Sure.'

'Are you seeing anyone?'

Aileen frowned. She hadn't heard the expression before. 'Oh, you mean, am I going out with anyone?' She smiled. 'Well, yes and no. There's someone back home I like. What about you?'

'We had a falling out last night. You know, and I'm still angry with 'im.'

'What did you fall out about?'

'He wanted me to stay over.'

'Stay over where?'

'Where do you think? At his 'ouse!'

Aileen wasn't sure how to respond. 'What about his Ma and Da?'

Val shrugged. 'They're away. Anyways, I said no. It's not as if we were engaged.'

'How long have you been going out with him?'

'Eighteen months. I wanted to get engaged on my birthday last March, but he wants to wait. "Wait for what?" I said. He keeps making excuses. What would you do?'

Aileen was in no position to give advice on boyfriends. She'd never had one for more than a week at a time at school and college until she met Dermot. 'I don't know, I–'

The phone rang out, and at the same time, Alan popped his head through the hatch, mumbling something completely incoherent. His voice was more garbled with the noise filtering through from the yard, and he had to repeat his request twice before she grasped what he wanted.

Her face flushed, she quickly flicked through to find the order then handed it to him. He crossed something out and scribbled in something else and handed it back, just as Val replaced the phone.

'Alan, can you write clearer until Aileen gets used to things?' Mumbling under his breath, he left. 'Take no notice,' Val said. 'He can be a moody devil. You'll get used to him.'

Aileen wasn't too sure about that, but seeing him reminded her of Bella. 'Val, have you seen Bella this morning?'

'No. Why?'

'She didn't come back to the boarding house last night.'

'I bet she's upstairs now. She'll have been with Alan. He's only just arrived.'

'What? You mean all night!' Aileen placed the advice note she'd just typed on top of the pile.

'Don't worry. We've all had words with her, but she's besotted. Anyhow, if Mr Bill finds out, it wouldn't be good for Alan. He's married, you know.'

'What about his wife?'

Val shrugged, picked up the notes, and placed them in the tray. 'Don't get me wrong, I like Alan, but he's, well, he's immature for his age.' Val shook her head. 'I'm glad she doesn't work in here; I'd never get ought done. She only has to bat those cow eyes of hers, and they all fall for her excuses. Miss Grimshaw is loath to lose any of the staff.'

'What's Bella's job?'

'She's just a junior. She sorts the post, makes the tea, and everyone upstairs feels sorry for her. Her snooty parents threw her out.' Val shrugged. 'I think she's a spoilt brat.'

'Umm.' The girl was trouble and Mary was worried about her behaviour, which was understandable. But Aileen found her fascinating and was looking forward to getting to know her.

By mid-morning, Aileen could hardly feel her feet, and she wished she had worn her ankle boots. She fetched her jacket, slipped her arms into it, and zipped it up.

'I've had more colds since I've been working here,' Val said. 'I should have told you to wear warmer clothes.'

Alan stopped in, leaving the office door open. He went to the cabinet and began rummaging through files.

'Shut the bloody door!' Val screamed.

'Keep yer 'air on.' He took a wad of sheets from his coat pocket and slammed them down on the desk, then closed the door none too quietly behind him.

Aileen sighed, flexed her cold fingers, and continued working. Time dragged. Typing advice notes all day was boring, but she needed to pay her way. She liked Val, admired the way she ran the downstairs office, and she guessed she could type with her eyes shut. She didn't appear to mind how many times Aileen interrupted her.

Val offered her the early lunch hour, and she went upstairs to see if Bella wanted to go to the Cape for a sandwich. 'No.' Bella yawned. 'I'm exhausted. Me head's splitting. I'm going back to the lodgings for a kip. I'll walk with you to the corner.'

She didn't look well. Strands of her beehive hairdo had come loose and dangled down both sides of her face. Her mascara was smudged, and her face needed a wash.

'Are you all right?' Aileen asked as they walked along.

'Yes.' She giggled.

'Mary worries about you, especially when you stop out.' Aileen wondered how she could come to work looking like she did.

'Well, she shouldn't. I'm fine. Alan and me had a bit of a wild night.' She giggled again.

'Where did you go, then?'

'To that new all-night club down the town.'

'Aren't you frightened of losing your job coming in late?'

'I don't care. There's plenty of jobs.'

Aileen couldn't believe her nonchalant attitude. She didn't appear to worry about anything.

They parted company on the corner. Bella yawned again. 'Tarra, might see yea later.'

Aileen shook her head and watched Bella totter unsteadily across the street, obviously suffering from a hangover.

# Chapter Sixteen

Later that day, Aileen let herself into the B&B. Mary was mashing potatoes in a big aluminium saucepan, her hips swaying to the Beatles' *Can't Buy Me Love* on the wireless. Aileen smiled and stood with her shoulder against the doorjamb. She was pleased to see Mary was in a good mood and wondered how she had reacted when Bella arrived back in the middle of the day looking like she'd slept in a barn.

Mary turned round. 'Spying on me, are yea?'

'Course not. I love that song, too. Can I help?'

'You're all right.' Mary placed the lid on the saucepan, picked up a string of fat sausages, and began to cut off a few links and place them along with a lump of lard into the black frying pan. 'There's tea in the pot if yea fancy one.'

Aileen sat down. 'Mary, have you seen Bella?'

'Not a bit o' 'er.' She emptied a plate of chopped onion into the pan and wiped her runny eyes with the bottom of her apron. 'I don't know what I'm goona do about that young 'un. Anyways, how'd yea get on?'

'Okay, I guess. Val, the girl I work with, is nice. Don't have any trouble understanding her; well, just a little bit. But some of the others, especially Alan, the foreman, he talks like his teeth are wired.'

'Ger off with yea.' They both laughed.

The smell of the fried onions made her hungry. 'I wonder where Bella got to then?'

'What'd yea mean? Didn't she turn up for work?'

'She left early. Said she was coming back here for a kip.'

'Did she now? Well, I've not seen 'err. What time was that?'

'Lunch time.'

'Keep yer eye on the pan, Aileen, I'll goo up and check. If she is up there, she'll feel the sharp end of my tongue.'

'I'll go, Mary.' Aileen placed her hand on the older woman's arm.

'Tell her, she's not getting out 'f 'ere tonight until we get a few things straight,' Mary called, as Aileen hurried out and up the stairs. She rapped on Bella's door.

'Who is it?'

'It's Aileen. Can I come in?'

There was no answer, so Aileen slowly opened the door. Bella sat on the edge of her bed, a letter in her hand.

'Are you all right?' Aileen sat down next to her.

'What's it to you?'

'Sorry, I was just trying to be friendly. Besides, Mary wants to talk to you.'

'What's she want now?'

Aileen stood up. 'Why don't you come down and find out?'

'Don't go.' She touched Aileen's arm. 'I've no-one to talk to. A letter arrived today from me mum. I was too tired to read it earlier, and I've only just opened it.'

'So that's good, isn't it?'

'Depends! She wants us to come 'ome. They threw me out when they found out about Alan. Now she's kicked me stepdad out, and she wants me back.'

'What will you do?'

Bella stood up and pulled at the sleeves of her oversized jumper, her short, black miniskirt barely visible under her long jumper.

'I can't goo,' she said. 'I wouldn't see Alan. We're goon' to have a baby together.'

Aileen's jaw dropped. 'No! You're not, are you?'

'Noo,' Bella giggled. 'But we're goona.'

Aileen shook her head. 'Why would you want a baby with Alan? He's already married, isn't he?' Aileen wanted to advise her.

After all, the girl was only sixteen and not very mature at that. But she hardly knew her, so maybe she should keep her thoughts to herself.

'Sometimes I think I love him,' Bella said dreamily. 'And other times I'm not sure.'

Mary called from downstairs, interrupting their conversation.

'What do you think I should do?' Bella continued.

'Me!' Aileen hadn't expected that. 'Well, I'd think about it carefully, especially if you're not sure how you feel about Alan.'

'Would you go back 'ome after being knocked about and thrown out?' She sat down at the dressing table and began to retouch her long lashes, already caked in mascara.

Mary called again. 'This tea won't stay hot for long. What yea doing up there, cookin' up a story?'

'Look we'd better go down before Mary comes up.'

'So, run along then, Miss Goody Two Shoes.' 'Please yourself,' Aileen sighed and went down alone.

\* \* \*

'Now,' Mary began when Aileen and Bella were seated in front of a plate of sausage and mash. 'Get that down yea.' Then she leant across to Bella. 'You and me's goon' to have an 'eart to 'eart. Okay?'

Bella nodded. She glanced across the table at Aileen, her large eyes misty, and Aileen saw a vulnerability she hadn't noticed before.

When they had finished eating, Mary took Bella into the front room and closed the door. Aileen sat in the kitchen, her fingers crossed that the girl wouldn't have to leave, although she knew that Mary had had enough of Bella's behaviour. From the room, she could hear angry voices—mostly Bella's raised in defiance as Mary spoke her mind.

'You're just jealous!' Bella yelled, then she stomped out into the hall, pulled on her coat, and went out.

'You're on your last warning, my girl,' Mary called after her, her face flushed.

*That went well then,* Aileen thought, as Mary turned towards her.

'She might not care about her reputation, but she's not giving this house a bad name.'

82

Aileen wanted to run after Bella. To try and persuade her to see sense. Instead, she ended up making a cup of tea for Mary, who continued to be infuriated by the girl's impertinence.

Later, as Aileen came out of the bathroom, she overheard Mary in conversation on the telephone. 'No. This arrangement isn't working,' she was saying. 'The girl's underage and she shouldn't be cavorting with a married man twice her age. So you'd better come and collect your daughter, or I won't be held responsible for what happens.'

* * *

The following evening, Aileen was surprised when Mary opened the door to a woman in her late forties. Her dress was impeccable, and she stepped into the hall wearing court shoes, gloves, and had a handbag dangling from her shoulder. She had a young girl of about ten by her side.

'I'm Bell's mother. Is she here?'

'I haven't told 'er you're coming,' Mary said. 'She's in 'er room, no doubt getting ready to go and meet him.'

'Can you let her know I'm here, or shall I go straight up?'

Aileen, who was standing in the doorway of the living room listening, said, 'I'll go and tell her you're here.'

When she knocked and popped her head round the door, Bella was looking in the mirror, pinning up her hair.

'Look, I'm in a hurry. What do you want?'

'Your ma's downstairs.'

'Me mum's here?' Bella frowned. 'She can't be. Who rang her? Was it you?'

'No. But you said yourself she wanted you to come home.'

Bella pulled a face and sat down. 'Tell 'er... Oh, tell 'er to come up.'

Aileen went back down, wondering if she could ever have broken down the wall Bella had built around herself.

'Well?' Bella's mother asked. 'Is she coming?'

'She's asked for you to go up.'

Not waiting to be asked twice, Bella's mother and young sister went upstairs. From what Aileen had seen of Bella's mother, she felt sure that she would easily persuade her daughter to return home. She knew that if her own da asked her to come home, she wouldn't hesitate. However, she felt disappointed not to have had time to get to know Bella.

'Come on, love.' Mary placed her hand on Aileen's arm. 'I feel like celebrating with a cup of tea and a Chelsea bun, don't you?'

# Chapter Seventeen

When Aileen had been working at the mill two weeks, Miss Grimshaw asked her how she felt about doing a few hours overtime on Saturday morning. 'Yes, I'd like that,' she said. 'What do you want me to do?'

The woman smiled. 'Can you come upstairs at nine tomorrow? You won't be on your own. It's just putting invoices into envelopes and using the franking machine.' She linked her fingers. 'They need to be in the post by twelve noon. Is that okay?'

Aileen nodded. The extra money would come in handy. She was saving to go back to Dublin for a few days. Dermot's letter had been full of news; not all good. The draper's shop had been closed for days, and when he'd asked her Aunt Lizzy if everything was all right, she had given him a load of abuse, telling him to mind his own business. He told Aileen that he understood why she had felt the need to get away.

So her aunt was still getting things her own way. Aileen wondered if she should have given in so easily.

Dermot's letter had increased her desire to see how her da was coping. Although she hadn't heard from him, she refused to believe he had completely forgotten about her.

* * *

Several times that week, Alan snubbed her, but Aileen just put it down to the fact that he was missing Bella. On Friday afternoon, she was outside in the yard when she bumped into him.

'Alan, have I done something to upset you? You seem…'

'You couldn't keep your pecker out, could you? Why did you have to interfere with something you know nothing about, eh?'

He turned and walked away towards the sheds.

Shocked, she followed him. 'What do you mean?' He tried to close the door in her face, but she pushed it open. 'This had nothing to do with me. Bella's mother wanted her to come home.'

'You and that Mary engineered it, though, didn't you?'

'No. It wasn't like that.' She wanted to say more, but this wasn't the time to get into an argument. 'Oh, think what you like,' she said and went into the toilet, bolting the door behind her. She took a few deep breaths until she felt calmer before returning to the office.

'Took yea long enough,' Val said, when she returned. The other girl was eating a sandwich with one hand and typing with the other; a pile of paperwork surrounded her. 'We must get this lot finished before we leave tonight.'

'Sorry. I was talking to Alan.' She said nothing more. She was still shaking from Alan's accusation. Why did he feel it was her fault? Had Bella been in touch and ended their relationship? As she typed, the keys kept sticking, and her fingers became covered in ink. Wiping them on a clean tissue, she glanced up at Val. 'Is Alan working tomorrow?'

Val shrugged. 'I guess so. He hasn't got Bella to distract him. Have you heard how she's getting on?'

Aileen shook her head while typing the orders as fast as she could. She wished now that she hadn't agreed to work. Each time Alan came to the hatch, he spoke directly to Val. He was acting like a huffy teenager, and she struggled to hold in the anger welling up inside her. This mess was all down to him. As far as Aileen was concerned, Mary had done Bella a favour.

\* \* \*

On Saturday morning, Aileen was determined not to let Alan intimidate her. When she arrived, the yard was quiet but she knew he was about because the shed doors were open. She quickly slipped upstairs. There was no-one in the office, and she felt vulnerable. The work was laid out on the desk, and she began to sort through it until she heard someone coming upstairs. She looked up, expecting to see the part-time lady, but was startled to see a man standing in the office. He wore a bright yellow jersey over a check shirt, beige casuals and suede shoes.

'I'm sorry, can I–?'

'Apologies if I startled you.' He held out his hand. 'I'm the company rep, Roy Pickering.'

'I'm Aileen. I've only been here a few weeks,' she said, shaking his hand.

'On your own then?'

Aileen shrugged. 'Looks like I am.'

He smiled. 'Well, I'll be around for an hour or so. If you need any help, give me a shout.' He moved to a bigger desk by the window overlooking the street and opened his leather briefcase.

Aileen sighed, pleased that she wasn't alone in the building. She glanced down at the work facing her and wondered how she was expected to get through it all, but she didn't want to let Miss Grimshaw down. When Alan appeared in the office, he walked across to where Roy was on the comptometer, his fingers quickly moving across the mechanical calculator.

Alan handed over an invoice, exchanged a few words, and went back down without so much as a cursory glance in her direction. *How rude*, she thought. The snub hurt her because he had always been polite to her before all this business with Bella.

By eleven o'clock Aileen had only got through half of the work, and she needed to get to the post by twelve. It was a ten-minute walk to the post office, so she decided to finish up, frank the envelopes she had ready, and go.

Roy Pickering finished what he was doing and shut his briefcase then looked over at Aileen. She was looking at the franking machine, a worried expression on her face.

'Need help with that?' Smiling, he came over. In spite of him being an older man, Aileen couldn't help noticing he was quite attractive, and certainly charming and polite. His ginger hair had a centre parting that needed a trim. He touched his hair and gave her a quizzical look. 'I guess you've not worked one of these before.'

She shook her head.

He explained about the dials and the pricing, and then asked her to place one letter at a time into the correct slot at the top and pull the handle. 'Would you like me to help you get the rest finished?'

Aileen smiled gratefully. She didn't want to be left alone in the building with Alan, and she would have used any excuse to keep the sales rep from leaving. 'I hope I'm not keeping you from anything.'

'A few household chores; nothing important!' He pulled over a chair and sat next to her. She could smell his aftershave but couldn't put a name to it. He chatted to her freely as they worked. 'So you're from Ireland? Do you miss it?'

'Yes, I guess I do,' she said, as they passed the envelopes back and forth. Half an hour later the work was finished and bundled together for posting. Aileen sighed. 'Thanks, I'd never have done it without you.'

'Pleasure. You shouldn't have been left in this situation.' He stood up and glanced at his watch. 'Quarter to! They close at twelve. You won't make it on foot.'

'I'm a good runner,' she said.

'Come on, I'll give you a lift.'

Aileen quickly put the bundles into her shopping bag, picked up her belongings, and followed him downstairs. Alan turned his back as she came outside.

A shiny black car was parked in the yard. Aileen knew very little about cars but when Roy opened the passenger door, she could smell the leather. 'I'll have you there in a couple of minutes.'

'I appreciate this. Thank you, Roy.' She settled back in the seat, holding the bag with the post on her knee as the car moved smoothly out into the avenue. She caught a glimpse of Alan standing watching with his hands on his hips.

When Aileen came out of the post office, she was surprised to find Roy was still there. The car purred softly, and he wound the window down.

'Have you far to go?'

'No. I'll be grand. I've some shopping to do.' Thanking him

again, she walked on, glancing into shop windows before slipping into the newsagents where she bought liquorice allsorts and the *Birmingham Post*. On the couple of occasions she had gone downtown to browse the shops, she had discovered it wasn't much fun on her own.

It had been especially lonely these past two weeks and, apart from Mary, she never saw a living soul all weekend. Sometimes she found herself wishing for Monday morning just to hear what Val and her boyfriend had gotten up to. But this morning, working alongside Roy had been pleasant, and she had enjoyed talking with him. Unlike Alan, his manners were impeccable, and she was intrigued to know why Val disliked him so much.

# Chapter Eighteen

On Monday morning, Miss Grimshaw was standing in the middle of the office with a folder in her hand. 'Oh, Aileen,' she said. 'I'm so sorry Eva didn't make it in on Saturday. Thanks for getting it all done, though. You did well.'

'Yes, it was a bit daunting, but the sales rep, Mr Pickering, helped. I'd never have got through it all without him.'

'Oh, I see.' She frowned and tapped her lips with her pencil. 'That was kind of him. Did he leave any paperwork?'

'I don't know, Miss Grimshaw. He may have left some with Alan.'

'Why he can't let me know when he's coming in, I don't know.' She sighed and went out into the yard.

'What was that all about?' Aileen asked.

Val shrugged. 'I don't think she likes Roy much either.'

There was obviously something in his character she had missed, but she would wait until she knew him better before making judgement. It could well be a personality clash; in Miss Grimshaw's case, that wouldn't surprise her.

'Why do people dislike him, then?'

'Don't know really. I rarely see him, but he comes over as a bit of a loner, if you know what I mean.'

'Really? He doesn't give me that impression.'

'Do you fancy him?' Val laughed.

'Don't be daft.' Aileen sighed. 'Anyway, what did you do at the weekend?'

Val stopped typing. 'We went dancing Saturday night at the Ritz social club, and on Sunday night we went to the Odeon.

We were in the back row.' She giggled. 'So, I've no idea what was showing.' She pulled the advice note from the machine and replaced it with another.

'Sounds grand.' Aileen was bored with staying in night after night. At least back in Dublin, she had Dermot to go dancing with. She missed him, especially at the weekends.

'What did you get up to?'

Aileen glanced up. 'Chance would be a fine thing. If you'd call writing letters, housework, and watching television with Mary, that's about it.'

'Drive me bonkers, that would.' Val looked up. 'I'll try and ditch Peter one night, and then you and me can go somewhere, if you like?'

'That would be great. I can't wait to see the city at night.'

\* \* \*

Later in the week, Aileen had just about had enough of Alan's rudeness, arrogance, and the snide remarks made when there was no-one within earshot. And she was at her wits' end as to how to deal with him.

'Oh, just ignore him. It's nothing personal.'

That was easy for Val to say. But Aileen couldn't forget it. She wanted to know why Alan was taking his frustration out on her.

'It is personal as far as I'm concerned, Val. And I don't intend to put up with it.' 'Look, let me have another word with him.'

Aileen shrugged. 'Ah sure, what good will it do?'

A few minutes later, Alan brought in a stack of orders. He handed half to Val and the rest to Aileen. She was still working her way through the previous lot and only gave the work a cursory glance.

It was much later that morning when she picked up the recent batch. The order on top of the pile was impossible to read. Although she was now familiar with the different kinds of seeds and grains, this just wasn't acceptable. He was deliberately trying to annoy her. She pushed a rubber thimble onto her middle finger and flicked through the rest of the batch. They were all the same.

A furious feeling knotted her stomach. She didn't want to

complain about him to Miss Grimshaw and be the cause of him losing his job, as well as his girlfriend. This was something she would have to deal with herself. Pushing down her anxiety, she gathered up the paperwork and went outside. She found him drinking tea with Bob, and she threw the sheets of paper onto the bench; some fluttered to the ground.

'You think this is funny? Well, I'm not laughing. I doubt Mr Bill will either when he hears what you've been doing.'

'Bitch!'

'Steady on, Alan.' Bob glared at him. 'That's enough. There's no need to speak to the girl like that.' Aileen bit her lip. At least now she had a witness.

'Rewrite these in a legible hand; it's the only way they will get done today.'

'Who the hell are you, telling *me* what to do?' He placed his hand across his chest to emphasise his importance.

'You might be the foreman, Alan, but it doesn't give you the right to take your childish pranks out on me.' Turning, she walked away. In spite of her limbs shaking, it felt good to have stood up for herself.

Val glanced up as she re-entered the office. 'What's up? You're trembling.'

'I'm furious.'

'Is it Alan? What's he said now?'

When Aileen recounted what had happened, Val got up. 'Really! He called you that? You're white as a sheet. Would you like some water?'

'No, I'm grand.'

Val sat back down. 'What are you going to do?'

Aileen swallowed, feeling a little dewy-eyed. 'Don't worry. I'll think of something.'

'If you complain to Miss Grimshaw, he'll probably get a good ticking off. Or worse, she'll report him to Mr Bill.' Val frowned. 'How he never got wind of the affair with Bella is beyond me. The boss is a deeply religious man, and he wouldn't condone it.'

Aileen couldn't reply. She reached across the desk and grabbed a handful of Val's work and began to type, taking her frustration out on the keys.

'I hope he won't be the cause of you leaving.'

'Who said anything about leaving?'

'Bella giving him the push must have hit him badly.'

Anger made Aileen snap. 'Oh, and that gives him the right, does it?'

'No. Course not. I never thought he was that serious about Bella.'

Aileen shook her head. 'It's his wife I feel sorry for.'

The phone rang, ending their conversation. There was only so much Aileen was prepared to take of Alan's abuse.

\* \* \*

Just before lunch, Val slipped on her jacket, took out her compact mirror, and smeared on a coating of red lipstick. Her naturally curly blonde hair was set close to her head, and Aileen had seen a similar hairstyle in Vogue. It reminded her she hadn't done anything exciting with her own hair for some time, and long hair had gone out of fashion.

'I'm meeting Peter and taking an extra ten minutes lunch. Will you be okay? And will you cover for me if Miss Grimshaw comes down?'

Aileen nodded.

'If I see Alan, I'll find out what's really bugging him.'

Aileen's eyes rounded. 'Don't bother. You've already tried, and he's still being obnoxious.'

After Val had left, Aileen worked solidly for over an hour, and in that time Alan didn't bother her. She thought about finding another job, but then Alan would have won. She couldn't let that happen.

When Val returned, Aileen was ready for a sandwich at the nearby café. But when Val stifled a sob and dabbed her eyes with a tissue, Aileen asked, 'He's not upset you, too, has he?'

'No. It's Peter. He still won't set a date. He swears he loves me, and he says that should be enough.' She sniffed.

'I'm sorry, Val. He's obviously not ready to settle down.'

Aileen thought about Dermot and how reasonable he had been when she'd told him she wasn't in a hurry to settle down. Unlike Dermot, Peter was making demands on Val.

'I don't want to lose 'im.' Val slipped off her coat and started typing.

Aileen sighed. 'Look, if he loves you, you won't lose him. Give him a bit more time and he'll come round.' She hoped she was right.

'I can't take that chance.'

Aileen wrapped her scarf around her neck and picked up her bag. She hesitated by the door and looked at her watch. 'I'll be back at two.'

'Oh, by the way, Aileen, Bob's just told me Alan's had a letter from Bella this morning. It's really rattled his cage. Her mother's taking her and her sister to live in Spain. Lucky mare!'

# Chapter Nineteen

Aileen was in the sitting room reading the *Birmingham Post* while Mary got on with her knitting. 'You know, Aileen love, I don't mind gooing down the mill meself and givin' 'im what for. After all,' she said, stopping to count her stitches, 'from what I've 'eard that young 'un was just looking for an excuse to throw 'im over. I'd enjoy putting another rip in his sail, so I would.'

'I don't think that would help, Mary. Besides, there's plenty of jobs going begging in tonight's paper.' She circled one. 'They're looking for an assistant in the laboratory at the Cape Hill Brewery.'

'There yea goo then. Why don't yea apply?'

A change of job wasn't ideal so soon after arriving in England, but if Alan continued his animosity towards her, she would have no alternative. 'I like Val, but the work is repetitive and boring.' Aileen sighed. 'I want something more challenging.'

'I know what yea mean. When I first came over, I used to work at the nuts and bolts factory. When Ken died, he left me a few quid, enough to put a down payment on this place.' She smiled. 'Now, that was a challenge. I was so busy I didn't have time to feel sorry for meself.'

'It must have been lonely. Did you ever feel like going back to Dublin?'

'Yea, but this is my 'ome now. I've 'appy memories of Ken here.'

Aileen nodded. She didn't want to spend the rest of her days alone without her family. She still felt the pain of losing her ma, and the deep hurt left by her da's rejection. Dermot's letters consoled her, and it was reassuring to know that he, at least, missed her.

'No news from your da then?'

Aileen shook her head. She didn't want to discuss him. It only made her angry.

'Look, Aileen, I've been thinking about what you asked me, about your ma, like. Just to set your mind at rest, why don't yea get in touch with the nursing 'ome where yea were born? They should have records.'

Aileen folded the newspaper and placed it back in the rack. 'I've thought about it, Mary. But I can't do much from here, can I?' She sat forward and cupped her face. 'Why did Ma go private? Most of my school friends were born at the Rotunda!'

Mary put down her knitting. 'Your da only wanted the best for Jessie. He booked her in for a week.' She laughed. 'Sure, I remember when she brought you 'ome. You were a lovely little thing. Everyone doted on yea.'

'Do you remember the name of the nursing home?'

'I'm afraid not. Your ma wasn't in there long enough for me to visit. She checked out before your da got to pick her up.'

'Really?'

'Sure, that was typical of Jessie, she loved her own 'ome and she couldn't wait to get back and show you off.'

Aileen smiled. That was true. Ma had loved her home. 'Can you remember where the baby clinic was?'

Mary placed her knitting on her lap. 'I think it was somewhere in Rathgar, or was that Rathmines? I'm not sure, love. It was a long time ago.' She picked up her knitting. 'As I remember, it was quite expensive at the time and might not be there anymore.'

'I'd like to go there, see what I can find out.'

'Hang about, yea've only been here five minutes.'

'I don't mean right now, Mary. But when I do, will you keep my room?'

'Course I will. Don't go getting your hopes up, love. As your da said, when people are dying, they've been known to hallucinate, even say things that don't make sense.'

* * *

During the week, Aileen noticed a change in Alan's attitude. He addressed her by her name for the first time in days. Even so, she couldn't look at him without thinking of how he had treated her and the things he had said. He hadn't apologised, and she guessed he wasn't capable of such pleasantries. However, she was happy that he was now writing the orders clearly and appeared to have stopped blaming her.

'Whatever did you say to him, Val?'

'I told him I knew about Bella's letter, and he said he was over that now. When I asked him why he was taking it out on you, he said, "So what? It was only a bit of banter".'

'He's got a nerve. Banter, my eye.'

'I think he felt threatened when you stood up to him. He won't want to lose his job. But don't expect him to apologise.'

Aileen was furious. 'I hope he keeps out of my way then.' She placed a sheet of paper between the silver rollers of her typewriter. Any conversation she had with him in the future would be purely work-related.

On Friday afternoon, Miss Grimshaw asked Aileen about working Saturday morning again, and she jumped at the chance. Time-and-a-half for working Saturday would boost her wage packet.

'It's much the same as last time,' the older woman said. 'The workload has increased and business in booming. But you won't be on your own this time, even if I have to come in myself.'

* * *

On Saturday morning, Roy's car was already parked in the yard when she arrived. Alan walked towards her, clutching a wad of orders, and pushed them towards her without speaking.

'I'm not typing orders today. I'm upstairs.'

'I know that! Just put them on the desk for Monday.'

If he expected her to do so without please, or thank you, he was sadly mistaken. She thrust them back at him. 'Do it yourself.' When she walked away, he uttered an expletive.

She glared back at him then continued upstairs. Roy greeted her in his usual friendly way. An older woman, whom Aileen hadn't met before, was sorting through the pile of invoices. 'Hello, is this your first day?' Aileen smiled.

'Yes, I'm from the agency. Miss Grimshaw booked me to help out this morning, so I'm all yours,' she said. Aileen was glad to have someone to help, with so much work to get through. And they even had time for a tea break.

Roy appeared busy, making numerous trips down to the yard while Aileen and the woman got on with folding invoices and putting them inside brown window envelopes.

By eleven thirty, the letters were franked, bundled, and ready to go, so Aileen pulled on her coat. 'I'll get off now to catch the post,' she told the woman.

Roy was on the phone; his briefcase open on the desk. Alongside his paperwork, Aileen glimpsed a Vernon's Pools coupon. So he was a gambling man. She smiled to herself. 'I'm off now,' she called, as he replaced the phone.

Aileen had reached the yard when he caught up with her. 'I might as well drop you off at the post office.'

'It's okay, Roy.' She glanced at her watch. 'I've plenty of time.'

'Don't be silly. I'm going that way.' He opened the passenger door. The inside of the car was spotless.

'Well, if you insist.'

Getting to the post office earlier wasn't such a good idea after all. The queue was out the door, and it looked like it was going to rain. She was about to step from the car when Roy placed his hand on her arm. 'Aileen, would you consider coming out for a meal with me some time?'

She turned towards him, unsure how to reply. She was longing to go to a nightclub, and anything was better than sitting in every night with Mary.

'Roy, I…'

'It's okay. I shouldn't have asked.' He sat back and straightened his tie.

The weekend stretched ahead of her, promising total boredom. A horn honked behind them, as she stepped from the car. Before she closed the door, she said, 'I'd like to go out with you, Roy.' She saw a smile play across his face as he drove away.

While she waited her turn at the post office, she wondered if she had been hasty in accepting Roy's offer then conceded it could do no harm. The post sorted and signed for, she headed for the travel agent, Thomas Cook, where she enquired about the ferry to Dublin. By the time she got back to Mary's, she was in a much more positive mood.

* * *

It was Friday of the following week that Aileen answered the phone, surprised to hear Roy's voice on the other end. 'Hello there,' he said. 'What are you doing for lunch?' Aileen felt her face redden, and Val stopped typing and looked up.

Aileen leant back in her chair. 'I've nothing planned. Why?'

Val pulled a face.

'Can you meet me in Victoria Park, at the bottom of Windmill Lane?'

'What time?'

'Can you take the early lunch? I'll bring something. What don't you like?'

She laughed. 'Cheese.'

'See you soon.'

She replaced the receiver and glanced at her watch. 'Do you mind if I take my lunch now, Val?' She stood up and slipped her arms into her coat.

'You're a coy one. Who's the secret admirer?'

'What?' Aileen shook her head. 'It's just Roy. I'm meeting him for lunch.'

'Roy?' Aileen saw the look of revulsion that crossed Val's face. 'Don't tell me it's Roy Pickering, the rep?' She ran her finger down the list pinned on the wall. 'What is he doing here? He's supposed to be in Stafford.'

Aileen shrugged. 'Well, he's back. He's down the road.'

Val sighed and shook her head.

'What is it you dislike about him, Val?'

She shrugged. 'There's something weird about him. Can't put my finger on it.'

'We're just friends. It's nothing serious.'

'I shouldn't have said anything.' Val looked contrite. 'I don't know much about him. Just be careful.'

'Don't worry. I will.' Aileen picked up her bag. 'See you later.' Val raised her eyes.

The weather had turned colder, and she didn't fancy sitting on one of those wooden park benches. When she got to the park, she couldn't see anyone apart from a woman walking her dog.

A horn beeped, and Roy waved a hand in her direction. She hurried across to where the car was parked. He swung open the door, and she got in. She might have guessed Roy wasn't the type to sit around on park benches.

'Glad you could come.' Smiling, he passed her a paper bag. 'It's ham. Hope that's okay!'

'I'm surprised you allow food in your car.'

'I have a small hoover in the boot.' That didn't surprise her.

She unwrapped the sandwich and took a bite. 'Umm. You didn't buy these from around here? They're delicious.'

'I know a little sandwich shop less than a mile from here. I was going to suggest the Seven Stars Inn for a snack. But then, I was outside the sandwich shop when I decided to phone you.'

'Val said she thought you were in Stafford today?'

'Spying again, is she?' He shifted in his seat. 'I finished early.' He chewed his salad sandwich, swallowed, and then wiped his mouth with a paper serviette. 'I wanted to see you, Aileen.'

'What about?'

'You've not forgotten you agreed to go out with me?'

'No. I've not forgotten.' She had thought he had when she hadn't heard from him.

'I've booked a table for eight o'clock tonight, and I wanted to let you know what time I was picking you up.' He leant his head to one side. 'That's if it's still okay?'

Aileen felt a flutter of excitement. She was looking forward to experiencing some of Birmingham's nightlife but had never expected it would be with someone as sophisticated as Roy.

'You haven't changed your mind, have you?'

'No. But you don't give a girl much notice.' She laughed.

'Sorry. With work and everything, I only managed to book it today. If you'd prefer not to, we can do it another time.'

'No, tonight will be grand, Roy.' She wasn't going to miss the chance of a night out.

'I'll pick you up at your lodgings, or we can meet somewhere else.' He finished his sandwich and screwed up the paper. 'I don't mind either way.'

Mary would probably have a fit if Roy turned up on her doorstep, especially as she hadn't been told. 'Outside the house will be grand. I'll be ready when you arrive. Is seven thirty enough time for us to get there?'

'Seven thirty it is.'

She put the remains of her sandwich back inside the paper bag. 'I must be getting back.'

Roy placed his hand on her arm. 'I'll drop you off.'

'Thanks, but I could do with the fresh air before going back,' she said, getting out of the car. She had only taken a few steps when he switched on the engine, gave her a wave, and moved off.

She needed time to consider the best way to tell Mary about Roy. Her landlady was bound to ask questions, but for goodness sake, it was only dinner. He was good company and, God knows, she hadn't had much of that lately. It wasn't as if she had feelings for him, not in the way she had towards Dermot.

She sighed. Dermot was miles away, she was lonely, and a meal with Roy wasn't a crime. But she wasn't looking forward to a lecture from Mary.

# Chapter Twenty

After work, Aileen sat in the kitchen with a mug of tea while Mary prepared their dinner.

'Don't put any on for me, Mary, I'm eating out tonight.'

'Oh, has Val given her boyfriend the night off?' Mary turned to face her, a potato peeler in her hand. 'Where are you gooin'?'

'It's not Val, Mary.'

'Well, who is it then?' She put down the potato peeler and leaned her back against the sink.

Aileen took a deep breath, stirred her tea, and placed the spoon on a saucer. 'It's the Sales Manager from the mill. His name's Roy Pickering.'

'Sales Manager, eh?' She sat down next to Aileen. 'I don't like the sound of this. How old is this Roy?'

'I'm not sure.' Aileen guessed he was in his thirties, but she wasn't going to admit that to Mary.

'Well, yea don't know much about 'im then.'

'It's just a meal!'

There was a slight silence, then Mary said, 'Well, I hope yea asked him to pick yea up 'ere?'

'I'm eighteen, Mary. You'll just have to trust me. I'm not Bella, and I don't want you to worry about me.'

'Oh, woman 'f the world now, are yea? Never mind Bella, you're family, and I will worry. Where does 'e live?'

Aileen shrugged, beginning to tire of Mary's questions. It was only a meal, for God's sake. Why would she feel the need to know everything about him?

'I'm going up to get ready, and if he knocks, please don't

102

embarrass him.' Aileen ran upstairs wishing she had said nothing.

\* \* \*

When she was ready, she hurried down and went outside. She waited on the porch until she spotted Roy's car coming along the avenue, and hurried towards it. As she settled into the plush leather seat, she saw the net curtain twitch. She felt bad and wanted to run back to reassure Mary. But when Roy turned and beamed her a smile and asked if everything was all right, she said, 'Yes. Fine. My landlady's a bit over-anxious, so I got out before she gave you the third degree.'

'Glad I didn't get as far as the door then,' Roy said. 'You look lovely.'

Roy looked immaculate in a grey pinstriped suit, pink shirt, and grey tie, in comparison to her black miniskirt and frilly white blouse under her black leather jacket. She wished now that she had bought herself something new. 'Is it a very posh place?'

He laughed. 'Well, not really. I thought we could eat and dance to one of the bands at the Locarno. Not sure who's playing tonight.'

'Sounds lovely.'

'It might be a bit crowded, that's why I booked in advance.'

She was pleased about that, and although she liked Roy, she didn't fancy going anywhere intimate with him. This place sounded just right, with lots of people around. She felt excited to see the city at night with neon lights flashing. Even New Street looked different, still busy with traffic and pedestrians.

Roy swung the car down Hurst Street, where he parked outside the Locarno. Aileen felt a frisson of excitement.

Brightly lit signs advertising dancing, dining and bands flashed on and off over the entrance as couples made their way inside. He guided her up to the bar. 'What would you like to drink, Aileen?'

She remembered Val saying she drank gin and tonic, and asked for the same. Roy had a pint of Mitchell's and Butlers and then they made their way down again. Tables for two with white covers surrounded the dance floor, and lights lit up the stage where the band members were tuning their instruments. It was very different to what she had imagined, and when she glanced around at the other girls with their fashionable hairstyles and short, colourful dresses, she felt out of place. A cosy two-seater sofa accompanied each table, suitable for courting couples. Once they were seated, Roy beckoned the waitress. 'I don't suppose you do vegetarian?'

'I'm afraid not.'

'What's on the menu?'

'Scampi and chips, steak and chips, or chicken in a basket.'

'Nothing outstanding then,' he said.

'Are you a vegetarian, Roy?' Aileen wanted to know.

'Mother and I often enjoy one when we're in London.'

Aileen nodded. 'Is it just vegetables then?'

His lip curled as if it was a stupid question, and she saw a faraway look in his eyes as if he had gone somewhere else. 'Roy... Roy, are you all right?' She sat forward in her seat.

The waitress sighed and chewed the end of her pencil.

'Sorry,' he said, blinking. 'What are you having, Aileen?'

She thought carefully before making her choice. She didn't fancy trying to eat chicken out of a basket, and she quite liked scampi.

'Well, I haven't got all night,' the girl said.

'Sorry. Scampi and chips, please.'

'Oh, nonsense!' Roy said. 'Have the steak. It's always excellent.'

'Thanks, but I'll stick with the scampi.'

He shook his head, and the waitress scribbled down their order, then hurried along to the next table.

'I hope it won't be too long,' he said, bringing his arm across to look at his watch. His shirt cuff inched up just enough for Aileen to see a heart-shaped tattoo with the initial 'M'; she quickly looked away. Aileen thought only sailors indulged in tattoos.

Smiling across at him, she asked, 'Where did you have your tattoo done?'

His eyes narrowed, and he shifted uneasily in his chair. 'It's nothing. It means nothing. You must take no notice of that,

Aileen. It was a long time ago.'

'Oh, I was just curious… I never–'

'Can we forget about the stupid tattoo? We're here to enjoy ourselves.' He gave a little laugh. 'I hope you like dancing. We can do that after our meal.' He glanced around impatiently, as couples around them had already started eating.

Although she was taken aback by his abruptness, she said, 'I love dancing, Roy. If I'd known, I'd have dressed up a bit.'

'You look lovely. Charming.'

His eyes moved down to her lacy blouse—the top button undone—and she felt a flush to her face. His odd behaviour was making her uneasy. What was the matter with him? This wasn't the same man who had helped her in the office. He was beginning to irritate her.

Their meal arrived. Roy didn't speak, and Aileen's attempts at conversation fell flat so she found herself eavesdropping on couples at nearby tables whispering sweet nothings to each other.

The drums and instruments now set up, the band members left the stage. Relaxing background music reverberated around the hall. Roy was subdued, and the music filled the void of silence between them.

'Roy, is there something wrong?' she asked. He tapped his fingers annoyingly on the table, and it wasn't to the beat of the music. 'Only, you seem agitated.'

'Wrong! Why should anything be wrong?'

Aileen lowered her gaze and prodded a scampi with her fork.

'This place was a bad choice.'

'I like it. It's nice.' She took a deep breath. 'I've never been anywhere like this before.'

'Well, in that case, if you're sure.' He picked up his knife and fork and started eating again, and Aileen was at odds to understand what was going on. However, in spite of her discomfort, she was enjoying the food.

'This is lovely.'

He chewed his meat and popped a chip into his mouth. 'I still think you should have had a steak.' How peculiar of him to be so persistent. He was on edge as if he didn't want to be here. 'I'm glad you enjoyed your meal, Aileen, but I don't like it here anymore.' He sounded like a petulant child.

'Do you want us to leave?'

'No. We haven't danced yet.'

His weird mood enraged her, and she would have been quite happy to leave then, with or without him.

The dishes were cleared away, and men began to move the tables to the side, leaving the small sofas as the band members assembled on stage. Aileen perched on the sofa, leaving Roy plenty of room, when the band began to play Chris Montez's *Let's Dance*. The lights were dimmed and before long couples were swinging and rocking to the music.

This was one of her favourite songs, but she had lost the urge to get out there and dance with Roy. But when he offered her his hand and led her onto the floor, she couldn't resist.

It didn't take her long to realise that Roy couldn't dance. He stood like a post, holding his arm in the air twirling her first one way, and then the other until she felt dizzy. She would need another drink if she were to get through the rest of the evening without saying something she might later regret. The music stopped and, with a sigh, she sat down. She thought about the time she had danced with Dermot in Dublin. Lovely, happy-go-lucky Dermot. What was she doing here with Roy? Was she really that lonely?

'I'll get us a drink,' he said. 'Don't dance with anyone while I'm gone.'

Aileen blew out her lips. Was this the same man she had eaten sandwiches with earlier today? His behaviour was beginning to worry her. The gin and tonic she had drunk earlier had given her a headache, and she would have loved a glass of lemonade. But when he returned with another gin and tonic and a pint of ale and sat down next to her on the snug sofa, she had no choice but to accept it. Most of the young couples around them were obviously in love.

She glanced up at the band members looking dapper in their matching black trousers and white jackets and took a sip of her drink. When she looked up at the glitter ball casting trinkets of light across the floor, she felt light-headed.

The band started to play *The More I see You;* it was certainly a Chris Montez night. Couples sidled onto the floor, held each other close, and smooched to the seductive tones of the singer. Some hardly moved, their eyes closed as if in a trance.

Roy got to his feet and put his hand on her arm. She shook her head, but he insisted, pulling her to her feet. He placed his arm around her waist and pulled her close. His bad breath fanned her face, and she drew back.

'This isn't a good idea, Roy.'

He pulled her closer. 'Don't be daft. It's only a dance.' He pressed his face against hers, and she turned her head away.

She wanted to get away from him. With only a small amount of change in her purse, would it be enough for the bus? She was angry with herself as much as with Roy. She hadn't noticed this side of his character before tonight and wished she was anywhere but here with him. The dance seemed to go on and on until she felt she would be sick.

'Excuse me, Roy.' She placed her hand over her mouth and rushed towards the Ladies.

She took ten minutes to compose herself and came back to find him sitting on the sofa, his legs crossed, his arm spanning the back of the sofa. There was no mistaking the scowl on his face.

'Can you please take me home, Roy? My stomach's a bit queasy. Something didn't agree with me.'

'Oh, that's a pity. I told you to have the steak.' It had nothing to do with the food, but she nodded then picked up her things.

'It wasn't me you were running away from, was it?'

'Of course not.' She forced herself to act normally.

Outside, she inhaled the cold night air and took a green chiffon scarf from her shoulder bag and wrapped it around her neck. He placed his arm around her shoulder, and a shiver passed through her.

'You're shaking. You're not frightened of me, are you, Aileen?'

She was stunned that he should ask her that. 'No. Why? Should I be?'

'I'd never hurt you, you know that, don't you?' He unlocked the car and she slipped onto the seat. 'I'll soon have you home.'

Anger sizzled inside her. Something about Roy didn't add up. 'Sorry... I'm... I'm just not used to alcohol.'

'Don't worry. It wasn't the best place I could have taken you to. Next time it will be a classier establishment.' He turned the ignition, and the car hummed into action. Tonight—all too late—she realised that Roy had a split personality.

The drive back from the city seemed to take longer. Their conversation was stilted. When, at last, he turned down the avenue, it was late and she knew Mary would be worried. He pulled the car to a stop and turned off the engine then he turned towards her. He placed his hand on her knee, and she swept it away. 'Aileen, I like you. I like you a lot.'

She turned to get out.

'Don't go!' He moved swiftly, pulling her towards him, he nuzzled her neck.

'Stop it, Roy.' Her heart pounding, she pushed him off. 'What do you think you're doing?'

'I'm sorry. I shouldn't have done that.'

'No, you shouldn't have. It was silly of me to think we could be friends.'

He hung his head and gripped the steering wheel, his knuckles white. 'Well, I feel a lot more than friendship for you, Aileen.'

'I'm sorry,' she said and pushed open the door.

At that moment the door to the guesthouse opened and Mary came outside, noisily placing milk bottles on the concrete doorstep. One fell over and rolled down the garden path. Mary bent to pick it up. Aileen was never more pleased to see anyone.

Her legs shaking, she walked towards the house. When she glanced back, Roy was sitting at the wheel, revving the engine unnecessarily. Aileen felt another cold shiver run down her spine and hurried inside.

# Chapter Twenty-One

On Saturday mornin, Aileen stayed in her room until she heard the teacher from the room along the corridor leave the house. Her head ached, and she swore she would never drink alcohol again as long as she lived. She slipped on her dressing gown, pulling the cord tightly around her waist then went down to the kitchen. Mary was cleaning the gas cooker and shaking Vim into the sink, and the smell caught the back of Aileen's throat. When her ma had used it, it always made her cough. Mary turned as she walked in.

'I'm sorry about the smell, love. It makes me cough, too. How are yea feeling?'

'No worse than I deserve.'

'Well, you had me worried. I'd no idea where he'd taken yea.'

Mary opened the cupboard and took down two mugs, poured tea in one and Camp coffee into the other. She milked and sugared them and pushed the coffee across the table towards Aileen.

'He took me to the Locarno, a dance hall on Hurst Street.' She shrugged. 'I'm sorry I went off like that, Mary. And to have kept you up.'

'From what I saw of 'im last night, you'd do well to stay well clear.'

Aileen sipped her coffee then pressed her fingertips to her forehead. She had already decided that for herself. One character change—as in her father—was enough for her to deal with. She certainly didn't need another.

Mary stood up and went to the cupboard again. 'Looks like yea need a couple of these.' She handed Aileen two Anadin, then half-filled a glass with tap water. 'What were yea drinking?'

'Gin and tonics.' She swallowed the tablets. 'Never again.'

'Well, if you're not used to it, you've only yourself to blame.'

Aileen couldn't argue with that. Grateful it was Saturday and she hadn't agreed to work, she declined Mary's offer of breakfast. 'I'm going back to bed for an hour.'

By lunchtime, she felt more like her self again, and when she went downstairs, Mary was out. She picked up the post. There was the usual weekly letter from Dermot, and the rest were addressed to Mrs Mary Reilly.

In the kitchen, she made herself some toast and sat down to read Dermot's letter.

*Darling Aileen,*

*I hope you are well. Things are okay here, but the street's not the same without you. You'll want to know that your father has had a For Sale sign posted on the wall of the haberdashery, and most of the neighbouring traders are anxiously waiting to see who will occupy it once your da moves out. I've tried to stay in touch with him, but you know what he's like, he doesn't encourage callers. He and your aunt have been seen at the pub on several occasions, and tongues are still wagging. I'm sorry, Aileen, but I know you wouldn't thank me for keeping this from you.*

*Look after yourself. I hope it won't be long before you come back to the Fair City. My feelings haven't changed, and I have in mind a romantic place where we can go when you return home.*

*Love Dermot*

She missed him so much and felt guilty to have been out with another man. Dear God! How could her da go and sell the shop and not bother to write and let her know? A lump formed in her throat. To stop herself dwelling on what was happening back home, she opened the cupboard underneath the stairs and took out the vacuum cleaner. It was the last thing she wanted to do, but Mary expected her to help with the chores, and it was the least she could do.

She hoovered the living room and then the hall; the noise made her head throb again. She was about to carry the heavy machine upstairs when the telephone rang. 'Hello.'

Aileen was surprised to hear Dermot's voice.

'Aileen, listen. Not sure if you've heard the news, or read this morning's newspaper. There has been a terrible disaster in Aberfan, South Wales. The slack deposited by the National Coal Board above the village has collapsed and buried the junior school. My ma's sister lives in Merthyr Vale and her eight-year-old granddaughter goes to the school.'

'That's awful, Dermot. No, I hadn't heard. God! Do you know if she's all right?'

'We don't know how bad it is yet, but Ma says her sister will need our support, so I'm taking her over there on the ferry today. Just wanted to let you know just in case you need me for anything.' She heard him sigh. 'I probably won't be home for at least a week, depending on how we find things.'

'Thanks for letting me know, Dermot. I'll nip out and buy a newspaper now. Take care. Let me know when you can.'

'Will do. Love you.'

The phone clicked off, and she replaced the receiver and sat on the bottom step of the stairs, pondering on the disaster. Her da selling the shop was small in comparison.

The vacuuming forgotten, she pushed her arms into her coat, tied a warm scarf around her neck, picked up her bag, and left the house. She only had to walk to the bottom of the road to the paper shop. Grabbing the last copy of the *Birmingham Post* from the shelf, she paid and left. Outside, she stared at the front page with the shocking picture of the buried school. *Dear God! All those poor kids.* She folded the paper and hurried back to Mary's to read it in detail.

An hour later, Aileen still hadn't absorbed the tragedy, so she switched the wireless on to hear more. The letterbox rattled. She switched off the wireless and hurried to open the door, expecting it might be Mary's sister Mavis, who often called at the weekend. Instead, the young boy from across the street stood under the canopy, looking up at her.

'Hello.' She smiled. 'Mrs Reilly's not in at the moment. Can

I help?' The boy glanced back over his shoulder. 'What is it?' The lad looked nervous, as if he had done something wrong. 'Look, what's wrong?'

'There's a man over there.' He pointed back down the street. 'He gemme two shilling to knock and tell you he wants to see yea.' With that, the boy ran back across the street.

Aileen's heart skipped a beat. Roy Pickering. Whatever he wanted, she wasn't going to find out. She shuddered and went back inside, closing the door behind her.

Upstairs, Mary's bedroom door was open, and Aileen took the liberty of going inside so she could look out through the bay window. She saw what looked like Roy's car parked a short distance from the house, and farther along she saw Mary lugging two heavy shopping bags. The car was turned in the opposite direction, with the driver's face obscured.

She drew back, hoping he hadn't spotted her. She wanted to go out and help Mary, yet how could she? As Mary drew closer to the house, the car drove slowly away and parked further up the street. This was ridiculous. He was beginning to give her the creeps.

As soon as she heard Mary's key in the lock, Aileen sighed and hurried to help her in with her shopping.

'What's up? Yea look like yea've seen a ghost.' Mary followed Aileen into the kitchen.

'He's outside.' She placed the shopping bags on the table while Mary removed her coat and hooked it up on the kitchen door.

'Who is?'

'Roy Pickering! He must have seen you and moved away.' Aileen sat down and placed her head in her hands. 'I should never have agreed to go out with him, Mary.'

'Well, you're as daft as a brush if yea think any man will go out with a woman for friendship.'

She knew that now. 'What am I going to do?'

'Has he been to the door?'

Aileen shook her head. 'He sent the kid from across the street.'

'Well, he's definitely gone now, and I dare 'im to come back.' Mary shrugged. 'Bloomin' cheek. I didn't like what I saw of 'im in the dark, Aileen.' She took a deep breath. 'There's something weird about 'im.'

Mary wasn't the first to see it. Why hadn't she noticed it herself?

'I didn't go on at yea last night, because I could see yea was upset. Did he upset yea?'

'I'm more annoyed with myself.'

She shook her head. 'The whole evening was odd.' 'I hope yea'll take me advice then and not see 'im again.'

'I've no intention of seeing him again.' Aileen hooked a strand of her hair behind her ear. 'One minute he's as nice as pie, and the next I don't know who he is.'

'Well, happen yea should pick your friends more carefully in future.'

'I'm sorry, Mary.' She pulled her cardigan around her and shivered. 'I guess you heard about the disaster? What with Roy Pickering making me jittery, I forgot to say.'

'What are yea on about?'

'There's been a catastrophe in Wales. Dermot rang to tell me. His aunt's granddaughter goes to the school.'

'A heard a few mutterings on the 'ill but didn't catch where it was like. I didn't get a paper because me 'ands were full.'

Aileen picked up the newspaper. 'Here, read it. It's heartbreaking.'

Mary shook out the paper, her eyes wide. 'God love them. How old are the kiddies?'

'Dermot said his aunt's granddaughter is eight.'

'Well, let's pray that they get the children out safely, although looking at this picture, it doesn't look good.' She put the paper down. 'I guess you'll be anxious to hear from Dermot again.'

Aileen nodded. 'I'll get on and hoover upstairs. It'll take my mind off things.'

'Hey, leave that. I've got a nice bottle of brandy in the cupboard me sister brought last time. I dare say it will settle your nerves.'

Aileen looked away. 'Not sure I should, you know, after last night.'

'Oh, a small glass will do you no harm under the circumstances.'

They sat in silence and sipped their drink. Then Aileen said, 'He can't dance, Mary.' Both of them began to giggle as she related Roy's efforts on the dance floor.

'Aye, it might appear funny to yea now, but my guess is it was the only way he could get his dirty hands on yea.' Mary drained her glass. 'Creepy little devil.'

The letterbox rattled, interrupting their conversation. Mary, her face rosy from the brandy, got to her feet followed by Aileen. 'If that's 'im, I'm in the right mood for 'im.'

'Mary, please let me deal with him.'

Her landlady flung open the door. A woman, who could easily have passed for Mary's twin, stood there looking at them. 'Well, what's the matter with yea? Aren't ye gooing to invite me in?'

# Chapter Twenty-Two

Sunday morning was wet and windy, and Aileen declined a walk to church with Mary. Now, as she languished in bed, she wished she'd made the effort and gone, because all she did was to ponder on those poor people who had lost loved ones in the Aberfan disaster. Dermot would be in Wales now, and she hoped that when he'd had time to assess the situation he would be on the phone to her. She couldn't relax until she knew how the little girl was. With that in mind, she threw back the covers and got up.

The teacher had gone away for the weekend, and while the house was quiet, Aileen decided to take a bath. Mary would have turned the immersion heater on before she left so the water would be hot. The bathroom was positioned on the first floor towards the back of the house, with a small frosted window that overlooked the back garden.

She turned on the tap and steam clouded the mirror. She sprinkled in a handful of Lily of the Valley bath salts, crumpled a scented cube into the water, and tested it with her toe before lowering herself into the hot, cloudy bathwater. With a happy sigh, she leaned her head back, letting her cares wash over her.

She stared up at the white plastic lampshade and the black and white tiles, wishing she could rewind time. How had her life become so complicated? If she hadn't come to Birmingham, she'd never have met Roy Pickering. She slipped down in the water and closed her eyes.

The sound of the doorbell startled her. She pulled herself upright; bubbles settled across her shoulders and under her chin. She stood up and grabbed her towel, wrapping it tightly around her. Then she tiptoed along the landing to Mary's room and took a look outside. The street was desolate and wet, but across the street, there was no mistaking a black car.

She held her breath as the bell rang for the third time. She gasped then covered her mouth. 'Please go away,' she murmured, desperately hoping that Mary hadn't left the back door undone.

Frozen to the spot, she stood hiding from view and shivering with cold until she saw the car move away, and then she hurried back to her room and got dressed. What did he hope to gain by making a nuisance of himself? If he had something to say, why couldn't it wait until she was back at the office? She couldn't relax.

It was still raining when Mary arrived home. She lowered her brolly, shook it, and stood it up on the porch. 'You won't see a stray dog out on a morning like this.'

Aileen sighed. 'I'm glad you're back.'

'What ails yea? You're as twitchy as that old cat we had years ago.'

Mary placed her handbag on the kitchen table and switched on the kettle. Aileen slumped into a chair. 'Roy Pickering's been here again. His car was parked outside. He rang the bell three times. I was terrified he'd come round the back.'

Mary spun round. 'Right!' She folded her arms. 'I've had enough of Mr No Good Roy Pickering. And I'll tell yea sommat else and all. When the rain stops, you and me's gooin' down the police station.'

'I'm sorry to have caused you trouble, Mary. I never expected he'd turn up on your doorstep.' Aileen dashed away a tear. 'Please don't involve the police. Let me deal with it on Monday.'

'I'm trying to run a business here, Aileen. I've just advertised the small bedroom, not to mention what will happen if Miss Brady gets wind of a prowler watching the house.'

'I'm so sorry,' she said again. 'Just give me until tomorrow to sort it before calling in the police. Please, Mary.'

'Oh, all right then, but it's against me better judgement.' She sighed. 'What if he comes back again tonight?'

'Then I'll go out and talk to him.'

'You'll do no such thing. You've no idea what you could be

dealing with. No! Let me think?' She scratched her head and then she turned back to the work surface and poured boiling water into the teapot. 'Right, you're coming wit' me to Mavis's. One more for dinner this evening won't bother her. That way I know yea'll be safe.'

# Chapter Twenty-Three

Aileen picked up a newspaper on the way to work and read it inside the shop. One hundred and forty-three people, mostly children, had been buried in the Wales landslide. The news increased her already fragile state as she made her way towards the mill, glancing over her shoulder. The area was busy with people on their way to work, and she arrived at the office without any sightings of Roy.

Alan was having the day off, and the desk was piled with orders. They came through on the office phone, keeping the women busy. Val only briefly mentioned the Aberfan disaster, and that suited Aileen as the mere mention of it upset her. However, as soon as they had a quiet moment, Val questioned her about Friday night.

'Did you go out with Roy at the weekend?'

Aileen wanted to say, 'Don't be silly. As if!' But what was the point in denying it?

'It was a big mistake.'

'Why? What happened? Don't tell me he tried it on.'

'Worse than that, he's been sitting outside the house for most of the weekend. I don't know what to do?'

'Good Lord! Told you, didn't I?'

Aileen related most of what had happened to Val, in between taking orders on the phone and typing. The other girl's reaction was one of disgust. 'That's creepy, Aileen. You'll have to report him.'

'I'm trying to avoid that. Besides, it's partly my fault for encouraging him.' She sighed. 'Val, have you got his work schedule for this week? I must talk to him before Mary goes to the police.'

'I wouldn't blame her if she did. I haven't got the sheet yet. Go upstairs and see if it's ready.' Aileen sighed, and Val gave her a sympathetic smile.

As soon as Aileen stepped into the accounts office, Miss Grimshaw pounced. 'Ah, just the person I want to see. Can you work this coming Saturday?'

She hesitated. 'I'm sorry, Miss Grimshaw. I'm afraid I can't. There's something I have to do.' She swallowed nervously.

The older woman frowned. 'Is there something wrong, Aileen? Only, you look a little distracted.'

This was her opportunity to ask for some time off. 'My father's not coping, and I need next week off to visit him,' she said in one breath.

'I'm sorry to hear that, Aileen, but this is very short notice.'

'Yes, I know, Miss Grimshaw. I've found out that my recently widowed father is selling the shop, and I don't think he has thought it through properly.'

'Umm, it's a bit inconvenient.' The older woman paused and tapped her pencil against her lips. She did this a lot when she was considering something, and Aileen crossed her fingers behind her back.

'You are coming back?'

'Yes, yes, of course.'

'Okay, I'll have your wages made up accordingly. As you're here, can you take Mr Pickering's work schedule down with you?'

She had made a snap decision, and it had worked. Now she hoped she would be in time to stop her da doing something he might later regret. With Roy's timesheet in her hand, she noticed his home telephone number alongside the works number at the top of the sheet, and she quickly scribbled it down before handing the paper across the desk.

'How far is Coventry from here, Val?'

'A good twenty miles or more, depends on what way you go. Why?'

'Well, if he's away, he won't be bothering me, will he?'

'Too right! He'll be there all week. The company won't pay his expenses for him to come home each evening then to go back next day, although he's brought in a lot of business from the Coventry area. He sometimes takes the train as he doesn't want to run up the mileage on his precious car.' She laughed.

'Well, that's a relief.' Aileen's face brightened. 'He'll have forgotten about me when he gets back.'

Val gave her a doubtful look. 'I'm taking an early lunch. Will you be okay?'

Aileen nodded. 'Before you go, I've asked for next week off. You remember me telling you about my da? I'm worried about him. He's acting out of character.'

'Oh, I'm sorry, Aileen. I won't half miss you. I'll have to manage with someone from the agency until you get back.' Sighing, she hurried out.

Knowing that Roy was some distance away would satisfy Mary, too. Next week, Aileen would be back in Ireland, and Roy Pickering would no longer concern her.

That night Dermot phoned with the news that both Aileen and Mary had been dreading. She could sense the shock in his voice and did all she could to console him. When she mentioned that she had booked a week off and would soon be home, his voice lifted.

\* \* \*

On Thursday of the same week, Aileen walked along Cape Hill on her way to the travel agents. With the return ferry tickets for Saturday night sailing safe inside her bag, she shopped for bits she needed to take away with her and then went into Timothy Whites for sea legs, just in case. It was the beginning of October, and a black cloud hovered overhead. She tightened her scarf around her neck and was about to make her way back to the office when the heavens opened, and shoppers ran for cover.

Aileen sheltered in a doorway, her hair dripping, her shopping soggy, and her handbag dangling from her shoulder. Why hadn't she taken a brolly? Mary had warned her it was going to rain. But that was her trouble, she never listened to good advice. Rain lashed the pavement, and she shivered inside her jacket.

On the opposite side of the street, a bus sloshed past and behind it, a black Ford pulled to a stop. It stayed long enough for her to glimpse the side view of the driver. Her heart lurched. Dear God! What was he trying to do to her?

A shiver ran through her body. Fearful he might spot her, she ran through the rain and arrived at the mill wet and miserable, her heart thumping. Once inside the yard, she went straight into the toilet and locked the door. She switched on the small electric heater, removed her wet jacket, and hung it up on the door. She stood directly underneath the heater to dry her hair and used the new Charmin toilet paper to dry her face and hands. When she felt a little warmer, she unlocked the door and went outside.

Alan walked across the cobbles, a cluster of dockets in his hand. 'Got caught in the downpour, did you?'

'Just my luck,' she said bunching her hair into a ponytail.

He handed her the paperwork. 'I've placed the urgent ones on top.'

'Alan, have you seen Roy today?'

'No. Why?'

'I thought… I'm sure I saw him on the Cape just now.'

He shrugged. 'He's in Coventry unless he's got a double,' he laughed and walked back towards the sheds.

* * *

By the time Aileen finished work, her mind was made up to speak with Roy. Drastic as she knew it was, she had to make sure he stayed away from Mary's place while she was away. If she had given him the wrong impression, she would apologise, and try to get him to understand that there could never be anything other than friendship between them. She owed it to Mary to try, even though Val had advised her against it. She didn't want to go away with an uneasy conscience.

She slipped into the first telephone box she came across and dialled Roy's number. It rang three times before being picked up.

'Hello.' The voice was that of a woman with an upper-class English accent.

121

Aileen swallowed. 'Hmm. Sorry. Have I got the right number? Is this Roy Pickering's?'

'Who is this?'

'It's Aileen from the mill. I'd like to speak with Roy, please.'

It went quiet at the other end, and then she heard hushed voices before someone spoke again.

'Don't you *ever* ring this number again. *do you hear*?'

The stressed words took her aback, and she winced at the abrupt way the phone clicked off before she had time to speak.

She felt a moment of terror. There was no mistaking the menace in the man's voice.

Her hands trembled as she vacated the phone box. Tears stung her eyes and unanswered questions fogged her mind as she hurried back to the lodging house.

# Chapter Twenty-Four

Aileen could hear Mary rattling around in the kitchen. She was determined not to let her landlady see how upset she was, especially with her leaving for Dublin soon. Picking up a letter from the hall table, she called out that she was home and would be down shortly, and then ran upstairs to her room. She needed time on her own before she had to pretend that everything was normal. With the door closed behind her, she struggled to control the feelings of rage that made her tummy tighten.

Dermot's letters were consistent, usually arriving on a Friday, and she looked forward to reading them. She took a few deep breaths, sat down on her bed, and opened the letter.

*Darling Aileen,*

*I'm sorry I was so down on the phone when last we spoke. The sight of all those bereaved parents who had lost children was heart-wrenching. My aunt is inconsolable, as you can imagine. We did what we could. I'm coming home, as Dad can't manage on his own much longer.*

*I'm sorry to be the bearer of more bad news, Aileen, but I feel I must tell you. Your father has sold the drapery shop and, as far as we know, the accommodation. He left a letter for you at the butcher's. I'm delighted to hear you are coming over for a few days. You know you are welcome to stay with us. I'll be home before you are. I can't wait to see you, and I'll be at the ferry port to pick you up.*

*Love and miss you,*

*Dermot x*

She folded the letter and felt sad for Dermot's aunt. Having experienced the loss of her ma, she could only imagine the unbearable pain of losing a child in that way. She realised that loss came in many guises; always painful, and some worse than others.

Aileen felt as if she had lost her da, too. He hadn't written to her in the eight weeks she had been away. The shop was their home. He couldn't have been thinking straight when he sold the business. She had never believed he would go through with it. How could he do this to her? Could she still stay with him? If not, she knew she could rely on her uncle and aunt. A tear ran unchecked down her face. Dermot was the only true friend she had, but would he still want her if he knew she'd been out with another man?

Lizzy was to blame for all this upheaval. And if it hadn't been for her manipulating her da, Aileen would still be in Dublin searching for her lost brother. To stop herself becoming maudlin, she began to sort through clothes she would be taking with her tomorrow. Feeling calmer, she went down to talk to Mary and managed to convince her that she'd had no more problems with Roy.

\* \* \*

On Monday morning, Roy Pickering dressed in the clothes that had been carefully laid out on his bed. His grey suit hung on the back of the bedroom door. He put on his freshly laundered pale-green shirt and matching tie, and clipped his gold cufflinks in place. He checked the crease along the sleeves, before slipping on his suit jacket—the one he had worn the previous week for his dinner date with Aileen. He ran his hairbrush over his hair and examined his nails, stopping to clip the middle fingernail on his left hand. He sighed then rearranged the items in his grooming kit so that they all faced the same way.

After admiring his image in the mirror, he hurried downstairs. His breakfast, consisting of one Weetabix and a black coffee, was set out on the table.

'Are you all right, dear? You seem a bit edgy this past couple of days. Has someone upset you?' The woman sitting opposite him threw him a cursory glance. Roy shook his head and sipped his coffee.

'You know,' she continued, 'if you're feeling unwell, I can make you an appointment with Mr Wainwright, dear, just to be on the safe side.'

He stood up. 'No, no need.' He smiled. 'I'm perfectly fine.' Then he leaned down and kissed her cheek before leaving the house.

He drove away from his secluded suburban home in Worley to the mill in Smethwick. The anger he had felt over Aileen ringing the house had subsided. And he wanted to apologise to her before leaving. He needed to gain her trust again and deter her from ever calling his home again. No-one had ever rung him his house, not even Miss Grimshaw, and he must make sure it never happened again.

He parked in the yard alongside Mr Bill's Rover. Ignoring Alan's call to him, he hurried inside. His jaw dropped when he saw a strange woman sitting at Aileen's desk; her head bent in concentration. Before he could ask any questions, Mr Bill's door opened.

'Ah, Roy. Good to see you. Pop in the office a minute. I've made two new contacts I'd like you to call in on while you're in Kidderminster.'

By the time Roy came out, he felt anxious and wished he had bypassed the mill. The old man had praised his efforts on increased sales over the past month and made an appointment for him with a new client for ten o'clock. Roy had smiled his thanks, but inside he was annoyed that he had to do all the running around while old man Bill sat on his arse all day, picking up the phone and giving orders. Kidderminster was, at best, an hour's drive away and if he were to get there in time, he'd have to shoot off without finding out where Aileen was.

The temporary typist glanced up as he walked through. He couldn't be bothered to raise a smile towards her. 'Where's Val?' he barked.

The woman frowned. 'Upstairs, I think.'

Without waiting, he hurried outside and got into his car. He took a few deep breaths to calm himself. Through the mirror he saw Alan and, revving the engine, he drove off.

He fiddled with the knobs of his radio and tuned into some classical music. It usually calmed his nerves. He could always phone Val when he arrived; she was sure to know where Aileen was. He wasn't going to give up on her that easily. He had been drawn to her from that first meeting when he had helped her with the franking machine. She was lonely, just like him. Having her around made him feel good. Had he spoiled things by rushing her? He'd make things right between them; yes, that's what he would do.

The traffic was beginning to irritate him, and he weaved between cyclists and changed lanes in order to speed up his journey. He must win her back, but he would have to be patient. Aileen wasn't like the others he had met. She was special. She wanted to make something of her life. He knew why she had come to Birmingham, and he had sensed her vulnerability being away from her family. He had plenty to offer her to make her happy.

He sighed. It was difficult not to think about her. She had an angelic face and long, golden hair that he longed to stroke. She didn't have a boyfriend. He paused at the traffic lights. Who was he kidding? A pretty girl like that? She could be two-timing him. Perhaps he was a fool and Aileen Maguire was just a tease. She had made him believe she liked him, wanted to be with him, and then humiliated him by refusing his advances. What was he to think?

Arriving hot and frustrated, he took more deep breaths, patted his hair in the mirror, then plastered on his best salesman smile before entering the building.

# Chapter Twenty-Five

Aileen arrived back in Dublin, fatigued after her journey. A sea of faces met her as she walked from the ferry dragging her case, much heavier than when she'd started out. Passengers rushed past her while others were greeted by smiling faces.

When she saw Dermot, her face brightened. He pushed forward and swept her into his arms. 'I thought you'd never get here. You look gorgeous. How was Birmingham?'

She lowered her eyes as colour flushed her face

'I'm sorry, I'm rattling on.'

'That's okay, Dermot. I'm pleased to see you, too. I wasn't sure you'd make it. When did you get back from Wales?'

'Last night.' He picked up her luggage, and they walked away.

'It must have been unbearable for your aunt.'

He nodded. 'My aunt's an amazing woman, you know, and the small community where they live is very supportive. But it'll take time for something like that to heal. Come on,' he said. 'The van's over here.' He unlocked the back and placed her case inside.

An air freshener dangled from the mirror, and the smell of lavender made her smile she got in. Dermot turned to her. 'It's so good to see you. I missed you, and I want to hear all about Birmingham.'

'We'll have plenty of time to talk later.' Aileen was in no hurry to discuss her experience of living in Birmingham; for now, she was more than happy to be home.

'Have you seen anything of my da, Dermot?'

He stopped at the side of the curb and pulled on the handbrake. 'Sorry, I almost forgot.' He pulled an envelope from his pocket. 'This is the letter he left for you at the butcher's. I took the liberty of bringing it with me.'

She turned it over in her hand, nervous about opening it. Then she glanced up at Dermot as he manoeuvred the van away from the docks, following the queue of cars towards the city. 'My da's not written to me once while I was away.'

'Don't worry, Aileen. Whatever it contains, you know already. Go on, open it.' He smiled reassuringly.

She swallowed and ripped it open. The single sheet of writing paper was neatly folded to fit the small envelope, and she noticed the new address on the top of the page.

*Dearest Aileen,*

*When I heard from Dermot that you were coming home, I quickly wrote this letter, as I didn't want you going to the shop and finding the locks changed. As you can see from the address above, we are now running a busy sweet shop on Camden Street. I'm sure you'll like it.*

*Lizzy has been instrumental in setting things up, and customers continue to come in—at first out of curiosity, and once inside they can't resist buying the confectionery. Which is good news for us.*

*I hope your stay in Birmingham was a happy experience, and that you will now see the sense of staying home and continuing your studies.*

*It'll be good to see you.*

*Your Da. Jonny Maguire.*

She folded the note and pressed it back into the envelope. Her father always signed off in that old-fashioned formal way. Aileen and her ma used to laugh about it, but now she felt totally ill at ease that there was no show of affection.

'Well, is he all right?' Dermot asked.

Aileen slipped off her Alice band and let her hair fall over her face, hoping to hide her tears. 'Yes,' she said, her eyes downcast. 'Would you mind if we don't go past the draper's shop, Dermot?'

'Sure. I'll go round the top end.' He drove the long way round and up Dominick Street, approaching Dorset Street from the other end. Then he stopped outside the butcher's.

Aileen placed her hand on his arm. 'Dermot, I can't stay at

yours.' He was about to speak when she handed him her father's letter to read. 'I'll say hello to your parents and then, if you don't mind, could you drop me off in Camden Street?'

He read the letter quickly, his brow creasing into a frown. 'A sweet shop!' He turned to Aileen. 'Your da will find that quite a change, then. I would never have called your aunt a sweet person. I mean...' Aileen couldn't help laughing. 'You know what I mean,' he said, opening the van door. 'I'll leave your case in the back, so.'

Dermot guided Aileen inside, where his mother came from the kitchen, wiping her hands on a tea cloth. 'Sure, it's lovely to have you home, Aileen. The kettle's on. Come on through.'

They sat round the kitchen table, and Aileen sipped a welcome cup of Irish tea and hospitality; she offered condolences to Dermot's mother for her sister's loss.

'Ah, sure the Lord works in mysterious ways, love, and we all get our share of grief.' She sighed. 'You know that as well as the rest of us.'

Dermot's parents wanted to know all about her time in Birmingham, but after an hour Aileen could hardly keep her eyes open. Fearing she might drop off the chair, she stood up, thanked them for their kindness, and asked Dermot if he would take her to her da's.

'Of course.' He got up and slipped on his jacket. 'You must be jaded after the journey.'

\* \* \*

The traffic was light as Dermot manoeuvred the van along O'Connell Street and Dame Street towards George's Street, along Angier Street, Wexford Street, and onto Camden Street on the south side of the Liffey. Aileen had no interest in sightseeing so she closed her eyes for most of the journey.

As they drew closer to the address, her heartbeat quickened; she was dreading going inside. She doubted very much that Lizzy would welcome her with open arms. What was her da thinking of, moving in with her? Didn't he care what people thought?

Their lack of conversation during the short journey didn't seem to bother Dermot. A look of concentration clouded his good looks.

'That's your da's red car parked outside, 'Dermot said and pulled up abruptly. His brakes made a harsh grinding noise and he apologised to Aileen, but she hardly noticed. She was already regretting coming here.

He placed his hand over hers folded in her lap. 'This is it, Aileen.'

Her heart raced. The brown paintwork around the shop window and door looked shabby, the paint blistered from years of neglect. It made her wonder what the inside was like. Her sigh was audible.

'Look, Aileen, if you change your mind, you know, just ring me, and I'll be over to pick you up.'

'I'll be grand. Thanks, Dermot.'

'I'll get your things.' He gave her a wry smile. 'You go on in.'

Aileen stepped out of the van just as the net curtains twitched upstairs. The street was quiet, apart from a couple of stray dogs and a few people making their way to early morning mass. A man coming out of the newsagent's across the street lifted his cap, and Aileen smiled. A strange feeling crept over her as she surveyed the shop window. Glass jars with different coloured lids, full to the brim with an assortment of sweets, adorned the window. They were arranged to attract and invite, and she could well imagine children coming in with their pocket money once the shop opened in an hour's time.

Before she had time to knock, the door opened. Her aunt framed the door, tugging her dressing gown across her chest, a scowl on her face. 'Oh, it's you,' she said. 'Pity you didn't give us more notice. Come in.'

She eyed Dermot. He shifted his stance and was about to step inside when Lizzy barred his way. 'Aileen can take that.'

Dermot shook his head and dropped the case by the door. Her aunt's manners were appalling, and Aileen was sorry she hadn't taken Dermot up on his offer to stay with his parents. She thanked him quickly before her aunt shut the door, leaving Aileen to carry her belongings through the shop.

The smell of sherbet and liquorice invaded her senses, and she just had time to glimpse the long counter to her left, with small boxes of sweets, including packets of pretend sweet cigarettes and silver mints. Too tired to linger, she followed her aunt and manoeuvred her way around cardboard boxes towards the living room, where she dropped her luggage.

'Well, don't stand there. Sit down.' Lizzy clicked her tongue and went through to the scullery where Aileen could see the gas cooker. She sat down on her ma's sofa, wishing she'd stayed longer at Dermot's. Her aunt returned and remained standing. 'The kettle won't be long.'

'Where's Da?'

'He's still in bed.' She gave a little laugh. 'Well, if you will call at this unearthly hour on a Sunday morning.'

'I'm sorry to have disturbed you, but it couldn't be helped. Can I go up and see him?'

'He'll be down soon. I'm sure everyone was awakened by that butcher boy's van. Noisy contraption.' Too tired to argue with the woman, Aileen stayed seated. 'How long are yea staying then?'

Desperately biting her tongue, Aileen said. 'I've come to see my da, and how long I stay will depend on him.'

'Well, I'm sure you'd like a drink.' She went back to the scullery.

Aileen leaned back on her ma's cushions, drawing what comfort she could from their softness, and closed her eyes.

When she woke, she glanced at her watch. Had she really been asleep for two hours? A mug of cold tea and toast was on the table next to her. She could hear children's voices coming from the shop, and was just about to go and look for her da when he walked into the room. Aileen stood up.

'I'm sorry I didn't hear you arrive. I sleep in the back bedroom.'

'How are you, Da?'

'You know, I'm getting there. And you, how have you been?' He came closer and put his arms around her. 'I'm sorry about before, love. I was crazy and out of my mind.'

She looked up at him. 'You mean, about Ma's baby?'

'No, about losing her. Now, I don't want to hear any more about a baby.'

'But, Da!'

'Come on, I'll show you round.' He led her through to the shop where Lizzy was serving a couple with two children. 'What do you think then?'

What could she say? 'It's lovely, Da. So you're in sweets now. Are you enjoying it?'

'Well, I'll soon find out, won't I?' He smiled, then took her elbow and walked her back into the room and out to the small scullery. 'We've a lot to do yet, but the shop had to take priority and Lizzy's been hard at it getting everything ready.' He chuckled. 'It's only been a short while, but already we're doing a good trade. By the way, the lavatory's outside.'

He led her upstairs. 'There's a small bathroom along the landing. We've only the two rooms, plus a box room up here, and I'm sorry I've not got round to getting it ready.' He pushed open the door, and she looked inside. 'As you can see, it's rather tiny, but maybe tomorrow you'll help me tidy it up. Your bed is underneath that mountain of clothes, bags and boxes,' he said with a laugh.

It was good to see her da laughing again in his old familiar way. Aileen sat down on the edge of a packing case. 'Da, are you and Lizzy together? I mean...'

'We're running a business together and we're living in the same house. That's it, okay? I'm past caring what people think. Your aunt's not happy with the set-up, but I'm not getting married again.'

Aileen thought it was a strange arrangement, but was delighted that her da hadn't married the woman. She bit down hard on her lip. In spite of the fact that she thought it was much too soon, she kept her own counsel. Her father was speaking to her more than he had done in months, and she didn't want him to stop. 'Are you happy, Da?'

He nodded. 'She looks after me, and we have a good little business going.'

'Da, can I stay for a few days?'

'Well, of course. This is your home, too, Aileen. If I'd known sooner when you were coming, I'd have made an effort to get the room ready.'

'I'll be fine,' she said and kissed his cheek.

After a wash, Aileen brushed her hair and went for a walk. It was Sunday, so everywhere was closed, and she was back sooner than she expected. Her da was doing a shift in the shop, and her aunt was sitting on her ma's sofa with her feet up.

'Can I get you anything?' Aileen asked, having decided to make an effort to get to know her aunt's better side, for her da's sake.

'The best thing you can do for me is to get yourself back to England,' the woman said. 'It was thoughtless of you to come before we had time to sort ourselves out.'

# Chapter Twenty-Six

Aileen couldn't sleep. She lay on the sofa wide awake, long after her da and Lizzy had gone to bed. Her aunt's words swirled around her head. Apparently, her da thought the woman was someone he could trust enough to live with and share a business. All she could do was hope that Lizzy's true colours surfaced sooner rather than later.

This was her home, too, her da had said. But it would never be home to her, not in the way it was above the haberdashery. How could it be when her aunt had made it blatantly clear that she wanted her to go? If she were to tell her father about Lizzy's overt act of intimidation, would he believe her? It might sever their already fragile relationship.

It was almost daylight when she finally closed her eyes but she still woke early, determined to be up before her aunt came downstairs. She folded the blanket and put away the pillow before making herself tea and toast. The cupboards were sparse, and she wondered if her aunt had any food in the place. She was munching her toast when her da appeared in the doorway, a smile on his face.

'Did you sleep okay?' He sat down opposite her at the small grey Formica table.

'Yes, it was fine thanks, Da.' She poured his tea.

'You know, love, it's really grand to see you again. As soon as I've drunk this, we'll get on and clear the box room. One night is long enough to sleep on that old sofa.' He swallowed his tea. 'Your aunt will be down in a minute to open the shop. Then we can make a start.'

While Lizzy was in the scullery, Aileen followed her da

134

upstairs. A large box was positioned in front of the bedroom door. It hadn't been there yesterday, and her da had to move it before pushing open the door. Inside, the single bed was littered with clothes and cases. Aileen couldn't see where they were going to put all the stuff once they cleared the bed.

'Look, Da, maybe I should stay at Uncle Paddy's, give you a bit more time to get straight.'

'Why would you do that? We'll have this room ready in no time. Help me with this box. Your aunt has marked all her stuff. I've forgotten what's in ours.' But when they had finished shifting stuff, the room looked no different. Boxes surrounded the bed, some piled precariously along the wall.

'As long as you can get into bed, you'll be grand for now.'

Aileen nodded. 'Thanks, Da.' At least, she had somewhere to hide from her aunt's disagreeable grunts when he wasn't around. 'As I said, Da, I can only stay until Friday, and I want to get started on Ma's last request.'

Although he nodded, his face clouded. 'Are you happy working in Birmingham?' His change of tact hadn't surprised her.

'Well, it's not what I hoped I'd be doing, but the girl I work with is grand. We have a laugh, like. The work is boring and repetitive. The papers are full of jobs, so I might look for something a bit more interesting when I go back.'

'Well, write and let me know how you get on.'

'I will, Da.' It was the first time he had shown any interest in what she was doing since her ma died, and it pleased her. 'Da, can I ask you something?'

He sighed. 'Go on.'

'Mary said that Ma had me in a private nursing home.'

'Not this again, Aileen.'

'Was it Rathmines, or Rathgar?' she continued. 'Mary wasn't sure. I want to see what I can find out.'

'It was Rathgar.' He took a deep breath. 'I wish you'd drop this. It'll only cause you heartache.'

'I'm sorry, Da. I can't.'

* * *

It was bitterly cold when Aileen stepped off the bus in Rathgar, but at least, it wasn't raining. She walked through the village until she came to the post office, which seemed a good place to start her enquiries, and the postmistress was eager to help.

'There've been a couple of new places in the past few years,' she told Aileen. 'I vaguely remember a private baby home. Well, if it's the one I'm thinking of, it's the only one around here at the time you're talking about.' She pursed her lips. 'I can't think what it was called. It's not there now. Replaced by one of them new buildings, I'd say.'

'Thank you.' Aileen was about to leave when an older woman, wrapped up against the cold, breezed in pulling a shopping trolley behind her.

'Hold on a minute,' the postmistress called. 'Mrs Murphy might know. She's lived in the village a long time.'

Aileen stepped aside as the woman bought stamps, and waited until she had finished her transaction. 'Excuse me. I'm trying to locate a mother and baby home that was in this area around 1948.' The woman's head shot up, and she moved her trolley out of the way of customers. 'I believe it was a private home,' Aileen added.

'Oh, do you mean St Anne's?'

Aileen shook her head. 'Unfortunately, I don't know what it was called.'

The woman sighed and sat down on the seat at the back of the shop.

'I believe I was born there, and I'd love to speak to someone who worked there around that time.'

'Ah, sure that was closed down years ago. The place has been done up and is now a home for the elderly.' The woman linked her fingers and twirled her thumbs. 'It's not far if you want to see it. Just carry on through the village, you can't miss it.'

'Thanks.' Aileen nodded. 'So you didn't work there then?'

'God, no! I'd hate to work with nuns.' She stood up and stretched her back. 'What exactly do you want to know?'

'I was hoping to get a look at the baby records.'

'Cant help yea there, love. One of them nursing sisters, retired now, lives around the corner from the home, at number twenty-nine. But if you take my advice you'll stay well clear. From what I've heard, she's a bit of a recluse.' She chuckled, and Aileen held the door as they both left.

Aileen followed the directions the woman gave her. Soon she was glancing up at the red-brick building in the quiet residential area, and it felt strange to think that her ma may have given birth to her here. She pulled the collar of her coat closer and walked to the end of the street then turned the corner. Some of the houses once owned by the well-off had been turned into student accommodation.

Number twenty-nine had St. Mary's inscribed on a gold plate attached to the black railing. This had to be where the nuns resided when the baby home was in use. Straightening her shoulders, Aileen pushed open the squeaky gate, closed it behind her, and then walked up the gravelled path and rang the bell. She heard it peal through the house. The door was opened promptly by a young girl, who appeared to be in a hurry.

'Oh, can I help you?'

'I'd like to speak to a nun who resides here.'

The girl sighed. 'Everyone has left for work now.' She frowned. 'But there is an older woman staying here; not sure if she's a nun, though. Lives on the second floor, first door on your right.' She shrugged. 'She's not very sociable, but if you want to go up.' She rushed past Aileen, leaving the door ajar.

Feeling a little nervous, Aileen went inside and upstairs. She knocked once and got no reply. There was no sound, and she wondered if the nun was asleep. To satisfy her curiosity, she rapped the door for the second time. Then she heard someone pulling back the bolt, and flinched when the door flew open.

A woman in her sixties stood glaring at her. She didn't look anything like a nun, dressed in a thick navy skirt and a cable knit jumper, her thinning hair scraped severely back from her face.

'Well, what do you want?'

Aileen, who still feared the nuns, began to stutter. 'I'm, I'm…

137

sorry to disturb you...'

'Pray, why do it then?'

'I'm desperate for information.' She swallowed nervously. 'I believe you used to work at the home for the elderly when it was a baby clinic.'

'How dare you come here, a complete stranger, and ask me impertinent questions!'

Aileen shifted uneasily. 'I'm sorry. I never meant to sound disrespectful. It's just that I was born there, and...'

The woman's face clouded, then she opened the door wider. 'And what, pray, can I do about that?'

Aileen offered a tight smile. 'Nothing, I guess, but if I could just talk to you. I promise not to keep you long.'

'You're not from the newspapers, are you?'

'No, I'm not. My name is Aileen Maguire.'

'Oh, you'd better come in. I can't stand here all day.' She walked back into the room and Aileen followed. 'You can leave the door open. Now, what is it you want from me?'

'My mother gave birth to me at St Anne's in 1948.' She fidgeted with her hands. 'She also had another child; a son.' She saw the nun's face darken, and Aileen frowned. 'I don't know when or where he was born. But if, on the off-chance, it was at the same home, I might be able to trace him through the records.'

The woman turned and walked a few paces, then raised her eyes. Aileen followed her gaze from the high ceiling and the white, plastic lampshade, to the holy picture of Christ hanging on the wall, a crown of thorns piercing his head, blood dripping down his forehead. A black crucifix hung above the blackened hearth. Aileen was unnerved by the image in the picture, and in the silence that followed, a clock ticked.

The question had obviously sparked some kind of reaction in the woman. The room was cold and sparsely furnished. In spite of there being chairs, Aileen hadn't been invited to sit. A yellow, wicker sewing basket was open on the table, alongside a garment that looked like a skirt with a measuring tape on top. She wondered why the nun lived frugally even in retirement.

'I'm sorry, Sister. Can you tell me anything about the time you worked at the home? My mother's name was Jessie Maguire.' Aileen held her breath, fearing she had asked another impertinent question.

The woman turned abruptly, her face expressionless. 'You expect me to remember your mother?'

'No. Of course not. It was eighteen years ago. But I would appreciate anything you can tell me. Do you know where I can look at the records?'

'Why you would want to look at records is most unusual.' She raised an eyebrow. 'I don't have access to records of any births that took place at that home. Besides, you don't know exactly when this boy was born.'

Aileen shook her head. The woman made a clicking sound with her tongue. 'Why come to me? The most natural thing would be to go straight to the registry office where records are kept.'

'Oh, I will, Sister. I wanted to see where I was born first.'

'I'm not a nun anymore. I would have thought that was obvious. My name is Miss Finch.' Her eyes narrowed. 'How did you know where to find me?'

Aileen bit her lip. This woman was hiding something, but Aileen had no idea what. 'Well?' She glared at Aileen.

'I, er, I made enquiries. Sure, I'll leave you in peace.'

'Yes, and please don't bother me again.' Aileen edged towards the door, desperate to get outside again. No sooner had she stepped onto the landing than the door closed quickly behind her.

# Chapter Twenty-Seven

Aileen avoided her aunt as much as possible; in spite of the clutter, she was pleased to have a room upstairs. It gave her time to organise the rest of her stay in Dublin undisturbed. The boxes were still unopened, and she guessed her da had been busy helping her aunt in the shop. Whatever was in them didn't concern her now. There was no way she could take anything back to England.

She hoped the registry office would be able to help her trace her brother. But, apart from her mother's name, what did she have to go on? Fearful of upsetting her da, she stopped probing him for more information, but the alternative was to return to England having discovered nothing at all about her brother. *Rome wasn't built in a day,* she told herself as she climbed over boxes into bed. She woke a couple of times during the night feeling claustrophobic.

The following morning, she left before her da and Lizzy put in an appearance. The weather continued to be cold, and she pulled the hood of her jacket over her head, tied it underneath her chin, and dug her hands into the pockets. The first phone box she came across, she rang Dermot.

'Aileen, I'm pleased you rang. How's it going?'

'Okay.' She apologised to him for her aunt's behaviour when he'd dropped her off, and asked if he could meet her after work.

'Sure. Just say where.'

She told him her plans, and they arranged to meet outside Trinity College. Then she caught the bus to Westmorland Street, where she couldn't resist the alluring whiffs of Bewleys coffee. Soon her cold hands were wrapped around a mug of hot frothy coffee. It was hard to beat it for taste, and the smell alone could

140

revive the poorest of appetites. Feeling warmer, she made her way via Pearce Street through to Lombard Street. She was handed a ticket and a form and sat down to wait her turn. Other than her mother's full name and their address in Dorset Street, there wasn't much else she could add.

'Do you have a rough idea when this baby boy was born?' the clerk asked.

'No. I know the information is vague, but could you check and see if he was born at St Anne's private nursing home in Rathgar.'

'What dates are we looking at?'

'Could you look at three years either side of my own date of birth, 1948.'

'If you want me to do a search, it'll cost you three shillings, and you'll have to call back tomorrow.'

'Umm!' She hadn't expected to pay that much.

He sighed. 'Do you want me to go ahead? There's no guarantee I'll come up with anything significant.'

She had to go through with it now, even if it came to nothing. She nodded, handed over the money and received a receipt, and went away hopeful.

She had plenty of time to spare before meeting Dermot, so she took the opportunity to visit her Aunt Bead. It started to rain, and she pulled a rain bonnet from her bag and queued for the bus to Finglas. She was looking forward to seeing her aunt.

Bead, as usual, was delighted to see her, and sat for an hour listening to Aileen talking about her life in Birmingham, about Mary and Bella; she left out the bit about Roy Pickering. Her aunt was pleased to hear that things were working out for her.

'Of course, there have been a few changes here, too. Well, sure, your da appears better these days. More like himself.'

Aileen nodded. 'He was happy when ma was alive.'

'Yes, I know he was, love.' Bead lifted the empty cups and placed them in the sink. 'I bumped into him at the bank in O'Connell Street about a week ago.' She sat back down. 'We didn't talk long. He did say he'd moved to a sweet shop on Camden

Street. I asked him if he'd heard from you. He nodded and, as he turned to leave, I asked him to stay in touch.'

'I've noticed his good mood, too, Aunt Bead, but he has no idea how devious Lizzy can be.' Aileen sighed. 'If only she wasn't living there, too.'

'I guess he's lonely, Aileen. Still, I'm surprised, so soon after Jessie.' She shrugged. 'Paddy went across to see them in Dorset Street a few weeks ago, and neither of them mentioned anything about marriage. He was under the impression, from what Lizzy said, that she was determined to get a ring on her finger.'

'I don't like it, Aunt Bead. I know she's not my ma's real sister, but it isn't right.'

Bead shook her head. 'Well, if I know your aunt, she'll want to stop tongues wagging by whatever means.'

'I hate leaving him again. What if it all goes wrong?'

Bead put her arm around Aileen. 'Your da will be grand. You should think about yourself and what you want. We'll let you know if anything major happens.'

'Yes, I know you will.' Aileen placed her elbows on the table. 'Why is he still reluctant to talk about my brother?'

'Maybe he doesn't know anything, love.'

'I've been to Rathgar, Aunt Bead.' And she told her aunt about the strange conversation she'd had with the woman who called herself Miss Finch and denied being a nun.

'Do you think she knows anything?'

Aileen shrugged. 'It's difficult to say, but she acted a bit shifty when I mentioned Ma's name and my brother. She told me to try the registry office. I'm going back tomorrow to see if they've managed to unearth anything.'

'I wish you luck with that, love. Sure, we don't know when the lad was born.'

'I won't give up looking for him, Aunt Bead.'

'Of course, you must keep trying.'

Aileen glanced at her watch; the time had flown. 'Aunt Bead, I'll have to dash. I'm meeting Dermot.' She pulled on her coat. 'Thanks for the tea and chat. It was good to see you. Tell Uncle

Paddy I'll come and see him before I leave.'

Bead walked her to the door and wrapped her in a hug. It was still raining, and she insisted on Aileen borrowing her brolly.

'I'll pop it back next time I call,' Aileen said and hurried towards the bus stop.

She sat on the bus looking at the rain dripping down the window and thought about her mother. *Oh, Ma! Why couldn't you have written a bit more on that note?*

\* \* \*

When Aileen arrived, Dermot was casually leaning against the railings surrounding Trinity College, one foot crossed over the other, his coat collar turned up, his hands deep in the pockets of his coat. He was soaked through, and people hurried past him out of the rain.

She hurried towards him, feeling guilty to have kept him waiting on such a miserable day. 'I'm sorry, Dermot. Have you been waiting long?' She placed the umbrella over his head and they huddled together.

'No. Not at all.' He smiled. 'It wasn't raining when I left the house, and then came down in buckets as I walked across O'Connell Bridge. Let's go somewhere out of the wet.'

'So, what did you find out?' he asked as soon as they were seated in a small cafe off Grafton Street and had ordered a pot of tea and scones.

'Nothing, as it turned out, but I met a very strange nun yesterday.'

'Oh.' Dermot cut into the fresh scone and plastered it with strawberry jam. And as they enjoyed their tea, she filled him in on her search for her brother. She rubbed her eyes with her fingertips.

'You're tired. Didn't you sleep well?'

'Not really. I kept waking up. I have a room upstairs, but there's stuff everywhere. They haven't had time to unpack yet. And the way Lizzy feels about me, I can't wait to get back to Birmingham.'

'What's she been saying now?'

Aileen shifted her chair closer to the table and sighed. 'Oh, you know. She can't wait for me to leave. She said as much to my face.'

'I'm sorry, Aileen. This might sound awful, but that woman has no soul.' He shook his head and leaned his elbow on the table. 'She's chasing you away again.' He sighed heavily. 'I take it you're going back then?'

'Yes. And time is flying past.'

'Well, I'm taking you out somewhere nice tomorrow night. Is that okay?'

'Just what I need, thanks, Dermot.'

'But you will come home for Christmas?'

'Christmas!'

'Well, it'll soon be upon us.' He chuckled. 'Dad's put in his order for geese and fowl.'

It couldn't have been further from her mind. 'I don't know, Dermot.'

He lowered his head and then drained his cup. Aileen licked the jam from the corner of her mouth. 'I'm not sure I can afford to come over again so soon.'

He moved closer and reached for her hand. 'I was thinking of coming over to you. When I mentioned it to Mam, she squashed the idea because she wants me at home when Liam comes back.'

'Liam! Is that your brother?' Frowning, she sat upright. 'Back, back from where? You never said where he'd moved to.'

'Well,' he said with a grin, 'you never asked. And besides, I wasn't keen to tell you.'

'Why?'

'I didn't want you to think that I might follow the same path.'

Her frown deepened. 'What has he done?' All manner of criminality raced across her mind.

'He's a priest. Newly ordained.'

Her shoulders relaxed. 'Well, that's wonderful. Your parents must be so proud to have a priest in the family.'

'Yes, they talk of little else now that he has finally taken his vows.' He rubbed his chin. 'I thought it would be nice for you to meet him.'

'Of course. I'll do my best, Dermot, but…'

He leaned in and hugged her. 'That's great.'

She loved being with Dermot. She felt at ease with him, and if it were not for her aunt, she would never have left Dublin.

'Dermot, you know, with me being away for weeks and months on end. I'll…' The words stuck in her throat. 'I'll understand if you don't want to wait. I mean…you might find someone else, and–'

He placed a finger across her lips and shook his head.

'I've told you before. There's only one girl for me.'

# Chapter Twenty-Eight

Aileen was first in the queue when the doors opened at the registry office and sat down to wait her turn. When her number was called she went to the window, her fingers crossed. As she waited, her heart raced.

'I'm sorry, Miss Maguire.' The clerk glanced over the top of his spectacles. 'There's no record of a male baby born to the lady in question.'

Aileen's shoulders slumped. 'What can I do now?'

'Have you tried getting in touch with the Civil Registry in Roscommon?'

'Do you think they might know?'

'Well, it's possible that your mother didn't register the baby herself, therefore it could have been registered by someone else.' He turned his back and picked up a leaflet. 'Here's the address and telephone number.'

Thanking him, she left. Her initial optimism was waning; after all, she didn't have much to go on. On her way back, she purchased some writing paper and envelopes. She would try every avenue to find her brother.

Back at the sweet shop, Aileen made no attempt to interrupt her aunt as she served two young girls with jelly babies and liquorice sticks. Her da was in the kitchen, eating his lunch of beans on toast, and his eyes lit up when he saw her.

'Ah, Aileen. Come, sit down and tell me what you've been up to. Have you been to the new Dunnes store?' He glanced down at the carrier bag.

'No, Da. It's just some writing material.'

'Have something to eat. We're still eating out of cans.' He got up and went into the scullery. As he opened the cupboard, she could see a row of canned soup.

'I'm grand, Da. I'll have a cup of tea, though. Dermot's taking me out for something to eat later, so I don't want to spoil my appetite.'

He brought in a cup from the scullery and poured tea from the pot. 'Young Dermot seems keen on you. Not a bad looking lad.' He sat down again. 'You should come home, Aileen.'

She milked her tea. 'I don't know, Da. I don't fit in here anymore.'

'Don't talk daft, Aileen. Lizzy's all right. Just cut her a bit of slack. She's overwrought with the new business and all.' He shifted in his chair. 'You could work here in the shop if you've definitely decided not to continue your secretarial course.'

She knew he meant it, but after what Lizzy had said, there was no way she could live here. 'I won't be finishing the course, Da.'

He nodded. 'I'm sorry, love. Everything changed when I discovered your ma had been keeping secrets.'

'She might have had a valid reason, Da. Can you remember anything else she might have said? I'm trying to make sense...'

He shuffled back his chair and stood up, and she could tell he regretted mentioning her ma.

'Da, please!'

At that precise moment, her aunt decided to enter the room. Aileen closed her eyes and sucked in her breath.

Lizzie placed the shop keys on the table. 'It's been non-stop out there this morning.' She placed her hand on Jonny's arm. 'When you've finished your lunch, we have an hour to sort out some of those boxes. Most of it is probably rubbish.' She glanced at Aileen as she spoke.

'Sure, will you sit down a minute, woman, and have something to eat.'

'No, I'm grand. I had a snack earlier. We'll eat later.' She turned back to Aileen. 'Are you going to be here for tea?' Tea?

Aileen hadn't seen a decent meal being cooked in the two days since she had been back home.

'No, thanks! I'm going out later.'

'Well, while you're here you can give us a hand upstairs.'

* * *

'You might like to keep your mother's jewellery,' her da said, handing over the jewellery box.

'Thanks, Da. That's grand.'

He glanced down at the floor and pushed a box towards her with his foot. 'This stuff belongs to you. What you don't want, leave in the yard, and I'll get rid of it.' Her aunt was busy rummaging through some of her own belongings.

An hour later, they could see the brown-patterned lino on the bedroom floor, and most items had found a home in the other two bedrooms and elsewhere around the house. Aileen pushed her case underneath the bed to make more room.

'Good idea,' her aunt said. 'We don't want the place cluttered up again.'

Her da folded the empty boxes. 'I'll take these down to the yard and then open the shop.'

Aileen pushed shoes and slippers underneath the bed then glanced up at her aunt who appeared to be supervising her every move.

'Don't get too comfortable,' the older woman said, opening a cupboard on the landing and placing an armful of blankets inside.

Her aunt's snide remarks had been delivered as soon as her da was out of earshot. Aileen knew she should ignore her, but this time her tongue preceded her reasoning.

'You think you've landed on your feet with my da, but he'll soon realise what a vindictive bitch you are.' Once she started, she couldn't stop herself. 'My ma was ten times nicer than you, and I'm glad you're not her real sister.'

Lizzy's mouth dropped. 'How dare you! I can make life very difficult for you. So watch your tongue.'

'And what do you suppose my da will say once he finds out what you say to me behind his back?'

Swallowing her anger, she went back to the bedroom and closed the door behind her. Damn the woman. She was determined to spoil things between Aileen and her da. If only she hadn't come home. But she was here now, and all she could do was to hope that her da would tell her what he knew before she went back to Birmingham. It was the only way she was ever going to find her brother.

# Chapter Twenty-Nine

Aileen removed her ma's wedding and engagement rings from the jewellery box, along with some gold earrings. As she fingered the pieces, a tear dropped onto her cheek. She slipped the rings onto her finger; they fit perfectly.

Her mother's oval-shaped topaz dress ring wasn't in the box, and she wondered if her da had given it to Lizzie. As a child, Aileen had loved to see her mother wear it as it meant her ma and da were going out to celebrate something special, and she would be staying with her Aunt Bead and Uncle Paddy. At least, she had the two rings that she would treasure. Removing them from her hand, she wrapped them in a tissue and placed them in the corner of her case.

That evening, for her date with Dermot, she wore a peacock blue woollen mini dress she had bought at C&A's. It felt warm and snug and clung to all the right places. With a multi-coloured scarf around her neck, she pulled on her jacket, slipped her feet into black high heels, picked up her shoulder bag, and went downstairs. Her da was sitting next to Lizzy on the sofa. He dropped his newspaper and looked round.

'You look lovely.' He stood up and kissed her on the cheek. 'Why not invite Dermot here for his tea before you go back?'

'That sounds grand, Da. I'll arrange something.'

His statement re-enforced her view that he had no idea how Lizzy felt.

Outside, Dermot appeared before she had time to close the shop door. He jumped from the van and opened the door. He had on a grey overcoat, and she could smell his aftershave—a new one she didn't recognise. Underneath, he wore his dark grey suit, white shirt and skinny black tie.

'Hi, gorgeous.'

Smiling, she got in. The van had been cleaned to within an inch of its life, and a lavender air freshener hung from the dashboard, and another one hooked over the mirror. It made her smile that he always went to so much trouble.

'Where are we going?'

He leaned across and kissed her. 'It's a surprise.' A mischievous grin creased his rugged face. 'Are you hungry?'

'Starving.'

'Good.' Dermot put the car into gear and soon they were heading towards Clontarf, along the Malahide Road.

Aileen was intrigued when they bypassed Portmarnock to arrive in Howth village, a popular spot with tourists and couples during the summer months. But it was a dark winter's evening, and she gave him a puzzled frown when he pulled into a parking bay close to the pier.

He got out and stood with his back against the van. Aileen followed. The sea air was bracing and almost took her breath away. She pulled her scarf tighter around her neck.

'Why have we stopped here?' She pulled her collar up around her neck. 'It's freezing.'

Dermot smiled. 'All in good time.' He wrapped his arm around her, shielding her from the strong wind as they walked towards the wall overlooking the sea. Even in winter, the view was stunning, with lights twinkling along the shore.

Dermot sucked in the fresh air. 'Come here,' he said, turning her round to face him. 'I wanted to have you to myself for a few minutes. Can you smell the sea?' He took a deep intake of breath. 'It's peaceful here, don't you think?'

'Yes. But it's also freezing. Can we sit in the van?'

He turned his face towards the sea. 'Aileen, when I said you were the only girl for me, I meant it with all my heart. Well, what I'm trying to say is, I don't want you to feel tied to me because of how I feel.' He drew a breath. 'When you go back to England, there's a strong possibility that you'll meet someone and want to settle over there.' He sighed.

Aileen quickly recalled her mistake with Roy, and it made her all the more aware of how much Dermot meant to her. 'What's brought this on, Dermot? I can honestly say I'll never settle anywhere but here, in the Fair City. I just need more time before making any kind of commitment, that's all.' She shivered and rubbed her hands together. 'I thought you understood?'

'I do.' He lifted her up onto the low wall and stood in front of her, holding her hands. 'I can wait, as long as I know you'll come back to me.'

She bit her lip. 'Dermot, there isn't anyone else I'd rather settle down with. And, of course, I'll be back.'

He lifted her down and held her close. 'Don't stay away too long. Promise?'

'I promise. Now, what about this surprise?'

He kissed her, then took her hand and they walked back to the van. He drove through the village and turned up Abbey Street, where cars lined both sides of the street. Dermot managed to squeeze into a tight spot between two cars.

Aileen stepped out onto the pavement and glanced up at the bright lights of The Abbey Tavern. Groups of young people and older couples were battling the strong winds as they headed towards the pub's entrance. With Dermot's arm around her waist, they joined the queue. She could hear American voices and smell the smoke from their cigars.

'I've heard so much about this place, but I've never been inside.' She arched her eyebrows. 'What's the entertainment tonight? Do you know?'

'I believe it's the Dubliners. That's why I bought tickets in advance, and you'll have noticed the crowd.' He guided her further inside. 'I thought you'd enjoy a real Irish night out before you leave.'

How thoughtful of him to remember that she loved the Dubliners.

'Thanks, Dermot.' She leaned forward and kissed the side

of his face. She needed cheering up, and the Dubliners would certainly do that.

'I've booked us a table for the entertainment and something to eat.'

In spite of the stonewalled interior and exposed beams, the place had a cosy feel. A turf fire crackled in the open hearth and smiling Americans already lined the bar.

'Grab a seat, I'll see if I can get us a drink.'

Aileen sat down at a small round table by the window and placed her jacket on a seat for Dermot. It was getting noisy, and she knew it would get worse later on once the Dubliners were on. They were very popular, and she loved the ballads they sang. She appreciated now why Dermot had wanted a quiet ten minutes earlier; there would be no chance of an intimate conversation inside the tavern. The Irish entertainment and the craic would be enough to keep them focused and sustain her for the journey back to Birmingham.

Holding a drink in each hand, Dermot made his way through the crowded bar to get to Aileen. He placed a glass of Irish coffee—mixed with whiskey, sugar and whipped cream—down in front of her. 'It'll warm you up.' He sipped his own drink—a large glass of creamy stout—leaving a white moustache across his upper lip.

Aileen laughed. 'You appear to read my mind, Dermot Brogan.'

'Oh, I wish I could.'

Aileen gave him a playful nudge before she sipped through the top layer of cream. 'This is delicious.'

They sat for a while with their drinks, then Dermot said, 'If you like, we can go through now and take our drinks with us.' He stood up. 'I was told the entertainment happens in a room at the back.'

'That makes sense.'

He picked up his pint and Aileen followed him through the crowded pub. Dermot handed the tickets to the man on the door and he told them they could sit wherever they liked. The room was enormous, and Aileen counted at least twelve oblong tables with four chairs on either side. The only thing that was small was the stage.

The room began to fill up until it was packed to the rafters. Aileen and Dermot sat in the centre of a middle table where they had a good view facing the stage, and other couples joined them. Thick white candles adorned each table, leaving every corner of the room bathed in soft yellow light. The flagged floor and stonewalls gave the place a rustic atmosphere. Chandeliers with candles hung from the rafters.

Aileen felt a frisson of excitement. The chatter of voices became louder as people ordered their food. The waiter came and took their order for more drinks, and told them what was on the menu. Dermot ordered another pint of stout and an Irish coffee for Aileen.

'I could get used to this,' she said.

Dermot placed his elbows on the table. 'So could I...with you, Aileen.' She reached for his hand.

The food was simple, with a choice of two main meals. Everyone had the same starter—a bowl of potato and leek soup. For her main course, Aileen had salmon with champagne sauce, carrots and mash, while Dermot had corned beef with parsley sauce, carrots and mash. With little time to digest the meal, it was promptly followed by a large portion of apple tart and custard.

When they had finished and the plates cleared away, Aileen felt fit to burst. She sat back in her chair. Couples around them were friendly, and it wasn't long before they were all singing along to the Dubliners. During the short break, people ordered more drinks, and the show resumed again. By then, they couldn't hear each other and Dermot's pretence at sign language made her double up with laughter.

Her night out with Dermot had cemented her feelings for him, and she was almost tempted to take him up on his offer of marriage. When he again told her that she was the only one for him, she regretted her date with Roy Pickering. Sooner, or later she would have to clear her conscience.

\* \* \*

With only one day left of her visit, she knew there was no point in questioning her da for more information, so she decided to find out how her college friend, Helen, was faring. It was nearly three months since they had bumped into each other on Dorset Street, and Aileen had often wondered about the girl, and if her parents had been supportive. She must be six months gone now. Aileen had heard of women binding themselves for months to hide their predicament.

When she arrived at Helen's house, she was invited in. 'I'm afraid she's not here,' the girl's mother said. Helen had often mentioned that her parents were quite strict, and Aileen noticed uneasiness in their mannerisms.

'Will she be long?'

'Can I ask how you know Helen?'

'We were at college together a few months back, and–'

'She won't be back for a while. She's staying with an aunt in the country,' Helen's father interrupted sternly.

'Oh, that's a shame,' Aileen said. 'I was hoping to see her before I went back to Birmingham.' A conspiratorial look passed between Helen's mother and father.

'How is she? Is… is she all right?'

'What do you mean?' her father asked.

'Well… Helen, I mean… we talked.'

'You knew she was?'

'Yes, she told me.'

'Just what did Helen tell you?' her father asked. 'Do you know who the blighter is? If I get my hands on him, I'll kill him and gladly go to prison.'

She felt at a disadvantage. 'I'm sorry, she didn't say, and I didn't ask.' She sighed. 'Can I write to her, or get in touch?'

'No.' Helen's father looked agitated. 'That won't be possible.'

'I'm sorry, love, you'd better go.' The mother ushered her towards the door. 'We have to try and put it behind us now, and get on with life.'

'Please tell her I called.' The door closed quietly behind her.

Aileen sighed. They had sent Helen away to hide the shame

she had brought on her family. That was what usually happened. Poor Helen! Where had they sent her? Was it one of those homes for unmarried mothers?

She wondered again about her own brother, and where he might be now. Life could be unfair, especially towards women. If it were to happen to her, where would she turn?

# Chapter Thirty

Roy Pickering drove from his home towards the city. He had an early appointment with Mr Wainwright, but as he was feeling good today, he decided to miss it. What did that shrink know, anyway?

He straightened his tie in the mirror. He was due in Tamworth and had enough calls to keep him busy all day, yet he couldn't resist dropping by the mill.

He swung into the cobbled yard and went straight in to reception, where Val was showing a temp how to set the tabs on Aileen's typewriter. She glanced up. 'Roy! We don't often see you on a Friday. Is anything wrong?'

'No. Why should there be? I just wanted a word.' He glared at the young temp.

She looked embarrassed and stood up. 'I'll go and see Alan for five minutes.'

Val placed her hands on her hips. 'There's no need to be rude, Roy. What is it? I'm up to my eyes here.' She held up her hands and shifted paperwork around on the desk.

'When's Aileen coming back?'

'Next week, I hope. I'm sick to death of having to train a new temp every other day.'

'Did she say what day? Only I thought I'd surprise her by meeting her at New Street.'

'Why? I mean... I assumed that you and she...' She bit back the rest of her words.

'What do you mean? What has she said?'

'Nothing.' She sighed. 'Look, Roy, can you send the girl back in, I've urgent orders to get out.'

'What day does she come back?'

'I don't know, Roy. The weekend, I guess.'

'Sure. Thanks.'

In the yard, he gave Alan a cursory wave and slid onto the driver's seat. Val knew something. Had Aileen been gossiping? He very much hoped not.

As he drove towards Tamworth, Roy planned his line of defence. Aileen wasn't going to forgive him easily, so he had to get his story straight. He'd grovel if he had to, anything to get her to trust him again. Flowers. Red roses should do it; she could hardly say no to them. He'd offer to take her for a meal and promise to drive her straight home afterwards. Yes, he was sure that would work.

His feelings for Aileen had grown, and he wanted to prove to his mother that he was capable of holding onto a relationship longer than a few weeks. Aileen was sweet, innocent, and she never mentioned a boyfriend. He'd felt sorry for her, losing her mother. Aileen didn't talk much about her family; too painful, he guessed. She was vulnerable, a bit like him. Perhaps that was why they had been drawn towards each other. She had gone away thinking he didn't care, and it wasn't how he really felt.

Anyway, he'd make sure he was waiting for her tomorrow morning, and if not then, the following morning. If she travelled on Friday, she would arrive on Saturday. He'd need to find out what time the boat train was due in and work out the connections from there. Roy enjoyed working things out like that in his head. Top of the maths class at school, he recalled.

As he neared Tamworth, with its busy roundabouts and byways, he put Aileen from his mind to concentrate on the day ahead. In the mirror, he practised his salesman's persona. He was adept at getting it right. Must keep the clients sweet, keep a cool head and, by whatever means, bring back as many new orders as he could get. It was dog-eat-dog out there these days, and he knew he was good at what he did.

# Chapter Thirty-One

Saying goodbye to Dermot proved much harder than Aileen had expected. They had clung together, and she had cried at the parting. Her da, although he hadn't come to see her off, wrapped his arms around her and kissed the top of her head as he had in the past, and told her to take care of herself.

The journey across the Irish Sea was rough. And by the time she finally stepped off the train at New Street station, she felt exhausted, vowing never to do the journey again. She jostled her way through the crowds towards the exit and out onto the busy street. Taxis drew up and car doors slammed, but Aileen only had enough money for the bus. She paused briefly to catch her breath, dropping her case by her feet.

When she glanced up, Roy Pickering was at her side. Taken aback by his sudden appearance, she picked up her case and turned away. If only she had spotted him earlier, she could have dashed for the Ladies.

'What are you doing here?'

He placed his hand on her arm, and she shrugged it off. 'I've come to pick you up.' He reached for her case, and she gripped it tighter. 'My car's around the corner, come on. Let me help you.'

'Just go away, will you? My bus will be here soon.'

'Don't be like that. You look shattered. I'll drop you off. I'm going that way.'

Where they stood, they were blocking the pavement and drawing attention. Sighing, Aileen backed into a doorway. 'You've got a nerve, after the way you spoke to me on the phone.'

'Aileen, what are you talking about?'

'You know perfectly well. We're no longer friends. You made that clear when I phoned you at home.'

'What?' He frowned. 'When, when was that? I've been away.'

'Look, Roy, I'm tired.' She moved along towards the bus stop.

'I never took a call from you at home.' He rubbed the side of his face.

She shook her head. She felt cold, hungry, and fit to drop. People pushed past them.

'Please, sit in the car, we can talk there.'

'Go away and leave me alone.' She turned away from him.

He continued to pursue her, moving closer. 'Aileen, can you remember what day it was that you phoned?'

'It makes no difference.'

'It does.'

'Friday, it was Friday. I rang to tell you to leave me alone, and I'm telling you now. There's no future for us. And why were you stalking my lodgings? I'm so angry with you for upsetting Mary.'

'That wasn't me. I did none of those things.'

A few more people had gathered by the bus stop, and she felt her shoulders relax. He linked his fingers. 'It could only have been my brother, Harold. He's... well... he's got problems. He's also very protective of Mother.' He sighed.

'How did he know about me and where I live?'

'I'm afraid Mother must have told him. With hindsight, I'd never have mentioned you.' He moved closer in the queue, continuing to plead with her.

Aileen had stopped listening. She could see the bus behind a row of traffic, and when it finally arrived at the stop she sighed and blew out her breath, but her heart still raced.

Determined to get away from him, she struggled to get her case onto the bus. He tried to help her, but she brushed him aside. The conductor took it from her and placed it in the luggage compartment under the stairwell, and she hurried upstairs.

'Aileen, wait!' he called after her, as the bus moved away.

A woman chatted to her non-stop about the weather and the price of coal, but Aileen couldn't rise above a nod and she was glad

160

when the woman got off.

She had been looking forward to coming back to Birmingham; now Roy Pickering had put her in a bad mood. It had infuriated her to find him waiting for her and she didn't want to believe him, yet he had an answer for everything and now she didn't know what to believe. Either way, he meant nothing to her.

She alighted the bus and walked through the side streets, glancing over her shoulder until she arrived at the top end of the avenue. She looked down at the empty street. It looked longer to her today. She placed her case down to stretch her shoulders and flex her fingers before walking on.

With every step, she expected to see his car parked up waiting for her. When it wasn't, she found renewed energy and her gait quickened. The walk helped her to regain her composure before arriving at Mary's. She hoped her landlady was home. She didn't want to be alone with the possibility of Roy hanging about outside. Quickly glancing over her shoulder, she pushed her key into the lock and went inside.

# Chapter Thirty-Two

She placed her luggage in the hall and Mary came to greet her. When she clung to the older woman longer than was necessary, Mary held her at arm's length and gave her a puzzled look. 'Yea look tired, so yea do. The kettle's on. I'm sure yea could murder a cuppa.'

The way she was feeling, a cup of tea would be lovely and then she would go to bed and sleep for a month. Mary placed cups and plates on the table. 'Well, sure, how was everyone back in the old country?'

'Good. They were all really well, thanks, Mary, especially Da. He seemed pleased to see me.'

'I should think so, too.' She poured the tea. Aileen's mouth felt dry as she milked and sugared it, then she sipped the hot liquid, warming her hands on the mug. 'Anyways, more importantly, did he sell the draper's shop?'

'Yes, he did, unfortunately. He's running a sweet shop with Lizzy.'

Mary's mouth dropped. 'No! A sweet shop! What in the name of God did he do that for? And with her! It's not as if she's loaded, or has property that would have influenced his decision.'

'What do you mean? Da's self-reliant, or at least, he was.' Aileen grumbled. 'More like the other way round.'

'I'm just sayin'. I wonder what made 'im do it?' Mary shook her head. Aileen felt a stab of pain at the reminder. 'I'm sorry, love.' Mary looked contrite, and she placed her hand on Aileen's arm. 'Me and me big mouth.'

Aileen stifled a yawn. 'I've lost my home, Mary. And worse

still, I think he'll regret it. From what I've seen of Lizzy, she's not right for my da.' She sighed. 'She's a forceful woman, and she made it perfectly clear that she doesn't want me around.'

'She said that? The vindictive bitch.'

Aileen stretched her back. 'If it's all right with you, Mary, can I stay here for a while longer?'

'Course yea can. I've got used to having yea round.'

'The problem is, I'm anxious to find out more about my brother, and I can't do that from over here.'

'Why? Have yea found sommat out then?'

Aileen told her about the strange nun she had met, and Mary was horrified. 'If I were you, I'd goo back and see that Miss Fish, or whatever she calls herself. Sounds fishy to me.'

Aileen laughed. 'It's Finch.' Mary was always getting names mixed up, and Aileen found it endearing. The woman had become like a second mother to her.

'Yea look bushed, love. Why don't yea go for a lie-down?' Mary stood up. 'I've prepared something to eat, but it can wait until later if yea like.'

'No, it's fine. I'd rather eat first, thanks.' She had to tell Mary about Roy, and was dreading her reaction. He could be so unpredictable, and could easily come looking for her. She took a deep breath and started. 'There's something I need to tell you first.'

'This sounds ominous,' Mary said, and began to put food on the table.

Over a delicious ham salad with homemade bread, Aileen told Mary about Roy turning up at the station to meet her. 'And yea believe 'im, do yea?'

Aileen shrugged. 'I really don't know, Mary. He's very convincing.'

Mary polished off a piece of tasty ham while Aileen struggled to keep her eyes open. 'I wouldn't believe a word that comes from that man's mouth.'

'He was the last person I expected to see when I got off the train.'

Mary shook her head and folded her arms. 'Well, you've a lot to learn about men like 'im. So, does this brother of his have a black Ford then?'

'Apparently. He said he copies everything, even his clothes.' Aileen glanced up. 'To be honest, Mary, I half expected him to come behind me as I walked down the avenue.'

'Whether he's telling the truth or not, you did the right thing making your own way.'

'I'm wrecked, Mary. Let's not talk about him.' Now that she was back, Roy Pickering was again causing discord between herself and Mary.

'I'm just looking out for yea, love.'

'I know that, and I'm grateful. But I'm not stupid. I can take care of myself.' Aileen stood up.

'Aye, yea'd better get some kip before yea drop.'

* * *

Aileen heard nothing more from Roy. His unnecessary visits to the office stopped, and any calls he made went straight through to Miss Grimshaw. Aileen couldn't have been happier. His name was no longer mentioned at home between herself and Mary, and Aileen's focus was on ways to find her brother. But to carry out her plans she needed to be in Dublin, and Christmas seemed ages away.

Weeks later, Aileen was helping Mary with the housework, and in the afternoon, they went to the local launderette to wash and dry the clothes.

'You know you should go out and mix with people your own age,' Mary said, as they folded the sheets and placed them in the wash basket. 'I'm sure that young feller of yours wouldn't mind.'

'Of course he wouldn't.' Aileen picked her winter jumper and placed it into the large dryer along with her work skirts, and pushed the coins into the slot. 'I'm saving for Christmas.'

'Are yea thinking of going home again then?'

'Dermot wants me to. His older brother, who has been studying for the priesthood, is now newly ordained.'

'Really!'

'Yes. Dermot would like me to meet him when he comes home at Christmas.'

'His mam and dad must be proud. You'll have to watch your p's, and q's, so.' Mary laughed.

'I know. Dermot says his mam talks of nothing else.'

'Have you heard ought from your da?'

Aileen shook her head. 'He asked me to keep in touch, and I've written a few times, yet I've not heard a word from him. Do you think he's all right?'

'Well, yea know what some men are like. Wouldn't write a letter to save their life.' Mary went and sat on the plastic chair. 'Pass me the *Tit-bits* magazine, will yea, love? Me dogs are killing me.'

\* \* \*

Mary was in bed with a chesty cough, and Aileen was in the kitchen pouring hot water into a mug of Lemsip when she heard the clatter of the post through the letterbox. She stirred the liquid and took it with her into the hall. A small stack of letters lay on the *Bless this House* mat, and she took them upstairs.

Mary was sitting up in bed, and Aileen placed the hot drink down on the bedside table. 'How are you feeling?'

'Oh, I'm fine. What have you got there? More bills, I reckon.' She removed the elastic band and fanned them out. 'There's one here for you, love.'

Aileen's heart skipped when she recognised her father's handwriting. Leaving Mary comfortable, she clutched the letter to her and went to her room. She had waited so long for a letter from him that she opened it slowly, fearful of what it might contain.

*My dearest Aileen,*

*I hope this letter finds you well. Forgive my tardiness in writing to you. After you had returned to Birmingham, you left me a great deal to think about. I'm not the best at expressing my feelings verbally, or otherwise. I have to admit that it is difficult for me to do so now.*

*I'm grateful for the way in which you took the news of my sharing the shop's accommodation with your aunt. I know it can't be easy for you. The drapers wasn't doing as well as you might have thought, even when your mother was alive. We'd have sunk had I not gone in with Lizzy's suggestion, and I'm pleased I did now.*

*Since your mother's deathbed confession, I have been distraught, unable to even speak of it in the hopes that it wasn't true. It's only now that I can...*

*On the morning your ma passed away, while we waited for the parish priest, she told me what she was about to confess. It knocked me for six. I couldn't speak. Not even to say goodbye. I remember how she struggled to get the words out, mumbled a lot, and I couldn't catch every word. 'We... had... a son, Jonny,' she gasped. 'Aileen's twin. I... I... left... him behind.' She could hardly breathe, and I eased her head back on the pillow. Then the priest came up. I was stunned, as if all the life had been knocked out of me. I don't know why she left him. I don't know why...*

*I remembered how she checked herself out of that clinic before I got to her. Said she wanted to get back to her own bed. At the time, I thought nothing of it, glad to have you both home. After all we'd shared, I couldn't believe that Jessie would keep secrets from me. Goes to show you can never really know anyone. I felt so angry, like I might explode if I didn't keep a lid on it.*

*Rightly so, you want to find your brother, and I'll help you all I can. I've refrained from mentioning any of this to Lizzy, at least until we know the outcome.*

*Your loving Da*

It was obvious that he had written it over several days, because it was three pages long. Now the ink was smudged with her tears. Unable to take it in, she read it through again. She was a twin, and her ma had rejected her brother? It didn't make sense. He must be alive somewhere, why else would her mother have asked her to find him?

Her head felt like it was about to burst. She massaged her temples against a headache that made her feel sick. Her mind raced. How could her lovely ma have rejected her brother? Why? There had to be a good reason.

# Chapter Thirty-Three

By Saturday, Mary was up and about again and swore the Lemsip had cured her.

'You still need to take it easy,' Aileen told her.

'Sure, I'm grand. Have yea thought any more about Christmas? Me sister's doing the honours this year, and she said you'd be welcome.'

'Thanks. That's kind of her, Mary, but I'm going to check out the travel agent today, see how much a return flight to Dublin will cost.' She sighed. 'I've never flown before and, to tell the truth, that plane crash at Luton has made me nervous.'

'Oh, yea don't want to dwell on that. When yer times up, there's not a lot yea can do about it.'

Aileen frowned. 'Well, I'm willing to risk it. I can't wait to see Dermot and my da again, especially now he's talking about ma.'

'I still can't believe it of Jessie. She wouldn't just abandon a babby like that. It wasn't in her nature. Someone must know what happened.'

'I intend to find out, and while da is in this frame of mind, we can work together and get to the bottom of it.'

'Aye, but that might prove difficult with Lizzy. If she gets a sniff of any gossip, she'll sharpen her tongue on it.'

Aileen nodded. She couldn't imagine her da discussing her ma with anyone. 'Well, unless there's anything else you want me to do round here, I'm off to town.' She put on her jacket and wrapped up warmly against the cold. 'Would you like anything brought back?'

Mary plucked a list from behind the clock. 'Can yea get me

these few bits? It'll save me legs.' She opened her purse and handed Aileen a pound note.

\* \* \*

There was an icy chill in the air that made her shiver, and she wished she'd worn her long coat. Frost was forecast for tonight, and Mary had left an extra blanket on her bed.

At the travel agents, she discovered she could afford a flight with Aer Lingus if she waited another week. After jotting the details down, she left. All she had to do was appeal to Miss Grimshaw's better nature when she asked for a couple of extra days off over Christmas.

Later, with the shopping done, shivering inside her jacket, she made her way back. She was halfway along the avenue when Roy's car pulled up alongside her.

'Hey, Aileen!' he called through the car window. 'How are you doing? Sorry, I've not been in touch. I've been busy.'

'I'm grand, Roy. And you?' She tried to act normally, but she wasn't interested in standing in the cold talking to him.

'I'm a bit down, to be honest. I'd love a chat with you. Are you free to come for a coffee?'

She shook her head and carried on walking. 'I'm sorry, Roy, I've a lot to do.'

'Oh, come on. It's been weeks. I feel lousy about what happened.'

She shrugged and continued walking, but he cruised along next to her. 'I wouldn't ask, only I buried a close friend yesterday and I need cheering up.' He offered a watery smile. 'Please, Aileen, just half an hour for a coffee.' Then he added, 'As a friend.'

She noticed he was wearing a black tie, and he placed his hand over it. 'I wear it as a mark of respect. I'll remove it.'

'Please don't. Not on my behalf.' She sighed, recalling that awful feeling in the pit of her stomach when she lost her ma. It wasn't a real comparison, but she still felt bad. 'Okay, Just a coffee mind. But, I'll have to take this shopping in first and let Mary know.'

Mary, nonplussed, clicked her tongue and shook her head. 'I

thought we'd seen the back of 'im. Why start all that up again?'

'Don't be like that, Mary. He's just buried his friend. He knows how things stand. Otherwise I wouldn't have agreed to have a coffee with him. I'll be back within an hour. You see if I'm not.'

'Aye, and I believe in Santa Claus.' She carried on spooning cake mix into a tin. 'Did yea remember to get me baking soda?'

Aileen nodded. 'It's in the bag.'

'Did yea book a flight then?'

'No, but the fare is cheaper than I expected. I'll buy a ticket next week when I get my Christmas bonus.' She felt Mary's eyes on her, disapprovingly, as she snuggled into her warm beige coat with the fur hood that made her feel like an Eskimo. She placed her purse into the large pocket, just in case. 'I won't be long.'

\* \* \*

'New coat?' Roy asked, as she got into the car.

'Yes, I suppose it is.'

'Thanks for being a friend, Aileen.' He had replaced his black tie with a bright yellow one that didn't look right with his black suit. She remembered the first time she'd met him at the office he had been wearing a yellow jumper. 'I don't know how I got through the funeral service,' he told her. 'I never expected to feel this emptiness.'

She nodded. 'It will get better. How long had you known each other?'

'Oh, years, we grew up together until he moved away. He was a heavy smoker. The doctors said it was his lungs.' He shrugged.

'I'm sorry.'

'Never mind. I don't want to make you sad. I know a coffee bar not far from here. Is that all right?'

She nodded. The coffee bar turned out to be a small restaurant on the Hagley Road that sold frothy coffee. She refused anything to eat. 'I'll be eating with Mary later and you can imagine how cross she gets if I spoil my appetite.' She laughed. It was an exaggeration, but it worked.

'Just two coffees,' he told the waiter.

'Has it been busy at the mill, Aileen?'

'Are you joking? Orders are coming in faster than we can type them.'

'That's good. Is the old man pleased?'

'I assume you mean, Mr Bill?' No-one ever referred to the boss as anything other than Mr Bill, and she thought 'the old man' sounded a little disrespectful. 'Well, I guess he is. How are you managing to get all these orders, Roy?'

'It's down to experience and know-how,' he said jokingly. 'However, it's always busy coming up to Christmas.'

'I guess so.' She removed her coat and relaxed back in her chair. Roy appeared more cheerful and she hoped her being there was helping. 'How is your brother? What did you say his name was?'

'Harold. He's gone away for a bit.' He shook his head. 'I'm sorry that I wasn't around to protect you from him. Naturally, Mother was pleased to have him home, but he should never have been released.'

Released. The word stuck in her mind and she wondered if he was a criminal. Being polite, she said, 'I'm sorry. That must be hard for her.'

'Why should you be sorry? He's caused you enough trouble.' The waiter returned with their coffee, and Roy paid, telling him to keep the change. 'How are things with you, Aileen? Have you decided to settle in Birmingham?' He leaned forward and slowly stirred his coffee, then fiddled with his watchstrap.

'I never intended to stay. I'm not living here through choice.'

He frowned. 'I guess you'll be going back at Christmas?'

She wasn't sure she should tell him. 'Well, maybe. I'd like to. I'll have to ask for extra time off first.'

He leant his elbows on the table and pulled on his bottom lip. 'Did you say you were flying?'

'I didn't.'

'When were you thinking of going?'

'I don't know. When we break up, I guess.' She sipped some of her coffee. It tasted delicious. 'This is good coffee.'

'I'm sorry, Aileen. I didn't mean to pry.'

'It's okay.' She remained nonchalant. 'What about you, Roy? Have you any plans for Christmas?' She drank the rest of her coffee.

He shook his head and looked pensive. 'No. I'll be working at home.' He shrugged. 'Just house maintenance stuff.'

'You're a workaholic. It's Christmas! What about your family?'

'That depends. Mother's not awfully keen on Christmas.' He sat forward. 'Aileen, I've been thinking of some way to apologise for my brother's behaviour that won't be construed the wrong way. What I'm trying to say is, if you were thinking of flying to Dublin, I can take you to the airport. As a friend, of course,' he added.

'You don't have to do that, Roy.'

'It would be my pleasure.' He ran his finger around the rim of his coffee cup. 'I wish I could have stopped what happened.'

'You can't be responsible for your brother's actions. I just hope he gets help.' She stood up. 'I must get back.'

'Okay. I feel better already. Thanks for being a friend.'

'I've a bet on with Mary that you'd have me back home in an hour.'

'In that case,' he got to his feet and helped her on with her coat, 'don't let's disappoint her.'

* * *

Mary's eyes widened and she dropped her knitting onto her lap when Aileen walked into the room. 'Well, I'll go to the bottom of our stairs.' Mary glanced at her watch. 'Maybe I was wrong. What did he want, then?'

'Just a chat! He was feeling down about his friend dying. I mentioned about going to Ireland for Christmas, and he offered to take me to the airport,' Aileen said.

'Well, I'm not sure.' Mary frowned. 'Can you trust him?'

'I'm sure it'll be fine, Mary. He's accepted how things are between us. I'm prepared to give him the benefit of the doubt, so to speak.'

'What about the brother, then?'

'Oh, he's gone away. I gather he's in some home or other. Roy

171

still feels the need to make up for his brother's actions.'

'Too right! Did yea tell him about Dermot?'

'No, but I will. He'll be happy for me, I'm sure.'

# Chapter Thirty-Four

Aileen had mixed feelings about her forthcoming flight to Dublin. She was looking forward to seeing Dermot and her da again—the two men she cared about most in the world. She hadn't heard anything from Roy all week, and on the Friday as she was preparing to leave for the airport, Mary suggested that she make her own way there and not depend on him.

'Now he knows there's nought in it for 'im, he might easily forget to pick you up,' she said.

Mary was leaving the following day to stay with her sister for Christmas, and was ironing a skirt to take with her while Aileen was tying a label with her name and Dublin address to the handle of her suitcase. 'The bus stops right across the road from the airport, me sister tells me.'

'It's all right, Mary. My flight is hours away yet. I'll phone a taxi to take me to the bus depot if I need to.'

An hour later, when the phone rang, Mary hurried out to answer it. 'Oh, it's you!' She glanced round as Aileen came into the hall. 'Okay, I'll give her the message.'

'Was that Roy?'

'Sez he'll be outside in half an hour.' Mary clicked her tongue and ambled back to finish her ironing.

When Aileen was ready, she stood in the hall, her luggage at her feet. She wore a warm black belted jacket over a cream woollen dress and knee-high black boots.

'Well, I expect yea better get off then. Have yea got everything?'

'I guess so. Happy Christmas, Mary.'

'You too, love. Give my regards to everyone. Let me know

173

when yea get there?' She held open the door and glanced outside to where Roy was parked up.

It was a damp, miserable evening and Roy got out as Aileen approached, and placed her luggage in the boot.

'All set then,' he said, opening the passenger door.

Aileen nodded. She had butterflies in her tummy about the flight while feeling excited at the same time. 'Thanks for doing this, Roy,' she said, settling into the leather seat. 'I hope it's not inconvenienced you.'

'Of course it's not, Aileen. I'd never break a promise to you.' He pushed the key into the ignition and switched his lights on full before moving away. 'You look lovely,' he said, glancing down at her new boots. 'I wish you weren't going.'

'It's Christmas, Roy. Besides, I haven't seen my boyfriend for nearly six weeks, and I'm looking forward to seeing my da.'

Roy went quiet. He changed gear then drove faster, weaving in and out of the heavy traffic.

Aileen glared at him. 'You're scaring me, Roy. What's the matter?'

'Sorry, Aileen.' He slowed down.

She glanced at her watch. 'What's wrong?'

He pulled into a layby and began to examine his inside pockets. 'Dash it.'

'What is it?'

Frowning, he stepped out and opened the back door of the car and began to search his briefcase.

'Tell me! What's wrong?' What was he playing at? At this rate, she could miss her flight.

'I've been so busy I forgot to fill the tank.' He scratched his head. 'I've forgotten my wallet.' He placed everything back neatly into his briefcase and got in the car. 'I must have left it at home.'

She tensed and felt a funny sensation in her stomach. She couldn't miss her flight; not for anything. 'Is there enough petrol to get us there?'

He restarted the engine so she could see the petrol gauge was low. 'I can't chance it,' he said, shaking his head.

'Can I help? How much do you need?'

'Oh, I couldn't let you do that.'

'Well, I'll get out here and catch a bus.'

He laughed. 'I wouldn't dream of letting you do that after I promised to drive you.' He patted her shoulder. 'Don't worry, you've plenty of time. I'm just annoyed with myself. We'll nip over to Warley. It's not far and I can pick up my wallet. Trust me!'

Aileen was nervous enough about the flight, and Roy's reassurance did nothing to make her feel less anxious. She couldn't speak and, after what appeared an age, he swung onto a gravelled driveway surrounded by high trees. The house was Tudor style; black timber crossed over white lime ash.

'You're so lucky to live in a house like this, Roy.'

He nodded. 'The house belongs to my mother. There's just the two of us, except when my brother arrives home unexpectedly. Why don't you come in?'

In spite of her curiosity to see inside, her mind was on her flight. 'It's all right, I'll wait here.'

'It's cold. Come in a minute.' He opened the passenger door and held out his hand.

Not wanting to appear rude, she stepped out onto the gravelled path and glanced up at the well-maintained house with its leaded light windows. A yellow night-light shone in the upstairs window, and a shadowy figure looked out then drew back and the curtains closed. She felt uneasy about going in.

'What about your mother, won't it disturb her?'

He shook his head. 'She retires early.'

He unlocked the front door and ushered her inside, switching on the light. Aileen stepped into a gloomy square hallway with heavy oak doors that led into a room on either side. The walls were bare. Her eyes swept up along the matching oak staircase with an attractive galleria that overlooked the main entrance.

She swallowed. In spite of the rich wooden floors and carpeted staircase, a shiver ran through her body.

# Chapter Thirty-Five

Aileen followed Roy into the dimly-lit sitting room, and he placed his keys down on the oak sideboard. The room was freezing. He frowned as if trying to recall something, then he walked across to the black marble fireplace, picked up his wallet, and slipped it into his pocket.

Aileen's sigh was one of relief. A strange fusty smell hung in the air as if the room hadn't been used for a while. The furniture was antique and undoubtedly expensive, but she could see no indication that it was Christmas. The walls were void of pictures or family portraits. It seemed odd that there were no ornaments anywhere. Then she remembered Roy saying he had maintenance to do on the house over the holiday. Could that explain why all the walls were bare?

Her throat felt dry, and an uneasy feeling settled in her stomach. 'Roy, shall we get going now?' She pulled the belt of her coat tighter around her waist.

'We've got time for a drink. Just a small glass will warm you up.' He opened a cupboard and took out a bottle of sherry, and held the stems of two glasses between his fingers.

'No, thank you, Roy, I'd rather we got going. You still need to fill up.'

He glanced at his watch. 'We've loads of time. It's Christmas; you said so yourself. Don't forget we have the motorway now. And I won't see you again until New Year.'

He had his back to her, opening the bottle. She felt her knees begin to shake and glanced over to the table by the window and the black telephone. If she could only...

He placed the drinks on a side table. 'Please sit down, Aileen.'

She remained standing and he picked up a glass and handed it to her.

'Cheers,' he said.

She gave him a watery smile, raised the glass to her lips and took a sip. She could have kicked herself for trusting him. Trying to keep her voice steady, she asked, 'So, how long have you lived here?' She glanced around her.

'Does that matter?'

She remembered how he hated questions about his personal life, and wished she hadn't asked. The ticking of the grandfather clock became more noticeable in the seconds that followed. She placed the glass down and glanced at her watch. 'I think we should go now. I don't want to miss my flight.'

'All this could be yours one day, Aileen.' He stretched his arms wide. 'Stay here and marry me.'

The colour drained from her day. She felt sick.

Taking in her shocked expression, his eyes narrowed. 'Oh, you'd prefer to run back to Ireland to what's-his-name?'

Her heart raced. 'His name is Dermot. What... What's the matter with you? You... You agreed to be friends. You promised.' Her hand rushed to her face. 'I thought I could trust you.'

'You can. You can.' He moved closer.

She shook her head, anger and fear making her shout. 'I'll make my own way to the airport!' She moved across the room and picked up the telephone receiver.

He snatched it from her. 'I can't let you do that, Aileen.'

'You're crazy.' She hurried to the door, but he pressed his hand against it. 'Let me out of here!'

He moved towards her. 'Don't you think it's time you told this Dermot about us?' He reached for her hand and she flinched. 'Why do you think I got you to come here?' he hollered, waving his arms. 'I'm asking you to marry me, you silly cow.'

Trembling, she screamed, 'Get away from me!'

'Ah, come on, Aileen. You like me, I know you do.' He took a step closer. 'I can't let you go, not now that you've been to my house.' He grabbed her arm, and she screamed louder.

Suddenly there were several loud bangs on the ceiling. Roy loosened his grip and straightened his shoulders, his eyes furtive. He picked up the bottle and quickly placed it back inside the cupboard. Aileen's heart raced.

The knocking grew louder. His face twitched. 'I'll see to it. You stay here!' He hurried out and ran upstairs.

Aileen grabbed his car keys from the sideboard, but couldn't stop herself from shaking. In the hall she heard Roy shouting, 'What is it, Mother?'

'Who have you got down there?'

'It's no-one. I'm all right. Go back to bed. I'm all right!' he screamed.

Aileen shrank back against the wall, Roy's keys gripped tightly in her hand. It was a reckless idea, yet her only means of escape. She could hear their voices as they rose in querulous tones.

'Shut up! Shut up, Mother. I've told you before, I don't need medication.'

Fearful he would come back down before she could get away, she tiptoed through the hall, her fingers clawing at the door as she let herself out of the house.

With trembling fingers, she fumbled to get the correct key, dropping them onto the gravel. She scrambled to find them in the dark, grazing her hands on the sharp stones. Glancing up at the window, she saw a face looking down.

Inside the car, her body shook and her hands jerked across the dashboard. She pressed the key into the ignition and turned the key. It started. She put it in gear and pressed her foot on the accelerator; the car shot through the gate, knocking over a large planter. Her breath came in gasps. Sweat broke out on her brow. God help me!

She could see Roy in the mirror, waving his arms. If he caught her, she feared what he might be capable of. She pressed her foot on the accelerator to try and put distance between them as the car juddered down the road then suddenly picked up speed. She was driving blind without lights, and pressed various buttons until the lights shone on the road ahead.

In a state of panic, her eyes searched for directions. A sign loomed for Birmingham and West Bromwich. Oh, Jesus Christ! Which way should she go? Her only hope was to keep going until she ran out of petrol.

Her heartbeat quickened when she met heavy traffic coming towards her. Were they going to, or coming from the city? Roy was bound to have a map in the glove compartment, but she was too nervous to stop and look. A car behind hooted and overtook her. Other car drivers blew their horns. Blinded by tears, she realised she was putting others in danger. Her hands shook as she gripped the steering wheel, willing the car to keep going. She then hit the curb and the engine cut out.

A police car with flashing lights pulled up behind her. On shaky legs she stepped from the car to retrieve her case, and then looked up into the face of a police officer. He glanced down at her case.

'Run out of petrol, have you, Miss?' She couldn't speak. The boot was open, and he leant inside. 'You do know that it's illegal to carry this much petrol around, Miss?'

She shook her head. Damn you, Roy Pickering, she muttered, and gripped the car door fearing she was going to faint.

'You do know you've enough petrol in there to fill a bus?'

She rubbed her temples. 'No, I-I had no idea.' Whatever she said would sound crazy, and already she could see disbelief on his face.

'Can I see your driving licence, Miss?'

She closed her eyes. 'I- I don't have one. This isn't my car.'

'Are you saying you took the car without consent, Miss?'

'Yes, no, I'm… I'm… well, yes, I borrowed it to get away… away from someone.' She wanted him to arrest her and take her somewhere safe where Roy couldn't find her.

'Can you step away from the car, please, Miss?'

She stepped back onto the grassy bank.

He scribbled a note and stuck it underneath the window wipers. Passing cars slowed down to stare and Aileen choked back tears of shame and frustration. She couldn't stop trembling, and wrapped her arms around herself.

'So whose car is it? Miss, can you hear me?'

Distraught, Aileen slid down onto the damp grass verge. 'My flight,' she sobbed, 'I've... I've missed my flight.'

## Chapter Thirty-Six

Aileen stood in front of the tall counter, feeling sick to her stomach as she stared at a row of keys hanging on the wall. The policeman who had brought her in had disappeared, and the bobby on duty appeared to be in no hurry. He was drinking hot tea from a Santa Claus mug and eating a piece of Christmas cake from his packup.

'Sit over there, Miss. Someone will see you in a minute.'

Above the counter were strewn a few wilting streamers from which six baubles dangled, in a mean attempt to cheer up Christmas. Aileen sat down, nervously locking and unlocking her fingers and biting back tears of frustration. If only she'd listened. What was she going to tell Mary?

A policeman walked towards her and directed her to a small room with a table and two chairs. 'Sit down. You look like you've seen a ghost. I'll see if there's a cup of tea going.'

He returned with the hot tea and left her alone. Aileen appreciated the warm, sweet drink that tasted like it had been stewing for hours, and wrapped her shaking hands around the mug. Roy would have rung the police by now, and he would make sure she was charged for taking his car without his permission. His car meant everything to him.

Dermot and her da would worry when she didn't turn up at the airport, and there was no way of getting a message to them, or to Mary. She glanced at the clock on the wall. Was it really eight o'clock? Her flight would be landing in Dublin now.

In her desperation to get away, she had only made things worse. And now everyone would think she was a thief who took cars and drove without insurance and a licence. Her good character would be sullied, and it was all her own doing. The thought of being locked up in a cell on Christmas Eve was a frightening possibility. She finished the tea and, with shaking fingers, placed it on the table in front of her. She picked at her freshly-painted fingernails, wishing someone would tell her what was going on.

The door opened, and the policeman returned, accompanied by a more senior officer.

'Right then,' the older man said. 'I'm Sergeant Jones and this is Constable Taylor. We need to ask you some questions, and warn you that anything you say may be taken as evidence. Is there anyone you would like us to contact?'

She felt vulnerable, not sure who she should turn to. Mary was the only one she knew who had a telephone, but she didn't want to worry her. Anyway, she would be disgusted and probably say, 'I told you so.'

'Miss!'

'I… I don't know.'

'I must caution you that, TWOC—taking without the owner's consent—is a serious offence,' the officer said. 'Can you tell us what happened to drive you to such lengths, Miss Maguire?' The policeman straightened his shoulders and sat forward, his pen poised over a notepad.

The senior officer's eyes narrowed, and Aileen was aware of his pale eyes watching her. It made her more anxious. She rolled her hands one over the other and linked her fingers, desperately trying to fight the urge to be sick.

The nice officer sighed and shifted in his chair. 'If you're telling the truth, you've nothing to fear, Miss. Carry on.' His words helped her relax slightly, and she told them everything about meeting Roy, his weird behaviour, and the cunning way in which he had lured her to his house.

'He hasn't hurt you, or threatened you in any way, has he?'

'No! Not exactly.' She leant forward in the chair. 'But he's not right in the head.'

'Well, that's not our concern,' the officer said. 'You taking a car without consent and driving without a licence or insurance is.'

A feeling of desperation swamped her, and she placed her head in her hands. 'I'm so sorry. I was… scared he was going to stop me from leaving the house.' She took a deep breath. 'I've… I've never done anything like this before.'

'A Mr Pickering reported his car taken from his driveway earlier.' The younger policeman rolled his pencil between his fingers. 'Can you tell me the address you took the car from?'

Glancing up, she shook her head. It seemed silly, but she had been in such a panic to get away that she hadn't taken no notice of street names. 'I'm sorry. It was dark, and I'd never been there before.'

The young policeman on the desk knocked and entered. He mumbled something to the senior officer, who scraped back his chair and stood up. 'Be back in a minute.'

PC Taylor pulled a face and blew out his lips.

'What will happen to me?' Aileen asked him.

The policeman sighed. 'It's difficult to say. You've admitted to taking a vehicle, and driving without a licence.'

Ashamed, Aileen lowered her head. Hearing her offences read out like that sounded dreadful. What on earth would her family say? Her ma would turn in her grave; she certainly wouldn't think her perfect now. Dear God, she was in such trouble. How would she explain all this to Dermot? She had never even mentioned her association with Roy Pickering.

Sergeant Jones came back into the room and spoke softly to his colleague. Aileen felt her heart race and could hear its beat in her ears. Were they going to charge her? Detain her overnight, or worse?

The sergeant cleared his throat. 'You ought to be more careful who you choose as friends, Miss.' Aileen was shaking so much she could hardly keep her head upright. 'As it's Christmas and I'm in a good mood, I'm going to caution you and warn you that if you ever drive without a licence or insurance again you won't get off so lightly. You're free to go!'

Aileen's hand rushed to her face and tears welled in her eyes.

'Thank you.'

'I'm sorry that you've missed your flight, Miss.' He closed the folder and passed it to PC Taylor, a smile lightening his face. 'My advice is that you get yourself out of here, and don't let me catch you doing this sort of thing again.'

Aileen couldn't believe what she had just heard. 'You're not going to charge me?'

'We have nothing to charge you with.' He walked to the door then looked back. 'Merry Christmas.'

The young constable gave Aileen a fleeting smile. 'You're lucky Sergeant Jones was on duty, and that the man you're so terrified of does not want to press charges against you.'

'Really! But does he mean it? He's deranged. He could change his mind.' Nervous, she pulled at the sleeves of her coat.

'He's been in and signed your release papers.'

Aileen gasped. 'He's been in here. When?'

'Just now.' He sighed. 'You should think yourself lucky to have gotten away with a caution.' The policeman got to his feet. 'Well, what are you waiting for?'

'I can't risk it. He'll be out there.'

PC Taylor shot her a puzzled look. 'Are you sure you're not being paranoid?'

She swallowed her anger. 'You don't know what he's like.'

'I suppose I could drive you home.' He glanced at his watch. 'If you don't mind being escorted back in a police car.'

'Thank you.' She picked up her bag and collected her case from the desk, desperately trying to hide the feelings of anger and rage tearing through her. 'Could I make a call to my landlady? She'll be going to bed soon…and…'

'Oh, go on. Make it quick.'

Aileen did her utmost to remain calm when Mary said, 'That was quick. Them planes are getting faster.'

'Mary, I'm still in Birmingham. I'm on my way back. I'll explain everything when I see you.'

Her landlady was sure to put two and two together when Aileen arrived back in a police car.

* * *

It was late when Roy Pickering drove his car back home and parked it neatly on the driveway. He sat a while, inhaling the sweet fragrance Aileen had left behind, and picked up a lipstick in a crevice on the passenger seat and put it in his pocket. His head ached, and he was in no hurry to go back inside the house or to listen to any more advice from Mummy Dear.

His attempts to bribe Aileen into marrying him had failed miserably, and he took several deep breaths to release the anger still raging through him. Couldn't she see how well they got on, and that he had more to offer her than that Irish guy? If only his mother hadn't interrupted him at that moment. Mother could be frustrating with her constant nagging. She owned the house, but that didn't give her the right to dictate who he could or couldn't entertain at home. Didn't she realise how hard he worked to pay the bills?

Yes, he had done the right thing by not pressing charges. When they had asked him if he was sure, he'd simply told them that he and the woman he loved had had a tiff. Just because she had borrowed his car without asking and subsequently run out of petrol, wasn't a good enough reason to land her with a criminal record.

'No,' he'd told them, 'you must release her.' One fresh-faced PC had gone as far as to say he must be mad, or in love. Although it had been said in a jokey way, Roy had taken offence. The cheeky young upstart; what did he know about loving a woman?

He pushed the seat back and stretched his legs. He had no idea how much of the argument Aileen had overheard, but obviously enough to make her drive off the way she did. She could have been killed, or killed someone. He had been relieved to discover she wasn't hurt; it was at that precise moment he knew he would always be obsessed with her.

He wondered if the stupid tattoo on his wrist with the initial 'M' had put her off, but his mother had become less important to him since meeting Aileen. He would have said anything to the police—even lied—to get her off. He smiled at himself in the mirror. Yes, she loved him really. She just didn't know it yet. Perhaps when she got back, she would see that turning him down had been a huge mistake.

He stepped from the car, locked it, and looked up at the sky. It was dark and brooding, which matched his mood. He ran his hands over the paintwork, glad to have found no apparent damage. He loved his car, but he loved Aileen more. He missed her already. An empty feeling swamped him, but he consoled himself with the fact that she would be in touch to express her thanks. With that thought, he filled his lungs with fresh air and went inside.

# Chapter Thirty-Seven

Mary opened the door in her navy candlewick dressing gown, a net covering her pink curlers, and she gasped when she saw a police car drive away.

'Glory be to God! What's happened?'

Aileen dropped her suitcase in the hall. She felt drained of energy. 'Can we go inside and I'll explain.'

As she went through to the living room, a link of Mary's Christmas decoration detached itself from the rest and fell across Aileen's shoulders. She shuddered, struggling to keep her emotions in check, and perched on the edge of the sofa. She began to tremble.

Mary opened the sideboard cupboard and took out a bottle of brandy, poured a generous helping into a glass and handed it to her. 'Drink this.' She pressed it between Aileen's hands and watched as she swallowed a good measure of the liquid, spluttered, and coughed.

'What happened, hen? I guess this has something to do with Pickering?'

Aileen took another gulp of the brandy then placed the glass down. It helped her to stop shaking. Angry to have missed her flight and full of self-loathing that she had been so gullible as to fall into his trap, she wanted to lash out at someone—preferably herself. Unable to stop herself, she picked up a cushion, beating it with her fists until the already dog-eared cushion split, and feathers floated everywhere.

Mary looked on astounded while Aileen stood up and paced the room like a caged animal; her eyes wide, she screamed and tore at her hair, tugging at it until Mary thought it would come out at the roots.

'Stop it, stop it!' Mary cried.

When Aileen dropped to her knees and sobbed, the older woman crouched down beside her, soothing her and gently stroking her hair. 'Tell me.' Mary sniffed. 'What has he done to yea?'

An hour later, when a distraught Aileen had finished recounting all that had transpired since leaving for the airport, a stunned Mary sat back and ran her hands over her face.

'He can't be allowed to get away with that, Aileen. God only knows what he's capable of.' She stood up. 'I'll make sure all the doors and windows are locked tonight. If the police won't arrest him, we can make sure his employers know what kind of a man they have working for them.'

'I'm an idiot and brought all this on myself. I…I thought he was genuine. I really believed I could trust him this time. He was very convincing. How stupid I am.'

'Don't waste your breath on the spineless creep. Dry your eyes and give that young feller of yours a ring. Tell him there's been a change of plan and that you'll try for a flight home tomorrow.'

'But…that's Christmas Eve.'

'It surely is.' Mary smiled and pulled Aileen to her feet. 'That blighter's not spoiling your Christmas or mine. Now, go and freshen up, then make that call and we'll get to bed. First thing in the morning you can see if you can get another flight to Dublin.'

* * *

The following morning, Aileen woke early with a thumping headache. She'd hardly slept a wink. The events of the previous evening had compounded in her head and she'd had to bury her face in her pillow to prevent Mary from hearing her loud sobs. She had sensed the disappointment in Dermot's voice when she told him that her flight had been delayed and she would try again tomorrow. She hated the lie, but what choice did she have?

Downstairs, Mary was cooking breakfast. A small portable

wireless muttered at low volume in the corner. It was Christmas Eve, and Aileen couldn't as much as raise a smile. A small Christmas cake and pudding Mary had cooked weeks ago were out ready on the worktop. Aileen guessed she was taking them to her sister's.

Miss Brady had already left to be with her family in Coventry. Aileen wanted to be with her family, but she wasn't sure that it was a likely prospect now. She would be alone in the house unless Mary invited her along to her sister's, and she didn't want to impose on their time together. She felt so wound up, and the smell of bacon did nothing to revive her appetite. 'Mary, don't cook anything for me. I can't eat. I'll do myself a piece of toast in a minute.'

'Drink your tea then.' Her landlady turned the flame down under the pan and sat down. 'Listen, Aileen.' She placed her elbow on the table. 'You're not going to let that nutter spoil your Christmas.' She took a piece of paper from the pocket of her Santa apron. 'Ring the airport direct. 'Ere, I've looked out the number for yea. Tell them it's an emergency, and they just might let you pay when yea get there.'

Aileen bit her lip. 'But... I...'

'Well, goo on then. What yea waiting for?'

'I haven't got enough money for another ticket.'

'Sure, I'll give it yea. Pay me back when yea can.'

'I can't let you do that. When could I pay you back?'

'Ring up and we'll worry about that another time.' She smiled and patted the back of Aileen's hand. 'I can't see yea disappointed.'

\* \* \*

Aileen could hardly believe her luck when, by midday, she found herself sitting in a window seat on an Aer Lingus flight to Dublin. Her previous worries about the aircraft crashing and the fact that this was her first flight were lost to her now. She focused her thoughts on seeing Dermot and her da again. After what she had been through, flying wasn't going to worry her. She still cursed her foolishness in trusting the sales rep, but it had taught her one of life's harshest lessons.

The people around her smiled and appeared to be full of the Christmas spirit, some carrying pretty packages wrapped in

Christmas paper. She thought about her own small gifts unwrapped in her case and closed her eyes. Before she knew it, the plane was touching down at Dublin Airport. A ripple of excitement went through her at the thought of seeing Dermot, and she hoped he would be there to pick her up.

She descended the steps of the aircraft to a grey overcast day. People waved excitedly towards the plane from the viewing tower but she couldn't see if Dermot was among them. Then she spotted him and stood a moment to wave, her pulse racing. She knew she would have to be truthful and tell him the whole story of how she'd come to miss her flight, but for now all she wanted was for him to hold her and to tell him how much she loved and missed him.

He was standing in the arrivals lounge, his shoulder against a pillar, his arms folded. He looked tired, as if he hadn't slept. She dropped her case at her feet, called out to him and waved, and then she rushed into his arms. Laughing, he swung her round, oblivious to holiday passengers hurrying past, carrying parcels and wearing colourful Christmas scarves and hats.

'Thank God you're here.' He kissed her and held her close. 'I was so worried you wouldn't get a flight. What happened?'

'It's a long story, but I'm here now. I'll tell you later.'

He picked up her luggage. 'You look amazing,' He was looking at her trendy outfit and high boots. 'Let's get home. Have you decided where you're going to stay?'

'With my da, I hope.' After what she had been through, Aileen wasn't going to be fazed by her aunt. She smiled up at him. 'That's if you don't mind taking me.'

As they walked towards the exit, Aileen felt her spirits rise at the sight of a huge Christmas tree in the centre of the airport.

'Sure, why don't you phone your da from here? Let him know you're on your way.' He paused to glance around. 'Look, there's a pay phone over there.'

Her father appeared happy to hear her voice, and she couldn't wait to see him again.

'Is everything okay?' Dermot asked, when she replaced the receiver.

'Yes, everything's fine.' She linked her arm through his, and they walked happily towards the car park.

'I really wanted us to have a little time together first, Aileen.' He sighed. 'Unfortunately, there's nowhere open on Christmas Eve. I can't even take you for a drink, but we can talk in the van.'

Aileen nodded. She was just happy to be back in the Fair City, and looking forward to doing normal things, grateful for her time here with Dermot. She tried to forget the previous day, but flashes of what might have happened at that house sent shivers through her body.

'What are you thinking?' Dermot, who had been concentrating on finding his way out of the airport, drove a short distance and then pulled into a gateway and glanced towards her.

'I was thinking how good it feels to be here with you.' She smiled.

'You don't know how good it is to hear you say that. I don't want to let you out of my sight. At least for now I've got you to myself.' He laughed. 'Now I sound like a love-struck teenager.'

She felt the same way, and never more than at that moment. Impulsively, she leant across and kissed him.

'Hold on.' He fumbled in his pocket and produced a crushed sprig of mistletoe. 'This has been in my pocket all night.'

Aileen laughed at the small, perspiring white flowers, crushed and wilted against the green stem. How romantic. It was her first time to be kissed under the mistletoe, and when he moved closer—his left arm around her shoulder, his right hand holding the mistletoe over her head—she experienced the same feelings of desire that had coursed through her the last time he had kissed her this way.

The mistletoe dropped onto her knee as his hand slid downwards to gently cup her breast. Aileen didn't object, and for a few short moments thoughts of the previous evening were wiped from her mind, like a duster across a blackboard.

# Chapter Thirty-Eight

When Dermot parked outside the butcher's shop, he turned towards her. 'I've got something for you.' He reached across her and opened the glove compartment. 'It's just a little something. By next Christmas, if you agree, I'd like to buy you an engagement ring.'

Her heart raced; it sounded wonderful. He handed her the small package and she ripped off the paper and opened the box. Inside she found a purple bottle of lily of the valley. She unscrewed the cap and dabbed a little behind her ears.

'I love it. Thanks, Dermot.' She replaced the cap and put it in her bag. 'You don't mind waiting then?'

'Waiting?' He frowned.

'To get engaged, silly.'

'No. It will give me time to save more money and buy you a bigger diamond.' He leant in and kissed her on the lips. 'I almost forgot. My brother is here. He's looking forward to meeting you.'

'Liam, isn't it?'

'He's fully ordained now. His name is Father Luke. Mam hasn't stopped singing since he arrived four days ago.'

'That's wonderful.' But she felt a little uneasy. Meeting Dermot's brother for the first time—and a priest at that—was daunting. As a layman, they could have joked and laughed about everyday things, but now she wasn't sure what would, or would not be appropriate.

Dermot locked the vehicle, and they both went around the back and stepped into the warm kitchen. The smell of roast chicken cooking in the oven was mouth-watering. The Christmas crib sat on the windowsill.

Dermot led her into the living room where a fire crackled in the hearth. A Christmas tree, with brightly coloured baubles and small neatly packaged presents underneath, brought a glow to her face. She wondered if her da would have kept up their tradition, knowing how her ma had loved Christmas.

'Oh, sure there you are.' Dermot's mother came forward and gave Aileen a hug. 'Sit yourself down. You must be perished. Get the girl a drink, Dermot.' Aileen perched on the comfortable sofa.

'Would you like a soda or perhaps a drop of wine, or sherry?'

'I'll have a wine, please, Dermot.' His eyebrows shot up and, smiling, he disappeared into the adjoining room. She wished now she had asked for a soda but felt in need of a little Dutch courage for what lay ahead.

'How was your flight? I heard you got delayed. It's not as if we've had bad weather, but we're glad you got here safe.' Dermot's mother said.

'Yes, it was unfortunate. I'm sorry Dermot had a wasted journey last night, Mrs Brogan.'

'Oh, get away with you. Call me Alice. Now, Father Luke is up at the church; sure he'll be down shortly to say hello.'

'You must be proud to have a son a priest.'

'Ah, sure indeed I am. I feel blessed, so I do.'

Dermot returned with a drink in each hand. 'Do you want one, Mam?'

'I'll wait until after lunch; otherwise the chicken will be nothing but a burnt offering.' Chuckling, she left them alone.

Aileen removed her jacket, and Dermot hung it up. He sat down next to her. 'Happy Christmas, Aileen.' He chinked her glass. 'I know you must miss your ma, but I refuse to let you feel sad for one minute.'

Alice insisted that she stay for lunch, and the five of them sat round the table to a tasty meal of roast chicken, roast potatoes and peas, with Bing Crosby crooning out *White Christmas* on the wireless.

When Aileen met Father Luke, there was no hiding the likeness of the two brothers with the same twinkling brown eyes.

Luke was older by about three years, and Aileen found him easy to chat to. She began to relax when the conversation didn't refer to her mother or her missing brother.

'What are your plans while you're here, Aileen?'

'I'm spending time with my da, and we're having Christmas with my Aunt Bead and Uncle Paddy.' She glanced towards Dermot. 'I'm hoping to fit in a lot in a few days.'

'Yes, I was sorry to hear about your loss. It can't have been an easy time for you.' Father Luke cleared his throat. 'I hope you'll find time for a night out before you have to leave, Aileen,' he said. 'I want to see as much of Dermot as I can, before I take my leave.'

Mrs Brogan sniffed and stood up to clear the dishes, but he reached over and touched her hand. 'I have to do God's work, Mam. You know that, don't you?'

'Course I do. Just wish you didn't have to do it in Massachusetts.'

Dermot's dad leant his elbow on the table. 'According to Billy Flood down the pub, yea can ask for a transfer after two years. Is that true?'

'I guess so, but I could be sent anywhere, Dad.'

As they chatted on, Dermot and Aileen asked to be excused and slipped out of the room. After using the bathroom to freshen up, they set off. Aileen felt suitably relaxed after two glasses of wine, but all the same, she wasn't taking anything for granted where her aunt was concerned.

'Well, then. What did you think of our Father Luke then?'

'He's really friendly, and nothing at all like I expected.'

'They're just flesh and blood like the rest of us, Aileen. But I know what you mean. Liam, or should I say, Luke hasn't changed a bit. We'll be going to midnight mass. If you fancy coming with us, give me a ring.'

'Thanks, Dermot, I will.'

When they arrived outside the sweet shop, it was late afternoon, and Aileen felt that sinking feeling in her stomach again. She was anxious to see her da but knew that once she set eyes on Lizzy, angry feelings would surface. Taking a deep breath, she stepped from Dermot's van.

He placed her case at her feet and then kissed her briefly before going back to sit in the van. He wound the window down. 'I'll wait until you're inside. And Aileen…' He winked. 'Ring me at any time.' She nodded.

Her smile wavered when she glanced at the glass shop door with the closed sign facing her. Her earlier resolve not to allow her aunt to intimidate her had been replaced by an anxious feeling in the pit of her stomach. She recalled the woman's hostility towards her on her last visit home.

Straightening her shoulders, she rang the bell. It pealed through the shop. Within seconds the door opened and her da stood smiling on the other side. He was wearing a silly Santa hat she hadn't seen for years. Laughing, he opened his arms, and she went to him. It was the first time she had properly felt his arms around her since her ma's death, and she clung to him, enjoying the scent of his aftershave for a few seconds, before pulling back.

'Oh, Da!'

'It's good to see you, love.' He placed his hand on her back and ushered her inside. Then he stepped out onto the pavement, gave Dermot a wave, and picked up her case.

Aileen knew she should ask about her aunt, but she didn't want to spoil the few minutes she had alone with her da. He led her through the passage into the living room, where Tom Jones was singing *The Green, Green Grass of Home* on the wireless. 'You were lucky to get a flight on Christmas Eve, Aileen. We were all a bit concerned when Dermot rang to say you'd been delayed.'

'I'm sorry, Da. This kind of thing happens at Christmas. Did you let Uncle Paddy know?'

He nodded and placed her case against the wall. 'I'll take it up later.'

A Christmas tree stood in the corner, and homemade decorations hung from the ceiling. 'Oh, Da, it's lovely.' She felt tears fill her eyes. Her ma's sofa looked inviting, and she sat down.

'Have you eaten?' he asked.

'Yes, I've had dinner at Dermot's. I'm going to midnight mass with him later.'

'Okay, grand. Now, I know you're anxious to discuss your brother.' He sat down next to her. 'I'll help you all I can. Together we'll get to the bottom of it.'

He had no idea how wonderful it felt to hear him say that.

'How long can you stay?'

Right now, she never wanted to leave, and she glowed inside with happiness and felt the urge to hug him again. 'Just a few days, Da.' There was still no sign of her aunt. 'Is Lizzy at church?'

'Lizzy doesn't live here anymore, Aileen.'

# Chapter Thirty-Nine

'What happened?' She really couldn't have cared less; Lizzy not being there was better than any Christmas present.

'We had a disagreement and she stormed out. To be honest, I felt a great sense of peace after she left.'

'Really?' Aileen wanted to add her own thoughts to that, but decided to keep quiet for now. She had thought her aunt had left before, but then she came back. 'What did you disagree about, Da?'

'We had quite a few argy bargies over the last few weeks. I discussed Jessie's request.' He shrugged. 'I know I said I wouldn't. Well, she ranted and raved when I said I was going to find my son, and bring both my children into the business if they wished it.' He shrugged. 'It wasn't just that, Aileen. I knew I'd made a mistake after you left the second time.

'I've been a fool, but I just couldn't forgive Jessie for keeping something like that from me all these years. I thought we were close. I'm afraid I let it get to me. It was Lizzy who got me to see a doctor. It turned out I was suffering from depression. I felt ashamed.' He removed his Christmas hat and ran his hand through his hair. 'I was deeply hurt by the fact that the woman I loved had secrets she never felt she could share with me. But that's no excuse for the way I treated you.'

Aileen gave in to the urge and hugged him. He held her at arm's length. 'I'll make it up to you, love.'

'You already have, Da.' She sniffed. 'You don't think Lizzy will come back, do you?'

He shook his head. 'She won't.'

'What about the joint business?'

'Don't fret, pet. I didn't put all my money into the shop. Lizzy doesn't know that, and she's taken more than her share of the profits. She won't be getting another penny, I promise you.'

Aileen let her shoulders relax. She would hate her da to lose everything he and her ma had worked so hard for over the years.

'I'm sorry for a lot of things, Aileen, and hope you'll forgive an old fool.'

She loved her da; forgiving him wasn't an option. 'I love you, Da. I always have.' She twisted round to look at him. 'Where's she gone? Did she go back to her old place?'

'I've no idea. She took everything she could carry, and she emptied the till as well.' He gave a little chuckle. 'Having you back in my life is all I care about now and finding my son.'

Aileen couldn't hold back the tears. This was the best Christmas homecoming she could have wished for. 'I've had no luck trying to find him through the normal channels,' she said. 'Perhaps we should start by going back to that residential home I told you about. Someone there must know something.'

'Fair enough then, we'll start with that. But with Christmas, it will have to wait, and you haven't got many days.' He rubbed his hand over his chin. 'We could try on St. Stephen's Day. We'll find your brother, I promise you.' He stood up. 'By the way, don't forget we're having Christmas dinner at your Aunt Bead's.'

'I'm looking forward to it, Da.' She placed her hand on his arm. 'Are you…'

'I've made my peace with them. Everything will be grand love.'

'That's grand.'

He picked up her case and she followed him upstairs. 'How long have you been on your own?'

'A couple of weeks, and it's been all right, love. I've put an advertisement in the paper for someone to help me in the shop. It's been busy.'

She wished she could stay and help him, but she'd put that right at the first opportunity.

The clutter had disappeared, and the bedroom she had previously slept in looked bigger and had a fresh smell. The apple green walls looked nice against the white candlewick bedspread.

'Sorry about the smell.' He moved across the room, undid the catch, and opened the window. 'I hope you like it.'

'It looks lovely, Da.'

'How is Mary?' He sat on the edge of the bed. 'It was good of her to take you in so readily. She was always a good sort, from what I remember of her. Jessie liked her, and they were friends for a long time.'

'She's fine.' She hung her coat on the back of the door. 'Speaking of Mary. Can I phone her and let her know I arrived okay?'

'Sure, use the shop phone. I'll make us both a Christmas ham sandwich. Then if you're not too tired, we can sit and chat for a while before you go to church.'

* * *

Later, Aileen rang Dermot and arranged to attend mass with him, his brother, and their parents. Just as she was about to leave, her da followed her to the door.

'Would you mind if I came along?'

'Da, are you sure?'

He nodded.

That night, Mr and Mrs Brogan, Aileen, her da, Dermot and his brother walked back home after attending midnight mass. Aileen couldn't have been happier, as she linked arms with her Da and Dermot. They had a nightcap and homemade mince pies at Dermot's before Aileen and her father walked home together.

She glanced up at the sky full of stars and pointed to one particular star that appeared to shine brighter than the others. 'Do you suppose Ma can see us, Da?'

'I'd like to think so, love.'

* * *

Christmas dinner at Bead and Paddy's was a special occasion. A Christmas tree decorated and trimmed with tinsel and fake snow graced the corner of the room. Small gifts were exchanged before the meal of turkey, with all the trimmings, and later they watched the Queen's speech and a little Christmas television.

It was difficult to believe all that had gone before, and no-one mentioned Lizzy. That suited Aileen fine. Her da partook of a few bottles of stout with Paddy while Aileen and Bead had a sherry and relaxed. What pleased her most was seeing her family together again.

Later, as Aileen helped her aunt with the dishes, she said, 'Thanks for a lovely Christmas dinner, Aunt Bead.' Aileen smiled. 'And isn't it great to see Da happy again?'

'It is that, love.' Bead hung the mugs back on their hooks and placed the dinner plates into the cupboard. 'Just like old times, isn't it? I don't think he was really happy with Lizzy. She got her claws into him when he was at his most vulnerable.'

'I wish I'd done more to protect him, Aunt Bead.'

'You did everything you could, love. We all did.' She dried her hands. 'But you can put all that behind you now. When are you going to start looking for your brother?'

'First thing tomorrow.' Aileen sighed happily. 'Da is as keen as I am to find out all we can while I'm here.'

'Bit ambitious, don't you think? Especially as you're going away in a day or so.'

Aileen chewed her lip. Returning to England was less exciting to her now, but she didn't want to let anyone down. Mary had been good to her, and she was happy enough at the mill. Still, she didn't want to think about leaving Dublin until she had to. 'We can make a start, though.'

'You'll let me know if there's anything Paddy and I can do while you're away, won't you?'

'Of course, I will, Aunt Bead.' Aileen leant across and kissed her aunt on the cheek.

\* \* \*

That evening, Dermot called over to Finglas. Aileen and her aunt made turkey sandwiches and brought in cake and slices of homemade Christmas pudding for tea. After a game of cards and

Cluedo, Uncle Paddy called for a singsong; everyone in turn had to do a party piece. Aileen danced the Irish reel, while Dermot clapped his hands and tapped his foot. Her da played the spoons, and Uncle Paddy played the fiddle. Bead sang *In Dublin's Fair City*, and they all joined in.

Paddy insisted they dance the four-hand reel, which Aileen could never get her head around. She partnered Dermot, her da partnered Bead, and Paddy gave instructions as well as playing the fiddle. No-one could remember how it was done. Hands and arms became intertwined, and finally, they all ended up in a heap on the sofa. Tears of laughter ran down Aileen's face. She couldn't remember when she had laughed so much, and it made her all the more aware of the family she was missing so much by living in England.

Soon it was time to leave, and everyone wished each other a Merry Christmas and a Happy New Year before Dermot drove them back home.

When he stopped the van, her da went inside leaving Aileen and Dermot to say goodnight.

He reached for her hand and pulled her close. 'God, I've wanted to kiss you all day.' He pressed his lips to hers and embraced her passionately. Everything that had happened in the last few months evaporated, and she felt a new contentment she hadn't known in ages.

Later, she sat in the scullery with her da, drinking hot chocolate.

'Jessie would have enjoyed today, so she would.'

'Yeah, she would have, Da.' It was the first time she had heard him mention her ma's name happily in ages.

# Chapter Forty

It was past midnight and Aileen couldn't sleep. A mixture of emotions unsettled her. Her da had admitted he'd had no idea Jessie was expecting twins and, in her ma's defence, he didn't think she had either until she was presented with the situation on the delivery table. So they were still in limbo as to why she had abandoned her son. It made no sense. Her mother had always been kind and caring, and for her to abandon her own flesh and blood seemed out of character. Someone knew the answer, and Aileen was determined—with her father's help—to find out.

It was after nine o'clock when Aileen woke. She glanced at the clock and swung her legs out of bed. Annoyed to have slept in, she pulled on her dressing gown and hurried downstairs to find her father sitting at the table hugging a mug of tea, a half-eaten piece of toast on his plate. 'Sorry, Da, I couldn't get off to sleep last night. Why didn't you call me?'

'I'm not long down myself.' He gestured. 'There's tea in the pot.'

'Have you any eggs, Da? I'll make you some scrambled eggs.'

He shook his head. 'I'd rather get going, love. It'll be after ten by the time we get there.' He stood up. 'I'll go and get ready. And afterwards, regardless of what we find out, I'm taking you somewhere nice for lunch.'

Aileen smiled. 'That sounds grand, Da. But there won't be anywhere open, will there?'

'We'll find somewhere.'

'Would you like me to ask Dermot if he'd give us a lift? I'm sure he wouldn't mind.'

'No, I'll drive. I was hoping we could spend today, just us, you know? You'll be gone back soon enough.'

Delighted to hear him say that, she finished her tea and went back up to get ready. When she came down, she was surprised to find her da waiting for her in the room. He had on a grey suit and an open-necked cream shirt, his overcoat slung over his arm. 'You look smart, Da.'

He smiled. 'You look nice, too, love. I like your hair up like that.'

'Thank you, kind sir.' She linked her arm through his, and he popped his hat on and threw a scarf around his neck as they left the shop.

After a couple of attempts to start the engine, the car spluttered into action with the help of the choke. A light coating of ice covered the windscreen.

'Get in, love. It'll clear in a few minutes.'

She blew into her hands and rubbed them together as she settled in the passenger seat. 'I hope Miss Finch is in, Da. What do you think?'

'First I'd like to call in at the place where you were born. There's always a chance that someone might remember something. Then we'll pay a visit to Miss Finch.' He changed gear and headed across town. 'I'm really puzzled as to why Jessie didn't bring the boy home.' He sighed, and Aileen placed a gentle hand on his shoulder.

'I know, Da.'

'If only she'd felt she could have talked to me, you know?' He broke off. The streets were empty, not a bus in sight as they headed towards O'Connell Bridge, stopping for lights at Trinity College.

Aileen had often wondered the same since discovering her mother's note. 'I hope we learn a bit more after today.'

'I wouldn't be too sure, Aileen. If there was any funny business, people can be tight-lipped.'

'What do you mean?'

'I don't know, love. I really don't know.' He drove up Dame Street.

Aileen frowned. 'Which way are you going?'

'I've not lived in Dublin this long and not know a few short cuts.'

She needn't have worried; her da knew Dublin like the back of his hand. Aileen relaxed, her mind full of questions that needed answers, and now she couldn't wait to speak to Miss Finch again. If she had any information at all, Aileen wanted to know—even if she had to plead with the woman. Where was her brother, and was he still alive? Thoughts of anything else would be too much after months of speculation.

* * *

When they arrived on the street, Aileen glanced up at the building as her da parked the car close by. They walked towards the home; the large bay window was lit up in true Christmas spirit with a brightly decorated tree.

'From the outside, it hasn't changed much since the day I took your ma here.' He straightened his shoulders. 'Let's see what we can find out, shall we?'

He rang the bell and they were admitted very quickly. The foyer was warm and pleasant, with sprigs of holly protruding from scenic pictures around the walls. The woman behind the desk glanced up.

'Who have you come to visit?'

Her father tipped his hat. 'We're not visiting.' He cleared his throat. 'I wondered if there's anyone here who might have information about this place when it was a baby clinic?'

The young receptionist frowned, obviously too young to recall the building's previous use. 'What is it you'd like to know, sir?'

'We're trying to locate what happened to a baby boy born here when it was run as a private baby clinic.'

'Sure, some of our staff are on Christmas leave, as are most of the residents.' She smiled. 'But please take a seat. I'll see if Cook knows anything. She's been here a while.'

'Much obliged.' Aileen's father tipped his hat again, loosened his checked scarf—a present from Aileen—and sat down. Aileen looked at the pictures on the wall; in particular, an old black and white photo in a gold frame. A nun stood on one side of an open door, and a nursing sister in a stiff-looking uniform stood on the other. They couldn't have looked more miserable if they had heard that they were to be shot at dawn. The date pencilled in at the bottom of the picture was 1935.

'Take a look at this, Da.'

Jonny Maguire moved closer to get a better look. 'Umm. That's interesting.'

'Excuse me. You wanted a word?' A small woman, her face flushed, stood in the reception. 'How can I help?'

Aileen explained their predicament.

'I wish I could help, but the baby clinic was before I came to work here, I'm afraid.'

Aileen's da exhaled. 'You wouldn't, by chance, happen to know who these two women are in this photo?'

The woman walked across to look. 'Well, they say that's the nun who ran the place when it was a baby clinic.' She shook her head. 'I don't know who the nurse is. The picture was left behind in one of the offices, and the new owner decided to hang it up here. I'm sorry I can't be of more help.'

'Thank you, you've been very kind.' Aileen looked again at the photograph on the wall. 'You know, Da, the nurse in this picture has a striking resemblance to Miss Finch.' Her da pursed his lips. However, Aileen now felt more positive about calling on her again.

It started to rain and they sat in the car discussing the photograph. 'It's her, Da! She has the same sharp features as the woman I spoke to, the same stance.'

'How can you be sure? That picture was taken years ago.'

'I am, Da, and I think she's hiding something.'

'In that case, what are we waiting for? Grab that black brolly from the back seat. If she's in, and she hears the car pull up outside, it might put her off answering the door, so we'll walk round.'

Her father held the umbrella over them as they walked the short distance.

'If she's not at home, will you come with me again tomorrow before I fly back?'

'Course I will, love. I can open the shop a bit later. Finding out what happened to my son is more important.'

Aileen recalled the squeaky gate and the blue Georgian door from her first visit. As she glanced up at the window, she saw the curtain twitch.

# Chapter Forty-One

Aileen felt like an intruder, calling on the woman on St. Stephen's Day, but what choice did they have? She rang the bell and shifted from one leg to the other as the rain dripped down the backs of her legs into her shoes. No-one answered, and her da rang again.

'It's possible that any students living here will have gone home for Christmas,' he said. 'She'll hardly answer the door if she's alone in the house.' He sighed. 'Drat! Well, we can't stand here getting soaked.'

They were just about to turn away, when the door opened. A thin man with white hair and a goatee looked up at them. 'Whoever you're looking for, there's no-one in. Apart from myself and the recluse on the first floor.'

'We're sorry to disturb you,' Aileen began. 'We've come to see Miss Finch.'

He gave a little chuckle. 'I wish yea luck. That woman hasn't a word to throw a dog, even at Christmas.'

Aileen shivered. 'Can we come in?' Her da folded the brolly, shook off the surplus rainwater, and left it outside.

The man stood back to allow them in, then closed the door. 'She never married, you see. Them's always the crabbiest.' He pulled on his beige waterproof and popped his felt cap on his head. 'It's weather for ducks out there,' he said, and let himself out of the house.

Aileen and her da breathed a sigh in unison, and paused a few moments before tentatively going upstairs. Aileen rapped on the door as her da removed his hat.

After several minutes, the woman shouted, 'Go away. I don't speak to reporters.'

'We're not reporters. We spoke before, Miss Finch.'

Aileen's father sighed impatiently and walked along the landing, examining the cracks in the plastered walls. 'Please, I just want to find my brother.' The door opened a crack, and Aileen beckoned her da.

'We're so sorry to have disturbed you, Miss,' her da said. 'I'm Jessie Maguire's husband, and this is my daughter, Aileen. My wife confessed to having another child, Aileen's twin, at the home where I believe you might have worked. We—'

The door was pushed to.

'We mean you no harm,' her da continued. 'We'd be grateful for anything you can remember. My wife lived with this secret until she felt forced to tell me on her deathbed that I had a son. She didn't live long enough to give me details. Can you imagine what that does to a man?' He swallowed. 'My daughter was deprived of a brother, and me a son.' Aileen heard the catch in his voice.

After a few seconds, the door opened slightly.

'What do you expect me to do? I told your daughter to go through the proper channels.'

'Nothing turned up from those enquiries.' Aileen was determined to keep her talking. 'I know you worked at the baby home when I was born. You're our only link to finding out what happened to my twin brother.'

Miss Finch stood in the opening, both hands holding the door as if she was about to close it again. She wore a dark brown suit with a green Paisley blouse, and a sparkly brooch lifting her bored expression. She shifted uneasily. 'I'm not sure I know what you're implying.'

Seeing her again, Aileen felt sure she was the woman in the photograph, that same expression on her face. 'We saw a photo of you hanging in the reception of the new residential home. It was taken in 1935. There was a nun in the picture with you. Do you know where she is now?'

The woman stayed silent.

Jonny Maguire sighed. 'Look, can we talk inside? It's bloody draughty standing here.'

'If you must.' She moved away and the door swung open. Aileen and her da hurried inside before she changed her mind. 'Don't expect me to offer you tea. I take all my meals at the nurses' home.'

'We don't expect anything except some honest answers.' Her father stood just inside the door, holding his hat in front of him.

The last time Aileen had been in this room she couldn't wait to get outside. Today it was slightly cheered by the nativity scene decorated with the smell of fresh holly. A copy of *Pilgrim's Progress* lay on the table. Aileen had only read the first few pages, more interested in the author, John Bunyan, who had spent years in prison. This place was Miss Finch's prison, and Aileen wondered if her choice of author was a coincidence.

The woman walked to the centre of the room, turned and faced them. 'Please sit down.'

Aileen sat in the old armchair and felt like she was sitting on the floor. Her da perched on the arm.

'You obviously worked at the private clinic when my wife, Jessie Maguire, went into labour. Tell us what you remember.'

She linked and unlinked her fingers. 'Can you promise me anonymity?'

'I'm only interested in what happened to my son. If you know and don't divulge what you know, make no mistake, I'll take it further.'

The woman eased herself down onto a hard-backed chair, plucked her embroidered handkerchief from the pocket of her jacket, and sniffed.

Aileen struggled to get up out of the low armchair. She stood next to Miss Finch and placed her hand on her shoulder. 'Do you know where my brother is?'

The woman shook her head.

Her da got to his feet. 'Look, Miss. My patience is wearing thin. Were you present at the birth?"

'Yes, yes, I was there.' She crossed her arms. 'Talking to you will cost me a great deal. I'll be opening gates I've kept closed for a long time.'

'We have the right to know.'

'Please, Miss Finch.' Aileen swallowed, and her throat tightened.

Miss Finch took a deep breath and shifted in her chair. 'When the second baby was delivered, half an hour after the first one, he… he, well, he was barely alive. He weighed less than a bag of sugar, had breathing problems, a weak pulse, and suffered from a lack of oxygen. Sister Amelia handed him to me and told me to take him away. Later, she told Mrs Maguire that she had a healthy girl and a boy who wouldn't survive the night.'

Aileen gasped. Her da paled, drew his fingers through his hair and moved across to the window. Aileen followed. Outside, a car swished past and heavy rain pelted against the window.

He turned back into the room, his expression intent. 'You've got it wrong. What proof do we have that you're talking about the same baby?'

'It was a long time ago but I've never forgotten that wee boy. You have to understand, Sister Amelia's word was law and no-one at that time dared question her authority.'

Aileen's father was silent as Miss Finch continued. 'I overheard her telling your wife to save her milk for her healthy baby.' She turned towards Aileen. 'Your mother begged to be allowed to hold her son, but she was refused.'

Aileen felt the room closing in on her. The cold, miserable place wasn't doing her father any favours either. He looked grey, and she saw that look of despair in his eyes she hoped never to see again.

'I tried to intervene, but Sister Amelia said it was kinder and would make it easier for Mrs Maguire to let go.'

'What are you talking about?' Johnny Maguire glared at the woman. 'You could have done something. And why did my wife discharge herself so soon?'

'I tried. When I went to check on your wife, she wasn't in her room. After I had checked the bathroom, I informed Sister Amelia immediately.'

Aileen's grief was such that she knew if she cried she would never stop. She glanced up at her da, his face creased in pain.

'You bunch of bloody hypocrites. It was a hospital, and you allowed my wife to walk out hours after giving birth.'

'It wasn't a prison; she was free to go whenever she wanted to.'

'She wasn't herself for weeks; sad and unhappy all the time. Didn't it occur to you to tell me?' His voice faltered. He straightened his shoulders, his breath coming in gasps, and Aileen feared what he might do. 'Someone will be held responsible for this!' he shouted.

Aileen stifled a sob at the enormity of her ma's suffering.

'I had no choice, you see…' the woman said, as if talking to herself.

The sound of a door shutting below alerted her. She stiffened. Footsteps hurried upstairs, paused on the landing, and went back down.

Aileen's father continued. 'You stupid woman! No choice? You could have told someone.'

Miss Finch stood up. 'If you'd be so kind as to let me finish, Mr Maguire.' She folded her arms. 'I invited you into my room because I felt you had the right to know what happened to your son.'

She walked across the room and stood with her back against the table, her hands in front of her as if addressing a group of children. 'There is something else that you need to know, Mr Maguire. Your son survived!'

'Are you saying my son is alive?'

Miss Finch poured water from a jug, sipped a small amount, then she sat down again. Her eyes closed, she folded her hands in her lap. 'After your wife left the home, Sister Amelia told me to stop fussing and to get on with my work. Later, I went into the small room where your son was lying in a cot. I bent to feel his pulse; it was weak, but he was still alive. I was astounded and quickly made up a small amount of milk, cradled him in my arms and fed him. I went back again an hour later and did the same.

'Sister Amelia was outraged, and berated me something awful

when she found out. She dared me to question her authority, threatened me with the sack and eviction from the home; she had the power to ruin my career in nursing if I said anything. I felt torn between that and my conscience. The following day, the baby had gone. Sister Amelia refused to disclose his whereabouts. I assumed she had him taken to an orphanage.' She sighed. 'I hated the fact that I was so compliant, but Sister Amelia, in spite of being a nun, was a manipulative woman.'

'So you did nothing?' Aileen snapped. Anger bubbled inside her. 'This is where you hide away with your so-called conscience, is it? This miserable room is all you deserve.' She stood up. She hated this woman's false assumption that she had made some heroic act of mercy. 'We should go, Da.'

He pressed his hand on her arm. She swallowed her anger and let her da takeover. Without this woman's co-operation, they would learn nothing more about her brother.

'Why didn't you tell us?' Jonny shuffled his feet on the cold linoleum floor.

Miss Finch's cheeks burned. 'I did what I could. The result of my actions is this two-roomed bedsit.' She stood up. 'I live on social handouts.' She knitted her fingers. 'God forgive me, but I felt elated when Sister Amelia died in May of this year. Her death released me fromf the fear she had bound me to for years.' She sat down again. 'I wrote to your wife immediately and arranged to meet her.' She joined her hands, sliding them against each other.

Aileen's throat went dry, and she thought she was going to be sick. Her da looked puzzled. Aileen could only guess what was going through his mind.

'What did you say to my wife?'

'I told her that her boy was alive and, when I saw him last, he was living in a Blackrock orphanage. But he still suffered with bronchial trouble. She was shocked, stunned. She lashed out, asking why I'd left it until now to tell her. I explained as best I could.'

'What did Jessie say?'

'Your wife kept repeating that it was too late and that her

212

health had deteriorated. She said she hadn't told her family, and it wouldn't be fair to resurrect the past after all this time. I never heard from her again.'

'Poor Ma!' Aileen swallowed. 'So where is my brother now?'

'I don't know. I stopped going to visit Tom at the orphanage in 1946.'

'Tom! Who called him Tom?' Aileen's da stood by the door and shuddered inside his damp coat.

The woman shrugged. 'He was named at the orphanage. I stopped seeing him when Sister Amelia found out. She left me no choice.'

'What was he like?' Aileen asked.

Miss Finch's tight expression gave way to a smile. 'He was a lovely little boy; bright as a button. Small for his age but holding his own.'

'Do… do you know what happened to him?' Jonny asked.

Miss Finch shook her head. 'I can only assume he was adopted. You can visit the orphanage and ask to see the records.' Silence hung in the air. Miss Finch glanced at her watch. 'I'm afraid I must ask you to leave now. I'm expected at the nurses' home.'

'Thanks for being so frank, Miss. I'm sorry I was impatient. I'm sure you appreciate how difficult this is for us.'

'If you find him, will you come back some time and let me know how he is?'

'That depends, Miss Finch, on where he is, and how he is.'

\* \* \*

Outside the streets were wet. A small stream of rainwater ran along the curb and down gullies. Too choked to speak, Aileen breathed in the fresh air, glad to be outside the confines of Miss Finch's room. Her da appeared subdued as they walked towards the car then drove to the hotel; it wasn't far.

'We don't have to if you'd rather we went home,' Aileen said. He shook his head. 'No, I'd like to, love.'

Aileen thought it was lovely that he had remembered his promise to take her for a meal in a hotel. But she felt numb. Her eyes stung from unshed tears, and the lines on her father's face told her he felt the same.

She had no appetite and was just about to say so when a porter walked towards them.

'Are you looking for somewhere to stay, sir?'

'No. We were hoping for a bite to eat.'

'Oh dear.' He shook his head. 'On a bank holiday. I'm afraid tea and scones are the best we can do.'

Her father glanced round at her. 'Is that okay?'

'Grand, Da.'

They followed him to the small dining room. It was empty, which suited them fine. There was no-one to stare at them and wonder why they were so glum. Aileen's head ached, and questions about the baby clinic tumbled around inside her head. What kind of a place was it that had so convinced her mother to leave without her baby boy?

When they were seated, she asked, 'Are you all right, Da?'

'To tell the truth, love, I don't know.' He took out his handkerchief and blew his nose. 'When your ma left that place, she must have thought the boy had died. She would never have left him if she had known there was a chance he might live.' He swallowed. 'That nun convinced her otherwise. Jessie, my poor darling.' He placed one elbow on the table and massaged his temple.

'We'll find him, Da.' Aileen forced a smile. 'The most important thing now is that he is alive, and we have to find out where he is. We owe it to Ma.'

The waiter arrived with a pot of tea and hot scones with jam and cream.

'Go on, tuck in, love. You've eaten nothing all day.'

Aileen reached for a scone and smothered it with jam and cream.

'Do you think we were a bit harsh on her?' She poured their tea.

He shook his head. 'It's no more than she deserved. She should never have kept that secret for all those years.' He sighed. 'Our life could have been so different.' Then he looked her in the eye. 'Aileen, never keep secrets. It only causes heartache.'

# Chapter Forty-Two

Inside the house, Roy went straight to the drinks cabinet and poured himself a large whisky. He swallowed it quickly and poured another. Only a short time before, the room had been cheered with Aileen's presence; now it appeared dull. He heard a loud bang on the ceiling and, gritting his teeth, he put down his glass and rushed upstairs. His mother was propped up in her four-poster bed.

'What is it, Mother?'

'Did you retrieve your car?'

'Yes, Mother.

'Has it been damaged?'

'No, I'll take it into the garage and have it checked as soon as this damn holiday is over.'

'Yes, and you don't know what harm that girl's done to the gears. I heard her screech out of the drive like a demon.' She patted the bed. 'Come here and sit down, Royston.'

He hated it when she called him that. It usually meant he had displeased her, or she had something important to discuss with him. Either way, he wasn't in the mood. Nodding, he sat down.

'Have you taken your medication?'

'Not this again.' He was sick of hearing her nagging him.

'Promise me you won't have anything more to do with that girl or any girl for that matter, and you know full well what I'm talking about.'

He folded his arms and tried to cover up his agitation. His plans with Aileen were ruined, thanks to his mother.

She had had him on the change, and these past few years

she spent most of her time upstairs, only coming down when she felt like it. It suited him fine, but he was beginning to find her tiresome. He blocked out her voice as she continued to harass him about an illness he didn't believe he had. He thought about Aileen.

He was sorry she had missed her flight to Dublin and wondered if she had managed to get another one. The next time she went he hoped to go with her as her boyfriend. He couldn't wait to hear from her. Of course, she would get in touch once she had time to reconsider his proposal.

'Royston, are you listening to me?'

'Yes, Mother. Excuse me.' He got to his feet. 'I have to go out.'

\* \* \*

The following day, he checked the phone in case he'd missed a call. There was nothing. He had expected her to be grateful; she owed him that much. After all, she wouldn't want her name splashed across the evening newspapers, and he had helped to divert that from happening. Why hadn't she had the courtesy to ring and thank him?

In spite of taking his medication, he knew he was getting worse. Nothing was going right for him. Lately, he had been hearing voices telling him he was useless, but he had swept them aside, putting it down to tiredness. He placed both his hands over his ears. Those pesky voices in his head were getting louder.

On Christmas Day, he watched his mother prepare their lunch. Since the last cook left, she had decided they didn't need one. His mother found it difficult to get on with anyone, and Roy was surprised she had put up with him for so long. When he offered to help, she shooed him away. It was a simple meal of cooked ham, peas, and mashed potatoes –similar to what she had cooked for him when he was a small boy—with jelly, set in a rabbit mould, and custard for desert.

He felt sick, but he didn't complain. He had offered to bring a turkey and all the trimmings from the market, but she wouldn't hear of it. So he had pretended to enjoy the food while the tension grew between them. He wanted to tell her about Aileen and his feelings for her, but Mother wouldn't be interested. Thank goodness he had his car; he wouldn't be stuck indoors with only her for company.

After their lunch, she said, 'Have you remembered to take your medication today, Royston?'

He felt his body tense. 'I'm doing fine, Mother, so stop talking about it.'

'You're not well. You know I'm right, and I dread to think what will happen to you after I've gone. No-one will care or love you the way I do. I've had words with your consultant, Mr Wainwright, on the phone. He suggested that you go somewhere relaxing for a while.'

'What?' He felt distracted. 'No, I'll not agree to that, Mother. I'm fine. Sometimes I have a wobble. It means nothing.'

'You've lapsed several times, and I can't keep reminding you about your medication. We've kept this to ourselves for years, and then you go and bring that girl back here. That was a bad move, Royston. If this gets out, you will not get a job anywhere. Mr Wainwright knows what's best for you. You'll be monitored closely, and once you've rested, you'll soon be back on top again.'

'There's nothing wrong with me. I keep telling you.' He rocked back and forth in his chair. Agitated, he tapped the table with his fingers.

'I'm sorry, son. As much as it pains me to tell you this, I've no choice now. Your father suffered the same mental illness and died in an institution.'

Roy jumped to his feet. 'You told me he died in the war. Why did you lie?'

'I was trying to protect you. Your father didn't develop the illness until after you were born. The medication you have wasn't available then. I had no choice but to have him committed. You showed no signs of the illness until you reached adolescence. Since then, your aggression has got worse, and when you refuse to take your medication...' She paused, sat back, and buried her tired face in her bony hands.

Roy couldn't speak. He just stared into space.

She glanced up, her face lined. 'You angered me by bringing that girl here, Royston. She heard too much, and she's bound to say something.'

Restless, he paced the room. 'This is all your fault, Mother.' He glared at her. 'You promised to keep me safe always, now you want to have me committed like my father, is that what you're saying?'

'No. It is not what I want, but if you continue to miss appointments…'

The rage in him grew; a rage fuelled by the news that his father had died in a mental institution. 'I have to get out of here.'

'Where are you going? There's nowhere open. Royston, come back!' The door slammed behind him.

## Chapter Forty-Three

Her father's words made Aileen think of Roy Pickering, and he was the last person she wanted reminding of. Should she have told Dermot about him? It wasn't as if she had had a clandestine relationship with the man. She loved Dermot, and felt sure that he loved her, too. But all the same, she couldn't be sure how he would react once he knew she had gone dancing with another man. If that wasn't enough, she had been foolish in letting him trick her into going with him to his house. The memory of it still made her shudder. What an idiot she had been.

No sooner had her da unlocked the shop door than the phone rang. It was Dermot.

'I miss you, Aileen. When am I going to see you?' Preoccupied with finding her brother, she hadn't given Dermot a thought until her da had mentioned secrets.

'Sorry. We've been finding out about my brother.'

'Any luck?'

'We've discovered where he might be.'

'That's wonderful. Can I come over and see you?'

'No. Don't do that, Dermot. We've had an exhausting, emotional day, and I don't want to leave Da on his own this evening.'

'But you're leaving tomorrow night, Aileen. We've hardly spent any time together.'

'I'm sorry.' She longed to be with him and feel his arms around her, but finding her brother had to take priority.

'Aileen, are you still there?'

'Yes.' She heard him drop more coins into the phone box

and realised that he wasn't phoning from home. 'I'll have time tomorrow when we get back from the orphanage.'

'So, what time will that be?'

'I don't know, Dermot. I'll tell you all about it when I see you.' She hung up.

* * *

Early the following morning, her da called the orphanage and made an appointment to visit. They had just finished breakfast when they heard a loud knock on the shop door. Aileen stiffened.

'Da, it might be her. Lizzy.'

He paused for a moment. 'Well, if it is, she won't be welcome, Christmas or no Christmas.'

With Aileen following, he went through to the shop and unbolted the door. Her shoulders relaxed when a small boy of about eight looked up.

'Are yea opening the shop today, Mr Maguire? I want to buy sweets with this.' He unfurled his fingers, showing a shiny two-shilling piece.

'Good morning, Walter.' Her da smiled. 'Come in.' He reversed the closed sign on the door. 'That's a lot of money. Are you sure you want to spend it all?'

'It's Christmas money, and me brothers are coming down an' all.' His eyes scanned the jars of sweets, then he pointed to the toffees on the top shelf. 'How many of them can I get for this?' Aileen smiled when he held up the polished coin.

'Quite a lot, Walter.' Her da went behind the counter and reached up for the jar. 'Why don't you mix them with your other favourites, the toffee bonbons?'

As Walter pondered, his two brothers bounded into the shop. Half an hour later Aileen was helping her da to serve customers and wondered if they were going to get to the orphanage at the appointed time.

At last, the shop emptied, and her da said, 'You run up and get ready, Aileen. I'll finish up here and put a sign in the window.'

'You know, Da. This place is a little goldmine.'

'Umm. I know, love. One thing your aunt was right about,

although I was dubious at first. I didn't believe you could make a living from sweets.' He laughed. 'And it's not just the kids who spend their money in here.'

\* \* \*

They arrived at the orphanage with minutes to spare. The nun who greeted them was nice, and Aileen began to relax. She knew from her school days that not all nuns were unpleasant. Yet, after what Miss Finch had told her about Sister Amelia, she felt she would never trust a nun again.

'We've had many babies come through this orphanage over the past twenty years or so. And to make it a little easier, I've put out the records for two years either side of 1946.'

'Thanks, Sister,' her father said.

'Right, if you'd like to come in here.' She opened the door. 'You won't be disturbed by the children passing through to their lessons.'

Two hefty brown ledgers lay on the table. 'If you need paper to write anything down, you'll find it on the window ledge.' She placed her hands into the large folds of her habit. 'I'll be back in half an hour to see how you're getting on.'

Aileen sat down next to her da in front of the open ledgers. She turned each page in trepidation and examined each entry closely. Her da was quiet as he turned page after page. After ten minutes, he glanced up and sighed. 'This is proving harder than I thought.'

'We'll swop ledgers in a minute in case either of us has missed something.' She eased her shoulders and flicked her long hair down her back. 'Don't just look at the date we were born, Da. It might have been days later when Tom was sent here.'

The clock on the cream painted wall ticked loudly in the silent room. Aileen glanced up. 'Lookat this, Da.' He leant across. 'It states here that baby Maguire, date of birth March 1946, was left behind by his mother. The date has been removed. And there's no guessing as to who made that entry.' Aileen felt a surge of annoyance and excitement at the same time. 'Oh, Da, we've found him!' She scribbled the page and the entry number down. Her father was visibly moved, and she saw him swallow. 'Jessie would never have left him, Aileen. It wasn't in her nature.'

The sound of children echoed up from below, and her da got up and looked out of the window. Aileen came and joined him. Children ran about playing with each other; they looked happy and didn't appear to have a care in the world. One or two huddled alone in the corner of the concrete yard. But they couldn't see any babies. Most of the children were five years and upwards. The large area was divided into two—girls at one end and boys at the other.

'You wait here, Da. I'll see if I can locate that nice nun, she might be able to tell us where my brother is.'

Aileen found her as she came out of the office. They talked as they walked back to where her father was waiting, his back against the table.

'I don't know the circumstances, Mr Maguire.'

'Well, I want that remark obliterated.' He pointed to an entry in the open ledger. 'My wife would never have left our son behind. That excuse for a nun, Sister Amelia—and I hate to speak ill of the dead—was not only cruel but a liar.' He straightened his shoulders.

'Entries can't be altered. I'm sorry.' She looked apologetic as she locked the ledgers away before taking out another even bigger one and laying it down on the table.

'This should give us details of what happened to your son, Mr Maguire. Most of the babies placed in our care are easily adopted. The ones that aren't, stay here until they are ready to go out into the world and fend for themselves.'

The nun was young, not much older than Aileen, with the sweetest smile she had ever seen. 'I'm pretty new and I don't recall ever seeing your son, Mr Maguire.' Her long slender finger slid down the entries. Then she glanced up. 'Your son, Tom, left the orphanage two years ago. It says here he was good with figures and a model student.'

'Really?' Aileen glanced down at the entry. 'It also states that he was a sickly child and didn't go for adoption. What does that mean?'

'Yes,' the woman said. 'He remained here, learned well, and passed his leaving cert with flying colours. He was offered a position as a bank clerk.'

Her da lowered his head. Aileen could hardly contain her own emotions. 'Isn't it wonderful news, Da?'

'It is indeed.' He blew his nose. 'Where's he working, Sister? Do you know?'

'Yes, he lives in a bedsit in Lucan, above the Royal Bank of Ireland.'

'I can't believe it. My son is well and working in a bank.' Sighing, he straightened his shoulders. 'Thanks so much, Sister.' He shook her hand. 'You've been most kind.'

Too emotional to speak, Aileen nodded her thanks and followed her father out of the building.

They sat in the car for some seconds, both a little overcome by what they had learned. Aileen leant across and hugged her da. He patted her arm.

'This is wonderful news, love.' He sniffed.

'It is, Da.' Aileen knew he was still upset about the entry in the ledger. 'We can tell Tom the truth when we find him.'

Aileen, emotionally drained, sat quietly while her da drove them back to the city. Persistence had paid off, and she was more than happy with the result.

'I'll go to Lucan at the first opportunity. Find out how he's doing,' her father said. 'I can't believe he's living just twenty miles away.'

'I wish I could come with you.'

'I know. Now I guess you'll be wanting to spend a few hours with Dermot before you catch that plane.'

'Da... I... well, I don't want to go back. But I must for now anyway.'

He remained silent, concentrating on his driving. Then he said, 'I don't want you to go either, love.' They were approaching the city. 'What do you say I drop you off at Dermot's?'

'Grand. I'll be back in time to pick up my case before I go.' She swallowed. 'You know, Da, this has been a wonderful

Christmas. I promise I'll be home for good soon. I can help you in the shop if you want me to.'

'Aileen. I don't expect you to give up your life.'

'I have no life in England, Da. Now that everything is coming together here, I'd like to consider coming back.'

He stopped the car outside the butcher's, and a smile brightened his face. She kissed his cheek and got out. It had been such a long time since she had felt so happy that she had forgotten what it was like.

# Chapter Forty-Four

Aileen's long chat with Dermot in his mother's back room hadn't gone well. Although he had been thrilled to learn about the news of her brother, he had constantly referred to their relationship and where it was leading.

'I thought we had settled this. You know how I feel, Dermot. With everything that's been going on, I would have thought you, of all people, understood. Was I wrong?' She sat down on the sofa.

'I do. But you're still going back, and you don't need to. Your da has recovered, and you've found your brother. Isn't that enough to keep you in the Fair City?' He came and sat next to her. 'If you go, where does that leave me?'

'Where you've always been, here, in my heart.'

'That's not enough, Aileen.' He moved closer, his eyes searching hers. 'Please don't go. Something's changed you. I don't know what it is, but it feels like you've been avoiding me.'

Guilt about Roy Pickering surfaced. She sniffed. If only she had more time, but it was too late now to bring all that up.

Dermot pulled her to him and buried his face in her hair. He kissed her cheek, and his breath fanned her face. 'I love you, Aileen. I want to marry you.' He held her at arm's length. 'I don't mind waiting as long as you're here, not miles away across the sea.'

She sighed, stood up, and moved across to the window that looked out into the darkness of the back yard. It was bleak. She wasn't looking forward to the flight that lay ahead.

Now Dermot's demands on her to stay only increased her anticipation.

She turned towards him. 'I have to go back, Dermot. I have commitments that I can't walk away from, but I'm thinking–' She never got to finish.

'Oh, well, if that's how you feel, don't let me keep you.'

Tears welled in her eyes. It was so unlike Dermot, but she wasn't going to back down. She picked up her bag and gloves and left through the back entrance. He didn't follow.

On the way back to the sweet shop, she felt torn by guilt. She wished she had told him how much she loved him and that she would make it up to him when she finally returned home. She had been consumed with winning back her father's affections and finding her brother. Now that things were just coming together, she had hoped that Dermot would support her. Together, or apart, she still loved him.

But tonight she had learned a valuable lesson, and she feared she might lose him. If only he hadn't taken on so, she might have told him that she was considering coming home for good.

\* \* \*

Her da was still up when she arrived home. He glanced outside then locked the door and followed her through to the back. 'Where's Dermot? I thought he was taking you to the airport.'

'We've had a row, Da. Dermot wants me to stay.'

He looked at her. 'Aileen, I'd love you to stay, too, but I don't want to influence your decision one way or the other.' He ran his hand across his forehead. 'You're cutting it fine if you still want to catch that flight.'

She rushed upstairs, threw the rest of her things into the case, and clicked it shut.

Her da came up behind her. 'I'll take that.' He walked ahead of her down the stairs. 'I'll keep you informed about your brother.'

She hugged him, choking back tears. 'I love you, Da.'

Nodding, he went through to the shop. Aileen checked her handbag for her plane ticket and followed him to the car.

At the airport entrance, he passed over her case then hugged her and wished her a safe journey. She felt him tremble.

'I won't come in with you. It will only make it harder. Phone me when you arrive at Mary's.'

'I will, Da. I'll see you soon.' As she disappeared inside the large complex, a tear rolled down her face. After checking in, she went to wait in the departure lounge. Going over in her mind every last word of her disagreement with Dermot, her anxiety increased. If only things hadn't gone so terribly wrong. Now here she was, returning to a life in England she didn't really want.

It was ironic that it was her da who knew her best. She wanted to make up her own mind about when to return home. Why hadn't Dermot realised that? She wasn't going to be pushed in spite of how she felt.

It wasn't long before her flight was called, and she followed the crowd across the tarmac towards the plane. The few days in Dublin had been successful. She had been re-united with her da and discovered the whereabouts of her twin brother. That happy thought would sustain her on the journey back.

As she boarded the plane, something made her turn and look up at the viewing window, and she was pleased she had. Someone was waving furiously. Although she couldn't recognise his face in the dark, it was his green and white scarf that caught her eye. She waved back, mouthing the words, 'I love you.' Once Dermot had time to calm down, she hoped he would understand.

The bumpy and unpleasant flight hardly bothered her. Her stomach lurched with every dip of the plane, but she centred her mind on pleasant things like her plans to return home and be with the ones she loved. And she couldn't help wondering what 1967 had in store for her.

When at last the plane landed, it was after nine o'clock, and she was looking forward to getting back to the lodging house. She hoped Mary had enjoyed Christmas with her sister. If it hadn't been for her landlady's kindness in loaning her the flight money, Aileen would never have been able to make the journey home.

She retrieved her suitcase and walked through the busy airport to arrive at the customs checkpoint. When she entered the green area, a security man asked for her ticket. This surprised her, as she had nothing to declare, then she was taken behind a screen where a PC stood waiting.

'Excuse us, Miss. Are you Aileen Maguire?'

'Yes. Why? Is there something wrong?'

'May we see your passport?'

Aileen's heartbeat quickened, and her fingers shook as she opened her bag and passed over the document.

'Miss Aileen Maguire, we would like you to accompany us to the police station for questioning.'

'What?' Aileen felt her face redden. 'What's this all about?'

'Let's go, Miss. It's best if you come with me. Everything will be explained at the police station.' He took her case and escorted her from the airport towards a waiting police car.

Petrified, she sat in the back. The PC refused to explain, instead concentrating on his driving. Aileen didn't know what to think. Had something happened to Mary?

It was only when they arrived at the station—the same one she had found herself in less than a week ago—that Roy Pickering sprang to mind. Had he changed his statement? Had he let her think she was free of all charges, and then hit her with them again? All manner of stuff shuttled through her brain: his angry face as he chased after the car; his arms waving for her to stop. It was the only explanation she could think of.

'In here, Miss,' the PC said, and Aileen went into the same questioning room she was now familiar with.

He pulled out a chair, and she sank down before her legs gave way. Aileen felt nauseous. The PC returned, followed by an older man in plain clothes, his coat over his arm as if he was about to leave. He hung it up and sat down.

'I'm Sergeant Ross,' he said, 'and this is PC Smith.' Aileen gripped the sides of the chair.

'We're sorry we had to send a PC to the airport. It was the only way we could be sure we wouldn't miss you.'

'But... why?'

'We just need to ask you a few questions, Miss.'

'What's this all about?' The sinking feeling in her stomach worsened.

'We believe you know a man by the name of Roy Pickering?' The PC took out a notebook and pen.

Aileen's hands shook. 'I, well yes, we work for the same firm.'

'Can you tell us about the last time you had contact with him?'

'He offered me a lift to the airport last weekend. He had no...' She paused, unsure how to continue without incriminating herself.

'It's all right, Miss. Take your time. So, did he take you to the airport?'

'No, no, he didn't. I went by bus.'

The Sergeant opened a folder and whispered something she didn't catch. He cleared his throat as he scanned the notes inside. 'We have it on record that you took Mr Pickering's car without consent, and that he dropped the charges against you. Why would he do that, Miss?'

Aileen's heartbeat quickened, and she played with the zip of her jacket, pulling it up and down. 'I've no idea. I only borrowed the car.' She swallowed. 'I was frightened. I had to get away from him. He...' She came over hot, and her hands felt clammy.

'So, after that incident, did you have any contact with him whatsoever?'

'No!' She shook her head. 'Of course not.' She loosened her red woollen scarf from around her neck. 'He was acting insane. He wanted me to marry him. I was frightened. It was a ridiculous suggestion; I have a boyfriend in Ireland. My friendship with Mr Pickering was purely platonic. I don't want to set eyes on him ever again.' She got to her feet. 'Look, please tell me why I'm here? Has Mr Pickering changed his mind about the charges?'

'No, Miss. Please sit down. Roy Pickering won't be making any charges against you or anyone else. You see, he's dead.'

* * *

Silence followed. She was aware of them watching her reaction. Aileen felt the blood drain from her face, and she slumped forward.

The PC rushed to get her some water and she sipped the drink with shaking hands, then leant forward, her face in her hands. This was a nightmare. Did they think she had something to do with his death? Dear God! Could this get any worse?

'We are still trying to establish why Mr Pickering took his life.'

Shocked, Aileen glanced up. 'He killed himself? How? I mean…when…when did this happen?'

'He hanged himself in the living room at his home on Boxing Day. We had a call here at the station from the hospital, and we were obliged to follow it up. When we called at the house, his mother gave us your name.' The Sergeant's eyes narrowed, and she was aware of him watching her. 'His mother is under the impression that you led him on, and then rejected him at a very critical point in his recovery.'

Aileen couldn't speak. Each time she tried to say something the words stopped at the back of her throat.

'Why do you suppose she'd say something like that, Miss?' Aileen's head felt dizzy, and she thought she was having an attack of vertigo. She took another sip of water. 'Did you know Roy Pickering had feelings for you, Miss?'

'Yes. No. I-I don't know. My God. I'm so sorry.' A sob caught in her throat. 'We were never more than friends. I thought he understood.'

'Did you know he was suffering from an acute mental disorder?'

'No. Not at first. He had been stalking me, and then told me that the man I had seen was his brother, who had taken his car and had problems.' She paused to massage her temples. 'He…'

'Take your time, Miss.'

'He totally convinced me.' She sniffed. 'I believed he was genuine.' She shifted in the chair, imagining the headlines with her name implicated as the cause of his death. She took a claming breath then straightened her shoulders; no way was she taking the blame.

'Go on.'

'On the night he was supposed to drive me to the airport, I-I overheard him and his mother arguing about his medication. That was when I realised he…he was the one with the problems, and that he didn't have a brother. I was frightened he would…try and stop me from catching my flight.' She sucked in her breath. 'I acted on impulse; we were in the middle of nowhere. I had to get away.'

'Well, it looks like you had a lucky escape, Miss. According to his physician, Mr Wainwright, our Mr Pickering was given to mood swings and could be a danger to women.'

Aileen sat back in the chair. She felt completely overwhelmed at the news of Roy's death. Frightened to ask, she took a deep breath. 'Am… Am I in any trouble?'

The Sergeant closed the folder and stood up. 'No, Miss, we are satisfied for now. As you were one of the last people to see him alive, we will need to speak to you again after we've questioned his mother. We found no suicide note, which is unusual in these cases. One of my men will escort you home.'

Aileen closed her eyes. She felt drained and, after what she had just heard, she wasn't about to refuse a lift. She stood up on shaky legs and followed the PC outside.

It was late when the police car stopped outside the lodging house. There was no-one around to witness her arrival, which was of small comfort. The light was on in the front room, and she walked up the path and opened the door. Mary heard her and came into the hall.

'Am I pleased to see you! I'm just about to phone our Bead.'

Uncontrolled tears ran down Aileen's face. 'Oh, Mary, you'll never believe what has happened now.'

'What is it?' Mary guided her into the room and sat her down. 'Is it your da?'

'Da's fine. Roy Pickering hanged himself on Boxing Day.'

# Chapter Forty-Five

Aileen lay awake, her mind churning with assumptions as to what had made Roy end his life. If it had been her fault, it would embed itself on her conscience forever. But she refused to believe that. Something else must have caused him to take such drastic action. From what little Aileen had witnessed at the house that night, she got the impression that his mother controlled him. Dear God! Poor Roy. If she had stayed, would he still be alive? She asked herself the question, knowing that she could never have done that. Guilt weighed heavily until she recalled what the PC had said earlier; he might have killed her instead.

Did they know at the mill yet? If not, how was she going to tell them without incriminating herself? They were bound to find out from the newspapers. Would she be mentioned as being at his house almost a day before he took his life?

Dark thoughts crowded in on her. Sleep was never going to come, and the way she felt she would never sleep easy again.

If she had only talked it over with Dermot, or her da, perhaps her conscience would be easier. It was too late now. Dermot might think she had only mentioned it out of guilt, and he would be right. Indecision swam around in her brain like tadpoles, and her eyes stung from lack of sleep until she eventually got up.

She threw back the eiderdown and blankets and slipped her feet into her slippers. Wrapping her dressing gown around her shaking body, she opened her door as quietly as she could. Mary was a light sleeper, and she didn't want to disturb her. Miss Brady was still away, so she crept along the landing and down the stairs.

In the kitchen, sobs choked her as she sat warming her hands on a mug of hot milk. How could she face them at the mill? She had been looking forward to working her notice and returning to Dublin, but now it would look like she was running away. The excitement of finding her brother had now been replaced with feelings of fear, guilt and frustration. Even worse was the fear of losing Dermot once the news broke. All she wanted to do was hide away from the world.

The milk hadn't helped, and back in her room she felt as wide-awake as before.

* * *

At seven thirty, Aileen heard Mary go to the bathroom and then descend the stairs, but she didn't move. At eight o'clock, she forced herself to get up and pull on some clothes. She wasn't sure how Mary might react this morning after sleeping on their discussion the previous night. She had so looked forward to seeing her landlady's face once she told her she had found her twin brother; now she felt a mess. Her life was in tatters and she couldn't rid herself of the black cloud now hanging over her. What this could do to Mary's business she hadn't begun to contemplate.

'Oh, you're up then?' Mary turned round as Aileen entered the kitchen. Aileen could hardly blame her for being annoyed.

'I can't apologise enough,' she said. 'Everything's a mess. I don't blame you if...'

Mary stood up and faced her, her back pressed against the worktop. 'Oh, give over, will yea? It's not your fault that the silly beggar decided to hang himself.' She sighed. 'What are yea goona do?'

'I don't know. I can't face work today. Look at me? I've not slept, and I look like something the cat dragged in.'

Mary sighed. 'I didn't sleep myself. I heard yea goo down in the night.' She turned back to the stove. 'This is a fine how-do-you-do, and I don't know how best to advise yea.'

Aileen sat down and leant back in the chair. How could befriending someone have led to this? She had let everyone down, and there was no way she could change things. 'I'll go in this afternoon and tell them everything.'

Mary shook her head. 'No, I wouldn't do that.' She filled a mug with tea and brought it to the table.

Aileen sat upright. 'Why not? Everyone will know sooner or later.'

'You don't know that, Aileen. Does this Val know Roy was taking you to the airport?'

She shook her head.

'Well then, say nought!'

'But what if it's in the newspaper?'

'Yea, well if it is, it doesn't mean your name will get mentioned. If it does, you'll have to tell the truth.' She stood up and went into the hall. 'I'm away to the shop. Freshen yourself up, and I'll bring back a morning paper.'

\* \* \*

That afternoon, Val seemed pleased when Aileen walked into the office, but Aileen could only muster up a watery smile. 'Didn't you have a good Christmas? You look proper poorly, I guess you're not over the journey yet.'

'I'm grand. I had a wonderful Christmas. How about you?'

Val flashed her hand across the desk. 'We got engaged.'

'Oh, that's wonderful. Congratulations. When is the big day?'

'In eighteen months' time, I guess. It'll give us time to save for a place of our own. How was your da?'

'He was wonderful, thanks.' Aileen smiled. 'And the best thing is, we've found my twin brother.' She went on excitedly, 'I haven't met him yet. I came back to give my notice and sort things out with Mary.'

'Oh, you're not leaving, are you?'

'Things have changed at home, Val, and I want to go back. Besides, I'm missing Dermot, and I think he misses me, too.' She smiled again, remembering how he had come to wave her off at the airport.

Val sighed. 'Can't blame you then. When are you going to tell Miss Grimshaw?'

They were both flicking through the stack of orders on the desk when the door opened, and Mr Bill walked in, his face grim.

He cleared his throat and both women turned their heads towards him.

'I'm sorry to be the bearer of sad news at the start of the New Year,' he said. 'Our rep, Roy Pickering, died over the Christmas holidays.' He shook his head, his face grim.

Val's eyes widened, and Aileen felt her heart thump in her chest.

'Oh, that's awful news,' Val said. 'What happened?'

'We don't have all the facts yet, but we are sending a wreath from the firm, and I've asked Miss Grimshaw to organise a message of condolence to his widowed mother.' Shaking his head again, he left.

'Good God!' Val exclaimed. 'How did that happen?'

Aileen, who was trying to stop herself from shaking, shook her head and forced herself to speak. 'It's... it's such terrible news.'

'When did you see him last, Aileen?'

She swallowed. 'Before I went away, but I didn't know he was ill.'

'Nobody knew anything about Roy.' Val leant her elbows on the desk. 'I always thought he was weird, but you liked him, didn't you?'

'Yes, as a friend, that's all.' A terrible feeling gripped the pit of her stomach, and she excused herself and hurried to the toilet.

For the rest of the afternoon, when anyone spoke about Roy she acted shocked as if she'd heard the news for the first time. But her heart was heavy with sadness that his life had ended in that way.

Just before they finished for the day, Val asked, 'Do you think we should go to his funeral?'

Aileen took a deep intake of breath before answering. 'I, well, I don't know, Val. We should leave that to Miss Grimshaw to decide.'

'Aren't you a bit curious to see his family?'

'Not really!' Aileen was determined to distract Val from talking about Roy. 'You never told me how Peter came to pop the question.'

Val needed no encouragement, and she made Aileen smile as they walked together up the lane. But when they parted, Aileen felt the weight of guilt pressing down on her like a heavy blanket.

# Chapter Forty-Six

There had been nothing about Roy's suicide in the morning or evening newspapers. Even the obituary column carried nothing about him. Aileen began to relax, although it might be too soon for the police to release it to the press. She had dreaded going home to Mary, knowing what a mess she had made of things. The older woman had been supportive and kind to her since her arrival in Birmingham, and in return all she had brought was the police to her door.

Aileen's plans of returning home for good would have to wait until all this was cleared up, and Roy Pickering had been laid to rest.

That evening, the two women sat in the lounge. Christmas songs played on the radio. Aileen was fidgety and restless; she couldn't settle to do anything.

'You know, you should take up knitting. It's very relaxing,' Mary said, stopping to count her stitches.

Aileen managed a weak smile. She had apologised to Mary so many times for the trouble she'd caused, and she was at odds to know what to do to make amends.

'Look, love. This will all blow over in a few weeks, and yea can get on with your life. In the meantime, stop maulding and put the kettle on.' She shook her head and carried on knitting. 'And can yea cut a couple o' slices of me Christmas cake?'

Aileen was glad to leave the room, as the clicking of Mary's needles was giving her a headache. In the kitchen, she almost spooned sugar into the teapot and just caught herself in time.

She was desperate to tell Mary about her brother. But the fact that Mary hadn't asked increased her reluctance to share the good news, in the light of what had happened. She took a couple of tablets to quieten her thumping head and checked the tray before bringing it in.

'Pop it over here.' Mary cleared a space on the table, gathering up the magazines and newspapers and placing them in the rack by the side of her chair. 'I'll pour, shall I? Yea haven't tasted me cake yet, have yea?' Aileen shook her head.

'Try and put him out of your head.' Mary passed her a cup of tea. 'You've done nothing wrong. Looking at yea, anyone would think you'd done a murder.'

Aileen let out a deep sigh.

Mary sat down with her drink. 'Where's the sugar?'

Aileen stood up. 'Sorry.'

'I'll get it,' Mary said, making for the kitchen. 'If yea want owt doing, do it yourself,' she mumbled. Aileen had grown fond of Mary; she had stood by her in all this, and she had to struggle to keep her emotions in check.

Over their tea and cake, Mary said, 'With all that's been goon on, I forgot to ask yea how yea got on in Dublin.'

'Oh, Mary, it was grand. I couldn't wait to get back to tell you about Da and my twin brother. But the joy I felt when I arrived at the airport, evaporated like sand through my fingers when I ended up in the police station. Dermot and Da want me to come home.'

'Did you say twin brother?' Mary sat forward eagerly, and Aileen related how she and her da had found her brother.

'God Almighty, that's grand news. So it is true, Jessie had another baby. Well, this calls for a celebration.' Mary went to the cupboard and took out a half empty bottle of sherry and two glasses.

After a few sips, Aileen felt the tension in her body ease and she relaxed back into the armchair. Mary listened intently as Aileen related everything about her happy Christmas back in Dublin, and most importantly the discovery and the whereabouts of her brother.

'Ah, sure isn't that just grand news? Have yea seen 'im yet?'

'No. I was planning to return home, for good, like.' She sniffed into her handkerchief. 'I can hardly do that now.'

'What do yea mean? Are yea goona let this business with Pickering ruin the rest of your life?'

Aileen sipped the rest of her drink and popped the last piece of cake into her mouth. 'I should have given my notice today, but when the news of Roy's death broke, I lost my nerve.' She lowered her head. 'I guess I feel partly responsible.'

Mary poured another glass of sherry and then she pointed her finger at Aileen. 'Now you listen to me, I–' The telephone rang out, stopping her in her tracks. She frowned. 'I'd better answer that.' She eased herself out of her chair and went out into the hall.

Aileen went as far as the door, hoping with all her heart that it wasn't the police. Dermot often phoned her late at night, and she would love to speak to him before she went to bed.

'Bead, lovely to hear from you,' Mary said. 'Yea, she got back safe. She's here with me now. Do you want a word with 'er?' Mary turned around and nodded to Aileen. 'Your Aunt Bead.'

Aileen took a deep breath before taking the phone.

'Hello, Aunt Bead. How are you? You heard then? Yes, it's wonderful. I know. I know. Yes. I'll be back home as soon as I can. I can't wait to meet my brother.'

Smiling, Mary left Aileen to chat. 'I'm away to me bed,' she whispered, and Aileen nodded.

'What's that, Aunt Bead? She's definitely emigrating then? Does Da know? Really! Oh, thanks for phoning, that's grand news.'

She felt better. Her chat with Bead had stopped her dwelling on Roy's death. So Lizzy was going to live in America? Where Aileen was concerned, it couldn't be far enough away.

# Chapter Forty-Seven

For the remainder of that week, the topic of conversation at the mill was Roy. Miss Grimshaw said she was flabbergasted to hear that he'd had a mental disorder. 'How did that go unnoticed?' she repeated several times. Val said it was obvious he had problems, but Miss Grimshaw said he had hidden it very well.

'Did you notice anything strange about him, Aileen?' the older woman asked.

Aileen sucked in her breath. 'Not at first. He could be moody; unpredictable, I'd say.' She was relieved to answer without the words choking in her throat.

'Anyway, the poor man's dead. Mr Bill and I will represent the firm at his funeral.' Sighing, Miss Grimshaw went back up to her office.

'I wonder what they'll do now without a rep,' Val said, placing her elbows on the desk and linking her fingers.

'There'll be no shortage of applications,' Aileen said.

'Orders are down already.' Val picked up a few from the pile and handed them to Aileen, and the rest of the day passed without much incident.

Roy's death was recorded in the newspaper as another suicide statistic. It only got a small notice in the newspaper, and if you weren't looking you wouldn't find it. Aileen felt an overwhelming sense of relief that her name wasn't mentioned. Only Mary and herself, and Roy's mother knew that she had been to his home days before he killed himself. That's how she hoped it would stay.

As soon as the funeral had taken place, she planned to give notice. She was longing to get back to Dublin and explain everything to Dermot and pray he would forgive her. She couldn't put back the clock, and what had happened to Roy would always be a sad reminder of her time in Birmingham.

* * *

A week after the funeral, Alan surprised both Aileen and Val when he walked into the office dressed in a smart suit and tie. 'Say hello to your new rep,' he chortled.

Val's mouth dropped, and Aileen glanced up. 'You've got Roy's job?'

'Not yet. I'm applying for it. How do I look?'

Aileen and Val exchanged glances just as the door to Mr Bill's office opened, and Alan was called inside.

'What do you make of that?' Val said. 'Who's going to take the orders? We're not taking them in here. We have enough to do.'

Aileen sighed and carried on typing. 'Sure, if he gets it, someone else will fill his job.'

'Yes, I know,' Val said. 'But that could take ages.'

Aileen wanted to mention that she was leaving, but thought it best to wait until Monday after she had told Miss Grimshaw.

On Friday, after work, she arrived back at the lodging house to find a letter from her father. Her excitement mounting, she opened it.

*Dearest Aileen,*

*I know it's only been a couple of weeks since you went back to Birmingham, and I wondered if you had thought any more about coming home. I don't want to put pressure on you in any way; perhaps you've decided to stay after all, and that's fine. I was thinking of employing someone full time as the shop is quite busy, and I'm run off my feet.*

*If you were planning on coming home, I'd keep the job for you; that's if you want it. You might have other plans.*

*Whatever you decide to do, can you let me know? I hope everything is well with you and Mary. If you feel that your life is in Birmingham, I'll come over for a visit in the summer months once I've got someone established here to look after things.*

*All the best*
*Your loving father,*
*Jonny Maguire.*

She folded the letter, not sure whether to laugh or cry. If only he knew how much she wanted to come home, help him in the shop, and be part of his life. She put the letter in the pocket of her dress and sat down on her bed. She would have been on her way home if it hadn't been for the tragedy that had met her on her return.

She wanted to tell her da, but not in a letter. Then there was Dermot. How could she expect him to understand? Once she told him about Roy, things might never be the same between them. There was only one way to find out. It was the time to end all secrets and come clean. However, if Dermot let her go, it would break her heart.

That night Aileen had a long talk with Mary.

'Sure, I'll miss yea, so I will, but I think it's for the best. You don't want to lose that young man of yours.'

Aileen shifted her gaze. 'I don't, but he knows nothing about Roy Pickering.'

'You've done nothing wrong, Aileen; perhaps just been a little naïve.' Mary looked at her with raised eyebrows. 'Sure, I was young meself once and know how it feels to be lonely.' She sighed. 'It's my guess you never wanted to come away in the first place. So there's nothing to stop you giving notice at the mill and goon back 'ome now, is there?'

'You're right. Thanks, Mary. I could stay until you get a new lodger?'

'Not at all. I'll soon fill that room. Sure, I'll be packing up in a few years. Me sister and me are going to retire to Rhyl. We've planned it a while back, so yea needn't go worrying about me.'

'Sounds nice.' Aileen reached for her bag. She always paid her board on Friday night, and she still owed Mary for the flight on Christmas Eve. 'I'll pay you back the rest of what I owe you next week.'

'Sure, yea can send it over when yea get home.' Mary stuffed the notes into her apron pocket. 'Don't forget, yea've another flight to buy.'

'That would be really helpful.' Aileen had been planning on

taking the ferry, but at this time of year the sea could be rough. She just might be able to buy a cheap ticket with Aer Lingus.

Mary got to her feet. 'Well, I'd better get back to me ironing.'

She made her way towards the kitchen, and Aileen picked up a magazine from the rack, but she couldn't concentrate. Her stupid friendship with Roy and his subsequent death had left her shaken. Now she could see things in perspective, she recognised how gullible she had been to have let herself be taken in by an older man and fallen for his lies. When she rationalised her own behaviour, it occurred to her that the loss of her ma, her da's unhappy state, and Lizzy's attitude, had all contributed to her lack of judgement.

The shrill of the telephone brought her out of her thoughts. Thinking it might be Dermot, she stood in the doorway as Mary lifted the receiver.

'What can I do for yea?' Mary was saying. 'What, at this time of the night? Aye, I don't know. Yes, she's here. Hold on.' Mary turned her head and beckoned Aileen to the phone. 'It's the police. They want to speak to yea.'

When Aileen replaced the phone, her face was white. 'What is it? What do they want from yea now?'

'They want me to call in at the station first thing in the morning, but they wouldn't say what it was about.' She placed her hands over her face. 'Mary, this is not going away.'

# Chapter Forty-Eight

'Please take a seat, Miss.' The older of the two policemen pulled out a chair and Aileen sat down, her hands folded on her lap. The younger man glared at her, and it made her feel uncomfortable. The older of the two cleared his throat.

'I'm PC Williams and this is PC Taylor, whom I believe you've met before.'

Aileen nodded.

'We're sorry we had to bring you down here again, Miss, but we have more news about Mr Pickering's death.'

Aileen's heartbeat quickened, and her hands felt clammy as she rubbed them together.

'Did you notice anything unusual when you visited Roy Pickering's house on Christmas Eve, Miss?'

Aileen frowned. She had noticed the strange atmosphere, but was that what they wanted to know? 'In what way?'

'Anything at all, Miss, about Pickering's mother, or Pickering himself, anything that you thought odd?'

'The house didn't look lived in, and it made me feel very uncomfortable.'

'My feelings, too,' the older PC said. 'What about the mother? How did you find her? Was she friendly?'

Aileen sat forward. 'Well, I never met his mother. I don't know anything about her.' She sighed. 'Why are you asking me these questions? Has something else happened?'

'No, Miss. When Mrs Pickering was first questioned, she was quick to blame you for her son's death. But we've since learned more about the family and discovered that Pickering left a suicide note.'

Aileen swallowed; her mind swirled with notions of what he might have put in the note. Would he have taken revenge on her for turning him down? He could be so unpredictable.

'Did you know that his father committed suicide, Miss?'

'No. As I've said, I knew nothing about his family. He never spoke of it. And, well, he always came over as a private person.' She sighed. 'He was friendly most of the time. When I told him I was going home to see my boyfriend and my family, his mood changed.'

'It's all right, Miss. We won't detain you much longer. We wondered if you knew anything about his home life; how he felt about his mother, for instance?'

'No, I know nothing at all. I only knew him for a short time. Why did his mother blame me?'

'Well, she had to blame someone. According to the suicide note, he couldn't go on after what he'd heard. It had nothing to do with you, Miss. Apparently, his mother revealed the truth that his father died in a mental institution, having previously told him he died in the war.'

Aileen was shocked to hear this. 'So, are you saying that is why he took his life?'

'It's very significant, Miss.' He sighed. 'I guess he was very disturbed and believed he would end up the same way.' The constable sat forward. 'Which goes to show that lying, no matter how well intentioned, doesn't pay.'

Aileen nodded and was reminded of her own dishonesty. 'Thanks for letting me know. I'd hate to have his death on my conscience. Can I go now?'

'Yes, yes, of course. Thanks for coming in. We are satisfied that this had nothing to do with you. Thanks for your co-operation, Miss.' He stood up and escorted her out.

# Chapter Forty-Nine

By the beginning of February, Aileen was finally back in Dublin. Miss Grimshaw had asked her to reconsider her resignation and offered her a wage increase, but Aileen's mind was made up. Val said she understood her need to see her twin brother and, after a tearful hug, Aileen had left the mill with their good wishes.

Reunited again with Dermot at the ferry terminal made her all the more aware that she didn't want to lose him. And when he dropped her outside the sweet shop, her da greeted her with a smile and a hug. It felt good to be home. A pleasant woman of about forty was working behind the sweet counter, and she stopped what she was doing to greet Aileen.

'It's nice to meet you, love. Your father never stops talking about you.' The woman seemed pleasant enough, and her da would need time off once they contacted her brother.

They walked through to the living room. There was the sound of a kettle boiling in the scullery. 'Is that it now? Are you home for good?'

'Most definitely, Da.' She removed her coat. 'By the way, has there been any news from Tom?'

'I'm anxiously waiting to hear from him.'

'Really? That's wonderful.'

'I wrote him a letter. Mind you, I found it difficult. I told him who I was and about you, and that we had just discovered his whereabouts.' He sighed as he placed a tea-tray on the table. 'I hope I did the right thing. I don't want to put pressure on him.'

He put a plate of ham and tomato sandwiches and a few fig rolls on the table, sat down, and linked his fingers. 'I included our

246

phone number should he wish to get in touch, and concluded that it would make us both very happy if he did.' He ran his hand over his face.

'You did well, Da. When was that?'

'Just after you went back. So far he hasn't phoned, or made contact.'

'Well, never mind. He'll need time to think about it. He might be nervous about meeting us.'

'I can understand that. I'll wait a few more days and then I'll phone the bank.'

Aileen frowned. 'I can't contemplate that he might not want to be part of our lives.'

Her da shook his head. 'Don't worry, love. I'm not losing him again, no matter how long it takes. He knows nothing about us yet, and he's probably cautious. We must take things slowly.' He placed a hand on her arm. 'I'd better go and take over from Fiona.' He glanced at his watch.

'Fiona, is it?'

He raised his eyes. 'She's just an employee, that's all.'

Aileen smiled. 'Are you going to keep her on?'

'Well, now, sure that depends on what your plans are. Look, when you've finished eating, have a lie down. Your room is ready. And later, why don't you go and see a film with Dermot? That young man's been missing you nearly as much as I have.' He laughed. 'Here, take this.' He handed her a ten-shilling note. 'Get some ice-cream on me.'

She kissed his cheek. How lovely it was to have her old da back.

\* \* \*

For her date with Dermot, Aileen wore a green, long-sleeved, woollen dress. It was short enough to show off her shapely legs. She wore the perfume he had bought for her at Christmas, and she left her hair loose, teasing it around her face the way she knew he liked it. A short leather jacket and heeled boots completed her outfit.

She was putting the finishing touches to her lips when Dermot's van rattled to a halt outside, and she hurried downstairs.

Tonight, if the opportunity arose, she planned to clear her conscience by telling Dermot everything that had happened during her stay in Birmingham. She had no idea what it might do to their relationship, but it was something she had to do.

'You sounded mysterious on the phone,' she said. 'What are you up to, Dermot?' He looked handsome in a grey jacket and open-necked blue shirt, his thick dark hair tousled as if he hadn't dried it properly.

'You remember I said I was planning something special for when you came home?'

'How special? Da's given me money for ice-cream.'

He laughed. 'Well, I don't think you'll need that.'

She frowned. 'Why, where are we going?'

He winked and drove the van down Camden Street.

'Oh, stop messing, Dermot, and tell me.'

'Be patient, Aileen Maguire. I don't want to spoil the surprise.'

She tried to guess, but each place she mentioned, Dermot just laughed and shook his head.

'Oh, go on,' she wheedled. 'You know I hate not knowing.'

He turned onto Dame Street and reversed into a parking space she was sure many drivers wouldn't attempt. Aileen shook her head and stepped out into the cold night air, a puzzled look on her face. The theatre came to mind. Yet Dermot gave her no clue. He took her hand, and they walked back along Dame Street.

They had only gone a few steps when he paused outside an Italian restaurant. The door opened and a couple stepped out. A chink of light shone on the pavement, and Aileen glanced up at the name above the door. 'You can't be serious, Dermot?' She placed her fingers to her lips. 'It's much too expensive.' Nico's was one of the first Italian restaurants to open in Dublin a couple of years before and had received great reviews.

'Let me be the judge of that. Your face is a picture.' Dermot laughed. He opened the door and ushered her inside.

'Are you sure, Dermot? It'll cost an arm and a leg...I...'

'We're celebrating your return to the Fair City, Aileen.'

Nico, the owner, greeted them as soon as they walked in. Tall and good-looking, his warm Italian personality instantly made them feel welcome. '*Buonasera!*' He took their coats and escorted them to a table for two in the corner.

'This is lovely, Dermot.' The place was small, intimate, and romantic. Colourful drapes looped along one side of the wall, and someone tinkled gentle melodies on a piano. Aileen glanced up at the overhead gas heaters and felt warm and cosy.

Nico handed them a menu. 'Take your time,' he said, in that lovely Italian accent. 'Call me when you're ready to order.'

Aileen glanced down the menu; everything looked delicious, but the prices made her eyes water. She could hardly expect Dermot to pay these prices, and wondered if she should offer to go Dutch, yet she would hate to embarrass him. He must have read her expression.

'Don't worry,' he said. 'I'm not without a penny or two. After all, what have I had to spend it on these past six months? Choose anything you like.' He glanced down the wine list. 'What would you like to drink?'

'Well, umm.' She wasn't sure she should, remembering the effect alcohol had on her. It was an episode she wanted to forget, but she felt happy here with Dermot and knew she was safe.

'Shall we wait until we order?'

He nodded. Couples were still arriving and being shown to their tables. The place was almost full, and she quickly counted a dozen couples dining. It made a very cosy atmosphere.

Happy and relaxed, she leant back in her chair, letting the muttering of intimate conversations, the chinking of glasses, and the gentle background music wash over her. Dermot bent his shoulders and took her hand. 'Have you eaten Italian before? No doubt you've been to a few fancy restaurants and nightclubs in Birmingham?'

'Well, no, not really.' She smiled. 'I don't expect you to take me to swanky places like this, you know?'

He released her hand. 'But you do like it here?'

'Of course, I do. It's a lovely surprise. I'm just saying.'

In spite of the subdued light, Aileen saw the lines on his

forehead relax. 'I wanted to do something special. You deserve it.' He studied the menu again. 'Now, I'm famished. What would you like to eat?'

'Nico's salad starter looks delicious, but I'll have the minestrone soup, I think. What about you?'

Dermot rubbed the palms of his hands together. 'Me, too.'

When they were ready, Nico came across and took their order. 'Can I try the spaghetti carbonara, please?' Aileen was surprised that Nico took the orders himself, and she assumed the woman who cleared the tables was his wife.

'Certainly, *Signorina,* and for you, *Signor?*'

'Spaghetti bolognese, please.'

Dermot glanced at the drinks menu. 'Would you like to try some Italian wine? I've had some before. It's quite nice.'

She nodded. 'Yes, please.' She felt relaxed and happier than she had in a long while.

'Splendid.' Relieving them of the menus, Nico retreated. Aileen remarked on his smart attire of black and white jacket. His black trousers accentuated his long legs as he made his way through to the kitchen.

Nico brought the wine—a squat bottle encased in a straw basket—and poured them each a glass. Aileen raised it to her lips and took a sip.

'Well, what do you think?' Dermot asked.

Aileen wasn't sure she liked it. The flavour was subdued, but she guessed it might taste better along with food. Smiling, she said, 'It's different.'

'It's not sweet. Would you prefer something else?'

'It's grand, Dermot, thanks.' She leant her elbow on the table, her fingers resting under her chin. 'I'm looking forward to trying my first Italian dish.'

'They do Irish as well as Italian.'

'I noticed.' Aileen raised an eyebrow.

Dermot sat back. 'I see you're not observing "no meat on Friday", then?'

Aileen laughed. 'No, I don't stick to it, and certainly not tonight.'

His shoulders relaxed. 'I'm sorry. I never thought to check with you first. Working as a butcher, I rarely eat fish. Ma keeps it up, you know, and with Luke being a priest and all, well, me and Da don't always get a choice.'

As they waited for their meal, he made her laugh at the silliest of things. 'You just wouldn't believe the stories the fish guy comes out with for being late with deliveries.' He leant forward. 'One week his horse went lame, another week the horse had a runny eye and he had to call in the vet.'

'Sounds like he needs a new horse.' They laughed.

Dermot was charming and funny. She glanced across at his rugged good looks and her heart swelled with love. He had made such efforts to please her. She glanced down at his strong hands, his nails looked like they'd had a manicure. She could see no traces that he had been working in a butcher's shop all day.

The atmosphere was so relaxing she was barely aware of other people around them.

'Is everything okay?'

'Wonderful.' She smiled.

Their food arrived, and they tucked in. Dermot tried to wrap the spaghetti around his fork, but after several attempts ,he gave up and scooped it into his mouth, the strips of pasta dangling from his chin. 'I'm sorry, Aileen. There must be a knack to eating spaghetti, just like with chopsticks.'

Aileen smiled and reached for his hand. It felt nice.

'It's so lovely to have you back home. Are you staying this time?'

She nodded.

'What are your plans? I mean... I can't see the sweet shop being enough for you. Will you go back to college?'

Right now, she would settle for anything so long as she was here in Dublin, close to Dermot, her da, and her brother. She swallowed. 'I don't see myself ever going back to England, Dermot, but I'm not sure what I want to do right now. Except, that is, find my brother.'

'Any word yet?' He asked sipping his drink.

251

She shook her head, frowning slightly. 'It's been weeks and we've heard nothing.'

'It's still not long, Aileen.' He placed his glass down and beckoned the waiter. 'Would you like dessert? I know I would.'

They both opted for Nico's special gateau with fresh cream.

Aileen picked up their conversation again. 'I know it won't be easy for him, Dermot, and he must be so confused.'

'Well, I can only go by how I might feel if I were in his shoes. I guess he'll be nervous and possibly take time to come to terms with the fact that he has a twin sister and a father, and at the same time wonder where they had been all his life.'

Aileen sighed. 'What if he never gets in touch? I can't leave it there, Dermot.'

'Just give him time, and then you can write again. Try and stay positive.' He moved his dish to the side and took her hand. 'I know it's not easy.' He lifted the chianti bottle. 'Would you like some more?'

'Okay,' she raised her glass. 'Just a small drop.' She sipped her wine and felt the smooth liquid ease its way down, then took another sip. 'I like the flavour; it doesn't taste like alcohol.'

'Oh, it is.'

She smiled. 'I've not been adventurous with alcohol.' She omitted to mention gin and tonic.

'I know. That's what I love about you. You're perfect. The most beautiful girl in the room and you're here with me.'

'Stop that, Dermot. You're making me blush.' She looked away. She didn't deserve any of Dermot's praise.

'I'm serious, Aileen. There's nothing I'd like to change about you.'

She reached across and touched his hand.

'You won't miss the friends you've made in England then?'

Their eyes met. His green and brooding, his dark hair and that lovely smile melting her heart.

'No,' she said. 'I've made the right decision.' She loved him now more than ever, and she dreaded having to tell him the kind of person she had made friends with back in Birmingham. But that would have to wait for another day.

Dermot ordered another bottle of chianti, and they sat sipping wine and chatting freely about the Aberfan disaster, her da, and mostly about Aileen's brother, Tom. When she glanced around her, the restaurant was almost empty. The time had flown, but she didn't want the evening to end.

She looked at her watch. 'Have we really been sitting here all this time?'

'I've hardly noticed.' He glanced around to where Nico was waiting patiently at the end of the room. 'I guess I'd better pay the bill, so.'

Outside, they huddled in the doorway as rain washed the pavements.

'Would you like me to call a cab, sir?' Nico asked, holding the restaurant door open.

Dermot glanced towards Aileen, and she gave him a knowing look. 'You've had quite a lot to drink.'

'What about the van?'

'It'll be fine where it is,' Nico said. 'As long as you pick it up in the morning.'

They didn't have to wait long. They sat in the back of the cab, where Aileen shook out her wet hair. 'Are you working tomorrow morning, Dermot?'

'I'm afraid so. But I'm free in the afternoon if you want to do something?'

'I'm going to see Uncle Paddy and Aunt Bead. Why don't you pick me up from there, and we can do something then?' She touched his hand. 'Thanks for a lovely evening, Dermot. I've missed you so much.'

'Not nearly as much as I missed you.' He pulled her into his arms. His kiss was full of passion, the end to a perfect evening. She couldn't spoil it by talking about Roy Pickering.

All too soon they were on Camden Street, and Dermot stepped from the taxi and asked the driver to wait. The rain was still pelting down, and they ducked into the doorway of the sweet shop. Giggling, Aileen fumbled for her key. When Dermot kissed her goodnight, she didn't want him to leave, but the taxi meter was ticking and he had to go. She watched him throw her a kiss from the taxi window as it sped away.

# Chapter Fifty

Dermot had fancied Aileen from the first moment he had spotted her walking past the butcher's shop, and he had never been able to get her out of his mind. Her angelic face needed no enhancement, and he loved her long, shiny blonde hair. He had thought her above him because she went to college and was studying a secretarial course; he, the son of a butcher, was happy and content with his lot. When she'd given up her studies to care for her sick mother, he had made every excuse under the sun to call in at the haberdashery. And he couldn't believe his luck when she had agreed to go out with him.

After she had left for England, he'd been lonely but he couldn't really blame her. If he'd been in her shoes, he would probably have done the same. But she was back now, her da had thankfully come to his senses, and they were on the verge of finding her brother; Dermot couldn't be happier for her.

At Christmas, he had thought her distracted. He had been sure she had found someone else but, fearful of the truth, he'd held back from asking. Now he realised how wrong he had been.

Once her brother was back in her life, he planned to ask her to marry him; perhaps get engaged. He had already saved a substantial amount towards a house. He sighed, reining himself in. He mustn't get ahead of himself. It was enough for now that she was home.

* * *

When Dermot entered the kitchen, he was surprised to find his mother still up, the ironing board out. She was steaming his dad's best trousers, a cup of hot cocoa on the table. 'I'm glad you're

255

back, son, only I didn't hear the van.'

'I left it in the city. It's quite safe. I'll pick it up in the morning. What's wrong?

Couldn't you sleep?'

'Your dad and I are taking the early morning ferry to Wales. Meredith is having a family service for her granddaughter, and we feel we ought to be there to support her. I spoke to her earlier, and they are struggling to come to terms with it all.'

Dermot sat down and rubbed his broad hand over his face. 'How long will you be away for?'

'Just the weekend; we'll be back Monday. Can you manage the shop until then? The orders are all done and in the fridge for tomorrow.'

'Don't worry. I dare say I can manage with the lad for one morning. Now you get yourself off to bed, Mam. What time do you have to leave?'

'Don't worry, your dad has booked a taxi. You just concentrate on the shop until we get back.'

* * *

Early the next morning, Dermot walked across town to retrieve his van. He found his vehicle where he had parked it overnight, close to Nico's; he was relieved not to have incurred a parking fine.

Before he opened the shop, he made a quick phone call to Aileen and confirmed that he would see her later at her aunt's house. The butcher's was always busiest on Saturdays, so he had little time to think about Aileen, but he whistled while he worked, and chatted with the regulars.

He closed the shop at midday, then had a bath and scrubbed his nails. One of the things he disliked about being a butcher was that it took him ages to get rid of the blood which became ingrained in the crevices of his fingers and underneath his nails. He knew some men had manicures, but that wasn't him. Instead, he clipped his nails short and, after a good scrub, they looked normal again.

When he was ready, he dabbed a splash of aftershave on his face. His newly-washed hair smelled fresh and clean, but it continued to stick up at the back. It was only then that he realised he had run out of hair cream. He dressed casually in beige cords, check shirt, and his dark, three-quarter length coat, felt his pockets for his wallet and left the house.

The strong, overnight wind had died down, and he hoped his parents' crossing hadn't been too arduous. He glanced at his watch. They would be on their way to Merthyr Vale by now. He sighed when he thought of what had happened there. The Welsh people were a resilient race, including his aunt's family, but he had to wonder how they would ever come back from this.

It was cold and the sky was cloudy; it looked like rain. He drove across town towards Aileen's aunt's. When he arrived, he rubbed his hands together and smoothed down the back of his hair.

Bead opened the door. 'Come along inside.'

As he walked through the hall into the front room, he asked, 'Is Aileen about?'

'I'm sorry, Dermot, but she's not here. Her da called, and she had to dash off.' Bead sighed. 'Please, sit down, I'll get you a hot drink.'

Dermot, unable to hide his disappointment, lowered himself onto the sofa. 'Don't bother with the drink thanks, Bead. Did she say what it was about?'

'No, her da appeared to be in a hurry and just said it was to do with his son. Oh, I almost forgot, Aileen scribbled a note for you.' She handed him a sealed envelope that had been propped up against the mantle clock. 'She said not to phone you as you'd have already left.'

Dermot scanned the note then, glancing up, he smiled. 'Just says she'll meet in Clery's tea room, and if she's not there by three not to hang about and she'll ring me later.' He stood up. 'I've a few things to do in town. Give my best to Paddy. Working today, is he?'

'No. He's down the bookies. Convinced he's onto a winner.' She laughed as she walked Dermot to the door.

On the drive back to the city, he felt curious to know what

Aileen's da had discovered about his son. He hoped it was good news; he was eager that Aileen should be reconciled with her twin as soon as possible.

His plan to take Aileen to see *The Sound of Music* at the Carlton had fallen flat, and he was keen to have time alone with her. He had something to ask her, and if he didn't do it soon, he might just lose his nerve. He picked up a few slices of cooked ham and a white, sliced pan loaf, along with a slab of fruit cake. He planned on making her tea. *How hard can it be?* he thought, as he began to prepare the sandwiches. He cut them dainty, the way his mam did when she had someone special coming to tea.

They were not as good as his mother's, but they looked all right, so he covered them and put them on the kitchen top for later. Then he switched the wireless on to listen to the match and closed his eyes.

\* \* \*

He woke with a start and couldn't believe it was two-thirty already. He freshened up, grabbed his coat and scarf, checked his wallet and keys, and hurried from the shop. He ran all the way, weaving through the crowds of Saturday shoppers and mothers with pushchairs and crying babies, to arrive with seconds to spare. There was no sign of Aileen.

He drew out a long breath, glad she hadn't arrived before him; she might think he didn't care enough to be on time. He sat facing the entrance to the tearoom so that he could watch her arrive—desperate to see her elegant walk in high heels, her bag swinging from her shoulder, and her lovely hair falling across her face. He ordered tea while he waited.

It was only when the waitress asked if there was anything else she could get him that he realised how long he had sat there. It was four-thirty, and the evening was closing in.

He gave up and left the department store. Things had obviously taken longer than expected, but he didn't want to go back home alone. Two of the day's plans had fallen flat, but there was still the evening. He decided to catch a bus across town to the sweet shop. When he arrived, it was all in darkness. They obviously weren't back yet.

Disappointed, he decided to walk home and wait for her to phone him. What if she got back too late? With all his plans ruined, he stopped at the first cinema he came to and went inside.

# Chapter Fifty-One

Aileen and her da stood by the river wall overlooking the Griffeen, in the small town of Lucan. The car was parked close by, alongside a row of elm trees. People were going in and out of shops on Main Street, and three lads sitting on the wall opposite the local pub whistled at Aileen. They were harmless, but she wasn't in the mood for their teenage banter. Her da appeared not to have heard them. He wasn't listening to anything she was saying either; he just stared into the fast flowing river.

The cold began to penetrate her coat, and a blustery wind swept through the bare branches and swirled around her feet. Shivering, she dug her hands deep inside her pockets. 'Come on, Da?' she repeated.

Finally, he straightened his shoulders and turned towards her. 'We shouldn't have come. This whole business was a mistake.'

'Of course we should have come. We're family.'

'He doesn't know us from Adam, Aileen. So, if we do as you suggest, we will be putting him at a disadvantage.' He sighed. 'Don't you see? I doubt he'd want to see us in his vulnerable state.'

In her eagerness, she hadn't thought of that.

'Please, Da. We should try.'

He walked towards the car and Aileen hurried alongside him, past the local lads who appeared to be waiting for the public house to open.

'How will you feel when we're turned away? Aye, tell me that.' He unlocked the car, and they got inside. Aileen rubbed her hands to try and get some warmth back into them. She had thought her da was going to stand by the wall all afternoon; he could be difficult when he was worried. She was just as anxious and somehow she had to convince him that going to the hospital was the right thing to do, even if they were turned away.

He started the engine, and she placed her hand on his arm. 'We can't give up now. At least, let's find out how he is?'

Her da sighed and pressed his back against the seat. 'And you think they're going to tell complete strangers that, do you?'

'You're his da, and I'm his twin sister; who else has he got?' She couldn't help the anger creeping into her voice.

'We've no proof, and I can't bear the thought of being turned away. I'd much rather we met him on his terms. Can you understand?'

She nodded. 'In the meantime, what if something happens to him?' She didn't want to give up and was getting frustrated with her da. Yet, she didn't want to fall out with him. 'Look, Da. Let's have something hot to drink at the tearoom. You're cold and…'

He nodded, and before she had time to finish, he stepped from the car. It was a busy little town and the tearoom was almost full. When they were seated with a strong cup of tea inside them, she hoped he would reconsider what she thought was a negative view, and take her to visit her brother.

When Tom hadn't been in touch, her da had suggested that they visit his place of work. They had arrived at the Royal Bank of Ireland earlier, but found it closed. Out of curiosity, they walked down the entrance to the flat and got no reply. A neighbour looked out from next door. 'If you're looking for Mr Miller, he's not in.'

'Miller.' Her father's brow wrinkled. 'Do you know when he'll be back?'

'That's anyone's guess. They took him away last night by ambulance.'

'Do you know what happened?' Aileen bit her lip. 'Is he ill?'

The neighbour shrugged. 'That's all I know.' She shook her head. 'Although, he didn't look all that grand when they carried him out.' Aileen's heart lurched.

'Where have they taken him?' her da asked.

'I'm not sure. It might be Steeven's.'

Aileen glanced at her da then, asked the woman, 'Do you know where that is?'

The woman shrugged. 'I'm not sure I should say.' She came out to the entrance, her arms folded across her chest. 'Who shall I say called?'

Aileen's da cleared his throat and turned to go.

'Oh, please yourselves.'

'Thank you,' Aileen called over her shoulder.

'Nosey neighbours, I can't abide them.' Her father walked across the street to the wall that overlooked the river and Aileen followed. His shoulders hunched, he leaned his arms across the wall, staring down at the fast flowing stream, looking at nothing in particular. Discovering that Tom was ill and in hospital had been a shock to them both. He may well have suffered ill health from his time at the orphanage. They knew nothing of what he may have gone through. All the more reason, to take this opportunity to find out.

* * *

They had almost finished the tea and cake before her da spoke. 'He hasn't kept the family name, Aileen.'

'Well, sure, he doesn't know who he is, does he?'

'Course, he bloody does!' he yelled.

'Da!' Aileen glanced around, embarrassed.

'I'm sorry.' He ran his fingertips along his forehead. 'He knows who his mother was. Didn't Miss Finch tell us so?'

'He was only a child then. We don't know anything about his life really.' Aileen leant across the small circular table and touched his arm. 'Please, Da.' She sighed. 'Let me find out where this Steeven's Hospital is. It sounds familiar.'

She left a shilling tip on the table and joined the queue at the counter. When her turn came, the portly woman serving the tea smiled. 'Another tea, love?'

'Actually, I wondered, can you tell me where to find Steeven's Hospital?'

'Do you mean, Dr Steeven's?'

Aileen shrugged. 'I guess so.'

'Well sure, that's away in Dublin, about seven or eight miles from here.'

Of course, now she remembered. 'Thank you.' She smiled towards the woman.

Her father joined her. 'If it's Dr Steeven's, I know where that is, Aileen. It just didn't register when the woman mentioned Steeven's.'

'Of course, it's that big building next to Euston Station.'

He nodded.

'Come on, Da. We can be back in Dublin in half an hour. We have every right to know how he is; we're not giving up that easy.'

The drive back to Dublin took longer, as they hit the teatime traffic. Aileen's da spoke little and only briefly answered her when she spoke.

'You do want to visit him, don't you, Da?'

He took a while to answer. 'I need more time to think this over, Aileen.' He turned right from Parkgate Street, and Aileen could see the hospital. But her da drove past and along the quay towards the city.

Aileen was furious but kept quiet. Her da was struggling with this and putting off the inevitable, and she had no choice but to go along with him. When he pulled up outside the shop, she turned towards him, unable to hold back her disappointment.

'Why didn't you want to go and see him, Da?'

He rubbed his hands over his face. 'You've always been headstrong, Aileen. Believe me, I'm right about this. We can't go barging in there without giving the poor lad some warning.' He sighed. 'I think we should give him time to recover and let him get in touch.'

'But, Da!'

'Will you stop going on?' He turned and stepped from the car, but Aileen couldn't help her feelings of disappointment. It started to rain as they went indoors.

'We don't know how ill he is, Da. It might be serious.'

He unbuttoned his coat and hung it up in the corridor before

263

turning back to her. Tears pooled her eyes.

'Look,' he said, more gently. 'If it will keep you from fretting, I'll give the hospital a ring. Pass me the Dublin directory.'

He went behind the shop counter and dialled the number. He took a deep breath and straightened his shoulders before speaking. 'I'm making enquiries about a patient, Mr Miller.'

He glanced down at Aileen perched on the shop stool, her eyes round in anticipation. 'I believe he was brought in some time last night. Can you tell me how he is?' He shook his head. 'No. I'm not a relative. I'm his father. Although… What I mean is. I've never met my son.' He tapped his fingers on the counter. 'No, not Miller, my name is Maguire.'

He nodded towards Aileen and placed his hand over the receiver. 'This is rather awkward.'

'What have they said?'

'Nothing yet.' He shook his head. 'They've put me on hold.'

Aileen felt the tension in her back watching her da. His face creased into a frown. 'Hospital policy! Never mind all that. Can't you make an exception? I want to know how…'

When her da let out a loud sigh, Aileen's stomach tightened. 'Can't you at least tell me what ails my son and if he's in any danger?' There was a slight pause. 'Comfortable! What does that mean?'

Seconds later, he replaced the receiver, lifted the hinged counter, and stepped out into the shop. Aileen got up and followed. 'What did they say, Da?'

He walked back into the sitting room and sat down. 'He's comfortable. They'll tell me nothing.'

'Comfortable is better than not knowing, Da,' she said reassuringly. 'He must be improving.'

Her da closed his eyes and rested his head against the back of the armchair. He looked tired. 'We still don't know what ails him.'

'I'll get you something to eat, Da.'

'No.' He waved his arm. 'I'm not hungry. You get off.' He glanced at his watch. 'I know you're anxious to see Dermot.'

# Chapter Fifty-Two

Despite not knowing what was wrong with her brother, Aileen was satisfied to know that he was comfortable; she hoped that meant he was out of danger. She felt bad about letting Dermot down and decided to go across and see him.

'Da, can I phone Dermot? I'd like to speak to him before I go over there.'

He nodded and closed his eyes again. Aileen kissed his forehead and went through to the shop. It rang out ten times before she put the phone down then checked the number again to make sure. His mother rarely went out of an evening, so why was no-one answering the phone? She looked at her watch. It was six-thirty and the shops were closed, so where was Dermot?

She made tea and placed a cup down next to her sleeping da, then took hers upstairs. The rain beat against the sash window, and she glanced up at the darkened sky before drawing the curtains. She could still smell the newness of the material. The green and white vertical stripes gave the window an elongated look. She appreciated the efforts her da had gone to on her behalf, and she was happy to be home. She decided to try phoning Dermot again later.

She slipped off her shoes and lay down on the bed thinking of her brother and praying that his illness wasn't serious. She wondered what he was like, tried to imagine his hair. Was it fair like her own? What kind of hobbies did he have? So many questions yet to be answered, and she was longing to meet him. She had heard that twins are often identical. She was five feet two inches in her stocking feet. Was Tom taller, like her da?

As much as she would have loved to see him today, she conceded that her da was probably right. Although, it wasn't easy, she would have to be patient.

She could hear the rain running down the pipe into the gully. There was no point in her going all the way to Dorset Street if Dermot wasn't in.

Downstairs, she found her da in the small scullery frying bacon, and the smell revived her appetite. 'I thought you'd gone to see Dermot?'

'He wasn't in when I phoned, Da. I can't figure out where he could be.'

'Happen he's gone to the pub with his dad.' Dermot rarely, if ever, went to the pub except on special occasions. 'Here you have this. I'll put more on.' He passed her his plate of bacon and egg. 'Do you still like brown sauce?'

She nodded. She was hungry now and enjoyed the meal with bread and butter and a mug of hot tea. When they had finished eating, Aileen said, 'How long do you intend to wait, Da... you know, before...'

'Just give it a few more weeks. I'm as anxious as you are to see him. We've waited all this time so, what's another two weeks? He may, if we're patient enough, get in touch with us before then.' He smiled. 'Look it's nearly eight o'clock. There's a play I want to listen to on the wireless.' He lifted his plate and stood up. 'Why not give Dermot another call? He might be home now.'

'Thanks, Da.' She kissed his cheek.

There was still no reply, and Aileen didn't know what to think. Had he gone back to Wales with his parents? Surely he would have left her a note. Sighing, she switched on the immersion and took a long soak in the bath. She so wanted to talk to him about Roy Pickering, but at the same time, she felt reluctant with each day that passed. Morally, she felt obliged to tell him, especially since she knew she loved him and wanted to marry him one day. Otherwise, it would hang over her for the foreseeable future.

She sighed. It was at times like this that she hated having a conscience. She needed to tell someone and thought of spilling it all out to her da, then changed her mind. Finding her brother was enough for him to cope with at the moment.

After her bath, she felt more relaxed and took out the clothes she would wear the following day. She unwrapped a new pair of American tan tights, and slipped her white lacy blouse and silky underskirt from the hanger and laid them across the chair before getting into bed. She felt tired, but her mind gave her no peace and she slept badly.

\* \* \*

In spite of the early hour, the morning was reasonably bright for February. She couldn't eat and scribbled a quick note to her da saying where she had gone. The Sunday buses were slow and she was anxious to get to Dermot's, to find out why he hadn't answered the phone.

On impulse, she hailed down an out-of-service bus heading towards the city, forcing him to stop. She made up an urgent excuse and the driver looked sympathetic. 'Oh, go on then, but don't go telling anyone or making a habit of this, young lady.'

'I won't.' She smiled and stepped on board.

The city had not yet come to life when the driver dropped her off in O'Connell Street. How strangely quiet everywhere was. Seagulls squawked overhead, their cry mingling with the chiming church bells that rang out over the city. It made her all the more aware that she had not been to church for some time.

It began to drizzle, which was no surprise. Ireland was capable of all four seasons in one day. She hated getting wet and hurried along towards Parnell Street, passing no-one apart from a woman in a heavy tweed coat and a headscarf, her chin buried into her chest. When she turned into Dorset Street, a cloud of sadness enveloped her. She hadn't walked down here since she had left for England, and it conjured up all kinds of emotions. But she had to see what had become of the haberdashery, her old home.

She paused to shelter in the doorway. The window that had once sported a treadle sewing machine, curtain material, silk ribbons, reels of cotton and boxes of buttons, had disappeared. In their place, hoovers, electric kettles, irons, and other electrical

267

items stood supreme. A lump formed in her throat. She glanced up at the warm yellow light coming from the upstairs windows and felt a stab of pain.

Choking back her feelings, she pulled up her collar and hurried towards the butcher's shop, hoping Dermot would be there. The rain increased, and she arrived feeling like a bedraggled cat.

She hurried down the side entrance and rang the bell, but there was no sign of life. Shivering in her wet clothes, she rang the bell again, this time with more determination. The door opened, and Dermot stood before her in stripey blue and white pyjamas, his navy dressing gown hanging open. She had to suppress the urge to giggle.

'Aileen!' After a moment of shock, he ushered her inside. 'Don't tell me you're still in bed?'

'It's only eight o'clock on a Sunday morning!' She saw colour flood his face. 'What… what are you doing here? Is there anything wrong?'

'I was worried when I couldn't get you on the phone.'

He stood looking at her, her hair dripping onto her coat. 'Sorry. Come on through.' He rushed to get her a towel.

She lowered her head and wrapped it turban-style around her wet hair then glanced up. 'Where's your mam and dad?'

'They're in Wales.' He bent and put a match to the kindling in the grate and placed a few pieces of coal on top. 'Look, you get out of those wet things.' He removed his dressing gown. 'Put this on, I'll make you a hot drink.'

She removed her coat and hung it over a chair. The rain had penetrated through to her thin blouse and skirt, so she removed them self-consciously along with her tights, underneath the dressing gown. It hung like a tent around her slim body. She drew it round her, and she could smell the scent of him, feel the warmth of him radiate through her. Dermot was still in the scullery, and she knew he would be giving her time before coming back in with the drinks.

When he returned, he placed the tray on the table and passed her the hot drink. As she reached for it, the dressing gown gaped open, revealing her lacy underskirt outlining the curves of her full breasts and slim waist. He diverted his eyes, and she felt a hot flush to her face. She couldn't do anything right these days.

'I'll just go and get dressed.' She watched him hurry upstairs, then sat down on the sofa to drink her tea. She should get dressed, but her clothes were still damp.

Dermot came back wearing casual jeans and a white polo shirt. 'Are you feeling warmer now?' He sat next to her.

She nodded. 'Dermot, I'm sorry things didn't work out yesterday for us, I mean…but…'

'Sure, it's okay, Aileen. When you didn't turn up, I went to the cinema. Just for something to do.'

'What? On your own?' She laughed out loud and her hair fell loose. She pulled the towel free, placing it across her lap.

'I know. Pathetic, isn't it? I couldn't face coming back to an empty house.'

'What was on? Was it any good?'

'You wouldn't have liked it. It was a war film. *633 Squadron.* I slept through most of it and ended up watching it twice, so got back late.' He looked contrite. 'I'd made plans for us and they all backfired.' He had a lost look on his face, and she reached over and kissed him.

He drew her to him and kissed her lips, but she felt nervous being this close to him when she was only half dressed. 'Dermot, I should go.' She picked up her tights.

'Don't go.' He reached out to her. 'That was so nice, and you are so lovely. I've wanted to kiss you from the moment you turned up at my door.'

She trembled beneath his touch. Dear Lord, she wanted him so much, and she found it difficult to resist him. Suddenly they were in each other's arms, kissing hungrily. His kisses aroused her. The dressing gown fell from her shoulders. His strong arms went around her and his warm hands slid up and down her bare arms, over her back, caressing the contours of her body. New and exciting feelings she had never experienced before coursed through her.

Breathless, she pulled back, frightened of where it would lead. They weren't even engaged! As much as she wanted to, she couldn't let this go any further.

'I'm sorry,' he said. 'I'm finding it very testing being this close to you.'

She wanted her first time to be special without guilt or secrets between them, and she knew she would have to tell him about Roy Pickering, sooner rather than later. She pulled the dressing gown around her.

'I don't feel that this is the right time for me to be reckless. So much is going on in my head.' She touched his hand. 'I do love you.'

'I love you, too, and I'd never do anything you're not completely happy with.'

She stood up, holding out her hands to the hot flames. Steam rose from her wet coat hanging nearby. There was a long pause, and she could feel his eyes on her.

'You're the only woman that's ever set my heart racing.'

When she turned round, she felt a hot flush across her cheekbones. He stood up and held both her hands. 'Tell me what's going on. I might be able to help. Is it your brother? You haven't told me how you got on?' The fire crackled and flames shot up the chimney. 'Did you get to see, or speak to him?' He drew her down beside him.

Tears welled in her eyes. 'No. We haven't seen him yet. He's in hospital, Dermot.' When she had finished bringing him up-to-date, her long lashes were wet with tears.

'Oh, Aileen.' He drew her close and caressed her damp hair. 'I'm sorry things didn't work out yesterday.' He looked into her eyes. 'Your da is right. You'll have to be patient a little longer.'

She sniffled and nodded. 'I know.' She stood up and gathered up her clothes. 'Can I?' She glanced towards the stairs.

'At the end of the landing,' he said. 'When you're dressed, we can talk some more.'

# Chapter Fifty-Three

The smell of cooked rashers met her on the stairs as she came back down.

'Come and sit down.' Dermot pulled out a chair. 'You must be hungry; I know I am.' He placed the food on the table and sat opposite her.

She smiled. 'I could get used to this.' The egg, rashers, sausage, and black and white pudding were cooked just right, with none of the black bits that accompanied her father's fry-up. 'I never knew you could cook, Dermot.'

'Ah, well, there's more to me than meets the eye.' He winked. 'Eat up before it goes cold.'

She didn't need telling twice. He'd also buttered a plate of wholemeal bread, and for a short time, they ate in silence. 'I doubt I could do better myself,' she said, leaning back in the chair. 'That was delicious.'

'The pleasure was mine.' He placed his hands under his chin and looked at her.

She gave him a quizzical look. 'What?'

'I was just thinking how nice it is having you here all to myself.'

She nodded and smiled. 'Like a married couple.'

'Now there's a thing!'

This was her opportunity to tell him what happened in Birmingham. He reached for her hand and her courage left her. 'I'll help you wash up.' She stood up, and together they cleared the table, piling the plates into the soapy water.

'Come and sit over here by the fire.' He patted the sofa. 'As we have the place to ourselves, I wondered how you felt about, I mean, about us getting engaged on your nineteenth birthday next month?' He placed his arm around her. 'Do you love me enough to become my wife in a year or so from now?'

She placed her finger across his lips. She wanted nothing more than to hear him say he wanted to marry her. 'I love you more than enough, and I'd be happy to marry you.' He was all she needed right now, and ever would need.

He kissed her, then pulled her to her feet. 'Let's go out and celebrate. You've made me a very happy man.'

\* \* \*

Back at the sweet shop, Aileen noticed how neglected their home had become from lack of a woman's touch, so she took over the household chores as well as the cooking. She also helped out in the shop. It felt a bit like child's play serving up sweets, and she missed the stimulus that the haberdashery had provided. But her da was content, and so was she. There was still no contact from her brother, and she was tempted to call at the hospital.

Although she and Dermot never had another opportunity to be alone, they spent their weekends visiting various jeweller's shops hunting for an engagement ring, finally settling on a sparkling solitaire that was a perfect fit. Aileen didn't want to remove the diamond from her finger, but Dermot reassured her he would keep it safe until her birthday.

There was never a right moment for her to offload her guilty secret to him. Her Aunt Bead hadn't mentioned Roy Pickering, and she was pleased that Mary had been discreet and said nothing. Yet each time she looked into Dermot's honest eyes, she knew she couldn't live with the secret.

Her birthday party was due to take place at Bead's house, where they planned to announce their engagement. It fell on the 18th March but, as always, it was brought forward a day to include St Patrick's Day, a national holiday.

\* \* \*

On the 17th of March, the morning was crisp and bright when Aileen waited for Dermot at the Parnell Monument; it was already surrounded with people, many of them tourists. O'Connell Street resembled a forest of green, but she spotted him pushing his way towards her.

'Sorry I'm late, Aileen. This holiday gets busier each year.'

'Don't worry,' she smiled. 'I was early.'

He had a sprig of shamrock pinned to the lapel of his coat, and his green and white football scarf around his neck. Everyone wore something green, and old habits were hard to drop. Aileen wrapped her own green scarf tighter around her neck. Dermot moved close and placed his arm around her, and they watched bemused as hundreds of excited spectators lined the pavement on both sides of the street, waving flags and banners. She had long since lost the allure for the St. Patrick's Day parade, but the majority of Irish loved it, as did visitors from around the world. From her experience, it always ended in drunken brawls around the city.

Dermot glanced down at her. 'There's another hour before the parade starts. What do you say? Shall we make our way towards Stephen's Green, and find a pub?'

A smile lit her face. She had been thinking the same thing but didn't like to say, as she was unsure how Dermot felt about the parade. They pushed through the throng and almost had to bribe a line of guards—arms linked to keep the crowd from spilling out onto the parade route—to allow them to cross the street. It was organised chaos.

Excessive noise rose into the air, and young men and women sat on top of what remained of Nelson's Pillar while other observers looked down from Clery's rooftop. They passed a platform decorated in green, white and orange, erected outside the General Post Office in readiness for the Taoiseach and other dignitaries; the area was heavily guarded. Smiling happy faces sang Irish songs, and a large white Stetson rose above the crowd.

'The Americans are here,' Aileen said with a laugh.

'St. Patrick's Day wouldn't be the same without some Yanks to join in the celebrations.' Dermot smiled and squeezed her hand as the sound of cheering crowds echoed around them.

'Perhaps we should have stayed put.' She clung to Dermot's arm. 'We'll never get across O'Connell Bridge. Look at it!'

'You wanna bet?' he said, and forged ahead.

\* \* \*

Later they joined some young people for a drink to celebrate their patron saint credited with bringing Christianity to Ireland. The men were drinking green beer, and Dermot couldn't resist ordering a glass. 'You'll have to taste it, Aileen.'

'How do they get it that colour?' she wanted to know.

Dermot laughed. 'Ah sure, it's only food colouring.' The bartender plonked the drink down on the counter and green froth oozed over the top of the glass. Dermot took a swig and wiped his lips with the back of his hand. 'It's not bad. Here, have a taste?' He put the glass to her lips.

She took a sip and wrinkled her nose. 'Yuk! This is not real Guinness.' The thick substance left her with green lips, and Dermot howled with laughter.

She nudged him. 'You did that on purpose.'

'I couldn't resist.' He kissed her cheek. The pub was heaving with noisy revellers, and it wasn't easy to find a seat, but eventually a couple of older women stood up to go.

'Those two old dears leaving when they did was a stroke of luck,' Dermot said, sliding in next to her. Aileen nodded and removed her coat, placing it across her knee. 'Well, are you all set for your birthday party tonight?'

'Yes, it'll be fun.'

'How do you think your da will take the news of our engagement?'

'I don't think he'll be surprised. What about yours?'

'Sure, it's a foregone conclusion as far as they're concerned. They will be thrilled I'm marrying a beautiful, well brought up, Irish Coleen.' He stood up. 'I won't be long. This time, I'll get you a proper drink.' Laughing, he disappeared into the crowd.

Aileen felt her heartbeat quicken. She didn't feel respectable anymore. Should she tell Dermot before they got engaged, or wait until afterwards? Somehow, that wouldn't seem right. Finally, he came back with a bottle of Cherry Bee, a Babycham, and a proper pint for himself. 'Wasn't sure which you preferred.'

She raised her eyebrows. 'Celebrating already, are we?'

'I wish it was real champagne. I was lucky to get a glass at all. It's bedlam at the bar.' Aileen poured her drink, and Dermot clinked his glass against hers. 'Here's to us, my beautiful fiancée.'

'Don't tempt fate. You've not put the ring on my finger yet!' She pushed her shoulder against his, making him laugh.

Sipping her drink, she sat back. In spite of the mayhem going on around them, she felt relaxed with Dermot, and she was sure that he felt the same. She noticed the way he looked at her, the love shining in his eyes, and she felt a stab of guilt.

He reached for her hand, and uncontrolled tears welled in her eyes. He gave her a quizzical look. 'What's wrong?'

They were surrounded by people. Voices grew louder and so did the music, drowning any conversation they might have had. She smiled and whispered in his ear that everything was grand.

'You're upset. What is it?'

Her decision to tell Dermot everything had now been foisted upon her, and she knew what she had to do. But it was impossible to speak inside the pub.

She leant in close. 'Would you mind if we went somewhere less noisy? There's something I have to tell you.'

# Chapter Fifty-Four

Aileen and Dermot sat on a bench in the park, facing the duck pond. It was cold, yet that was the last thing on her mind. She couldn't imagine what must be going through Dermot's head. He moved close and placed his arm around her shoulder.

'Is this about your brother, Aileen? Is he... has something happened?'

She took an intake of breath. 'This has nothing to do with Tom, Dermot.' She looked down. 'It's difficult, I've been wanting to say something for weeks.' She sniffed. 'I've done something I'm not very proud of and I...' She paused.

'It can't be that bad, Aileen?' He frowned. 'Is it?'

'I went out with someone, for a meal, but it didn't mean anything. We were just friends.' She paused again when she saw the confused look on his face.

'What! What are you saying? You mean when you were away?' His arm fell away from her shoulder. 'You've been out with another man, is that what you're saying?' He looked aghast.

Children ran past, bread for the ducks dangling from their small hands.

'Dermot, don't look at me like that.'

'You've met someone else? Is that what you're trying to say?'

She swallowed. 'No, no, of course not.' She glanced down to hide her tears. 'Please, let me explain?'

He shook his head. 'I knew there was something. When you came home at Christmas, you were distant. We hardly spent any time together. Is that... is that why you went back, to be with him?'

'Oh, no, no. Not at all.' She looked away from his shocked expression. His eyes sought answers, yet he wasn't prepared to listen to her.

'As I recall, you couldn't wait to get back.'

She glanced up. 'That's not true. You need to hear me out, Dermot, please.' But she could see he wasn't listening. He had gone somewhere else in his head.

He leant forward and cupped his face in his hand, then abruptly got to his feet.

'I'll walk you back to the city. I need time to think.'

She remained sitting. 'Please, Dermot. I need to tell you more.' He threw her a furious glare. She'd never seen him like this; she felt tremulous. 'Let me explain.'

'Like I want to hear it.'

Aileen stared at him, then got up and walked alongside him in silence.

The celebrations were in full swing—marching bands and happy people decked in green while children sat high on shoulders squealing with delight as the last of the floats passed by.

Aileen couldn't raise a smile in any direction, regretting every word that had brought them to this. A trust had been broken and she had no idea how to repair it. He walked with her as far as the shop, his expression one of contempt. Then, without a word, he turned round and stormed off, his hands deep in his pockets, leaving her bereft.

Aileen rushed upstairs to vent her frustration out on her pillow. Her da was outside tidying the yard. They were due at her aunt and uncle's house at six, and she was only grateful that she hadn't mentioned her engagement to anyone. Dermot had wanted to keep it a secret until the party. Now she had no inclination to go at all.

She had bought a new green and white check dress from Dunnes Stores for the occasion, but the incentive to have a bath and get ready had left her. She had always thought she could talk to Dermot about anything, but she hadn't expected him to react the way he had. Now she wished she'd said nothing.

A solitary feeling gripped her. What if she lost him? She had come back to Dublin for her father's sake, but Dermot had been a huge part of her plans, too. How could she make him understand that her life had little meaning without him? A birthday party was the last thing on her mind. What excuse would she give to the family if he didn't turn up? And if he did, she would have to pretend for the whole evening that everything was all right between them.

When she heard her da come out of the bathroom, she knew she had little choice but to get up and make herself look presentable. After a bath, she felt better and decided that she had no choice but to face the consequences. She got dressed and piled her newly-washed hair on top of her head, sprayed it with lacquer, and placed a diamanté hair clip in the side. She painted her nails and applied the same red to her full lips.

Her da looked good in a new charcoal suit. 'You look lovely,' he said. 'Your mother would have…' He paused. 'Well, we'd better be going. We don't want to keep people waiting.'

She forced an involuntary smile and joined in light conversation with her da on the way, but her thoughts were with Dermot.

* * *

They arrived to the usual warm welcome from Bead and Paddy, who ushered them inside and took their coats. The front room was warm and cosy, and Aileen suppressed a sob when she saw all the baking her aunt had done. The table was groaning with delicious food. Bead had made neatly-cut sandwiches, apple pies, small cakes, and pastries. It looked perfect, with a birthday cake with cream icing sugar in the centre of a table.

'It looks lovely, Aunt Bead. Thank you. But you shouldn't have gone to such trouble.'

'For our favourite girl.' Paddy hugged and kissed the top of her head. 'We're so pleased to have you home, Aileen. We haven't half missed you.'

'Help yourselves to drinks,' Bead said. 'I've got in extra bottles of stout as it's St Patrick's Day and all.' Paddy put a record on the radiogram and Bead slapped his wrist. 'Oh, Paddy, what are you like? Aileen won't want to listen to classical music on her birthday. Here, put this on. I got it especially for the party.' She smiled. 'It's the new single by Nancy Sinatra, *These Boots are Made for Walking*. You can take it home with you.'

Aileen smiled her thanks, but inside she felt sick, wishing for Dermot to come through the door with that lovely smile of his and let her know that everything between them was all right.

'Where's Dermot?' her da said, glancing towards the door.

'He'll be here soon.' She looked at Bead, who was still putting out food. 'Thanks for doing all this. It must have taken you ages.'

Bead beamed her a smile and then pointed towards the kitchen. 'I've got chicken pieces in the oven.'

There were a few awkward moments where she struggled to remain positive, when after what seemed an age, the doorbell rang. Her heart did a somersault. She swallowed and quickly checked her make-up in the mirror over the fireplace. 'I'll get that.' She hurried to the door and admitted Mr and Mrs Brogan. Dermot hung back, and Aileen wondered if he was going to refuse to come in.

'I'll just check I've locked the car.' She waited for him to return while Bead welcomed the guests. He walked slowly, hesitating on the doorstep.

'Come in, Dermot, please.' She touched his hand, but he didn't respond; he didn't speak. Aileen felt as if a knife had pierced her heart. Dermot walked past her into the room and apologized for coming late.

The evening was torture, and at times, she wanted to make an excuse to leave. Most of the time, he sat in a corner of the room, his face in shadow. It wasn't until towards the end of the evening that an opportunity arose for them to be alone. Dermot nudged her and, making her excuses, she followed him out to the hall. Her head ached with tension, and she was glad to leave the room.

She sat on the stairs next to him. She felt fearful, her nerves shattered, her hands folded in her lap. She longed for his touch, but he made no attempt to sit close to her and kept his eyes downcast.

'Dermot, please speak to me. Say something?'

'I came out here to save the embarrassment of pretence between us.' He lifted his gaze. 'Under the circumstances, I can't put an engagement ring on your finger, in spite of how I feel and as beautiful as you look.' His eyes misted, and Aileen felt a sob choke the back of her throat.

She moved in close. 'But we can still be civil, can't we?'

Someone passed through to the kitchen, and Dermot stood up. She thought he was going to leave, and her heart raced. He shuffled his feet. 'It's cut me up something awful to think of you seeing another man.'

'But, I'm not. I wasn't. Not in that way, Dermot.'

He put his hand up for her to stop. 'I don't know if I can forgive you.'

She stared at him, a host of thoughts flashing through her mind. She got to her feet and placed her hand on her forehead. 'I don't need your forgiveness, Dermot, because I've done nothing wrong.'

He glared at her. 'I can't do this, Aileen.'

'Me neither, and I can't go back in there now.' She swallowed. 'Can you at least drive me home? They'll understand, and think we've gone off somewhere to be alone.' Her heart heavy with disappointment, she choked back tears. 'When you come back for your parents, you can say I had a headache?'

# Chapter Fifty-Five

The following morning, Aileen couldn't raise enough interest to get out of bed. The world was a different place without Dermot. His reaction yesterday had shocked her, leaving her with feelings of shame and regret. How was she going to face today, of all days; her birthday? Her da was bound to notice something was wrong if she didn't put in an appearance. After last night's charade, she felt mortified.

She pulled the bedspread over her head when she heard a tap on her bedroom door, and her da walked in, a smile on his face as he carried a breakfast tray. 'I thought as you weren't up yet I'd surprise you for your birthday.' He placed the tray down on the bedside table.

'Oh, Da.' She swallowed. 'You didn't have to do that.' It was so nice of him, and brought a smile to her face.

He sat down on the bed. 'This is from me.'

She sat up, propped her pillow behind her head and unwrapped the small gift. Her eyes brightened. 'They're beautiful, Da.'

'They belonged to your mother. She would have wanted you to have them.'

Aileen clipped on the pearl earrings set in the centre of a cluster of tiny diamantes. Then she leant across him. 'I'll treasure them.'

He sniffed. 'Well, I'm glad I kept them safe for you.' He stood up. 'Bead asked me to give you this. She said you can change it if you don't like it.' He passed the wrapped package. 'She also hopes you're feeling better.'

281

Aileen sighed. 'I'm sorry if I let people down, Da, but…'

'Oh, that's all right. They understood. Dermot's mam grumbled a bit when Dermot wasn't there, but once he returned she was full of sympathy for you. Said she suffered with bad heads when she was younger and had to lie down in a darkened room.' He chuckled. 'Me, I ate too much cake.'

'Thanks, Da.'

'I'll see you downstairs.'

When he had left, she felt overwhelmed by his understanding. In an attempt to cheer herself up, she switched on her transistor to the Beatles singing their latest hit, *We Can Work It Out.* The words seemed poignant in her present dilemma; if only she could make Dermot understand.

The song gave her a new determination. She straightened her shoulders, trying to regain some semblance of control, then finished her tea and toast and got dressed. She pulled the blue angora jumper over her head—the present from Aunt Bead. It matched her new cream skirt she had bought the previous week. As she went downstairs, she wondered if her twin was doing anything special today.

She placed the dishes into the sink and began to wash them.

'Leave that, love. Why don't you get off, go somewhere nice with Dermot? Weather-wise, it's not a bad day for a drive along the coast.' She gave him a weak smile but carried on drying the dishes and putting them away. 'You've no need to worry about me.'

'It's not that, Da.' She pulled out a chair and sat down.

He arched his eyebrows. 'Aileen, it's your birthday, and somehow I get the feeling that something's bothering you. Am I right?'

By opening up to her da, she risked being alienated from his affections, but she had to tell someone. She sighed, wishing that she had some good news to impart. 'Da, can I talk to you about something delicate?'

'Good Lord! You're not?'

'No, Da. It's nothing like that.' She couldn't imagine feeling any worse if it was. With a heavy heart, she moved across the room and sat down next to him on the sofa.

'Well, what is it? Whatever it is, you'd better spit it out.'

\* \* \*

Half an hour later, Aileen sat fidgeting with the rib of her jumper. She glanced across at her da, his expression strained, his brow furrowed. Her story had stunned him into silence, and it filled her with dread. What if he, too, turned away from her?

'Oh, Da.' She stood up. 'Please don't hate me.' A sob caught the back of her throat.

He held out his hand, and she sat down again. 'Hate you? Don't be silly. You have to admit you were naive in the way you thought about this man.' He shifted, and then he placed his arm around her. In that solitary moment, she felt her shoulders relax. 'I've no right to judge you,' he continued. 'Sure, we all react differently to grief and loneliness. You could have killed yourself in that car, and God only knows what that lunatic was capable of.'

He removed his arm and cleared his throat. Linking his fingers, he twirled one thumb over the other.

'I really love Dermot, Da. Now he hates me.' She sobbed. 'We were supposed to be getting engaged last night.'

He nodded. 'Well, to be honest, I thought he looked uncomfortable last night. Dermot's behaviour is understandable. Look how I reacted when your mother, Lord rest her soul, told me a secret she'd kept for years. Sure, I didn't know the whole story then, did I?'

'Oh, Da. what am I going to do?'

He stood up, walked to the window, and glanced out at the cloudy sky; something he did a lot when he was thinking. He turned back into the room. 'Dermot doesn't know the whole story either. He's a man, as stubborn as I was. If it hadn't been for me, you wouldn't have gone away in the first place. I can't bear to think of how lonely you must have been over there. I'm so sorry, love.'

'Don't blame yourself, Da. It wasn't you who drove me away.' She hooked her hair behind one ear. 'I've grown up a lot in the past few months.'

He sat down again. 'You're lucky you didn't end up with a criminal record. Thank the Lord the blighter dropped the charges before he…'

'I still can't believe he did that, Da.'

'The mind is a complicated machine, Aileen. I've found that out by talking things through with the doctor. It's a mistake to bottle things up.'

Aileen reached out, linked her arm through his, and nodded. 'I only hope that Dermot will come to realise I've not been unfaithful.'

'I can have a word. Make things right between the two of you before this gets out of hand.'

'No, Da.' She sat upright. 'You've helped me by understanding what I've been going through. I just couldn't keep it to myself any longer.'

'What about Dermot?'

'If he loves me like he says he does, he'll give me the benefit of the doubt.'

Her da shook his head. 'I don't agree, love. If he's as stubborn as me, you might wait a long time.'

\* \* \*

Aileen was in the kitchen making a drink and her da was reading his newspaper when Fiona came through from the shop and tapped lightly on the open door. 'I thought you'd like your post, Mr Maguire.'

He turned and looked over his shoulder. 'Thanks, Fiona. How's it going out there?'

'Busy enough. The liquorice allsorts are running low.'

'Make a note of it and I'll be out to relieve you shortly.' He picked up the post as Aileen walked in balancing a tray of tea and biscuits.

'I've just made tea if you'd like a cup?' She smiled at the other woman.

'I'd better not.' The shop bell chimed, and Fiona gestured with her eyes before hurrying out.

Aileen placed the tray down. 'They're nearly all for you today, love.' Aileen sat down to open her cards, but the one she wanted most wasn't among them. 'How nice of Val to remember my birthday, Da.'

He nodded then got up and fetched a knife from the kitchen to open his post. His eyes scanned the length of the handwritten letter.

'My word, Aileen, it's from Tom.' He sat down again to read it, his face a mixture of emotions.

Aileen sat next to him. 'What's he say, Da?' She tried to read over his shoulder until he passed it to her. The fact that it was written a day before their birthday and on hospital notepaper did not detract from the beautiful handwriting, or the very formal way in which it was written.

*Dear Sir,*

*17th March, 1967*

*Forgive me if my approach appears formal, Mr Maguire. As we don't know each other, it wouldn't feel right for me to address you any other way. I thank you for your letter and for the information it contained and trust it to be genuine. I apologise for my lack of communication until now.*

*I expect to be released from the sanatorium in the next few days, and, please can I ask you not to come to see me here. I will be in touch with you again shortly, if for no other reason than curiosity. I want to know my background and how I came to end up in a children's orphanage.*

*This is all very strange to me, as I was never told anything about you.*

*Sincerely,*

*Tom Miller.*

'Oh, Da. Poor Tom.' She felt sad for her brother's life and that he had missed so much of theirs. Her da didn't speak for several minutes, and she could see he was struggling to put his feelings into words.

'We've made progress, Da.' She passed back the letter. 'I can't wait to see him.' A tear trickled down her cheek and she dashed it away.

He nodded. 'He's ill, Aileen.' He cleared his throat and folded the letter slowly and put it back in the envelope.

'What do you suppose is wrong with him?'

'Could be tuberculosis. He must have been bad to spend time in a sanatorium. If he accepts us, I'll make sure he never wants for anything; you neither, love. I'll get him the best care I can afford.'

Aileen placed her hand on his shoulder. 'We both will. You know, Da, although I feel sad for Tom, this is turning out to be a memorable birthday after all.'

Her da shook his head, and a gentle smile lifted his face. 'Yes, indeed it is, love.'

# Chapter Fifty-Six

Days passed with no word from Dermot, and Aileen convinced herself that their relationship was over. Each time the phone rang out, she rushed to answer it in the hope that it was for her. Each time the post dropped through the letterbox, she scanned it for another letter from Tom. Hopes of seeing her brother took the edge off her longing to hear from Dermot.

During the long evenings, she wondered what he was doing; she found it difficult to accept that maybe she had been wrong in assuming his feelings for her were sincere. If he truly loved her, how could he stay away like this? And if he no longer loved her—the thought pained her more than she could bear—she would have no choice but to find a way of getting on with her life without him. Being open and honest had done nothing but make everyone unhappy. *How many people actually managed to keep secrets?* Her ma had for eighteen years. Now Aileen wasn't so sure that honesty was the best policy.

She spent her days cleaning the house and working in the shop when her da needed a break. Talking to and meeting new people, as she served them confectionery, helped her to focus on something other than herself. Locals were forever gossiping and bringing in snippets of interesting news that kept her amused.

One afternoon, Aileen was serving in the shop. She unscrewed the lid from a jar of bonbons and tipped some onto the scales, adding a couple extra for good measure before sliding them into a paper bag. 'Will that be all?' she asked the man.

'No. Gimme four ounces of liquorice allsorts as well.'

Aileen lifted the jar from the shelf. 'Oh, I'm sorry, we appear

287

to be almost out.' In the excitement of Tom's letter, her da must have forgotten to re-order when he went for the Easter eggs.

'Oh, dear, I can't go back without the allsorts. They're the wife's favourite, and she enjoys them while watching the television.' He chuckled. 'I tell yea, since I rented the thing, she's been glued to it. We watched *Cathy Come Home* the other night and she cried all the way through it.' He clicked his tongue. 'Women.'

Aileen turned the jar sideways. 'There's about two ounces left, will that do you?'

'Grand. And gimme four ounces of treacle toffees and the same of jelly beans.'

Smiling, the man paid and left, leaving Aileen smiling. The rest of the afternoon was busy, and she was glad of the distraction. So when the letterbox rattled, and a customer picked up an envelope and handed it to her, she knew straight away who it was from. With a happy sigh, she placed it underneath the counter to open later.

'Ah, from your feller, is it, love?' the woman customer cackled. A typical Dubliner from the liberties, who loved to gossip, she called in every Saturday for pear drops and six ounces of cough and throat tablets. Most of the time, Aileen was happy to chat, but today she couldn't wait for her to leave.

It wasn't until her da came through an hour later that she finally got the opportunity. In her desperation to read Dermot's note, she ripped open the envelope.

It simply said:

*Aileen, can we talk? Please phone me. I miss you.*
*Dermot x*

She pondered on the scarceness of his words, but he missed her and sent a kiss. Did that mean he still felt something for her? In the evening, after the shop closed, she lifted the phone and dialled his number.

\* \* \*

Aileen walked through the gates of Stephen's Green and spotted Dermot walking towards her; her heart raced. It was two weeks since she had last seen him. As he reached her, he took her hand

and they walked a few steps in silence before sitting on one of the wooden benches.

'I've missed you so much.'

'Me, too.' She stifled a sob.

'I'm sorry I was such an idiot. Can you forgive me? I love you, and my life means nothing without you.'

Aileen wept softly. 'I love you, too.' He drew her close, and she placed her head on his shoulder. It felt so good to be here with Dermot again; she couldn't speak.

'Aileen, I should never have... I mean, I knew there'd be other admirers, and in my heart, I knew you would never... I don't know what possessed me. Please say you forgive me for doubting you?' He drew breath. 'If you agree to marry me, I promise never to mistrust you again. If you refuse,' he paused, 'I shall remain a bachelor for the rest of my life.'

'Oh, Dermot.' Aileen straightened up and blew her nose. 'What changed your mind?'

'I was wrong to react in the way that I did. I felt consumed by jealousy.' He sighed. There was no doubt in her mind that his words were sincere. But all she wanted to do now was to forget the whole sorry episode.

'Aileen, tell me what you're thinking?' He looked into her eyes and took hold of her hand. 'Am I forgiven?'

'What do you think, you daft hapeworth?' It was a phrase she had picked up in Birmingham. He gave her a puzzled look and pulled her to him, then he reached into his pocket and presented her with her engagement ring. As he placed it on her finger, sheer happiness made her cry. They had a lot of making up to do, as well as plans to make for their future, and it was getting dark as they left the park.

'I've no doubt that we love each other, Aileen, but can I ask you just one thing?'

She frowned. 'You can ask me anything!'

'Should I feel threatened in any way by this other man?'

She shook her head and swallowed. 'He's dead.'

Dermot's face paled with shock. 'Jesus Christ, Aileen. How did it happen?'

'Before you ask, it had nothing to do with me.' She sighed. 'Sure, if you take me to the pub, I'll tell you everything.'

'I don't need to know. It won't make any difference, honest.'

'I think you do, so we can put it to rest. I don't want us to have any secrets from each other ever again.'

It was much later, over a pint of Guinness, that Dermot finally heard the whole story. Visibly shocked, it was moments before he spoke. He lowered his head into his hands and Aileen held her breath. When he glanced up, his arm went around her. 'My God, Aileen, I've been a stupid idiot!'

'So was I, but it's all right, Dermot. It's in the past.'

'I should have been supporting you, and I pushed you away. Darling Aileen, I don't deserve you.'

'Yes, you do. Can we close the door on that now and never mention it again?'

When Dermot finally walked Aileen home, it was getting on for midnight. With the man she loved back in her life, she felt happier than she had in months. If she could just have her brother in her life, her happiness would be complete.

\* \* \*

Aileen's da was delighted to hear of the young couple's engagement. 'How long before the big day then?'

'We thought eighteen months, Da. Just before my twenty-first birthday. Dermot has saved a down payment on a house. They're building new houses about ten or so miles from here, on the east coast.'

'They'll be pricey. You don't want to stretch yourselves.' He smiled. 'But I guess you can't go wrong in bricks and mortar.' She leant in and hugged him.

'Are you planning to go on working after you're wed?'

'Yes, we don't want to start a family straight away.'

He nodded. 'I take it you won't be returning to Birmingham?'

Aileen laughed. 'What do you think?'

'Good. There's something I have to do in the morning. Can you look after the shop?'

'Sure.' She removed her coat and hung it up on the peg. 'Is everything okay, Da?'

He got to his feet. 'Never better, love.' He kissed her forehead. 'I'll head up now.' He placed the shop keys on the mantle. 'Just in case I've left before you surface.'

Aileen was looking forward to spending time in the shop, yet she couldn't help wondering why her da hadn't said where he was going. Surely if he had heard from Tom he'd have said. A knot of uncertainty clenched her stomach.

* * *

It was lunchtime before he returned. He wore a serious expression as he walked through the shop wearing his business suit, overcoat, and trilby hat. 'Close up, love. I want to talk to you.'

Aileen's heart somersaulted. What was this all about? She followed him through and was about to switch on the kettle. 'Don't bother with that for now, love. Sit down.'

She perched on a chair. 'What is it, Da? You have me worried. Are you ill?'

He laughed. 'No, it's nothing like that. It's good news. Well, I hope it will be.'

Aileen's eyes brightened. She placed her hands on the table. 'You've found Tom?'

His face clouded. He removed his hat and placed his coat over the chair and sat down. 'No. I've heard nothing more. And, before I get carried away, are you planning on working at the butcher's after you marry Dermot?'

She brushed back strands of her hair. 'What a terrible prospect. Whatever gives you that idea?'

'Well, it's a family business. Are you sure Dermot won't ask you to?'

Aileen laughed. 'Are you joking, Da? Dermot knows me better than that. Why are you asking?'

He stood up and cleared his throat, his hands clasped behind his back. 'I've taken the lease on a small shop on George's Street.'

Aileen's eyes widened, and she sat back in the chair. 'And I want you to take it over; run it, like.' He smiled. 'What do you say?'

Tears brimmed in her eyes. 'Oh, Da. That's wonderful. Are you sure?'

He nodded. Aileen jumped up and kissed his cheek, inhaling the familiar smell of his shaving cream. 'What sort of business do you want it to be?'

'It can be whatever you want. It's completely empty. I don't have access to upstairs, but there's a small yard out back.'

'Really!' Bubbling with excitement, she said, 'When can I go and see it?'

'I've already done the deal and have the keys here.' He dropped them into her lap. 'You have a good head on your shoulders, Aileen. I've paid the first year's lease. What happens after that is up to you.'

She pulled on her coat.

'Before you dash off, love. It'll need a lick of paint and a good scrub out before you can put stock in. Of course, I'll help you get started.'

She lifted her hand and brushed a few tears from her cheeks. 'I don't know what to say.'

'You don't need to say anything. I'll be interested to see what you make of it. Here's the address.'

\* \* \*

Aileen stood in the empty shop, then she swung round to take in every inch of the place. She ran her hand along the dusty shelves and the glass top counter, and wondered how long the place had been idle. But she didn't care. It was hers now, thanks to her da. He had more than made up for his behaviour after her ma died. It made her wonder if he regretted letting the haberdashery go, and how he might react if she suggested what was going on in her brain.

Casting her mind back, she vaguely recalled that there had once been a jeweller's here; she remembered passing it many times. A small room at the back of the shop led out into the yard where weeds and dandelions had begun to sprout up between the concrete paving. There was also a useful wooden shed against the back wall.

Excitement almost made her dizzy, and she couldn't wait to show it to Dermot. He would help her to get it smartened up and then she could start with a small amount of stock. With all kinds of plans swirling around in her head, she locked the shop and glanced upwards. The name of the jeweller had worn off, and the front of the shop was in need of a coat of paint.

As she walked back home, she thought about Tom and wished he would get back in touch.

# Chapter Fifty-Seven

When Aileen showed Dermot the shop, he was impressed. 'So, you're going to be a businesswoman? I'm pleased for you. What are you going to trade in?'

'Well, I'm not sure.' She looked pensive. 'I have mixed feeling about it.' She glanced around the empty shop. 'You remember how upset I was when da sold the haberdashery.'

He nodded.

'I wish I knew what Ma would want me to do. I want her to be proud of me.'

'Sure, she is. Look, don't think I'm interfering, but bear in mind the reason your da sold up in the first place, Aileen.'

'That's nonsense, Dermot. Da just lost interest. I think he secretly wants me to open one again.'

'Just don't rush into anything.' He put his arm around her shoulder. 'Whatever you decide, I know you'll make a success of it.' His words brought the smile back to her face. 'Let's go somewhere and celebrate.'

Arm-in-arm they walked towards the city. 'You know, they say that good things come in threes. Here's the second. I've been making enquiries about those new houses and arranged for us to look at one of the show homes at the weekend. If you like the show house, we can even look at the plans. A small deposit secures a plot. Then we could watch our house going up brick by brick.'

She paused. 'Oh, Dermot. Sure that's grand.' She kissed his cheek. 'I love you, Dermot Brogan. I'm so happy I'm frightened something will go wrong.'

'Nothing is going to go wrong, or stop us feeling happy.'

He placed his arm around her waist, and she laid her head on his shoulder. 'Now stop worrying, and give your future husband a kiss.'

* * *

After a chat with her father, Aileen found herself facing a bout of indecision. She conceded that small drapery shops were slowly going out of fashion; many department stores provided the needs of the majority. Her head swirled with possibilities and the idea of opening a wool and baby shop interested her. The outlay would certainly be less.

The following week passed in a whirl of excitement as Aileen's da and Dermot helped her to clean and paint the premises inside and out.

'So, a wool and baby shop it is.' Her da stepped down from the ladder, his dungarees spotted with blue and pink paint. 'It should do well along here. I'll take you with me to the wholesalers next week, and you can start stocking up.'

'Thanks, Da. I'll work hard and repay you every penny. Would you mind if I put my name above the door?'

'Well, "Aileen's" sounds grand enough to me. Dermot's doing a great job painting the outside, and a cup of tea wouldn't go amiss. Did you remember to bring the kettle?'

* * *

A week after Easter, Aileen's shop was up and running. She stocked every shade of yarn, knitting and crochet patterns, books on needlework and crafts, and knitting pins of every size to satisfy the fussiest of customers. She also stocked baby layettes, nylons, and small household articles that women liked to buy. It was early days, and she wasn't going to take anything for granted. Every day she noted what sold and what didn't do so well. She even stayed open until six to catch the workers on their way home from the city.

One Friday evening, when Aileen was closing the shop, Dermot pulled up outside in a red Mini.

'What's this?' Her eyebrows shot up.

'I thought it was time I drove my future wife around in a proper car.' He laughed. 'What do you think?'

'It's wonderful. It's practically brand new.' She looked it over, then got in and examined the interior. 'It's lovely, Dermot. It must have cost a fortune.'

'Not really. Dad knew I was looking for a car, and he told me about a friend of his who was selling a Mini. I got it at a knockdown price.' He sat back. 'The thing is, Aileen, do you like it?'

Aileen chuckled. 'Of course I like it. It's smashing.'

'How would you like to drive it?'

'What? You know I can't... I...,'

'I'll teach you. Once you have your provisional, you can drive around in it. And we can go to the seaside at weekends, and see how the house is progressing.'

'Oh, Dermot, that would be wonderful.' They were kissing when there was a sudden build up of traffic behind them, and irate drivers threw them angry looks until Dermot was forced to drive away.

\* \* \*

The following Monday morning, Aileen was about to leave for the wool shop when her da came through holding a letter. 'It's from Tom, Aileen. I've closed the shop so we can read it without interruptions.'

Aileen closed her eyes as if offering up a prayer in thanks, but still she felt her throat tighten. She sat with her da on the sofa, as he slit the envelope open. He took a deep breath and they both read in silence.

*Dear Mr Maguire,*

*23rd April, 1967*

*I was grateful to receive your letter and to know that I have a twin sister, Aileen. Knowing this doesn't make the pain of being abandoned any easier. And the reason I've delayed getting back in touch is purely selfish. I can't bear the hurt of another rejection.*

*However, I would like to meet you both. I exercise, for my health, on Sunday mornings in the Phoenix Park, and if you are agreeable, I will wait for you on the steps of the obelisk at eleven o'clock.*

*If this is not convenient, please let me know, and we can arrange to do this at a time more suitable to you.*

*Sincerely,*

*Tom Miller*

Aileen sobbed into her handkerchief, and when she glanced

up, she saw sadness in her da's eyes. 'It's going to take time to convince Tom he is loved and wanted.'

Aileen nodded. 'We'll have to tell him everything, Da, and then pray that he will understand the circumstances.'

She tried to imagine how her brother might be feeling. If she were in his shoes, she would want questions answered, too. But would what they knew be enough to satisfy him?

## Chapter Fifty-Eight

It was a sunny but chilly Sunday morning when Aileen and her da walked through the gates of the Phoenix Park. Her da was deep in thought; she was trying to focus on her brother's feelings while struggling with her own. They walked along tree-lined avenues that stretched over acres of grassland, with flowerbeds just coming into bloom and hedgerows bursting into life. A grey squirrel climbed a tree, and in the distance wild fallow deer grazed. A cyclist passed along a nearby path. Through a gap in the hedge, Aileen glimpsed a group of young boys preparing for games.

She shivered in spite of the sunshine and her da remained quiet as they walked further into the park. She knew he was apprehensive, but so was she—and she sought reassurance. 'I'm nervous, Da, and I don't know why.'

'I guess Tom's feeling much the same.' He touched her arm. 'Don't worry, just be yourself.'

His words helped a little, and she checked her jacket pocket for a tissue just in case.

Tom had chosen the Phoenix Park. The vast oasis in the relatively quiet of the morning was the perfect place for their first meeting, where they could talk openly. In a few hours' time, the park would be busy with visitors and families picnicking. As a child, Aileen had loved coming here with her parents to visit the zoo.

She could see the Wellington Monument up ahead. Her da glanced at his watch. 'We're a bit early, love, but we don't want to keep him waiting.'

Feeling warmer after the walk, Aileen glanced around her for sightings of her brother. 'Will we recognise him?'

'I'd like to think so, love.'

As they approached the obelisk with its wide, steep steps on all sides, her da cleared his throat and straightened his shoulders. She touched his arm. 'It'll be grand, Da. Let's just sit on the step and wait.'

They had just sat down when they spotted a young man sprinting towards the tower. Aileen gasped. 'Da, is that him?'

They got up and walked across the grass, but the runner carried on. Aileen sighed. They turned back, and Aileen glanced towards the monument. A young man was sitting on the top step, his head down, his hands resting on his knees as if trying to catch his breath.

Aileen nudged her da, who was looking at the deer. 'Look, up there, Da.'

The young man looked down, hesitated, then brushed his hand across his blond hair and walked down the steps towards them. 'Mr Maguire?'

'Yes, and you must be Tom.' The men shook hands. 'This is Aileen.' She held his hand longer than she should have. 'I'm so happy to meet you, Tom.'

She leaned in to kiss his cheek noticing his blue eyes, the same blue as her ma's. She felt a lump in her throat and took a deep breath.

'I'm happy to meet you both. Thank you for coming.' He wore a navy running outfit and light-coloured shoes with laces. 'Please excuse how I look.' He smiled. 'Doctor's orders.'

Her da cleared his throat. 'How have you been, you know, since your stay at the sanatorium?'

'As much as I hated being in there, it's done me a power of good. I'm back at work, and that helps.'

'That's good.'

Aileen was taking in every facet of her brother's appearance. She felt unsure what to say, yet her da was doing brilliantly. She felt lost for words and just wanted to hug Tom and never let him go.

'Are you happy to talk here, or,' her da asked, 'would you like to walk?'

'We can sit here on one of the benches, Mr Maguire.'

As the three sat side by side on the long bench, Aileen suddenly recovered her power of speech. 'Is running helpful?'

'Yes, I believe so. I was sceptical at first.' He paused. 'I also play a round of golf, once a week. A more sedate pastime.' He smiled.

'They say it's good to exercise,' Da said. 'I liked running myself as a young man.'

'Yes, I think it's been beneficial since I came out of the sanatorium.'

Aileen said. 'I'm sure you have questions to ask us, Tom, and we're here because we want you in our life.'

Her da cleared his throat. 'I want to help you in any way I can.'

Tom glanced down at his hands, his shoulders slumped.

'I know it will take time for you to accept us as your family. Can I assure you,' her da went on, 'we are genuine.'

'Why did my mother abandon me?' He glanced towards Aileen. 'If we are twins, and it appears we are, it doesn't add up.'

Tears welled in Aileen's eyes. 'We knew nothing of this until July of last year when Ma died.' She glanced at her da.

'I'm sorry.'

'It wasn't until your mother, Jessie, lay dying that she told me about you. She left a note for Aileen, asking her to find you and to beg for your forgiveness.'

A host of emotions shot across the young man's face, but he stayed silent.

'The whole business was a huge shock to us both,' their father continued. 'It sent me into months of depression. Aileen was desperate to find you but, to my shame, it took me longer to accept that Jessie had kept such a thing from me for eighteen years.'

'What you say only proves she didn't want me. Why take one twin and leave the other?' Tom got to his feet. 'I'm sorry, I can never forgive her for that.'

Their father got to his feet and placed his hand on Tom's shoulder. 'Please, Tom. What we discovered since your mother's death shocked us, and you will be, too, when you hear the full story. In tim, you'll come to realise that your mother wasn't the monster you believe her to be.'

Tom sat down again, his breathing a little erratic.

'Look,' his father said, 'we don't have to do all this today. Now that we've found you, we're not going to lose touch again.' He glanced towards Aileen, who nodded in agreement. 'Let me drive you home.'

Tom looked pale as they walked slowly back towards the gates of the park.

'You know what, Mr Maguire? I've hated my mother for years, and if what you have to tell me helps to ease how I feel right now, it will be worth it.'

## Chapter Fifty-Nine

The following week, Aileen was in a happy frame of mind and hummed to herself all morning as she worked. She loved being in charge of her own business, and that her da had trusted her to make a go of it. She was happily engaged to a wonderful man who made her laugh, and she had at last met her twin brother. She'd felt a surge of joy when she'd first glimpsed him sitting at the top of the Wellington Monument. There was no mistaking that Tom was her brother, and she had bonded with him instantly. But there was still a lot to discuss, and it was going to take time for him to come to terms with what had happened to him.

When they arrived home that evening, her Da had been reflective. 'You know, Aileen, he's the spit of me when I was his age.' He swallowed. 'I only wish…'

'Yes, he is, Da. He's a Maguire all right. And doing what he can to control his bronchitis. You have to admire him.'

'Yes, I was surprised to see him so well. To be honest, I wasn't sure what to expect.'

'I know he still feels a great deal of anger, but that's to be expected, don't you think?' Aileen put a mug of tea down next to him and sat down.

'I could see the anger in his eyes, Aileen. Sure, what he can't get his head round is, why Jessie didn't do more to get him back after she'd discovered he was alive.'

'I know, Da. It's going to take time.'

'I think he understands that his mother wasn't a bad person, just manipulated by a callous nun into thinking that he had died.'

'I'll talk to him some more and hopefully, he will come round.'

She had been over the moon when Tom had asked her if they could meet again, just the two of them, the following Saturday.

Today, nothing could dampen her happy mood, not even the irate customer who had stomped into the shop to complain about the knots in the wool Aileen had sold her. When Aileen apologised and replaced the wool, the woman went away looking a smidgen happier than when she had walked in. She was gaining new customers each day, and she had devised a chart so she could watch the sales grow each week.

That evening, she had her first driving lesson. It was fun, and she laughed so much she couldn't remember anything. In the end, Dermot decided to wait until early Sunday morning with less traffic. The fewer obstacles, the better, she had agreed.

\* \* \*

The next morning there was a chill in the air, though it was already the first week in April. Aileen was wearing a brown tartan miniskirt with a summer jacket and black high-heeled shoes, with a matching shoulder bag. She wanted to look her best to meet her brother.

She closed the shop early and walked the short distance along the quay where Tom's bus from Lucan was due to arrive. Excitement and anticipation churned her stomach. She was waiting when he stepped off the bus wearing a light grey jacket and a stripey scarf that partly hid his white collar and tie. His black winklepickers, with a slightly pointed toe, looked like they had seen better days.

'Hello.' He smiled. 'How are you?'

'I'm fine, thank you, Tom. How are you?'

'Good, good.' He smiled again, and she instinctively linked her arm through his.

'If you like, I know where we can go for a coffee.'

'Lead on then.'

It was as if they had known each other all of their lives, and Aileen was sure Tom felt the connection, too. The town was always busier on Saturdays, but today it was positively bustling. Hardly aware of the noisy traffic, she wanted every minute of her time with her brother to last forever. 'How have you been, Tom?'

303

'Sure, I'm grand. The new inhaler is a godsend.' He inclined his head. 'How…how is your da?'

'He's your da, too, Tom.' She kept a smile on her face. 'He's fine, and, like me, delighted to have met you at last.'

They approached the cafe and went inside, where Aileen found a table in the corner and they sat down. The waitress said she would be with them shortly. 'What do you drink, Tom, coffee, or would you prefer tea?'

'I like coffee when I'm out, but I'm normally a tea man.'

Aileen ordered coffee and Danish cakes, and Tom insisted on paying. As they enjoyed their coffee, she felt none of the unease she thought she might have felt in his company. They chatted about the charts and who they thought might make it to number one next week. It was as though he had always been around.

When they had finished eating, Tom leant back in his chair, took out a packet of Craven A—a popular brand amongst young smokers—and lit up. She watched as he drew heavily on the cigarette. Surprised that he should smoke with his condition, she nevertheless kept her own counsel. It wasn't her place to lecture him about his habits.

He leant towards her. 'Aileen, will you come to see a film with me?'

She sat back in her seat. 'You mean now?'

'Yes, if that won't be a problem. Are you, I mean…if you have other plans…'

'No. That's absolutely fine, I'd love to. I'll just have to phone Dermot.'

Tom frowned. 'Are you courting then?'

'Yes, I'm engaged to be married.' She held out her slender hand.

He touched her fingers to glance at the diamond. 'Umm. When is the big day?'

'Oh, not for a while yet. We're saving for our own home.' She pushed back the chair and stood up. 'Shall we go then? What film had you in mind?'

He stubbed out his cigarette. 'What films do you like?' He pulled on his jacket and wrapped his scarf around his neck then followed her outside. 'It seems unreal that we know little about each other.'

Aileen smiled. 'We have plenty of time to put that right, Tom.'

They walked towards the general post office. 'I'll just nip in here and phone Dermot.'

He nodded. 'I'll wait for you by the bridge. I want to buy a newspaper.'

\* \* \*

Later they walked through the city centre, her arm linked through his as if it was the most natural thing in the world. 'I hope Dermot didn't mind too much?'

'Dermot was fine. He's teaching me to drive tomorrow morning when the streets are empty.' She laughed. 'He's not taking any chances, in case I run over someone.'

'He sounds like a nice chap.'

'He is.'

Tom shook open the *Evening Press* then moved into the doorway of Tyler's shoe shop to read the cinema listings. Aileen glanced over his shoulder.

'Why don't you choose?'

She smiled. It was hard to decide on a film suitable to view sitting next to the brother she had only just met, unaware of his likes and dislikes. *The Sound of Music* would have been an ideal choice if she hadn't promised to see it with Dermot. 'What kinds of films do you like, Tom?'

'Me, oh, most things. I'm really gone on 007. Let me see.' Their heads almost touching, he ran his finger down the column. 'How about *Born Free*? Would that appeal to you, Aileen? Do you like animals?'

'Yes.' She nodded, feeling relieved. 'I love films about animals.'

'So do I, yet from what I've heard, this one's sad. Are you okay with that?'

'I'll cope.'

He folded the newspaper, placed it in a nearby litter bin, and they headed for the cinema.

* * *

It was still light when they emerged, and Tom appeared subdued. 'Are you all right, Tom?' She paused to glance at him.

'Yes, I'm fine,' he answered, as if coming out of his thoughts. 'You know, Aileen, I'd love to go to Africa one day and see the lions. Beautiful creatures, all of them, even the wild ones.'

She agreed and hooked her arm through his. It was such a lovely moment that she didn't want to spoil it by asking Tom questions about his life, although she longed to know more about him and the orphanage where he grew up.

Heading along O'Connell Street, Aileen was oblivious to her surroundings, or that the wind had turned keen, until she saw her brother wrap his scarf tighter around his face.

'What time's your bus, Tom?'

He looked down at his watch. 'There's plenty of time yet. I'll walk with you to yours.'

Although she shouldn't have been surprised, his next words made her heart skip. 'What was it like growing up with a mam and dad?'

She swallowed and looked down; black spots of chewing gum stuck to the pavement like a disease. She clutched his arm tighter. How could she say how good her life had been before their ma had died, without making him feel left out, frustrated and even angry?

She paused on O'Connell Bridge, turned, and glanced into the Liffey. This evening she was less bothered by the pungent smells that rose from the murky water, as Tom stood close to her.

'I'm sorry, Aileen, I need to know.' His voice rose above the noise of traffic. 'Did you ever consider that you might have a sibling?'

She turned her head towards him. 'No. Never. I had no reason to.' She turned her back on the river and leant against the bridge. 'There is so much we haven't yet discussed, Tom,' she said, opening the flap of her bag.

The note her ma had left her was tucked safely inside a zipped pocket. 'This is the note Ma left me before she died. Please read it, Tom.'

# Chapter Sixty

When Aileen arrived home, she found a note from her da saying he had gone for a drink with Bead and Paddy. She was pleased that he was socialising again. She knew, too, that he needed to discuss Tom with someone other than herself. She made something to eat and then rang Dermot.

He arrived in the Mini and they drove somewhere quiet to sit and talk. Dermot wore jeans and a white collared shirt, open at the neck. Aileen also had on jeans and a floral summer top. He wanted to know all about her meeting with Tom.

'When am I going to meet him?'

'Soon, I hope. I'm sure you and he will hit it off. Already I feel a special bond with him. I guess it's because we are twins.'

'It's bound to make a difference, Aileen. What film did you see?'

They talked at length about Tom, until Dermot assured her that her brother would eventually understand the circumstances their mother had been in. 'After all, it's early days.'

'Yes, you're right. I just hate to see him so sad.'

'Look, I've got some good news, Aileen. I went to the housing site this afternoon. They've started digging out the foundations.'

'Really! That's exciting.' She snuggled close and felt the hair on his chest tickle her ear. She glanced up. 'At that rate, we might have to get married sooner.'

Dermot did that funny thing with his eyebrows. 'I'm all for that.' He lowered his head and kissed her passionately. Before long the car windows were steaming up, and Aileen had to come up for air.

'My goodness, Dermot, you almost took my breath away then.' She blew out her lips. 'I love you but…'

He squeezed her around the waist. 'Don't worry. I love you, too. This is driving me crazy.' He straightened his hair with the flat of his hand. 'What's stopping us from getting married now?'

'Don't be daft. Where would we live?' She shook her head. 'No, let's wait. I want a proper wedding.' She glanced down at her engagement ring. 'The time will soon go.'

Dermot wound down the car window and leant his arms across the steering wheel.

'A year seems a lifetime away.'

Aileen sighed. She had still to find herself a bridesmaid. She couldn't ask Val to come all the way over from England, and her friend Helen would be too busy looking after her baby; if she got to keep it. When Aileen had called at Helen's parents' house a week ago, they'd refused to tell her anything. Aunt Bead had suggested asking her sister-in-law's daughter in place of Helen.

'What are you thinking of, Aileen. You're miles away.'

'Oh, just wondering about a bridesmaid, and if you'd any idea who you might approach as your best man.'

'I want to talk to you about that.' His brow furrowed. 'I can hardly ask my brother.'

Aileen's eyes widened. 'Could he marry us, do you think?'

'You wouldn't mind?'

She laughed. 'Mind? It would be marvellous. You still don't have a best man, though.'

He took her hand. 'What about Tom? Do you think he'd do it?'

Aileen leant in and kissed him. 'Why didn't I think of that? I'll ask him. Or, better still, you can ask him when he comes for tea at the sweet shop tomorrow. Da wants the four of us to have Sunday tea. There's something he wants to discuss with Tom.' She shrugged. 'What do you think? Will you come?'

Dermot nodded. 'It sounds like a good plan,' he smiled. 'Now, before you get me going again, I'd better take you home.' Aileen shook her head as the car roared into life and moved off to a belch of smoke. 'Are you still on for a driving lesson in the morning, Aileen?'

'Are you kidding? I can't wait.'

* * *

Dermot's attempts to teach Aileen the three-point-turn ended in frustration. After several attempts, she conceded she would never get the hang of it. She kept hitting the curb. 'Those wing mirrors are too low,' she complained.

'No, you're not concentrating,' Dermot said. 'You can't expect to do it right the first time. Besides, you're too impatient, Aileen Maguire.' Annoyed at having to give in before she had succeeded, she saw the relief on Dermot's face. 'You'll get better with practice, you'll see.' He placed his arm around her shoulder and changed the subject. 'I haven't been to church for weeks. I guess I'll have to start going regular. What about you?'

She lowered her head. 'If I'm honest, I'm just as guilty.'

Later that morning, Aileen and Dermot decided to go to St Mary's Pro-Cathedral to hear mass. Because they both lived within the city boundaries, they had a choice of churches in which to marry, but it was too soon to make a decision.

* * *

Aileen wanted to make sure everything was perfect for tea with her brother. She worked hard all afternoon baking fairy cakes and scones, and made a variety of small sandwiches with the crusts cut away.

Tom and Dermot arrived, and when the preliminaries were over, they all tucked in while Aileen poured tea into her ma's best china teacups. Tom and Dermot chatted as if they had known each other for years, soon polishing off the sandwiches before starting on the scones with butter and jam.

'These are delicious,' Tom said, turning towards Dermot. 'You're a lucky man.'

'Don't I know it.' He winked at Aileen.

She smiled. The old saying, the way to a man's heart is through his stomach, must be true. Her da looked pensive and ate little, but after the lunch he had eaten she wasn't surprised.

Later, Aileen, Dermot and Tom sat on the sofa listening to *Top Twenty* on the wireless with Alan Freeman, while Da offered to wash up. Straight after that, it was *Sing Something Simple,* with the Cliff Adams Singers and Jack Emblow on accordion, playing sweet melodies. After pop music, Aileen thought it sounded rather dreary, but her da loved it. Her ma used to call it, *Sing Something Sinful,* and they would both giggle.

Just then, her da came in carrying a tray with a glass of beer for the men and a small glass of sherry for Aileen.

'What's this, Da? Are we celebrating?'

'Well,' he said with a smile, 'it's not every day that a man finds he has a nineteen-year-old son he never knew about. I'd say that was cause for celebration.' They all chinked glasses.

'Hear, hear!' Dermot said.

The wireless was turned off, and Aileen glanced towards Dermot. She had no idea what this was all about, and it gave her an uneasy feeling in her stomach. She hated surprises, especially if they turned out to be disappointing, and she certainly didn't want Tom upset now that she had discovered his sensitive side.

'I've something I want to put to you, Tom.' Their father leant forward in the armchair.

Tom's head shot up.

'Sure, it's just an idea, and please say no if it doesn't appeal. I wondered if you'd consider coming into the sweet business with me?'

Tom looked taken aback, and Aileen held her breath while Tom took a few seconds to answer. 'Oh,' he said. 'Thank you, sir. I, well to be honest, I love my job at the bank. It's what I do best, and I have,' he gave a little laugh, 'aspirations of moving up the ladder one day.'

'I'm proud of you, son. That's very commendable.'

Dermot glanced at Aileen. 'We might be coming to you for a loan then, Tom.'

Tom nodded and their da cleared his throat. 'I was just thinking that, you know, with your weak chest, the shop would be easy work. You could take time off whenever you needed to, without the added worry of losing wages, and...'

'Please don't patronize me, sir.' Tom sat forward, his back stiff with indignation, and placed his glass down on the coffee table. 'I'm sick to death of hearing about my bloody illness. It's always been poor Tom, the sickly child, or poor Tom wasn't well enough when the adoptive parents came to see him. He'll never be fit enough for hard labour.'

Tom's words cast a cloud over the evening, and the room sank into silence. Aileen quickly placed her hand over his.

'We understand, Tom. Da was only trying to help.'

'I'm sorry, I didn't mean to be disrespectful, sir. I've been told I have a stubborn streak, but it's not just that, I want to prove to myself that I can make it on my own.'

Aileen glanced at her da and thought how alike father and son were.

Their father nodded. 'It's all right, Tom. I'm sorry, I should have been more tactful.'

Tom excused himself and went outside to have a smoke. Dermot gave Aileen a knowing look and she shrugged.

'I didn't know Tom smoked,' her da said. 'It won't do his chest any good.'

'He's nervous, Da, that's all. He's had a lot to contend with these past few weeks. I'm sure he'll give them up when he feels more secure.'

'Aye. You're probably right.'

When Tom returned, their da offered more drinks, and they chatted as easily as before. Tom talked about his work at the bank, and it was obvious to those listening that he had a passion for what he did.

When the subject of family life was broached, Tom was willing to share a little of what living at an orphanage had been like. 'Sure, I've never lived in a normal family, so it's difficult to judge one against the other. The nuns were good to me and made sure I had a good education. They taught me most of what I know. I'm afraid I missed a lot of schooling, but,' he chuckled, 'I guess I was useful to them around the place. Healthwise, I had many good days when I did gardening and light maintenance, but my heart was always in bookkeeping and commerce.' He lowered his head and sipped his drink. 'I'm more than happy to know I have a family.' He smiled towards Aileen.

'Thanks for sharing that with us, Tom,' their father said. 'I'm only sorry that we didn't know of your existence earlier.'

When it was time for Tom to leave, Aileen and Dermot said they would walk with him to the bus.

'You are welcome here at any time of the day, or night,' their father said.

Tom smiled. 'Thank you. I hope you know how much I appreciate your offer, even if…'

'It's okay, son, I understand. Just wanted you to know that you're family now.' He smiled, and they shook hands.

As they walked to the bus, the young ones talked about Aileen and Dermot's forthcoming wedding. 'I'd be delighted to be your best man, Dermot. What do I have to do?'

'Just make sure he turns up,' Aileen said.

'Have you set a date yet?'

'No, but we're planning for early next year.' Dermot took Aileen's hand as they crossed the Ha'penny Bridge. The town was quieter now, with just a few people running to catch their bus home. 'I'd marry her tomorrow, and to hell with all the trimmings.' He raised his dark eyebrows. 'But you know what women are like.'

'I don't, but I'm beginning to.' Both men laughed.

Before Tom boarded the bus, he kissed Aileen on the cheek. 'See you, sis,' he said and waved from the window.

\* \* \*

That night when Aileen got home, her da was still up. 'Did Tom get off all right, love?'

Aileen nodded. 'The evening turned out well, Da.'

'Aye. If only he'd stop calling me sir! It makes me feel like his schoolmaster. I want to be a father to him if he'll let me.'

'You are. Give him time.' She sat down. 'Do you know what he told me, Da?'

'What was that, then?'

'Apparently, when Tom was about ten, the nuns sent him to a farm in Cork for a week's holiday. The couple, Mr and Mrs Miller, had a boy around Tom's age, and they got on really well. He was sent there each year until he was about thirteen.'

'He wasn't abused, was he?'

'No, Da. It's nothing like that. Tom loved it there so much that he started calling the boy's father, Da. The man rebuked him for it and told him to call him sir.' Sighing, she slipped off her shoes. 'So you can kind of understand why he's wary, can't you, Da?'

Her da shook his head. 'Poor lad.' He sat down next to her. 'I've something here to show you.' He took a small photo from his wallet. 'I came across this while you were out.'

Aileen looked at the black and white snapshot—a picture of her da, around Tom's age, walking across O'Connell Bridge.

'Gosh, Da, what a striking resemblance! Will you show it to Tom next time he visits?'

'Yes, it will be interesting to see what he thinks.'

Their evening together had given Aileen and her da a much clearer insight into Tom, the man. Being overlooked for adoption because of his bronchial troubles had made him vulnerable.

'I would feel exactly the same way,' her da said, putting the photo back into his wallet. 'In his shoes, I'd hang on fiercely to my independence. Well, I don't intend making things any tougher for him.' He stood up. 'I'm away to my bed. Before I do, I want to say I'm proud of your efforts to make the wool shop a success. Keep up the good work.'

With everything else going on, she had quite forgotten how busy the shop had been lately. 'Thanks, Da. At this rate, I'll soon be able to pay you back.'

He leaned down and kissed the top of her head. 'Goodnight, Aileen.'

'Night, Da.'

She sighed. It had taken months, but this was the father she had known and loved from childhood. Today had been an amazing day for them both, and had made her more aware of the privileged life she'd had compared to Tom's.

Although it was only a short time since she had first met her twin brother, already she loved him as if she had known him all her life. He would always be part of her and her family now, and she would make sure never to lose sight of him again.

# Chapter Sixty-One

Aileen reversed the Mini into a small space in line with a row of cars outside the park.

'Well done,' Dermot said. 'I couldn't have done better myself.'

'Really!' Aileen beamed and stepped out onto the pavement. She locked the car and handed the keys to Dermot.

It was Sunday morning, and she had on jeans, a frilly white blouse, and her white flat shoes for driving. Dermot wore dark jeans and a patterned short-sleeved shirt. It appeared that everyone was taking advantage of the nice weather. Young people had gathered in groups outside the park; some were looking at the art exhibition secured to the railings.

'Once your provisional licence comes through, I'd like you to keep the car; get used to driving it to work and back. I think you're safe enough now.'

She nudged him, then linked her arm through his. 'That's grand, Dermot. Are you sure? How will you manage?'

'I'll manage. You can drive me for a change.'

'I can't wait.' She kissed his cheek. 'I appreciate you doing this for me.'

He beamed as they walked along the tree-lined pavement towards the park's arched entrance.

'Now that I'm feeling more confident, I can pick up my own supplies. What do you think?'

He nodded. 'You had a good tutor. I'm not saying it wasn't hard work, though.'

She slapped his shoulder playfully, then, laughing, circled away from him until he chased her through the green oasis of the

315

park's interior, past the duck pond and through the trees until she collapsed in a heap on the grass.

Dermot lay down next to her, kissing and hugging her close, a tree obscuring them from view. Aileen loved him with a passion that at times she found hard to control. Soon he was nuzzling her neck, fondling and caressing her until she bolted upright. Sighing, she bunched her long hair together and let it fall down her back. Dermot ran his hand down its shiny length.

'What is it? What's wrong?'

'Nothing's wrong. Everything's grand, Dermot.'

'I just want to look at you. Touch you; be alone with you. I'm sorry if I…'

'Really, it's fine. I know. I feel the same.' Each time she was alone with him they struggled to keep their hands off each other. With months to go yet before their wedding, she wondered if they should see less of each other. But her heart said otherwise. To distract from what they were both feeling, she said, 'Dermot, there's wedding stuff we need to talk about.'

'Good idea. Come on.' He pulled her to her feet. 'Otherwise, I'll be having to go to confession again next week.'

They walked hand-in-hand across the grass where sleeping ducks and pigeons lay side by side. Families picnicked on the grass and children kicked a ball around.

'Hang on a minute.' Aileen paused as a young woman rushed past them, her dog straining at the leash towards the duck pond. 'You've been to confession already?'

Dermot laughed. 'Aileen, your face! You're so easy to wind up.'

She sucked in her breath. 'You had me worried then.'

They reached the bandstand close to the river's edge. Dermot sat with his feet either side of the bench, and Aileen rested her back against his chest, his arms wrapped around her shoulders.

'It was generous of Tom to agree so readily to be my best man. He's a truly nice guy.'

'Yes, he is, isn't he?'

'Have you called to see Helen again?'

'She wasn't at home. And I doubt her family will have her back.' Aileen looked down at her engagement ring, the diamond sparkling in the sunlight.

'Sure, that's a shame.'

'Her parents are staying tight-lipped about where she is. I don't even know if she got to keep her baby.' She sighed. 'It's so unfair you know, Dermot. All this hypocrisy makes my blood boil.' She stood up. 'I'll keep calling until they tell me what's happened to her.'

'I'm sorry, Aileen. They're obviously feeling embarrassed and secretive, you know how people are.'

She turned to look at him. 'Would your parents shun you if it happened to us?'

He blew out his lips. 'Gosh, Aileen, I never gave it a thought, but maybe.' He shrugged. 'With Luke being a priest and all.'

'You'd better behave then.'

He did that funny thing with his eyebrows that always made her laugh. 'Anyway, Aunt Bead's sister's daughter, Fiona, has agreed to be a bridesmaid. We haven't seen each other since we were nine or ten.'

'Well, you'll have plenty of time to get to know her again.' He stood up. 'Let's walk. Who else are you inviting, apart from Mary and her sister?'

'Oh, there won't be that many. What about you?'

'Mam was saying she'd like to invite Meredith and the family. There'll be quite a few of them.' He frowned. 'Is that okay with you?'

'Grand, I'd love to meet them.'

'Aunt Meredith will be looking forward to the wedding. It will give her something to focus on.'

'In that case, we should go ahead and book the church. You need to give at least six months' notice for a church wedding.'

'Really! Look, why don't we make it a spring wedding? What do you say?'

'I'd love that, Dermot. Will the house be ready by then?'

'Well, sure if it's not, we won't be stuck for somewhere to stay now, will we?'

She linked her arm through his, and they walked towards the small stone bridge that spanned the pond. They stood a while looking down at the water. 'Dermot, would you mind if I was to meet Tom a couple of nights a week? There's still so much I want to learn about him.'

Dermot's jaw dropped. 'You mean as well as the night to stay in to wash your hair?'

'Oh, don't be like that.'

He paused and drew her close, caressing the side of her face with his fingertips. 'Of course, I don't mind. You're a terrible temptation to me anyway.' He glanced up at the now overcast sky. 'I guess we've soaked up all the sun for today. Right, no more worrying about weddings and stuff. I'm taking you for a coffee if I can find somewhere open, and then you can drive me home.'

Smiling, they walked out of the park. Traffic was building up, and a bus filled with passengers turned down Grafton Street. Distant church bells rang out the Angelus. 'Is it twelve o'clock already?'

'There's no time for coffee then. I told Da I'd cook him lunch.'

Dermot looked disappointed. Drawing her into a shop doorway, he said, 'I love you, Aileen Maguire. I can't wait to make you my wife.'

'I love you, too.'

He encircled her in his arms, and as his lips crushed hers, she felt a warm glow run the length of her body.

She drew back. 'I can't wait to be Mrs Brogan, and I promise to be the best wife I can be.'

'What more could a man want?' Smiling, he took her hand and they headed back towards the car as drops of summer rain began to fall.

# Chapter Sixty-Two

With her wedding plans in place and her business making a small profit, Aileen couldn't have been happier as the weeks flew past.

Tom and Aileen were in constant touch, and their closeness grew. At times, she felt that she almost knew what he was thinking. Yet Tom had never said he had forgiven their mother for leaving him behind at the baby home. Nor had he made any attempt to visit her grave.

Alone in bed at night, she acknowledged that sometimes you had to accept that things didn't always work out the way you would like them to. Right now she was happy to have found her brother and fulfilled part of her mother's last wishes.

Tom had at least stopped referring to their da as sir, and sometimes called him Jonny. They had all come a long way in a short space of time. At best, the three men she loved were close.

\* \* \*

It was the first anniversary of her ma's passing. Aileen arranged for a special mass to be said for the repose of her soul, and later she would visit the graveside.

As far as she knew, her da hadn't visited the cemetery since the funeral. She had assumed he had stayed away because of his guilt over Lizzy.

The night before, after tea, he said, 'It's been a sad yet wonderful year, Aileen.' He paused. 'Jessie, your ma, would be proud of you—and Tom, had she known him.' He drew in his breath. 'Did you remember to order flowers for the altar, love?'

'Yes, don't worry, Da. Will you visit Ma's grave with me

tomorrow after the mass?'

He nodded. 'Paddy and Bead are attending the mass and said they would meet us back at theirs later for something to eat.' He cleared his throat. 'Has Tom… you know? Has he said anything about his mother?'

Aileen shook her head. 'We should leave him, Da. He'll come to terms with things in his own time.'

\* \* \*

It was warm and humid the following morning as Aileen and her da placed white lilies and red roses on the grave.

They stood in silence, their heads bowed, deep in their own private thoughts. Aileen sniffed back tears of utter sadness. Her father's shoulders shook, and he took out his handkerchief and blew his nose.

Aileen felt a lump in her throat. It was the first time he had shown any outward sign of grief in front of her, and it stirred her deeply. She moved closer and linked her arm through his. When she glanced up, Tom was walking towards them carrying a wreath made of fresh lilies—her mother's favourite flowers.

As he bent down and placed the wreath alongside theirs, tears of joy ran down Aileen's face, and her da gave a little cough and straightened his shoulders. Tom lowered his head and held his hands as if in prayer. Then he turned to face them.

'Da… Aileen.' His eyes fixed on them both. 'I'm sorry I'm late. The bus broke down, and we had to wait ages for a replacement. That must sound like a cliché.'

His father smiled. 'Sure, not at all, son. That's Corporation buses for you. Thanks for coming. It would have meant a lot to her.'

He placed his hand firmly on Tom's shoulder and the other around Aileen.

The three of them stood close together. Aileen sniffed back tears. No-one spoke for a very long moment. And in that miraculous few seconds, Aileen knew that her Ma's last wish had finally been fulfilled.

'Rest in peace, Ma,' she murmured.

# ABOUT CATHY MANSELL

Cathy Mansell writes romantic fiction. Her recently written family sagas are set in her home country of Ireland. One of these sagas closely explores her affinities with Dublin and Leicester. Her children's stories are frequently broadcast on local radio and she also writes newspaper and magazine articles. Cathy has lived in Leicester for fifty years. She belongs to Leicester Writers' Club and edited an Arts Council-funded anthology of work by Lutterworth Writers, of which she is president.

# GET IN TOUCH WITH CATHY MANSELL

Cathy Mansell
www.cathymansell.com

Facebook
www.facebook.com/cathy.mansell4

Twitter
twitter.com/ashbymagna

Tirgearr Publishing
www.tirgearrpublishing.com/authors/Mansell_Cathy

# OTHER BOOKS BY CATHY MANSELL

SHADOW ACROSS THE LIFFEY
Released: February 2013
ISBN: 9781301231720

Life is hard for widow, Oona Quinn. She's grief-stricken by the tragic deaths of her husband and five-year-old daughter. While struggling to survive, she meets charismatic Jack Walsh at the shipping office where she works.

Vinnie Kelly, her son's biological father, just out of jail, sets out to destroy both Oona and all she holds dear. Haunted by her past, she has to fight for her future and the safety of her son, Sean. But Vinnie has revenge on his mind . . .

HER FATHER'S DAUGHTER
Released: November 2014
ISBN: 9781301256402

Set in 1950s Ireland, twenty-year-old Sarah Nolan leaves her Dublin home after a series of arguments. She's taken a job in Cork City with The Gazette, a move her parents strongly oppose. With her limited budget, she is forced to take unsavory accommodations where the landlord can't be trusted. Soon after she settles in, Sarah befriends sixteen-year-old Lucy who has been left abandoned and pregnant.

Dan Madden is a charming and flirtatious journalist who wins Sarah's heart. He promises to end his engagement with Ruth, but can Sarah trust him to keep his word?

It's when her employer asks to see her birth certificate that Sarah discovers some long-hidden secrets. Her parents' behaviour continue to baffle her and her problems with Dan and Lucy multiply.

Will Dan stand by Sarah in her time of need? Will Sarah be able to help Lucy keep her baby? Or will the secrets destroy Sarah and everything she dreams of for her future?

GALWAY GIRL
Released: May 2014
ISBN: 9781310901614

Feisty Irish gypsy girl, Tamara Redmond is just sixteen when she overhears her parents planning her wedding to the powerful and hated Jake Travis. In desperation, she leaves Galway, a place she loves, and stows away on a ship with disastrous consequences. On her release from a cell in Liverpool, she takes refuge in a travelling circus and falls in love with Kit Trevlyn, a trapeze artist.

Accused of stealing, she is thrown out. She sleeps rough in Covent Garden where her fear of Jake Travis finding her dominates her waking hours. When he kidnaps her and keeps her captive, her life spirals downwards. Then Tamara hears a truth, a truth that will change her life and her very existence forever.

WHERE THE SHAMROCKS GROW
Released: September 29104
ISBN: 9781311081100

Set in 1917 against the backdrop of the Irish civil war, young Jo Kingsley is transported from her turbulent childhood of domestic servitude, to the sophisticated life of the upper classes at the beautiful Chateau Colbert. Here she meets Jean-Pierre, the grandson of her employer, Madame Colbert, and visits Paris where she discovers the desires of men. But Jo's destiny takes her to America where she experiences more than her dreams of becoming a music teacher.

During prohibition, in the mysterious haunts of Greenwich Village, she falls deeply in love with Mike Pasiński, a free-spirit; and a son of Polish emigrants. However, loneliness, loss and hardship follow during the Wall Street crash.

Will the beautiful Jo let go of her demons and learn to love again?

Lightning Source UK Ltd.
Milton Keynes UK
UKHW020952100519
342458UK00014B/149/P